The Wall Plug Boys

Peter Sandor

The Wall Plug Boys, 1st Edition.

Rev. 14, 05-13-25

ISBN 978-0-9917954-2-0

Copyright 2019 by Peter Sandor

Read other books by Peter Sandor

The Wyld Wynd Trilogy
Book 1 – Wyld Wynd The Rising
Book 2 – Wyld Wynd The Unrest
Book 3 – Wyld Wynd Unleashed

The Talus 3 Series
Book 1 – Arctic EMP
Book 2 – Galactic Illusions
Book 3 – Forsaken Drifter

Ebooks and paperbacks by Peter Sandor are available in all marketplaces through Amazon.

Contents

Acknowledgments

I would like to thank Randall Cousins—song writer, recording artist, musician and music mixer for allowing me to incorporate his song titles into this novel as chapter titles.

I would also like to thank Linda LaForge for the fantastic cover art.

Chapter 1: Chaotica

"What type of sandwich did your mom make?" Shoe asked.

BB pulled apart the wax paper and lifted the top slice of brown bread. He looked at Shoe from under his afro boasting six-inch-long strands of jet-black hair. The globe was impressive for anyone but awesome for a 15-year-old. As he did constantly, BB pushed his square, metal-rimmed glasses up the bridge of his nose. "It looks like roast beef."

"Pass it over," Shoe chirped as he circled his fingers toward himself.

"What do you mean?"

Shoe formed an angled smirk on his face that matched the heavily-gelled spikes of jet-black hair atop his head. Shoe was nicknamed *Shoe* because he always wore Converse running shoes. There were different colors, but it didn't matter where he went, the Converse brand was always on his feet. He said, "You probably figured having your mom put roast beef on brown bread would throw me off, but it's not working. We agreed last week, when I bought you fries in exchange for your chicken sandwich, that I would have dibs on another trade when I saw fit to take it. I'm taking it now." To ensure BB understood, he pushed his own peanut butter sandwich across the table toward BB.

BB whispered, "Ya *gobshite*."

"Piece of shit," Shoe responded.

Yes, BB's skin was dark-colored, but he was born in Ireland. His foster parents brought him to America when he was ten years old, and he never lost the Irish accent nor the words coming with it.

"Shoe, why don't you give him a break," Mario interjected. "It's roast beef, and you know that's his favorite." Mario was easily identifiable as Italian descent. He sported a mullet of tight, black curls and wore flashy, bright clothes. The name *Shoe* was already taken, otherwise Mario might carry the nickname on account of his perpetually-worn, white, patent-leather loafers. His look matched who he was as the son of a well-to-do construction contractor, and his family lived in an over done mansion in the countryside outside Canton, Ohio.

"A deal is a deal, and as best buds, we keep deals." Shoe ignored Mario and turned his hand over while angling his open palm toward BB.

BB rewrapped the roast beef sandwich and placed it in the open palm while his other hand pulled the peanut butter sandwich toward himself. "*Bollocks,*" he muttered.

Jack was the fourth boy sitting at the table in the high school cafeteria. He didn't join the group until grade ten at Canton High School South. In the little over a year since the day he met the other three boys, there were many quirks and strange events they had shared, but his fondest memory was still the strange sequence of events on that fateful day they met.

Jack remembered that Electronics Class sounded like a lot of fun, so he signed up for it as one of his electives, early in the school year. Mr. Lee was a reasonable teacher and offered up, since each person had to participate in a project, if they had an electronics device at home they wanted to improve, they could bring it in. Immediately, Jack thought of the old, lacquered stereo cabinet, inefficiently taking up space against the wall of their living room. It was older than he was, and he didn't remember it ever working. When he asked his parents if he could take it in to try and fix it, his father thought it was a great idea. However, his mother was relieved to just get it out of the house. Although she wanted her son to succeed in all things, this was an instance where his failure to bring it home would not be totally disappointing.

Jack was teamed with a classmate on his project, and they were both excited, but neither had a clue what they were doing. The stereo still had an old manual, and they tried to follow it, but their efforts were no more than random wire reconnections done as best guesses.

After a few classes, Mr. Lee came over to check on their progress. He leaned over, carefully poking and prodding. The antenna wire was in his way, so he gently grasped it between thumb and forefinger to move it aside. However, as soon as contact was made, his head jolted backwards, and his glasses fell from his face. This occurred at the same time his hand was thrown back with the 120-volt electrification.

Mr. Lee settled his hands on his hips while his eyes bored into both boys, but since Jack owned the stereo, eventually his focus centered there. It was at that point Mr. Lee noticed Mario, Shoe and BB, in another project group across the room, snickering. They were having difficulty keeping their emotions from breaking out into full-blown, uproarious, side-splitting laughter. Jack realized the three boys and Mr. Lee all thought *he* had connected the hot live-wire to the antenna wire intentionally, but in reality, it was pure ineptitude and bad luck.

Mr. Lee realized he played a part in the stupidity by touching a live wire. After all, he was the teacher and was expected to know better. After quick consideration he decided to just shake his head as he looked at both boys and mumbled, "*Youz Guyzzz.*" His head was still shaking as he walked away, deciding he had already spent too much time on the matter.

As Jack walked from the Electronics Lab to his Math Class, Mario, Shoe and BB caught up to him.

BB said, "That was fierce—right savage!"

Jack looked up at BB who even at this young age was already six-foot-one-inches tall. Jack realized, if he told the truth indicating it was a fluke, they would think he was a moron. Instead, he replied, "It took a bit of work, but everything worked out as planned."

From that instant in time, Jack was part of the group. He was not just bad, but he was now *bad-ass*. They now did everything together, both in school and out, and they ate lunch together at school every day as they were doing right now.

"Let's go for a stroll," Shoe suggested when they finished eating.

They gathered their garbage, tossed it in the garbage can, then proceeded toward the exit doors at the far end of the cafeteria.

Suddenly, there was a hesitation in BB's pace. "There she is—Mary Ellen—Mary Ellen Perfect Tits."

They slowed their walk as Mary Ellen walked toward and then past them.

With his eyes glazed over, Mario said, "They look even more amazing in the tight, thin sweater."

"I think I saw a bit of nipple protrusion," Shoe added.

Mario, in an annoying, jealous tone, chirped, "She isn't your type. You're much shorter than she is." He turned and looked at the jeans hanging off Shoe. "And you have no ass. She would not depreciate your black, spikey hair!"

Shoe was about to respond when he heard Jack chuckling. "Mario, you said 'depreciate.' It should have been *appreciate*. You always try and use big words to sound smart, but often you just sound like a dick."

"Full on *whanker*," BB added.

Mario's thick, black eyebrows furrowed.

Jack saw Mario's disappointment. To pick him back up, Jack admitted, "I wouldn't go near Mary Ellen, notwithstanding the large breasts."

"Are you kidding me?" Shoe asked in astonishment. "She's blazin bad-ass. I would give my left nut to touch those breasts— even for two seconds. What's wrong with you?"

As they continued down the hallway outside the cafeteria, Jack responded, "Chill. She has big feet. I mean, not just big, but huge. I can't handle feet that size."

For a few seconds the other three boys all stared at Jack in amazement. If there was a thing called mental telepathy, surely at this point they would have been voting to banish Jack from their group.

Finally, Mario looked at Jack much as an owner looks at a sick puppy that accidentally pooped on the carpet. "Are you okay? She has beautiful breasts, and you wouldn't touch them because she has big feet?"

"Not big—huge," Jack corrected.

Shoe wasn't as sympathetic. "Close your freaking eyes then!"

BB added, "Buy her boots to wear. I wouldn't care if she had a head like a bag of spuds."

Jack considered this. "Maybe if they were high boots, the height to length ratio would make her feet look smaller, but I don't think it would work. I'd be touching her breasts, and all the while have the mental image of her huge feet with thin, dirty toes as long as my fingers."

"You're a putz. There's no hope for you," Mario concluded as he opened the door leading to the interior hallway where all the shop classes were located.

"We're not allowed down there at lunchtime. It's off limits," BB reminded them.

"Chicken," Shoe challenged.

The word strengthened their collective backbone as they walked through the door and strolled down the hallway. Fortunately, all the shop doors were closed, and someone was using a grinder in the Auto Shop at the end of the hallway. Consequently, their movements were unseen and unheard.

Almost at the end of the hallway, there was a stairway leading up to the second floor, and they made their way upwards where they came upon a short hallway leading directly away from the stairs. At a right angle to it was another longer hallway, and at the end of it was an identical stairwell leading back down to the first floor. They peered around the corner of the block wall and down the longer hallway with their four faces lined up one on top of the other. Shoe was at the bottom and BB at the top. Mario and Jack jostled for the spots in between with Jack finally achieving the higher position.

"The classroom doors are all closed except the one halfway down. Whose class is it?" BB asked.

"I had Math in that class before lunch," Jack answered. "It's Mr. Keswick's class."

Mario whispered, "The math teacher with the condition—the vibrating eyeballs?"

"Yeah, that's him," Jack replied.

"Those eyes make him look as mad as a box of frogs," BB quipped.

The group had been tight for long enough to know what they were going to do next. Without words said, like a well-oiled commando team, the four boys slid into the hallway. The action began with a slow-paced jog, but quickly it changed to a gallop and finally to an all-out dash toward the opposite stairwell. Jack was quick and slightly in the lead. BB's legs were gangly and awkward, but notwithstanding their extraordinary length, they gave him superior speed. But it didn't change the unsightly appearance akin to a crazed, brown giraffe with an afro. Shoe was surprisingly quick for a short kid, but you could see by the look on his face, he was scared, and it was that fear now propelling him forward. They were in a tight formation with Mario in the rear, easily identifiable by his white, patent-leather shoes rotating at phenomenal speed. Even though his hair was a mass of tight black curls, they were wind-blown as he ran with his forehead held back, his mouth wide open and his slightly protruding teeth doing their best to stay the laugh that was on the edge of breaking free.

The four delinquents flew past the door as Mario's arm stretched out sideways. There was no reason to push, as his speed created sufficient momentum for the door to be pummeled closed when his hand made contact. The group was already several yards down the hallway when they heard the shattering *crash* of the small window inset within the heavy door. That was their cue as they all started howling. By now they were taking the stairs, three at a time, down to the first level.

They separated quickly, and Jack headed straight to the bathroom by the cafeteria. He sat down in the stall and could finally release the spurts of pee that started with the crash of the window. The left inside thigh of his jeans was wet. Sitting on the toilet, with his elbows on his knees while holding his head, he mumbled, "What the hell just happened?"

It was a weird moment for Jack. He just pissed his pants with his buds. *Who does that?* he thought. After a few minutes, he came to the realization he truly was part of the team. If he had ever questioned it before, this event surely bonded the four of them for life.

The turbulent bump pushed Jack's chin up off his chest and brought his eyes back to life. His conscious mind kicked in, and he realized he had been asleep.

The little, old lady sitting beside him on the plane had tight, white curls of hair and black-rimmed, round glasses. She smiled at Jack. "I think you were dreaming, and it must have been good because at one point you were chuckling."

Jack tilted his head to face her. "Sorry about that. I was having a weird dream about my friends from high school, so I think I must be looking forward to seeing them more than I envisioned. Where are you going?" Jack asked.

"Just travelling," she responded. "I travel around the country staying at different hotels. I'm retired and considering the seniors discounts I get on flights, hotels and the great meal deals they have at Bob Evans and Perkins, it actually costs me less than living in a retirement home."

"Wow!" I never really thought about it before, but when I do, it makes perfect sense. There are no discounts for seniors in senior's homes, are there?"

"Nope." She chimed.

What a sweet, intelligent lady, Jack thought.

They were sitting on the left side of the DC-9, two-thirds of the way back. Up front, the door of the cockpit opened, and a tall, good looking pilot exited. He looked sharp in the grey uniform as he walked slowly back to a spot even with the wings.

Of course, all passenger eyes were locked on him as he took off his hat, leaned over and peered out the window at the left wing. Then he turned and did the same while scrutinizing the opposite wing. After a few seconds, he straightened, affixed his hat back on his head and headed back to the cockpit. Considering the pilot's actions, Jack didn't think it unusual that the silence in the cockpit, caused by his appearance, was now broken by the rapid cadence of many seat belts closing almost simultaneously.

Jack turned to the sweet lady beside him. "I'm sure that was nothing. It's probably just a routine inspection."

"Fucking pilots—fucking airlines!" she said through a scowl.

Jack's eyebrows rose.

"They do this shit on purpose," she continued. "I bet they're both up there right now laughing their guts out. Fucking morons."

Prudence told Jack to stay quiet for the rest of the flight. The fucking morons got the plane on the ground at the Akron–Canton Airport, after which the stair truck bumped up to the exit door. It only took a few minutes to walk to the brown, brick terminal building just as the sun finally poked out from behind a huge cloud. Looking up, Jack saw there was nothing but blue skies now. *It's a good omen*, he surmised.

Mario was one of Jack's all-time buds, so he knew it wouldn't be hard for Jack to recognize him, but Mario might as well have worn a bright-red, flashing light on his head. There were about 30 people in the terminal waiting for passengers. However, only one man wore white and light-green plaid pants and a bright green shirt. And, of course, the man still wore the white, patent-leather shoes with the squared off toes that was still very sheik in 1978. As Jack smiled toward him in recognition, Mario hurried forward, passed the hand Jack held out to shake, and gave him a huge hug.

"You're back. Awesome possum!" Mario roared. "I hope this time you're staying for longer."

"I hope so too, Mario. I was in Philadelphia for a year, and I found it wasn't for me at all. In fact, I think big cities aren't for me. With luck, I'll find a great job locally and stay for good."

Mario's eyes smiled wide. "Excellent, my friend. Shoe and BB are working, so we'll meet them later. I can't wait to tell you all that has perspired."

At first Jack just kept his eyes forward and thought about what Mario said. Mario was an inch taller than he was, and even though he could tell Mario just shaved, he had a dark shading of unremovable stubble on his face. At 23 years old the changes from his adolescence were obvious, but apparently, he still had the affliction, and even the heavy, gold chain around his neck didn't help or cure his mixed-up words. "Mario, you said 'perspired.' It's not *perspired*. You meant *transpired*."

"C'mon, you knew what I meant, so who cares about a few wrong letters. Don't be a chump."

It seems some things haven't changed, Jack thought.

The pair made their way to the luggage pickup. Jack only had one checked bag that Mario grabbed before Jack could do so, leaving Jack to carry his leather briefcase. They made their way to the exit doors where Mario spotted the minibus.

"My car is at the far end of the parking lot, so let's take the shuttle," Mario suggested.

They moved through the doors and took seats along the side-wall of the vehicle. The driver said, "We're just going to wait a minute, as there's another plane that just landed."

"Cool," Mario said.

A young woman scooted up the steps and took the seat opposite them. She was cute, looked good in her tight jeans, and she looked even better to Jack when she smiled at him. "Where did you fly in from?" she asked Jack while peering at the ticket stub still held in his fingers.

"Philadelphia," he said.

"Coming back home?" she questioned.

Jack had a better look now and enjoyed her extremely light-blue colored eyes complementing her dark-blonde hair. "How did you know?"

"Not many people come to Akron or Canton for vacation," she said through a chuckle.

A rush of eight people hopped on the shuttle, and as the vehicle moved forward, the ticket stub fell out of Jack's hand. He leaned over to pick it up, but as he did so, the girl was quicker and picked it up for him. She rose and handed it to him, saying, "Have a great day."

She moved to the door, telling the driver, "Right here is good." She exited as did several other people after her.

"We're getting close to my car," Mario said as he stretched his neck upwards, searching for it. "There it is." He got up as did Jack, and they exited the shuttle.

Mario opened the trunk of a bright-silver Chevy Vega. The back end was jacked up extremely high, and each wide tire was on a bright chrome rim.

"Ace car," Jack stated. "Daddy still looking after you?"

"Of course." Mario chuckled. "To Italians, family is everything."

After his suitcase and briefcase were placed in the trunk, Jack slid into the super-compact passenger seat and realized he still had his ticket stub in his hand. But there was also a note he didn't see before. It read,

Carley. 555-2701. Now that you're back home, don't be lonely.

Jack smiled as he squinted at the sunshine, thinking of her pretty blue eyes. *Yes, it's definitely a fantastic day!*

Chapter 2: Traumatic

"Hi. Is Jack in?" Mario asked.

"Oh, sure Mario. Come in. I'm sure he will be down in a moment," Mrs. Decker said. "We just ate dinner, and I still have some perogies. Would you like some?"

Jack's mom made great homemade perogies. Even though his belly was full from his own mother's veal parmesan, it was tempting to say, yes. "I'll take a rain check for sure," Mario replied through a smile.

Their banter was interrupted by the creaking of upstairs floorboards in the 50-year-old house situated in the Polish district of Canton. The eerie sounds came closer as Jack descended the stairs.

"Hey Mario," Jack said.

Before Jack could step out the door, Mrs. Decker said, "Mario was just going to come in for some perogies."

"Oh no. We're a bit late, so we need to bug out," Mario answered, apologetically.

"Later Mom," Jack said just before planting a kiss on her cheek, then he scooted out. He yelled back, "I'll be late. *Monday Night Football* is on tonight!"

The boys slid into the Vega, and Jack smiled back at his mom waving from the doorway. She was doing well considering the recent changes in her life. When Dad died two years earlier, it changed her life in many ways, and some were quite unexpected. She quit her job at the bank where she worked for 15 years. She took a yoga class that Jack thought, at the time, was a real waste. But little did he know how many people were interested until she achieved her instructor certificate and offered classes from home. She was doing great, not only physically and emotionally, but financially as well.

The car lurched forward. It had good initial pep, but, after that, it was gutless for sustained, top speed. Jack wouldn't say it to Mario's face, but GM made a car that looked good, for a good price, but the performance was more than lacking.

A few turns later, they were on the highway heading to Wooster, a 30-minute drive east of Canton. "Why do we have to pick up Shoe in

Wooster?" Jack asked.

"Because he lives there."

"I know he lives there, ya spaz," Jack admonished Mario.

The transmission screeched as Mario attempted to shift it into a higher gear and missed. A second attempt found the correct position. "Chillax. He wants you to see his pad and the Shrine," Mario stated through his chuckle.

"Shrine? What Shrine?"

Momentarily tilting his face toward Jack, Mario winked at his friend. "An exclamation would not do it justice. You have to take it in personally."

Rolling his eyes, Jack responded. "There you go again!"

"What did I do now?" Mario was puzzled.

"Do you know what an *exclamation* is?" Jack questioned.

"Sure—something that would not do justice to Shoe's pad," Mario said as he snickered.

"Just sit on the funny stuff, you moron," Jack said. "You meant *explanation*. The explanation would not do it justice—that makes sense. *Exclamation* makes no sense at all."

Mario mumbled, "Maybe that's what I meant."

The remainder of the trip to the college town of Wooster was without words. They just listened to the pop music on the radio until they pulled up to an older, two-story house on a quiet lane. Mario parked the Vega on the road, and they walked up the drive to stairs along the side of the house, angling down to a basement-level door. After making their way down, Mario knocked. The door creaked open, and the visage of Shoe filled the doorway.

Oh my god, Jack thought. Shoe was exactly the same as he remembered in high school. He wore a similar black, leather jacket and black jeans that looked painfully tight at the ankles. Where the hem ended, there was a splash of color. The weathered, Converse running shoes were yellow, and carried the familiar white ball on the side, emblazoned with a blue star. Shoe still had a full head of pitch-black hair formed into spikes by an excessive amount of gel. The only noticeable difference from his memory of Shoe was the significantly larger head on the same size body. Shoe moved forward, gave Jack a huge hug, then pulled back slightly. He tilted his head to peer suspiciously up the stairs before pulling Jack into the basement apartment.

Mario followed and closed the door. "What about me? No hug? Not even a hello?"

Shoe pushed Jack down into his one and favorite reclining lazy-boy chair. As Shoe pulled the lever, Jack's feet shot up in the air. With Jack settled, he finally turned back and responded to Mario, "Piece of shit," he muttered.

Mario scratched his head as he sat down on the couch opposite Jack, and he looked at Shoe who was now at the fridge getting them cans of soda. "You always say 'piece of shit.' I don't get it. I've never really seen a *piece* of shit. When you look in the toilet, there's a *whole* shit. When you see a dog take a shit in the park, it's a *whole* shit. You don't say, 'Oh look. There's a piece of dog shit.'"

Shoe handed Jack a soda, and as he passed another to Mario, he stated, "You make sense. You're not a piece of shit. You're a whole, big, smelly Italian shit."

Thinking it an opportune time to interrupt, Jack said, "Great pad. How did you score this?"

"I work at the college here in Wooster where I do basic maintenance and handyman work. One of the Professor's and his wife own the house and live upstairs. They gave me a great price for rent as long as I do the same maintenance and garden work here."

"Outstanding," Jack said while tipping his soda can toward Shoe.

"Over there is the eat-in kitchen, and I have this huge living room area. Down the back hallway are two bedrooms and a phenomenal bathroom capable of handling *pieces* of shit or *whole* shits with equal capability." Shoe snickered at Mario as the words spilled out.

Jack thought, *wow! Things sure haven't changed. Mario and Shoe give each other these friendly insults, seeing who can top the other just like when we were in high school.*

"If you have two bedrooms, why do you have all those boxes piled up on the far wall of the living room?" Jack questioned.

"The second bedroom isn't used as a bedroom. It's a shrine," Mario interjected.

Shoe squinted at Mario. "What's wrong with that?" He turned and headed toward the hallway, poking Jack in the shoulder on the way. "C'mon. I'll show you."

Mario followed, whispering in Jack's ear, "Prepare yourself."

Shoe turned and waited at the bedroom door with his fingers around the handle. When his two friends arrived at the doorway, Shoe grinned and said, "Get ready for the grooviest freaking thing you've ever seen."

After Shoe opened the door, his hand reached around the jamb and flicked on the light. At ceiling level, from each corner of the room, white floodlights broke the darkness. In addition, the floor was covered with a brilliant-white shag carpet, the color of which matched the high-gloss white paint used on the ceiling and walls.

With the burst of white and light, Jack's pupils narrowed, and his hand came up to deflect the visual onslaught. "Holy shit!" he exclaimed.

"Holy shit? Now, that's a whole other version needing to be evaluated," Mario mumbled.

Shoe bent down and started undoing his yellow shoe laces. "Take off your shoes."

"You're kidding?" Jack replied.

Kicking off his own runners, Shoe ordered, "Take them off. No one goes in with contamination."

Soon, they were all in their sock feet on the plush carpet. Jack moved over to the wall where there were seven long, white shelves, and on each sterile ledge, meticulously aligned, were ten sets of Converse running shoes. Within the total of 70 pairs was every color of the rainbow in a mix of high-top and sneaker versions.

Jack moved to touch a beautiful silver pair when he felt the slap on top of his hand. "No touching," Shoe chastised.

Mario was waiting at a small, white table in the middle of the room. On it sat a glass cube similar to what would be seen in a museum. There was a pair of used, white Converse shoes stored within its confines.

Followed by Jack, Shoe walked over to the table. "This is the finest piece in my collection."

Jack's stomach took a tumble. "These must be at least size 18. They're huge!"

"Quietly please." Shoe hushed them as if they were in a library or a church. His voice turned reverent, and the words flowed much differently from the earlier "piece of shit" banter. "Look at the autograph on the side. These were worn by Wilt Chamberlain who is the greatest basketball player of all time, and he wore these during the 1961 season for the Philadelphia Warriors. It was one of the greatest sport performances of all time where he averaged 50.4 points per game."

Jack eyes were now wide in amazement. "How did you get ahold of these?"

As his eyes turned and bored into Jack's, Shoe said, "I could tell you, but then I would have to kill you."

"Oh Christ," Mario chirped. "Hurry up and show him your big finale so we can get out of here." Mario moved to a specific spot half-way between the wall and the trophy case. "Jack, you have to come and stand beside me."

Jack moved to the designated position as Shoe moved to the door, closed it, and turned off the light. Jack couldn't even see the end of his nose with the complete darkness.

Across the room, Jack heard Shoe's proud voice. "Watch this."

There was a *click* of a switch, and several things went into motion. The large disco ball, adorned with a multitude of small mirrored faces, hung above the trophy case in the middle of the room, and it began to rotate. The light, hanging from the left wall at the roofline, pushed a red beam toward the globe resulting in a myriad of thin, red light beams scattered around the room after reflecting off the mirrored surfaces of the disco ball.

Jack stood there open-mouthed.

He heard Shoe whisper, "Wait for it."

The red changed to green and then blue, as the kaleidoscope in front of the light source provided many brilliant colors. The shards of reflected light danced across the 70 pairs of running shoes, but the effect in the glass enclosure was most amazing. Similar to a crystal effect, the light separated into other colors within it, giving the illusion the Wilt Chamberlain Allstar Specials were floating in outer space.

The show lasted 30 seconds before Shoe changed the room back to the sterile white light. "That's enough. What do you think?"

As they walked down the hallway, all Jack could say was, "Unbelievable. I now understand why the boxes are in the living room."

"Two minutes of my life I'll never get back," Mario muttered.

"Pieces of shit," Shoe grumbled.

The silver Vega sped down the highway on the return trip to Mario's house, carrying the three occupants. Jack was in the front seat while Shoe was compressed in the tight back seat.

"What time does the game start?" Jack asked.

Mario spoke in a raised tone to overcome the radio and road noise amplified by the deep sound from the high-tech muffler affixed to the vehicle "It starts at 9:00 p.m."

Focused on the game about to come, Jack continued, "Jets and Bills, right?"

"Change the station." The words floated from the rear seat.

"I think the Bills will take it," Mario forecasted.

"Change the radio station." The words repeated from the back seat.

"Not sure I can agree. The Jets have won three straight games," Jack offered.

"Hey! Change the radio station! God damn and please!"

"Chillax already!" Jack yelled back. "What's the big deal?"

"I don't want to hear boy bands in the car," Shoe demanded.

"Boy bands? I don't get it," Jack answered, puzzled.

Pointing his finger at Mario, Shoe said, "He drives like he's in Italy. I don't want to die, but for sure I don't want to die with a boy band song being the last thing I hear!"

"If you were dead, why would you care? It won't matter." Mario stated.

Shoe put one hand on each front seat back and pulled himself forward. "How do you know? How do you know what happens to us when we die, or where we go?"

Jack said, "You really think, at that point, the music matters? Do you think, in Heaven, Nirvana or wherever we end up, that we'll be grouped by musical tastes?"

"I don't know and either do you," Shoe retorted. "But if we are, I don't want to take the chance of being with the gay guys listening to boy bands and wanna-be-bands from Sweden."

Mario laughed. "Someone will say, in a deep voice, 'Walk toward the light,' and at the end of that tunnel will be 'Puppy Love' being sung in an adolescent voice."

"Just do me a solid and change the station," Shoe repeated through clenched teeth.

Mario finally pushed a button on the radio, and instantly, the music became more raucous.

Shoe fell back into the rear cushion. "Finally. See, if I die, I want to be with these guys—Nazareth—playing 'Hair of the Dog.'" Shoe began to sing, "Now you're messing with—a son of a bitch—now you're messing with a son of a bitch! Good old American boys."

"They're Scottish," Jack corrected.

"Don't mock my patriotism."

They all thought the silence was better than the banter for the next few miles.

Mario gave a slight upwards cock of his nose as he looked out the passenger side window. "Shoe, keep your eyes open. That's Amish country to the south."

Jack was confused. "Amish—who cares?"

Shoe had his face pressed up against the side window. "We do and you should as well." His voice lowered in tone and volume. "There's weird stuff going on over there. Men won't shave. Women won't look in a mirror. We haven't put all the pieces together yet, but we're almost ready to *bust a move* on the Amish."

Bust a move was the term the four of them used when, in their youth, they would plan out and conduct a really well intentioned, but ultimately stupid event.

"You guys haven't changed. You're still as crazy as ever!" Jack held his gut as he laughed. "The Amish conspiracy! Tell me—Amish don't wear hoodies, do they?"

"You sound like you're the one who's gone crazy," Mario said. "Hoodies?"

Jack's laughter subsided to a chuckle as he rubbed a tear from his eye. "I was not sure whether or not I should mention it, but both of you are so suspicious. So…"

"What already?" Shoe pressed.

"Around the corner from your house, there was a guy in jeans wearing a hoodie with the hood up. I thought it odd since it's June, and it's not raining," Jack answered.

"It's not that odd, and you're right. It has nothing to do with the weird happenings in Amish country." Mario stated.

"The weird thing is the *Hoodie Guy* was there when we arrived at your pad. He was still there on the same corner when we left," Jack explained.

"There's a lot of strange stuff going on Jack. When we're all together, and we have just a few more pieces, we'll share the intel," Mario responded.

Intel, Jack thought. *What the hell are they up to? Whatever it is, it sounds like nothing but trouble, and I'll just keep my distance from it.*

The Vega veered off the main highway onto a smaller road and finally to a lightly-used, gravel lane. The large, red-brick mansion on the left was their destination. The long, oak-tree-lined driveway led to the four-door garage at the side of the house.

Jack jumped out of the car and spun on his heels for a 360-degree view. "The house is the same and as large as I remember, but back there—what's that?" His finger pointed at the building behind the garage alongside the pool.

"That's my pad," Mario proudly replied. "Dad built it for me when I finished the accounting course. He told me I could live there as long as I did his books for him."

"Sweet deal," Jack commented as he began walking toward the gate.

The guest house was smaller than Shoe's pad, but it contained top notch furnishings and the latest conveniences including a hot tub just outside the front door. The overhanging roof, covering the front porch area, ensured that even in inclement weather, the tub was very useable.

Jack changed into the swim suit he was told to bring with him, and Shoe also donned the swimsuit he permanently left at Mario's pad. Mario joined them, and all three enjoyed the hot water expelling from three jets toward the submerged benches they now sat on. There was a huge TV under the canopy, angled precipitously at the edge of the hot tub. Mario reached over and turned it on.

"Are you crazy!" Jack hollered. "If that falls in the water, we'll all be electrocuted!"

Mario turned the channel until football players appeared on the screen. He turned his face back to Jack and shrugged. "No risk, no reward."

Suddenly, Shoe's body jerked as if he *did* receive an electrical charge. "*String Bean*, you know better than to sneak up on us—especially when it's dark."

BB was standing at the side of the hot tub, already in his swim shorts. "Don't call me String Bean. You know I hate that name."

"Sometimes you can really freak me out," Shoe said. "I don't know if that means you're Mr. Stealth or Mr. Creepy."

As BB walked up the step and then into the tub, Mario laughed. "Did you drive here in your swim shorts?"

"Nope. Changed in my van."

Mario continued the questioning. "Why didn't you change in my place?"

"I hate your pad as well. Reminds me of a hospital."

BB lowered himself into the tub and smiled wide as he approached Jack. "Hey, Blood. How have you been?"

Rising, Jack moved forward with both arms out to give the last friend of their adolescent group a hug. BB was even taller now, closer to six-foot-five-inches, and his height extended significantly further with the huge afro globe still maintained on his head. Jack canted his head for a better look at the side of the fro. He thought, *wow!* On the side of the afro was a cowlick— a huge one. Jack couldn't remember seeing an afro with a cowlick before. He kept his amusement to a grin but thought, *it looked similar to a hurricane on a weather map.*

BB grasped one of Jack's outstretched hands, preferring to shake it from a distance. "Sorry guys, but even best buddies don't have unclothed skin-to-skin contact—especially in front of the *himbos.*" BB's other hand splashed a wave of water, hitting Shoe and Mario.

Shoe shook the water from his black spikes of hair. "I think BB changed in the van, so we wouldn't see his black ball.

A scowl came across BB's face. "Not that you would see anything, but if you did, it's a blue ball, not a black ball."

Oh no. It only took a few minutes, but here we go again, Jack thought. When they were younger, the four of them played a game, and as young boys will do, sometimes they play very curious games. Often, how much pain or embarrassment one can take is at the root of the competition.

On that particular day, not much unlike the September day just passed, they were outside throwing a couple of tennis balls. The simple game of catch quickly became competitive, and the result was the four boys standing in a square with each boy at a corner, 20 feet apart.

What increased the adrenalin was the fact there were two balls in play. The goal was to hit your friend in the groin, and this was made more difficult for the recipient with both balls moving at the same time. You covered your jewels as best you could, but again, the difficulty was always the lack of focus on the second ball. Such was the case when BB was protecting himself from the tennis ball flung from Jack. It only took a momentary lack of focus and BB's hands shifting a little too far forward and to the right to block the initial ball. Unbeknownst to BB, the second ball was hurling on its way, directly on target.

There was a sickening *thud* as the tennis ball made contact followed by a second louder *thud* as BB dropped to the ground. Groaning with considerable pain, he lost all sense of modesty and held his precious balls. Once he recovered sufficiently, he saw the left testicle was swollen and blue. Later, it clearly turned dark-black against his brown skin, and the color change never reverted back.

Jack's reminiscing was broken by BB's continuing explanation. "I've told you guys enough times. I 'm a black man, and it makes no sense that a black man can have a bruised, black ball."

"But you're not black. Your color is more light-brown. You might be better described as a negro with a black ball," Mario explained.

"Ya *eejit!* In case you haven't noticed, this is 1978, and we're not negroes. We're black since this was affirmed by my brother, Malcolm X, over ten years ago."

"What's wrong with *negro*? It was okay a few years back?" Shoe asked.

BB pushed his glasses up the bridge of his nose with his forefinger. "*Negro* was better than *colored*. Times change. Today we're black and I'm black with a blue ball, not brown with a black ball. Who knows? Maybe in a few years there'll be a better term, but for now BB is short for blue ball. It's the only thing that makes sense."

"Touchdown!" Mario yelled while creating a splash as both fists shot out of the water to a position raised above his head.

"Go Buffalo!" Jack added. He looked at his friends—the ones he said long ago would always be his best friends—come what may. Pressing his fist out in front of his chest, he said "Hey guys."

It was their thing, and they had done this since the year they bonded as teens. First Shoe, then BB and finally Mario placed their fists on top of Jack's. They knew there would be kidding all the time, the way great friends do, but they also knew it didn't matter what their skin color was or their religion. Even though they would joke with each other, they would always watch out for each other and be best buds.

Their fists lowered slightly and raised once. The second time the movement was a bit higher, and on the third lift, their fists opened as their fingers flew apart. In unison they whooped out a, "Hoorah!"

Each of them had a wide smile on their face with the identical thought in their minds. *Oh yeah, the boys are back!*

Chapter 3: Just About Almost There

Jack honked the horn of his mom's yellow Jeep Cherokee Chief. Looking up through the windshield, he saw a curtain on a fourth-floor apartment draw open, then quickly close. *I suspect that was her,* Jack thought.

A minute later, he saw Carley walking from the building's front entryway toward the car. She quickly made her way into the passenger seat and swung the door shut.

"You found the place okay?" She asked.

Jack didn't want to sound smart-assed in the first minute of the date, but he thought, *the answer is obvious since I'm here.* Alternatively, he said, "No problem. You look great."

"Well, you did say casual." Carley turned toward Jack, giving him a beaming smile that made the clothing inconsequential. "So, where are we going?"

If the word *multitasking* was more commonplace in the 1970's, surely Jack would now understand the theory where men have difficulty with such complicated activities. He was trying to drive, answer her question and also keep one eye on her attractive appearance. Her attire was simple with a light-blue halter top matching her light-colored eyes, and she wore cut-off blue-jean shorts. They were well worn with white, frayed edges along the line where the pant legs were cut off, and at the end of her shapely legs were two Jesus sandals. The soft, light-brown leather sole had a band across the top of the foot and a leather tie from this to a toe loop. The final look was simple but suited her very well. *Thank god,* Jack thought. *She has small, cute feet.*

"I'm not sure if I would call it home sick or maybe nostalgic, but I'd like to show you some of my old hangouts. We'll start with dinner, if you're hungry."

"I'm famished," Carley responded as she settled herself into the wide seat of the large vehicle.

Dusk had set in by the time they arrived at the drive-in restaurant. "I love Sonny's!" Carley said.

"I haven't been here for a long time, but it was a favorite of mine, especially on weekends if we needed a midnight burger after a night of partying," Jack explained.

They both exited the Jeep, and once out in front of it, Jack put his hand on the far side of her waist. She didn't resist and leaned in a bit closer to his touch.

"The place hasn't changed at all," Jack said as he undertook a momentary examination. The back two-thirds of the small building was made of dirty-white cinder blocks. The front third was primarily glass with a door on either side. Along the top was a huge sign with red lettering on a white background, spelling out - *Sonny's*. There was a small ordering area inside in front of the long counter, and only take-out was available. You either ate in your car or at one of the six wooden picnic tables in front of the building.

Sonny's was owned by a Greek family, and as Jack entered the building, he recognized the owner. His hair, both on top of his head and in the moustache above his upper lip, had turned from black to grey over the years since his last visit. Just as in the past years of Jack's memory, the place was bustling with activity. Between the workers yelling orders at each other, the banter of the customers and the cheesy music playing from the old speakers, it certainly brought back fond memories. There were two couples ahead of them, but finally they were at the counter.

"Order please," the owner said as he wiped down the counter.

"Cheeseburger, fries and a Coke for me," Carley answered.

Jack took a moment to review the menu. "Steak on a bun with fried onions. Fries and a coke as well."

Quickly, two thin, cardboard boxes were popped open and placed on the counter. The owner went to the cooking area where he set the meat on the grill and placed three handfuls of fries down in the fryer.

"Not the healthiest eating," Carley murmured.

"Would you rather get a salad somewhere else?"

"Absolutely not. I was making an observation, not a complaint." She looked over at Jack and gave him that great smile again.

The two boxes were filled with food, and they carried them outside to a vacant picnic table. They unwrapped their sandwiches, and once Jack completed his first bite, he asked his first question. "When we met at the airport the other day, were you flying in?"

Carley answered between bites, "No, I was seeing a friend off who was flying out of town for a week. How about you? What was in Philadelphia?"

"I was working there. It was my first job out of college, but it wasn't for me, so, I think to the benefit of myself and my employer, I moved on."

"It sounds like you didn't like it. What were you doing?"

"I worked for a major power tool manufacturer. As a lowly engineering assistant, I was completely lost in the mass of people. I have some good ideas, but, no one listens to you until you're at least 35 years old," Jack explained.

"You're an engineer?"

"Yes. I spent four years at Rensselaer Polytechnical Institute in New York State and received a degree in Electrical Engineering."

Moments of silence passed as Carley chewed her food while staring at him. He did the same except his eyes were more furtive with the discomfort of her steady gaze. Feeling he was being evaluated, or maybe even judged, he desperately needed a diversion.

"You know the saying about the optimist thinking the glass is half full?" Jack asked.

"Of course."

"Here is a different twist on it," Jack added. "The optimist says the glass is half full. The pessimist says the glass is half empty. What does the engineer say?"

Just finishing the last bite of her food, Carley wiped the corners of her mouth with the napkin. "I have no idea."

Jack leaned forward, knowing, in his mind, this would impress. "The engineer says, 'Why the hell are they using a glass that's too big?'"

She smiled. "That's cute, but, honestly, engineers are boring."

The corners of Jack's eyes drooped, not knowing if it would be better to challenge the comment outright now, or let it pass—at least for the time being. He chose the prudence within the second option. "Are you ready to go?" he said.

"I just need to use the bathroom. Where is it?" she questioned as she cocked her head from side to side, searching for a sign of it.

Chuckling, Jack replied as he rose to his feet, "They've never had a bathroom here. You eat here at your own risk, so I'll stop at a gas station along the way."

Carley entered back into the Jeep after the gas station stop, saying "Where to now?"

Jack smirked. "Somewhere boring, I'm sure." His eyes went wide thinking, *was that my out loud voice?*

Carley raised one eyebrow, and now it was her turn to let the comment go and see where the night would lead. After five minutes of driving, they were in the parking lot of the new Canton Mall. The Jeep was driven down a long parking lane until it was directed into a parking spot under the glaring, large, red sign above the store. It read – *Kmart.*

Carley's brows were now furrowed, and her fingers were curled into tight fists pressed into her waistline. She glared at Jack. "You're bringing me to Kmart for our date? Really?"

"Chill and don't be like that," Jack replied. "I need a few minutes to pick up a pair of jeans, so think of this as a time out from the date." Without waiting for a possible barrage of comments, he exited his door. He walked around to the other side of the Jeep and opened Carley's door for her.

They both were thinking similar thoughts.

Jack thought, *hey, I'm opening the door for you. This should get me some brownie points.*

Carley thought, *idiot. He thinks opening my door for me will get him some brownie points.*

"I will be really quick," Jack said as he led her down the store aisles until they both stood in front of the shelves holding many pairs of jeans. It didn't take long for Jack to find his size and pull a pair off the shelf. He opened them and held them up against his waist. He was six-foot-tall, weighed 190 pounds, and he surmised these would fit just fine.

Carley, with a scowl on her face, pulled the jeans from his grasp and threw them back on the shelf. She grasped his hand and pulled him further up the aisle to the lighter-blue, weathered-look jeans. She grabbed the same size in the lighter color and pushed them into his chest. "These ones—they're not as boring."

"Okay—okay I get it!" Jack answered through a laugh. "I'm going to try these on," he said as he continued walking toward the four little stalls against the far wall.

Jack slid into the compact booth and thought it would be best not to take up too much time. In the present circumstances, it was of the essence. Without a bench in the change room to sit on, he hopped up and down while pulling one leg of his older jeans over his left sneaker, and then performed a similar feat to remove the other pant leg. Now, he considered the new jeans, realizing these jeans weren't as flexible, and the ankle hem was a bit thinner. He cursed himself, thinking, *shit—maybe Carley is right. My engineering mind is evaluating putting on a pair of freaking jeans.* He turned off the analytics in his mind as he aggressively jabbed one sneaker-shod foot into the left pant leg. It got caught and Jack jumped with his effort to push it further through. His ass banged off the walls twice before the shoe shot out of the lower cuff and hit the floor.

He took a moment before undertaking the second half of the adventure. He raised his right foot and pushed it down into the pant leg. He pulled and pulled from the waist while mumbling curses, as the sneaker moved slowly through the leg of the jeans. His body was spinning as he jumped once again on one leg. His face turned red. The challenge was no longer about being an engineer. It was about being right and winning!

Carley was patiently waiting outside the change room where she heard the bangs from within. When she finally heard the curses, she leaned toward the wall. "Are you okay in…"

Before the sentence could be finished, Jack's ass hit the door, and it sprung open. In slow motion, his red face passed right in front of hers and then continued by. Both his hands were on the waist of the jeans where they had been pulling. His one foot was still caught as he toppled over, and his body made one complete roll followed by his crash into the clothes rack on the other side of the little aisle.

Jack looked up at Carley, at first not sure what to do since he was in this awkward position with his new jeans still around his ankles. Earlier in the evening, as he prepared for the date, he sorted through his underwear and finally selected the sleek, green speedos. Now, as Carley, with her arms crossed in front of her, smirked, he thought, *nope. There isn't anything remotely sexy about this.*

Carley said, "Now, *that's* not boring!"

Once Jack collected himself and was properly dressed, they were making their way to the cashier when Carley said, "Hold on. You need to buy me something."

Jack grinned. "I thought I embarrassed myself enough."

"Not even close," she replied as she led him down an aisle into the Women's Department.

Jack followed but as he saw her leading him toward the lingerie and underwear area, he hesitated. "I think I'll wait for you here."

She slid her arm around his waist, and with her other hand, placed his hand on her far shoulder. Her sweet voice floated toward him. "Honey, did you really think you would bring me to Kmart for our first date, and there would be no consequences?"

Jack was getting flustered. "Not a first date—just a stop…"

She pulled at his waist, moving them down an aisle until they were in front of a section where thongs and G-strings abounded. Carley pulled a hot-pink, next-to-nothing thong off the hook and held it up in front of him. In a loud voice she said, "Are these what you were thinking, sweetheart?"

Two younger ladies further down the aisle started to giggle. One of the women cupped her hand in front of her lips and whispered to her companion while looking at Jack.

Carley slung the pink thong over his shoulder. "Hold these for me." She then pulled another thong off a hook. It was mint-green and was made of soft material resembling bunny fur. Rubbing it against his cheek, she said, "Feel how soft it is!"

Jack tried to pull away, but Carley's hand held tight onto his waist. He rolled his eyes and caught sight of an older lady with white, curly hair, two aisles over. She turned her cart and was racing away as if the plague was behind her.

"I think I'll take these two," Carley said through her smile as she finally released his waist and led him back toward the cashier.

Jack followed behind her, rolling his eyes. He thought, *I guess I deserved that.* But the thoughts changed quickly to a vision of her first in the pink thong, then in the green one. With his embarrassment over, he hoped the shenanigans would be an investment toward future relations.

As they approached the short line-up to the cash, Carley turned, placing the two thongs on top of the jeans slung over his forearm. "I'll wait for you by the car," she said while her eyes glinted with mischievous evil.

His mouth opened to respond, but before he could do so, she turned on her heel and walked out the doorway of the store. Left with the two thongs, it seemed like an eternity to get to the cashier. He quickly placed the thongs down on the table and covered them with the jeans. The middle-aged cashier picked up the jeans without looking. She placed the tag in front of her horn-rimmed glasses and read the price. After keying it in, her hand felt for and retrieved the pink thong. She pulled the second price tag in front of her eyes, but her peripheral vision caught the hot-pink color. She froze, first turning her eyes to look directly at the thong in her hand, then the green thong still on the table. The corner of her mouth lifted when her eyes came up and met Jack's. With her initial shock now over, her entire face joined the smile, and the mischievous glint in her eyes matched what Jack saw in

Carley's only moments before.

Oh my god, he thought as he waited for her to finish ringing in the items. She handed him the bag. Her hand brushed his, and she let it linger there, causing Jack to pull back and rush out the door.

"Come back again soon!" she yelled after him.

Jack hustled back to the Jeep where Carley was leaning up against the door. "Nice one! You can open your own door," he said as he moved around to the driver's side.

Once he unlocked the passenger door, Carley giggled as she scooted in. Her eyes smiled at Jack, and he burst into his own boisterous laugh.

"Okay, I admit that was good," Jack considered. "But remember paybacks can be very bad, and one day, you'll be reminded of this one. I'm an engineer. As such, there won't be a quick, emotional repercussion. Rather, I'll make a plan. It might be days, months or even years from now." He leaned toward Carley with his lips very close to hers, pressing her back. Jack whispered, "Every time you wear either the pink or green panties, think on the payback. Look over your shoulder because I might be right there about to unfold a repayment of historic proportions."

Her moist lips were slightly parted, and her gaze was lost in his. She didn't know if he would kiss her before her restraint withered, whereby she would have no choice but to reach up and initiate the delicate contact herself. Their lips were only a breath away when her anticipation overtook her, and she closed her eyes.

She felt the slap of his hand on her knee as he pulled away, grinning. "We better get moving," he said as he put the key in the ignition and roared the engine to life.

Carley opened her eyes and blinked several times. Straightening herself in the car seat, she said, "Where are we going now?"

"More shopping? Just kidding—definitely not more shopping," Jack replied. "I think a picnic is in order."

"Now you're kidding." She chuckled. "It's 10:30 at night."

"If you recall, having just returned home, I'm a bit nostalgic. There's a place we used to go as teens to have a couple of drinks."

"That's fine, but by now, you do realize you're on a very short leash."

Jack directed the Jeep to the local Minimart where he purchased a pint of rum and a large bottle of coke. He slid back in the car and handed the bag to Carley. They drove down the highway for five minutes and then veered onto a smaller country road. After another few minutes, Jack slowed the vehicle, finally muttering, "There it is."

As they turned down the dirt lane, Jack turned off the car lights. "This is old-man Macmillan's peach orchard. Make sure you're quiet. It's beautiful in there, but if the old man hears us, he'll send out his dogs."

Jack drove another quarter mile before he pulled over against the white board fence and turned the engine off. They both exited, and Jack retrieved a blanket from the rear compartment of the Jeep. He had a last second hesitation and turned to Carley. "You sure you're up to this? We can go back if you like."

Carley jumped up, leaning her waist against the edge of the top fence board. She swung herself over until her toes hit the tall grass on the other side. "This sounds like fun," she offered.

Jack handed her the blanket and the bag of drinks. Jumping and placing one foot on the top board, he propelled himself overtop to a landing beside her. "This way," he said, "But keep quiet."

They walked through the ankle-length grass between two rows of trees in the darkness only broken intermittently by the light of the half-moon. He led, searching, and after a few minutes, said, "There it is." They walked another 30 feet to a spot under a huge peach tree growing from a slight rise in the terrain. There was a long-forgotten, overgrown hedge beside them, breaking the slight breeze coming from the west. Jack took the blanket and laid it out against the protected edge of the hedge.

Carley handed him the bag and stated, "Mr. Engineer—there's a flaw in your plan. You can't drink since you have to drive me home later."

Jack scratched his head and finally pulled the pint of rum from the bag. He walked to the hedge, unscrewed the cap, and turned the bottle over. The rum spilled out as Carley's eyes went wide. He continued until only a small amount was left in the bottom of the bottle. "Hand me the coke," he said while holding his open hand out to her.

She unscrewed the cap of the coke bottle and handed it to Jack. Very carefully, he tipped the coke bottle over the rum bottle allowing a thin stream to flow down and mix with the rum. Once the rum bottle was once again full, he handed it back to Carley. "It'll be safe enough to drive with that small amount of rum, but at least drinking out of the bottle will bring back the memories."

"Fair enough," Carley responded. She tilted her head back and took a long swig of the mixed drink. She replaced the cap and threw the bottle back to Jack before finding a comfortable spot on the blanket.

Jack joined her, and it wasn't long before half the bottle was gone. They were both lying on their backs, looking up at the moon through the branch tips. "So, tell me about Carley," Jack said.

"It's a pretty simple story. My family have been farmers in Ohio for several generations, and we still have a large farm south of Canton, growing wheat, cabbage and cucumbers."

"Why aren't you there?" He tilted his head up off the ground and took another drink from the bottle.

She looked over at Jack. "My fingers just aren't into farming as the rest of the families are. I have an older brother who works the farm with my father. I received a small inheritance a couple of years ago from my grandmother, so that keeps me off the streets."

"Are you working?"

"I'm between jobs right now, but I'm thinking I might go back to school. I'm not sure. I have more time to think about it before my inheritance runs out," Carley answered. "How about you? Tell me what happened in Philadelphia."

Jack shifted onto his side with his head held up by his arm propped on his elbow. "I told you before, my employer and I didn't see eye to eye, so I left."

"There has to be more to it than that." She laughed as her finger poked him in the rib.

He couldn't hold back his own laughter and grabbed her hand before it could pull away. He let the contact linger before he released her. "I have a lot of ideas in my head. One I've had for a while is what I call a *variable speed trigger.*"

"Say what?"

Jack shifted a bit closer to explain. "All power tools have a trigger you push, and it turns the tool on, or when not depressed, it is off."

"That's easier to understand," she said, now propped up on her own elbow facing him.

"I had a concept I proposed to my senior management. It's for a trigger that's variable. That means, as you push it, the speed ramps up. Push it just a little and the speed is slower. As you push it further in, the speed increases. Once fully depressed, you have full speed."

"That sounds very complicated," she responded.

Jack chuckled. "That's what they said— 'too complicated.' Since they didn't want any part of it, I made all the drawings myself, on my own time, and applied for the patent, which I received."

She grinned. "Complicated to impressive—I like that."

"My management team didn't think my independence was impressive. Once they heard about the patent, they said they owned it since I was working for them when I applied. I told them to show me the hiring document I signed indicating patents were transferred to them. It was actually a hole in their hiring process, and they couldn't produce it. But it didn't stop them from asking me to leave."

Jack was passionate about his patent and didn't notice, as he was explaining, that her hand had been placed over his. It had been there for some time, until now, when she reached up and tickled his ribs. She laughed. "Such boring engineering stuff!"

"I won't let you get away with that a second time," he scolded just before his own laugh broke out. Jack rolled over half on top of her with both of them tickling in one location, then another as their fingers searched out the most vulnerable spots. They rolled over several times, consumed with laughter until, suddenly, Jack put his finger to his lips. "Listen," he said.

Off in the distance, they could hear a dog barking and snarling. They both turned on their stomach and peered through the hedge's lower branches toward the source of the sound. They both jolted, and Carley screamed when a bright light was turned on in the distance.

"Holy shit!" Jack cried.

They both scurried to their feet, picked up their belongings and made a speedy retreat back toward the car. "Hell!" Jack yelled as a shotgun blast cracked the darkness.

The sound of the shotgun had an impact on Carley. Her legs spun faster as she pulled away from Jack. He strained and was barely able to keep up to her.

The voice in the distance carried to them. "Get out of here you god damn kids! The next shot won't be in the air!"

Carley bounced over the fence in an efficient style reminding Jack of a military maneuver. He also bounced off the fence and over, but not without damage. His gut hit the top board in a manner knocking the wind from him. They both knelt with one knee on the ground as the quiet once again overtook the orchard. They waited a couple of minutes, making sure there were no more indications of the farmer or the menacing dog.

They smiled at each other as Jack's breath came back to him. He said, "It's a good thing the farmer didn't let the dog out after us. You're really quick, but I don't think we could have out run the mutt."

Carley chuckled while they both rose to their feet. She peered over the fence, then returned her gaze back to him. "I wouldn't have to out run the dog. I would have only had to out run *you*!"

She leaned in as her fingers came up to his cheek. She gave him a fleeting kiss—quick but soft with a meaning. She pulled away, grinning. "Okay, maybe you're not so boring."

She turned and got back in the car, leaving him standing there bewildered. A wry smile slowly came onto his face as he thought, *I think I like her.*

Chapter 4: Esoteric Stew

The final whistle blew, indicating the *Monday Night Football* game was at an end. The final score was *Pittsburg Steelers* - 24 and the *Cleveland Browns* - 3.

Jack leaned back in the hot tub and sighed. "Some things don't change. The Browns are still one of the worst teams in the league."

Mario, who was an avid Brown's fan, said, "Don't badmouth my team. They had a lousy night, but they'll bounce back."

"Dream on! They're all pieces of shit, and they bounce the way shit bounces—with a *splat*!" Shoe said.

BB laughed as Mario walked down the steps into the hot tub, carrying the four cold cans he retrieved from his fridge. "Pass the beers. We can drown our sorrows," BB said.

Mario had a scowl on his face, and it turned sinister. "Fish for your beers boys!" With that, he threw the four cans into the hot water.

"No! Ya eejit!" BB yelled. He went under, head first, followed by Shoe, then Jack. When the three came up shaking their heads like dogs, Mario had a puzzled look on his face, as he realized he threw his beer in as well.

"Damn!" Mario yelled just before he dove under the water to retrieve the last can.

"You're a moron, Mario," Shoe said. "You can't do anything right."

"If you don't like it, give me back the beer," Mario retorted.

Jack started laughing. It started as a chuckle, but soon it was uncontrollable. It only took a minute of hearing Jack, for BB, Shoe and Mario to also be roaring, even though they had no idea why.

BB, tried to get the words out while attempting to hold back the sobs. "What—" It was no use. He couldn't continue as another explosion of laughter came from his lungs.

Jack lifted his hand from the water and pointed at BB's head as another even louder roar came out.

Shoe was panting since he had very little air to support more laughing. The opportunity was there, so he quickly asked, "What is it?" The words came out just in time before another howl was let lose.

Jack, BB and Mario almost regained control, but Shoe's howl set them off once again, and it took another five minutes before their hysteria quelled.

"What was that all about?" Shoe asked.

Jack took a long sip of beer before answering. "It suddenly struck me that all four of us have wet hair, but only I have hair that actually *looks* wet."

BB, Shoe and Mario all tilted their heads slightly to the right, similar to what a dog does when it has a lack of understanding.

Jack clarified, "Look at my hair! It's still sopping wet, and it's flattened to my head the way wet hair should. Now, for the three of you, as soon as you came up, your hair looked instantly dry."

"What kind of *bolloxology* are you talking?" BB said as he looked into the water trying to see his reflection.

Jack continued. "As soon as you came out of the water and gave your head a shake, there was a slight jiggle of the frizzy afro and bam—instant dry!"

Mario laughed as he looked at BB, confirming Jack's observation.

"Mario, you're no better with your tight Italian curls. Your hair is like a helmet. If you hit your head into one of those concrete walls your dad builds, your skull would fracture, but not one hair on your head would be out of place. What chance does a bit of water have!"

"I know—I'm next," Shoe predicted.

"When I think about it, Mario and BB were born with their hair being what it is, but you—you had to learn how to do what you do to your hair. It took a plan with training and tubs of hair gel for your hair not to budge when wet. It's a consciously learned trait."

"That's not funny Jack. You're a *rale* barbarian, ya are." BB said.

"Piece of shit," Shoe muttered.

BB took a deep drink from the beer can. "There's something that's been bothering me, and it's more important than wet or dry hair."

"What's up dude?" Jack asked.

"Back in the day there were four of us, but when you left, we became three. Now we're four again, and it's taking some getting used to. In some ways, three is more natural," BB answered.

"That's stunned, you goof," Shoe said. "What does it matter—three or four—as long as we're friends?"

"Have you ever heard of The *Three Caballeros*, or *The Three Musketeers* or even *The Three Stooges*. It's always *three*." BB laid out the theory.

"And the *Three Little Pigs* or *The Three Bears*," Shoe added with a snicker.

BB ignored the malcontent. "There doesn't seem to be anything important until we get to higher numbers. We can remember *The Magnificent Seven* or The *Dirty Dozen*. I can't think of anything with four, five or six except a quartet, and that's embarrassing. I don't want us to be compared to barber shop singers."

"Your mind goes to places where no man has gone before," Mario said.

It was very strange to Jack, but BB was his good friend. Ever since the day he pee'd his pants, Jack knew if he was ever in trouble, BB would come running as would Shoe or Mario. A few quirks were easily overlooked, and Jack needed to come up with a solution to BB's predicament.

"You mentioned the *Three Musketeers*. Did you forget about d'Artagnan? There were actually four of them," Jack offered.

Tapping his finger into his chin, BB thought about it. "That's brilliant! You're right! We are the *Four* Musketeers!"

"Right on," Mario said. He turned his gaze to Jack. "I assume you are d'Artagnan since you have a lady friend."

"Nice play Mario. You always have a roundabout way of putting your nose into my business," Jack said.

Mario shrugged. "I try."

"We did go to a movie on Saturday night. She's a lot of fun."

"What movie did you go see?" Shoe asked, "I haven't been to a movie in forever."

"*Superman*," Jack replied.

"You took a girl to a cartoon movie?" Mario's eyebrows were raised in astonishment.

"No, you idiot! It's a regular adult movie. Christopher Reeves has the lead." Jack wondered why he gave them even this little piece of information. They were asking questions like little old ladies.

Shoe laid out his thoughts. "I can't believe they made a real-life movie about a cartoon character. I love comics—all kinds of them, but that's where superheroes belong. Pulling superheroes out of comics into the real world—well there's something deeply wrong with that."

Jack crossed his arms. "Well, they did."

"Mark my words. The movie will be a flop. It's the first and last superhero movie you'll ever see. Superheroes on the big screen—what were they thinking?" Shoe finished by shaking his head.

"I'm bushed guys, so I need to boogie," Jack said through a yawn.

Mario put a hand on Jack's shoulder. "Stay a few more minutes. I want you to watch something I taped from the TV. It's hilarious."

Jack settled back down. "Okay, as long as it's not too long."

Mario shuffled over to the TV, leaned behind it, and pulled a VHS tape machine to the front. He picked up the tape on top of it. Giving it a little shake, he looked at Jack and said, "It's a skit from the *David Simpson Variety Show*. It really is hilarious!"

"I haven't seen him in a while," Jack replied. "There's a lot of really good British comedy on his show."

The tape was inserted into the machine, and Mario pressed the play button. The skit started with David Simpson, in a red, military-style uniform, sitting at a large desk, reading reports. Then, there was a knock.

"Come in," David said.

A door opened and another man in a similar uniform, but blue, entered the room. He saluted David under a silver cap identical to the one David wore.

David smiled wide and shook the other man's hand. "Please sit down. Larson, how long has it been—ten years?"

"Captain Razor, it has actually been 12 years since my last report from Earth."

"Amazing," Captain Razor said. He tapped his finger on the report on his desk. "I am impressed with your evaluation of the Earth people."

"Thank you," Larson replied. "I've been living among the Earth subjects for 24 years now, and I believe, as my recommendation states, they're ready to be educated regarding the *Alliance of Planets*. They've come a long way since my last report, and they'd make an excellent addition as the 354th world of the Alliance. Unfortunately, there are still wars but nothing nuclear. The different countries, and now even the different races, live together somewhat cohesively. Although there are always improvements possible, they've progressed very well."

"It does appear so," Razor said. "How about family values?"

Larson leaned forward. "Again, much improved. There are divorces, but it's probably better than people living together unhappily."

"Captain Razor raised an eyebrow. "Unhappily?"

"It's nothing to worry about because the divorce is now seen as acceptable to most."

Captain Razor nodded and raised the rubber stamp in his hand, imprinted with the word - *Approved*. It was on its way to Larson's letter of recommendation when Larson chuckled and said, "Husband and wife used to fight like cats and dogs."

Captain Razor's hand came to an abrupt stop an inch from the paper, and he placed the stamp on the table. "Cats and dogs?"

"It's nothing important. Humans have pets. Cats and dogs are two species they prefer."

"So, cats and dogs are animals?"

"Yes. Both species are four-legged, cute, furry animals. As such, humans keep them in their homes."

Captain Razor's eyes grew a little wider. "You're kidding? They keep animals in their homes? These dogs, as you call them, what do they do when they need to defecate?"

"It's difficult to explain if you haven't seen a dog on Earth."

"Try," Razor said.

"Well, a dog can be well trained. When they need to defecate, they go to a back door, and this signals the human owner to let the dog out to the backyard."

"They shit in the backyard? Isn't that awkward for the owners and their children, who might want to enjoy the yard?" Razor asked.

"Larson started to fidget. "Well, intermittently, the owners go out and pick up the poo."

Razor jumped to his feet. "Humans pick up the dog shit! Great Saturn's Ring!"

"Please, calm yourself Captain," Larson said. "You must understand the relationship between humans and dogs is very special. There's a saying that 'a dog is man's best friend.'"

With his elbow on the desk and his finger pressed to his temple, Razor asked, "Isn't there a problem with the dogs propagating? After all, most animals have temperamental urges on a cyclic timetable."

"The humans have a solution. It might not sound elegant, but it does work. The dogs are either spayed or neutered to relax their temperament."

"The words are foreign to me. What is 'spayed and neutered?'"

Larson thought for a second. "There's only a crude but simple explanation available. The humans cut out their genitalia."

Captain Razor's face pitched forward as he choked on a breath. "They cut off their nuts!"

"Or their ovaries, if the dog is a female."

"Larson, I am getting confused and this gives me some hesitation. You say dogs are man's best friend. You do not cut off your best friend's nuts. Tell me about cats. Hopefully they have a less torturous story."

"Cats are similar furred animals although they are typically smaller than dogs," Larson explained.

"Why aren't they man's best friend?"

"Many people own cats, but they're more temperamental than dogs. They aren't easily trained and are more likely to destroy objects such as chairs and curtains with their sharp claws. Nevertheless, some cats are very cuddly and affectionate, but some just prefer to be left alone," Larson said.

"I take it humans also cut out cat's genitals for the same reasons as stated for dogs," Razor said.

"That's a fact," Larson said. "They will also cut out the cat's claws if the damage they might inflict becomes excessive."

Captain Razor chuckled sarcastically. "Of course they do. After all, they aren't man's best friend now, are they?"

"Not all cats have their claws removed. Some cats are outside cats, and they need the claws to protect themselves from dogs and other cats," Larson explained.

Razor took a deep breath. "I understand one species might not like another, so they fight. But you said, 'outside cats.' That implies there are inside cats, and the concept is increasing my confusion."

"You're correct. There are inside cats. It can be dangerous outside, so some humans cut off their cat's claws and cut out their nuts, and in this case, they're safe exclusively in the home of their human owner."

"If someone threatened to cut out my finger nails, toe nails and my balls, I would not feel very safe," Captain Razor offered. "If they are in the house all the time, where do they defecate?"

Finally, able to offer a sensible answer, Larson smiled. "The humans train their cats to urinate and defecate in a box in the house."

"And, of course, the humans clean it up for them." Razor shook his head. "I think you have your facts mixed up. You said dogs were easier to train, yet they shit in the yard. Cats, on the other hand, are not easy to train, but they are smart enough to shit in a box, like some kind of vulgar circus trick. I take it outside cats shit in the backyard?"

"Actually, outside cats shit anywhere."

Correct me if I am wrong Larson. Are you telling me dogs shit in their owner's yard, and cats shit in anyone's yard? This is the accepted practice?"

"Well, yes." Larson realized he was failing miserably in explaining the story of cats and dogs, so he decided to move the conversation down a different path. "Dogs and cats can be very beautiful animals, especially if they are purebreds."

"That's a term we in the Alliance of Planets have not used in a long time. Please explain." Razor leaned closer to listen to the details.

Larson thought carefully as he organized his words. "For example, there are many sub-species of dogs. Humans make efforts to keep the breeds pure by only raising offspring from a pure line of the sub-species. If a new-born dog, known as a puppy, comes from such a pairing, they're considered purebred. They're highly prized and very valuable. In other cases, if two different sub-species propagate, the offspring dog is considered a *mutt*."

Razor opened a drawer in his desk and pulled out a book. "Remember this? It is the Earth dictionary you gave me on your last visit, and now, I finally have the chance to use it." He opened the book, turning page after page. "Mutt. Ah, there it is. Mutt—a mongrel dog or a stupid or insignificant person."

The captain smashed the book closed, and his eyes were afire. "I have heard quite enough. The human race is bizarre. That is the best word I can come up with. They pick up animal shit. They cut out their balls! Some of their pets shit in a box. Some shit in their yard, and some shit anywhere. But now, you tell me a dog is man's best friend, and I see this means a friend that is stupid or insignificant! Unbelievable!

However, the last straw is hidden in your words. You have told me racism is dwindling on Earth, yet here you are telling me of man's efforts to create pureblood races of dogs and cats. Are you telling me man is cured of their need to create the super race, and at the same time these same humans are creating super races of dogs and cats?"

Larson's mouth opened in an effort to respond.

"Don't bother to answer, Larson. I think you have been on Earth too long, and you stumble over your own words." Captain Razor flung open another drawer and pulled out a different stamp. He slammed it down on the report. Your recommendation for Earth to be assimilated into the Alliance of Planets is—rejected!"

Throughout the comedy skit the audience laughed, and BB, Shoe, Mario and Jack joined them. Now, with the skit ended, there was polite applause from the audience, cut short by Mario pressing the *off button* on the VHS machine.

"What did you think of that?" Shoe asked Jack.

"It was hilarious! I'll never think of cats and dogs in the same way ever again."

"I was busting a gut as well," Mario added. "But what did you think about the rest of it—the whole theme of aliens deciding the fate of Earth?"

"Aliens? I'm not sure what you're getting at?" Jack replied with a curious look on his face.

Mario continued. "Do you think it could be true? Are there aliens out there watching us?"

"Probably," Jack replied. "We know by now there are billions of planets. It would be naive to think we're the only sentient beings in all of that expanse."

"True enough, but do you think they might be already here in Ohio?" Mario asked.

Jack's finger pointed downward. "Here—aliens in Canton?" He smiled and soon was laughing uproariously for the second time this evening. If his laughing wasn't so hysterical and his head wasn't thrown back with his eyes closed, he would have seen, this time, he was the only one laughing.

Chapter 5: Iguana Sex Dance

Tilting his wristwatch toward his gaze, Jack asked, "What time is BB picking us up?"

A horn sounded twice from Mario's driveway.

Mario Popped up from his leather couch. "Psyche! That's him now."

Jack and Mario hustled out of Mario's pad, walking through the metal gate toward BB's van. It was a 1973 Chevy van, but it was anything but ordinary. Painted metallic-brown and supported by wide, black tires on solid, white rims, Jack realized it was as much an art piece as a mode of transportation. As he moved closer, he could now make out the amazing detailed mural on the side body metal. There was a fierce looking horse's head with wild anger in its eyes and hot air curling from its nostrils. Slightly faded in the background was the shadow of a dark rider wearing a low-brimmed cowboy hat while holding a flaming lasso in a raised fist. Just behind him were three more dark riders at a full gallop, racing after the first rider. Above them, the metallic-brown melded and then changed into a midnight-blue night sky lit by a full moon.

BB smiled wide. "What do you think?" The slight breeze buffeted the whirlwind cowlick in BB's afro as the question was asked.

"Outta sight! What do you have inside?" Jack replied.

Opening the driver door, BB offered, "Hop in and have a look."

Stepping up into the van, Jack put one hand on the back of each front bucket seat and looked rearward. The inside was as impressive as the outside. A bed ran the entire width along the back of the smartly-trimmed living space, and the floor was covered with gold, shag carpet. There was an additional, smaller bucket seat on the left side behind the driver while on the right side there were oak cabinets and a mini fridge.

By now, both BB and Mario had entered the van. "Help yourself to the rear seat," BB said to Jack.

Jack lowered himself into it as the van started to move down the driveway. "Did you win some money?" Jack asked.

"I got a line on this van from a friend. A dude in North Dakota wanted rid of it, and the price was really sweet," BB replied.

Jack leaned left as BB took a right turn onto highway 30. "I don't get it. Why such a good deal?"

BB laughed. "Well, it was in a police impound yard. This dude had been running a hooker ring out of the van until he got busted. Since there were all kinds of strange activities going on in the van, no one in the entire state wanted it, but for an out of state guy, it was a steal of a deal! I just had to pay the impound fees and *BABAM*—I was the proud owner of the *Shaggin-wagon!*"

Jack lifted his ass off the seat cushion with the news of unknown, seedy activities.

"Chillax. Everything is copacetic since I had the van professionally cleaned, and the mattress at the back is new. You won't catch anything," BB assured Jack.

"Listen to this," BB said. "I just had an eight-track player installed two weeks ago." He pushed in a tape, and Pink Floyd vibrations pushed into the van from the four speakers, one mounted in each corner of the rear compartment. "Just sit back and hang loose."

Jack leaned forward. "I would enjoy this a lot more if you guys told me why we have to go to this place in Dalton. I have a girl now, and you're taking up valuable time."

Mario interjected, "You haven't said very much about this girl. What's the skinny on her?"

"We've been on five dates now. It's getting pretty hot, but that's all you need to know," Jack answered with a smug grin.

Mario turned, pointing a finger at Jack. "Don't beat the bush around! We've been your friends a lot longer than your time with this flash in the can girl! You, at least, need to give us the sorted details."

BB lifted his hand from the steering wheel into the air, checking Jack before he could speak. "Let me handle this one," he said.

In what began as a soft, sympathetic tone, BB explained. "I know from time to time you mix up a few words, but often we ignore it, knowing your family mainly speaks Italian in your home. It can be a handicap." BB put his hand on Mario's shoulder. "Sometimes we feel the need to correct you just so you learn, but right now you hit the motherlode of fucked up words, and it's difficult to overlook." He lifted his hand and smacked Mario in the ear. "You made not one, not two, but three mistakes in the same breath. For most people the odds of that happening would be unimaginable."

40

Mario flinched from the whack in the ear.

BB continued to drive and spurt the onslaught at Mario while occasionally glancing over at his Italian friend. "You're thick as a brick, Mario. Don't say anything and just listen. *Beat the bush around*—ya eejit! It's *don't beat around the bush*. Next, it's flash in the *pan*, not flash in the *can*. Finally, and I think I heard you right—no one *sorts* their girlfriend details—ya gobshite! It's *sordid*, meaning dirty. Dirty girl details make sense."

Jack kept quiet and smiled, but he did feel sorry for Mario who, as usual, was just trying too hard.

Mario grumbled, "Minor details—that's all it is."

Jack chuckled as he reversed his thoughts of sorrow for his friend who just didn't know when to leave it alone. "I've got this one BB. Mario, there's a saying you should consider."

"What is it?" Mario retorted while rolling his eyes.

"Better to stay quiet and let them think you a fool than to open your mouth and remove all doubt!" Jack chided.

Mario turned, looked at Jack, then snapped his head and his attention toward BB. "And what kind of guttural back alley English is 'gobshite!' What about 'whanker?' Talk about my use of English and…"

BB reached down and turned up the music volume, drowning out whatever else Mario had to say.

It was 15 minutes later when they reached their destination, and Shoe was already at the reststop on highway 30. He waved from a picnic table under a large maple tree. Jack, BB and Mario walked over with each taking a seat on the wooden boards of the bench, next to him.

Jack began. "Is someone going to finally tell me why you three are acting so weird, and why we're here out in the middle of nowhere on a beautiful Saturday afternoon?"

Shoe looked at BB and then Mario. "Is he ready?"

BB shrugged. "As ready as he'll ever be."

Jack threw up his arms. "Ready for what?"

"Shut up Jack," Shoe whispered as his dark eyes looked furtively from side to side. "I mean—be quiet. We have some stuff to tell you, but it could put you in danger. There has been some really weird shit going on since you've been gone."

"Okay. I'm all ears," Jack responded.

"If we tell you absolutely all the information we have, we would be here a long time. We need to show you—show you the proof that the unbelievable story we're about to tell you is true. First, we need to…"

"Stop acting the maggot and cut to the chase," BB interrupted. "We are after aliens and the Amish."

Jack didn't say anything for a few moments, hoping someone would correct BB. It didn't come. "What do illegal aliens have to do with the Amish?"

Mario pointed a finger up toward the sky. "Not illegal aliens—space aliens, and no, I'm not mixing up my words."

Before Jack could reply, Shoe continued. "Do you remember when we were in grade 11, and we did a science project on UFO's and alien abductions?"

The memory brought back a smile. "Sure. It was a lot of fun, and we put together a real good story. Wait—you don't really believe that stuff, do you?"

"Initially, no. But we were never satisfied, so we kept visiting Professor Johansen at Wooster college. He had huge amounts of very compelling documentation. You remember him, don't you?" Shoe queried.

"Sure," Jack answered. "He was impressive and very smart."

"Well, he is impressive, smart and very dead," Mario continued.

"Under very mysterious circumstances," Shoe added. "If you recall, he was a Professor of Astronomy at Wooster and spent most of his time in the mini-planetarium."

Jack said, "Sure. It was a very cool place."

Shoe's eyes narrowed, and once again, he inspected the reststop before quietly continuing. "Then you remember he was 62 and in good shape. It wasn't like him to fall off the walkway running around the inside perimeter of the planetarium since the walkway is only three feet off the ground. How likely would it be to suffer a broken neck from such a low fall over a waist-high, sturdy railing?"

"That is odd," Jack muttered.

"That's all we should say for now," BB said. "We think there are people following us, so we have to be careful. That's why we talk about it in places like this where there are no electronic bugs. We do see shadowy people from time to time, but we should not get into that right now. Just bear with us as we show you more evidence at a pace that won't overwhelm you."

"No problem. I can see by the look on your faces, this isn't some practical joke. I'll tag along until we prove or disprove your theory," Jack concluded. The thoughts going through Jack's head didn't match his words. Right now, he thought his friends had lost their marbles, but they were his *best* friends, so he would play along—if for no other reason than just that alone.

They arose from the picnic table and headed back toward the parking area. Shoe pointed. "That's my bike."

"Wow—nice! What is it?" Jack questioned.

As they moved closer, Shoe said, "It's a 1970 Triumph Bonneville, and it runs great."

As Shoe lifted the seat, Jack noticed the slippery oil spot under the engine. "Bummer—it leaks a bit."

Having retrieved the object from the storage compartment, Shoe fit it down over his head.

Jack laughed. "What the hell is that?"

"What does it look like? It's a helmet," Shoe said as he tightened the chin strap and put on a cool pair of mirror-faced, air-force-style sunglasses.

Jack answered. "What does it look like? It's boxing headgear! It has two inches of black padding all the way around your head with a big hole at the top. You look stunned."

Shoe tilted his head down and peered at Jack over the rim of the flashy glasses. "Do you know what a full motorcycle helmet does to the gel spikes on the top of my head? It looks pathetic."

Jack started walking backward while holding two thumbs up. Sarcastically, he said, "It's a good trade off. Right now, you look terrific!"

From the reststop, BB's van barreled south, followed by the noisy motorcycle. After five minutes, they came to a crossroad in the heart of Amish country. On one corner was a gas station while on the corner, opposite to it, was a restaurant. On the other two corners were a Mennonite furniture store and the biggest hardware store Jack had ever seen.

In front of Miller's Hardware were two lines of large pine trees in an elegant setting of mulch and intermingled shrubs. Between the foliage and the store was a large parking lot, and, at the time, it was filled equally with motorized vehicles and the wagons and buggies used by the Amish. In the vacant far corner Shoe parked his motorcycle alongside the van. He stored the helmet and flashy glasses under the motorcycle seat before pulling a second set of dark sunglasses over his eyes.

Jack turned to Shoe and said, "Why the switch to dark glasses?"

"We don't need any unwanted attention, so inconspicuous is the name of the game," Shoe answered.

Jack glanced at Shoe. The hair on the side of his head was pressed flat against the side of his head. The spikes had been pressed perfectly vertical out the top of the helmet so that his hair looked like a crown of black glass shards. His gaze lowered. "For god's sake. You have silver running shoes on!" Jack said. "That's real inconspicuous." He just shook his head as he followed his three friends to the front door of Miller's Hardware.

As they were about to enter, Shoe muttered, "Time to bust a move."

Crap. Here we go again, Jack thought.

As they entered the door, Jack now saw a small tool bag swung from Shoe's hand. "I'm going to attend the small how-to class at the front of the store," Shoe declared. "Hardwood flooring installation is the topic. You guys see what you can find out roaming the aisles."

The store was busy with about one third of the patrons easily identifiable as Amish. The rest looked like typical farmer folk.

"The first observation is evident when you see the Amish families here," Mario said.

There were indeed quite a few Amish families wandering the store. In the main aisle, families were in discussion while others were looking for items to purchase. "They look normal enough to me," Jack concluded.

"Sure, if we were in Sears, but this is a hardware store," Mario offered.

"Why does that matter?"

Mario said, "Do you see any toys here? Do you see chocolate bars or candies on a rack? Why do the Amish parents bring their kids, or their wives for that matter? There isn't anything for them here, but the bigger question is, why aren't the kids whining and complaining? They're quiet and smiling and that's just not normal."

BB gave Jack's shoulder a shake. "Quick, we need to follow that Amish family down the shoe aisle."

They tried not to look hurried, but they still took quick steps to the target aisle. They pretended to look at the work boots on the shelves while constantly glancing toward the Amish family at the other end of it.

"What are we looking for?" Jack whispered.

"See the mirror at the end of the aisle—just watch," Mario whispered back.

The Amish father, having tried on a sturdy pair of work boots, was looking at them in the mirror at the end of the aisle. His son was looking into the same mirror, also admiring the foot wear. The mother and another woman, both had their heads tipped down under their bonnets, and it appeared they were making a conscious effort to not look into the mirror.

Jack raised a corner of his lip, thinking, *what's that about?* His train of thought was broken by the tug of BB's hand on his shoulder as he was yanked out of the shoe aisle. BB's hand slid across to the other shoulder, and Mario joined the huddle.

"You saw it?" BB whispered.

"Yeah," Jack responded. "The women won't look into the mirror."

"We have seen it many times. The younger women will, but the married women won't," BB qualified.

Mario whispered, "I only know of one group of people who don't look into mirrors."

"Jack's eyes widened. "You can't mean…"

"Vampires." BB finished the sentence for him. "Blood-sucking vampires…"

"Maybe even blood sucking vampires from outer space," Mario added.

Jack rose out of the huddle. "That's a bit of a reach."

Mario placed his hand on Jack's shoulder. "We're just pointing out observations, Jack, but we have more to show you."

They walked down the main aisle until BB veered down a side aisle. There were three Amish men, and two others who didn't appear to be Amish, looking at various power tools. One Amish man was holding up an electrical drill to show his friend. The third Amish man was holding up a circular saw close to his eye and listened to the *click* as he practiced pulling the trigger.

"I don't get it," Jack said.

BB leaned in toward Jack. "That's because you haven't done the hundreds and hundreds of hours of recon we have." BB's voice lowered as he continued. "Amish people don't use electric power tools because they don't use electricity."

"Then, why are they looking at power tools?" Jack questioned.

"Exactly," Mario said, his eyes narrowed to suspicious slits. "It's a very good question." The words sent a chill down Jack's spine.

"The next aisle—leg it," BB blurted.

The three young men moved into the neighboring aisle where a sign above it read - *Tool Supplies*. The men who had been inspecting the electric drill, were now slowly walking down the aisle toward them and intermittently pulling boxes off the shelf. They weren't finding what they were looking for until they were half-way down the aisle. They stopped and pulled several larger boxes off the shelf, inspecting each before selecting one. They were discussing the boxes and finally kept the larger one as they walked down the aisle past Jack, BB and Mario.

"C'mon—quick," BB said as he led Jack and Mario to the spot where the two Amish men had been contemplating the different sized boxes.

"I'm still confused," Jack said.

"And we have told you why," Mario offered.

"Shut up, Mario," BB said. "Look at the boxes they were looking at and the bigger box they finally left with."

Jack leaned forward, peering at the different boxes. "They're all wall plugs. They bought a box of 500. So what?"

BB poked Jack in the chest. "So what? How many pictures do you think Amish families have to hang in their houses?"

"Or mirrors," Mario added. "They don't seem to like mirrors."

"Well, it's weird when you put it that way," Jack agreed.

"You're finally starting to catch our drift," Mario said. "There's a pack of weirdness going on in this store."

"Pack of weirdness?" BB looked at Mario. "Is *weirdness* even a word?"

"Buzz off," Mario replied.

BB grinned. "To add to the weirdness, look at the quantities. There are smaller packets of wall plugs, but here are quantities of 250, 500, and look, there's even a 1000-piece box."

Jack scratched his head.

"We've done research, and this is the only hardware store in Ohio that carries these larger quantities on the shelf—right here in the middle of Amish country where they don't use power tools so don't have a need for wall plugs," Mario explained.

"So, here's the answer, Jack," BB interrupted. "These Amish people maybe aren't all Amish. Our info says there are space aliens hiding in the Amish community—hiding in plain sight!"

Jack's mouth involuntarily moved to its extreme open position and expelled the loudest laugh. "Ha Ha Ha Ha!" After 30 seconds, he was able to quell the laugh. "That makes no sense at all, so you can't be serious. Why would aliens hide out with Amish?"

"Because Amish don't use power tools. You see, the conspiracy is even deeper and more convoluted." BB leaned in close to Jack and tapped his forehead. "The alien minds are different. We have solid evidence their brains get discombobulated when they're within range of very specific electromagnetic frequencies, and they happen to be exactly the frequencies produced by the high RPM motors in typical power tools."

"Can you dig it?" Mario asked Jack.

Jack stood there with his mouth half open.

Mario continued. "The people who, no matter how hard they try, can't use power tools without hurting themselves, well, it's not their fault. They aren't idiots. They're idiot aliens! And the wall plugs—that's for the kids. The aliens have been here for a long, long time, and their numbers are growing. Those sweet, innocent Amish-looking kids are alien offspring. Their parents are training them so they can survive and, one day, assimilate with the rest of us. It must be torturous as the parents force those kids to install wall plug after wall plug, day after day, week after week and month after month. With constant intermittent exposure to the debilitating electromagnetism, they are trying to create an immunity to their affliction. If they succeed in overcoming the power tool syndrome, humanity won't be able to stop them."

Jack was still standing on the same spot, but his mouth was still open very wide. "That's fuc…"

The awkward conversation was broken by a commotion at the front of the store. As the three of them moved toward it, the commotion heightened into all out yelling. They cleared the last side aisle and heard the noise coming from a group of chairs at the how-to class. Moving closer, they saw a man in front of a bench, and on it was a long piece of hardwood flooring and a circular saw. The man looked angry and was glaring at Shoe.

Shoe had his knees bent and was balanced on his toes like a lion about to pounce. "I said, pick up the freaking saw, and use it, you piece of shit!"

The store facilitator stepped between them with his hands holding Shoe away from the other man. "It's okay. Not everyone is ready to use a power tool."

From his tool bag on the chair, Shoe whipped out the item. He clicked on the switch, and a deep vibrating *burr* erupted from the baseball-size orb at the business end. The Amish women watching the commotion looked at the odd device curiously while shrugging toward each other with their confusion.

A younger woman, lacking the Amish bonnet, suddenly held her fingertips to her cheek. Her eyes opened wide and through trembling lips she yelled at the top of her lungs, "Oh my god. It's a vibrator!"

Shoe glanced at the woman with an evil smirk on his lips. "Not just a vibrator. It's the Hitachi Magic Wand—the most powerful vibrator sold in the pornographic world!"

The woman screamed a second time as the Amish women continued with the look of confusion on their faces.

Shoe lunged forward under the facilitator's arm, using the vibrator like a sword, trying to prod the vibrating ball into contact with the older man. "How do you like that! I'm going to turn your brain into scrambled eggs!"

Jack was in a full run by this time, when a figure caught his peripheral vision. His head turned and there was the same person Jack had seen before. It was the mysterious person wearing the blue jeans and the black hoodie. Oddly, once again the hood was pulled up over his head. Jack thought, *I don't have time for that right now* as he jumped the chairs and grabbed Shoe by his shirt collar. Shoe almost fell before he managed to gather his feet back under him as Jack dragged him out the front door. BB and Mario were close behind. BB grasped Shoe's empty tool bag on the way by and yelled out, "Apologies!" as they sped past the baffled shoppers.

The shoppers and workers in the store were in a state of shock, not knowing what to do, but surely, not following the crazy young pervert with the dark glasses and spikey hair, was the correct choice.

As they were speeding away from the scene, Jack was as shocked as those in the store. Aliens, power tools and wall plugs were a connection he could not have conjured up on his very best abstract-thinking day. He just shook his head, first thinking, *what have I got myself into*. But after a few more seconds of thought, the endorphins started to flow through his body—more potent than cocaine or heroin, but natural and free. Jack sat back, enjoying the moment. He heard BB and Mario laughing uncontrollably, and finally his own burst of laughter exploded from his lips. Jack's thoughts changed from foreboding to exhilaration as he thought, *wow! That was a gas!*

Chapter 6: Trouble Started with Hello

"How much further?" Jack asked.

"It's only about 15 minutes more, but look up ahead. There's a traffic jam," BB said from the driver seat of the Shaggin-wagon.

Mario was lying down across the bed at the rear of the van. He rose up, looking at the long line of traffic blocking the two lanes of the highway they were traversing on their way to Beach City. Normally, the drive took 30 minutes, but it appeared they were going to be delayed.

Now blocked by the cars ahead, BB slowed the van to a crawl. "Bollocks! We're going to be late for sure."

Shoe, from the front passenger seat, glared at BB. "I told you this would happen if we made this trip on a Friday afternoon—fool that you are."

"Chillax. We'll get there eventually," Jack offered.

"It won't be good enough. The man we're going to visit runs a very tight ship. He'll think we're dorks if we're late," BB explained.

"There's lots of campers and families in cars," Mario observed. "They're going away for the weekend."

"We need to bust a move," BB stated. "Shoe, grab the microphone and do me a solid."

Jack leaned forward and his brow furrowed with curiosity as he watched Shoe take action. There was a CB radio hanging under the center of the dash, and hanging from it by a curly cord was the microphone. Shoe flicked one switch on the CB and turned the volume button to its highest position.

Shoe looked back at Jack and said, "In emergencies, we've used this process in the past. This is an emergency, so here goes." He looked over at BB. "You ready?"

"Ten-four—Roger—Roger. Ready when you are," BB replied.

Shoe cleared his throat once and then a second time. He pressed the button on the side of the microphone and placed his lips against it. Parting his lips, a low sound was emitted. Then, it was repeated louder and louder still. As the volume increased, the pitch increased as well.

"*Rrrroooaaarrr! Rrrroooaaarrr! Wooot! Wooot!*" The sounds repeated from Shoe's throat.

Shit! Jack thought. *The CB radio is also a loudspeaker, and we sound just like a police car!* "Does this work?" Jack asked. "We don't look like a police car."

It only took a few seconds for the answer to be evident. Driver's heads spun from side to side in their search for the emergency vehicle. Of course, there wasn't one, but they heard it. As BB veered toward the center line between the two lanes, cars, vans and campers all creeped onto the shoulder along either side of the highway.

"*Rrrroooaaarrr! Rrrroooaaarrr! Wooot! Wooot!*" Shoe continued the police siren impression to perfection.

The traffic parted for Shoe's wails just as Moses parted the Red Sea with his beseeching. Jack and Mario were howling hysterically in the rear compartment. Shoe continued, but upon hearing the laughter from the back, he sputtered and stuttered the sounds as little balls of spittle dropped from his lips.

Finally at their exit, BB veered down the side road, and they sped toward their destination. Before arriving at Beach City, which really was no more than a small town, they turned off onto a second side road, then a third and, finally, a fourth.

"I have no idea where we are." Jack stated.

"That's the idea," Shoe said. "This is top secret, and you can't talk to anyone about what you're going to see today."

"Get real," Jack said as he rolled his eyes.

BB slowed the van. "This is serious, Jack, so no more acting the whanker. You're either with us, or we turn around now."

"Relax. You guys are really tense about visiting this fellow, but I told you I'm in, so I am," Jack responded.

One hundred yards later, BB turned off onto a rarely used driveway defined by two lines of gravel still visible through the grass and weeds trying to overrun it. Ahead, the driveway just seemed to end at a thick line of trees, but as the van's bumper almost hit the first tree, BB turned the steering wheel hard to the right. The driveway continued in this direction for 30 feet until, again, a thick line of trees blocked their path. This time, BB made a hard left in a complete *U* turn while maintaining the tires on the gravel tracks. This back and forth pattern continued three more times before the van cleared the dense vegetation and popped out into a large clearing. Ahead, there was a large ranch house surrounded by a six-foot-high, steel, mesh fence.

BB continued driving down the gravel tracks to the large gate. He honked the horn and pushed his afro-shod head out the window while looking up at the camera attached to the fence post.

After a moment, the sound of a small motor could be heard as it pulled the gate open.

"Okay, we're in," Shoe said.

Once the van was near the front porch, they exited the vehicle and walked up the three steps to the faded, front door under a rusty metal canopy. Shoe pushed the doorbell, resulting in a loud chime followed by the speaker, hanging off the wall, crackling with static.

"Who the hell is he?" the voice asked.

"A new recruit," BB said. "His name is Jack Decker. He's a friend of ours, who just returned from Philadelphia."

"You vouch for him with your lives if need be?" the voice asked.

New recruit—vouch with your life? What kind of shit is this? Jack thought.

In unison, BB, Shoe and Mario said, "Yes."

For at least three minutes, there were the sounds of one lock after the other being unbolted from the other side of the door. Finally, the door swung open, and a man stepped into the doorway. He was of medium height, very thin with curly, white and grey hair well past his shoulders. The mound of hair was parted at the side and rose in a wave over the top of his head to slide down to the opposite shoulder. He wore flip flops, yellow beach shorts and a red and green, Hawaiian style, button-down shirt.

"Quick—quick!" he said as he pushed the four men into the small front hallway. He poked his head back out, looking from side to side before pulling himself back in and slamming the door shut. "You weren't followed?"

"Not a chance, Commander," BB answered.

Commander? Jack thought.

"Awesome!" the commander said as he smiled wide at Mario, BB and Shoe. "Glad you're back since we have a lot to do."

After they shook hands, Shoe turned and said to Jack, "This is Commander Peri Winkle."

Jack pressed out his hand and said, "Hello. My name is Jack…"

The commander raised his own hand, but instead of shaking Jack's hand, he pointed at Jack's watch. "Take it off. Put it in this tray along with your belt and any other change or metal objects you have in your pockets."

Jack smiled courteously and did as the man asked. Once everything was in the tray, the commander put it on the side table before opening one of the drawers. From it, he pulled out the portable metal detector and slid it up and down Jack's body.

"Really! You don't have to do that," Jack suggested.

The commander's pitch-black eyes bore into Jack. He didn't say a word while he thoroughly continued the inspection.

Once he put the detector back in the drawer, Jack reached for his watch. The commander smacked his hand. "Everything stays here until you're ready to leave."

"What about them?" Jack asked, pointing to his friends.

Commander Peri Winkle leaned forward until his nose almost touched Jack's. "They've been my soldiers for a while. I don't know you at all."

Jack was about to respond when the commander turned quickly and started down the hallway. "Follow along!"

Peri Winkle went through the doorway of what should have been a back bedroom, but when they entered it, there was a desk and two chairs facing a row of six filing cabinets. Turning, Peri Winkle said, "I want to make sure I heard you three boys right. You all vouch for your friend. He'll make a good soldier?"

Jack said, "I'm not sure…"

BB interrupted in a loud voice, "He's good to the max."

Jack looked from the commander to BB in wonderment.

"What did you say your last name was, boy?" The commander asked.

"Decker, but we're moving…"

There was a loud grating sound as the commander opened a drawer of the second filing cabinet. "Decker!" you said. "Let me see." He pulled out a file folder and read off the paper within it. Running his finger down as he read, he finally snapped the folder closed before putting it back in the drawer. "Congratulations! Your name isn't on the list." He walked over to Jack and slapped his hand down on Jack's shoulder. "Welcome to the Alien Resistance, Ohio Battalion."

"Resistance—Battalion—What is that?" Jack stuttered.

"It's what you just signed up for," Peri Winkle said through a smile. He winked at Jack with his hand still gripping his shoulder. "It's probably the best decision you've ever made." He looked at Jack's friends. "Haven't you told him anything?"

BB replied, "We went to Miller's Hardware. He saw the Amish and some suspicious activities, but we need you to give him the full lowdown."

The commander brushed past Jack as he headed out the bedroom door while snapping his fingers above his head several times. The four boys followed him across the kitchen area, then into a large, dark room on the other side. The commander said, "This is Central Command. From here, there's no going back."

Before Jack could object, the light was switched on and the door slammed shut behind them. Peri Winkle pushed down a large metal bar into hooks on this side of the wall, ensuring they would not be interrupted.

"Holy crap!" Jack shouted as he looked around the room. The large conference table, with numerous chairs around it, was normal enough, but it was the walls and the ceiling that had him dumbfounded. Every visible surface was covered with sheet upon sheet of tin foil. Looking closer, he could see the strips were stapled onto the wall, the ceiling, the door and even the boarded-up window.

"It's awesome, isn't it?" Peri Winkle said as he threw himself down in a chair.

"Unbelievable is a better word," Jack offered.

BB pointed at a world map on the far wall. "Show him the organization. It'll give Jack a scope of the work we're doing."

The commander popped up from the chair. "Sure."

Once they moved over to the map, Jack saw it as a regular world map, no different from one you would see in any high school geography class. The exceptions were the little flags pinned to it, and on each pin was a name.

"I'm not the only commander," Peri Winkle said. He pointed to the flag pinned to Beach City. "See, here I am. The Northeast is my territory." His crooked finger pointed to Las Vegas. "This is Commander Mul Berry's cell." His finger slid up to Edmonton, Canada. "The commander here is Aqua Marine." Not bothering to point any longer, he continued. "In France, Australia and South Africa we have Commander's Golden Rod, Bitter Sweet and Flesh Tint, respectively."

Jack's eyes went wide. He looked at each of his three friends and then back to Peri Winkle. "This is ridiculous. Peri Winkle—Mul Berry—Aqua

Marine and Flesh Tint? They're all crayon colors! You're pulling my leg," Jack said before he started to laugh.

"You don't think we would use our real names, do you?"

"Okay, but crayon colors?" Jack repeated.

"Isn't it brilliant? It's a worldwide standard and right in front of everyone's nose. No one would give it a second thought."

Jack thought, *they wouldn't have to, as everyone's first thought would be these guys are stunned.*

BB's eyes looked angry. "Flesh tint isn't a color—at least not any more. Malcolm X put an end to that shit."

"What are you talking about?" Shoe asked.

BB pointed to his forearm. "Does my skin look flesh color? Well, by definition, it does. It's black, but I know that's not what you're thinking. You're thinking of the color that went from *flesh-tint* when my people were colored, to *flesh* when we were called negroes. Now that we're black, and proud of it, there's no more *flesh* color. It's now *peach*, and my skin isn't the color of a *peach*. Problem solved except for the *effin* commander dude in South Africa who is working with a very old box of crayons. It doesn't sound like he's quite the full schilling."

Peri Winkle interrupted. "We're talking about the future of the world as we know it, and you're talking semantics about colors. Let's look at the big picture and move on."

Mario pointed down to a flag pinned into Brazil. "Everyone has a double name except this guy. Why?"

"We communicate through the U.S. Postal Service and sometimes couriers. They won't deliver anything unless the recipient has a first and last name," Peri Winkle explained.

"That doesn't explain—Mr. Maize," Mario continued.

"You're not very worldly Mario. Remember, we're talking Brazil." The commander was now in teach mode.

"So what? Just explain it already!" Mario threw up his arms.

The commander just shook his head in frustration. "Brazil uses single names."

The four boys still looked confused.

"C'mon. Do I have to spell it out for you! Pele! Zico! All the important people in Brazil have a single name."

"Gotcha—so he's just Mr. Maize?" Mario asked.

"No, he's not Mr. Maize. He's just—Maize," the commander said with finality.

Jack said, "Okay, I might be as slow as a space cadet, but is there some evidence for this theory of Amish and aliens?"

Over and over, the commander started snapping his fingers above his head. "You guys sit in these chairs and pay attention." He turned and pulled down a white projection screen. Lowering himself to a squat, he pulled a transparency projector from under the table. He lowered himself a second time, and from under the large wood table, he pulled out two banker boxes. Popping the lid off one, he fumbled through it and muttered, "There it is." After turning the projector light on, he pointed to BB. "Turn off the room lights."

When BB returned to his chair, the commander had a transparency on the projector and was adjusting the focus. Projected onto the big screen was a world map with many, many small circles on it. "Each circle represents a report of a UFO sighting or an alien abduction," the commander said.

"Where does the information come from?" Jack asked.

The commander slapped the top of the first box. "These are records from Area 51." He slapped the second box. "These are CIA records, and there are many more boxes under the table from all over the world."

"Where did you get them?" Jack continued questioning.

Peri Winkle sat down and closed one hand over the other as he rested on his elbows. "Son, I'm going to give you some direction. I'm going to tell you two words and then ask you to repeat three words back to me."

Jack tried to make his smirk look like a smile. "Okay."

"Remember these two words," the commander said. "Plausible denial."

Jack chuckled until Peri Winkle said, "Be quiet and listen."

Crossing his arms, Jack slouched back in the chair.

"Now repeat these three words after me," the older man said. "I don't know."

"I don't know," Jack said.

"So, what are you going to say when anyone asks you anything about your activities today, including these boxes of records?"

"I'm guessing—I don't know."

"Louder!"

"I don't know!" Jack yelled.

"I don't freaking know!" the commander yelled back at Jack.

Mario raised his hand. "That's four words."

"Let's take it down a few notches and fall back in line," Peri Winkle said in a low voice. "Notice, on this world map, the high concentration of activities in Northern Ohio." Before anyone could answer, he pulled the slide off the projector and replaced it with another.

This guy is bipolar, Jack thought. *He just went from super high to Mr. Calm in two seconds.*

The commander picked up a long, wooden pointer and tapped the screen. "This line chart shows UFO and alien occurrences in Northern Ohio over the last 20 years. You can see the chart is irregular, but quite obviously it goes upwards from 1955, on the left, to 1975 on the far right." He pulled another slide from the folder and overlaid it on the present slide. "This slide has the increase in Italian immigration into the area over the same time period. Do you see a correlation?"

BB saw the new Italian immigration line was level while the Alien line slanted up. "They don't match."

The second slide was removed and a third was placed on the projector. "This shows Polish immigration. Any similarity to the Alien line?" Peri Winkle asked.

"'Negatory,'" Mario said.

"Guys," the commander said. "I have slide upon slide in the boxes here. Everything from different immigration patterns to food purchase patterns. I have slides showing car purchases, house sales, college applications and even pet ownership charts. Nothing matches except these two charts I am holding in my hand."

Peri Winkle placed one of the new slides on top of the Alien chart, and after aligning them properly, the lines matched almost perfectly. "Do you know what this line represents Jack?"

"No idea," the younger man answered.

"This is from Ohio census results, and it shows the increase in the Ohio Amish population," The commander answered.

You could have heard a pin drop until BB said, "That's effin savage, it is."

The commander leaned in slightly, and the projector light caught his face, giving it a red glow. That, along with the long tendrils of grey, curly hair, gave him a satanic look. "That's nothing. There is a third slide." Peri Winkle slid back as he placed the third slide over top of the other two. "*Voila*," he said.

Now, all three lines matched very well, and even the year to year spikes that appeared along the upward trend, matched. "Do you know what this third trend line is?" the commander asked.

BB held his hand over his mouth in shock.

Mario's eyes were so wide it looked like they would fall out of the sockets.

Shoe had that classic smirk on his face. "Power tools," he answered.

"Exactly," the commander affirmed. "There is an indisputable correlation between alien sightings, Amish population growth and power tool sales!"

The awkward silence was broken by a loud chime echoing within Central Command. "That's another one of my assets. I'll be back momentarily," Peri Winkle said as he pulled up the iron bar and exited the room.

Five minutes later, the commander reentered the room followed by a tall, leggy woman. She had strawberry blonde, shoulder-length hair, and she was wearing a leopard-print, short dress accenting the shapely legs on top of stiletto high heels. The front of the dress was lacking material, and the woman's large, lily-white bosom was making an extraordinary effort to spill out. The four younger men, jaws slack and mouths open, gazed upon the finer sex as she sat down.

"This is Red Velvet," the commander said. He waved a hand at the boys. "This is BB, Jack, Mario and Shoe."

The woman smiled wide, showing perfect teeth through deep-red lips. "Hello boys. Shoe sounds interesting but not as interesting as BB. What does it mean—perhaps—Big Boy?"

BB coughed into his hand while thinking, *deflect—deflect!* Then the light bulb went off. "Red Velvet isn't a crayon color."

Peri Winkle laughed. "That's because she's not a commander. She's one of my informants. You wouldn't believe the information a stripper can obtain at a dance club."

Red Velvet chuckled, then her gaze fell on Jack's handsome face. "Red Velvet is my stage name, and I much prefer being referred to as a dancer in a strip club. It looks better on my business cards."

The commander interrupted. "Enough chit-chat. You told me you had important information, and it was so important you had to tell me in person."

"Of course, Darling," She purred.

Jack raised his hand. "Can I ask something? Nothing personal, but how reliable is information from a strip club?"

She shrugged and then leaned forward, resting her breasts on the table, directed at Jack. "I work at a finer establishment. The men coming in are company directors, government officials and owners of large businesses, who more than anything, need someone to listen to them. I dance for them and impress them just as they then want to impress me. There's so much information. I could tell you which car models are being cancelled next year, or would you like to know which pitcher will be starting for the Indians on Monday night?"

"You're kidding," Jack muttered. "The Indians?"

Red Velvet laughed until the commander got her attention. "Enough teasing! What news do you have?"

"There are two things, Darling. First, there are two CIA agents who come in regularly from the Columbus Field Office. I give them a little rub, and their secrets release from the confines of their minds—especially when I tease them with a little illegal peek while asking the right questions."

"Get to the point," Peri Winkle coaxed her on.

"There's a task force of agents assigned to the troubling trend of UFO sightings in Ohio. There are six agents in total, and last week they came across what they think is a break through."

"Yes—yes," the commander said.

"Apparently there's a processing building for aliens coming into Ohio. They know it's somewhere in the farmland southwest of Canton, and it's called - *the House of Aliens.*"

Peri Winkle jumped up out of his chair. He turned and continued jumping several times before thrusting his fist in the air. "Yes!" he yelled. "I knew there must be a central point for the aliens. Now we have confirmation!"

"There is a second piece of information you should know about," Red Velvet offered.

Peri Winkle sat back down. "Right. Please continue."

She took a deep breath, whereby Jack thought, *surely more flesh will pop out from the tight dress.*

"Sometimes people have meetings at my club," she continued. "Another dancer and I were attending two men who were discussing business. You know the one man. He is Bart Wilkins, the real estate broker you see on TV all the time."

Mario chuckled. "You mean the stunned putz in the green blazer and yellow tie, who yells out, 'If you want to roam, I'll sell your home!'"

"Exactly. He was having a drink or two with a Japanese fellow who, from what I overheard, is an associate of the governor."

"Governor Carter Breed of Ohio?" Jack asked.

"The one and the same," She answered. "It was very clear they were discussing some very shady dealings. It had to do with land the governor's office wanted purchased, and Bart Wilkins was pressuring the landowners in support of that goal."

"God damn Japanese are getting their nose in everything," Shoe quipped. "There's more and more Japanese stuff for sale all the time. I bet you it won't be long before they'll be building Japanese cars here in the good old United States."

"You can go now Red. Great intel, but there's always more. Keep your nose to the—well, just keep your nose in—just keep bringing me good reports."

Once she left, Jack said, "The governor is the real deal. Why would he be getting involved? It's not making sense."

"Jack, along with your three friends, you're a soldier in the alien resistance now. It's now *your* job to do the leg work out there and to make sense of it."

"What about you? Aren't you going to be working with us?" Jack questioned.

"We all have our tasks to perform, so the big machine keeps moving. I'm the planner, and you guys are the doers," The commander answered.

"Plan—what plan?" Jack's voice was edged with irritation.

The commander sighed. "Don't have a cow. Do I have to spell it out for you guys? You have two tasks. First, find this House of Aliens. It sounds really big, so how hard can that be? Second, it shouldn't be hard to find out who is behind the strong-arm land purchases Red Velvet told us about."

Jack got up from the chair, thinking, *this was more than enough time wasted.* "There isn't a lot of detail in the plan, Commander Planner."

Sensing the irritation within the new recruit, the commander turned to Mario. "You've been here several times before. By now, you know, so what's rule number one?"

Mario replied. "The commander is always right."

"And what's rule number two?"

Mario took a deep breath. "If the commander is wrong, refer to rule one."

Peri Winkle laughed. "Exactly. Continue on," he said as his hand waved them out of the room. "And Jack, welcome to the team!"

Chapter 7: Into the Rhubarb

Bart Wilkin's real estate office was on Jenson Drive in Canton. It was a large, two-story house converted for commercial use. Behind it and the other buildings on Jenson Drive, was a pot-hole-filled laneway used to access the garages facing away from the buildings.

BB's van inched down the laneway, stopping four houses away from the real estate office. The van was parked off the edge of the laneway between two lilac bushes, making it difficult to see it in the dark, moonless night.

BB turned to Shoe who was sitting in the passenger seat. "Do you think anyone noticed us?"

"It's 3:00 a.m. on a Thursday morning. Everyone's sleeping, so don't worry."

BB felt the need to remind Shoe and said, "It's not every day we do a break in."

"You heard what Commander Peri Winkle said. There are suspicious land purchases happening in Amish country. We need to get the lowdown, and the first step is to find out who's making the buys," Shoe responded.

"Then, let's get it over with. I'll keep a lookout from the laneway, and you go into the house through the broken basement window we saw when we cased the place this morning," BB offered.

"Dream on you piece of shit!" Shoe said through clenched teeth. "Who decided I was going in?"

"It makes perfect sense since you're much smaller than I am. My six-foot-five-inch frame won't make it through the small window."

"Your height has nothing to do with it. You're so skinny you don't even have to hop the fence. You can just slide through the gap between the wood slats!"

"Ya eejit! We're as crazy as a box of frogs for doing this. Maybe there's another way." BB was trying anything to get out of doing the break in.

Shoe pulled the newspaper from the dashboard, rolled it up and smacked BB in the shoulder. "Did you read the Derek Stankowski story on page three?"

BB rubbed his shoulder, "No, why?"

Shoe opened the paper, turned to page three and read the headline.

"Canton Man Killed by Electric Toothbrush."

This moron was using an electric toothbrush and somehow managed to unhook the tip while it was in his mouth. It got lodged in his throat, and he choked to death."

"That's daft," BB said.

"I've met some really smart people at Wooster College, and I've met my fair share of space cadets, but I have a hard time thinking of any normal person doing this," Shoe said. "It has *alien* written all over it! Aliens in our backyard! They could even be living right next door to us with their alien kids going to school by day, and then the electric drills are going all night as the alien parents push them to see how many wall plugs they put in before collapsing. It's a tragedy that has to stop. That's why you're going in that freaking window."

"I know what we'll do," BB said. "Give me a dollar bill."

Shoe laughed. "What—if I give you a dollar—you'll do it?"

"I have an idea on how we can settle this, but I don't want you to cheat. Give me a dollar," BB insisted.

Shoe's hand searched in his pocket, then pulled out a crinkled dollar bill and handed it to BB. "As long as this gets us moving," Shoe muttered.

BB pointed to the glove box. "There's a pen in there. Write a number on your hand between one and ten. I'll also pick a number, and whoever has the number closest to the fourth number of the serial number of this bill is safe and doesn't have to go in through the window. That means the other person has to do it."

Shoe opened the glove box and retrieved the pen. After a quick thought, with his tongue hanging out the corner of his mouth, he printed a number on his palm. He handed the pen to BB. "Your turn."

BB already knew his number and quickly wrote it on his palm. He handed the pen back to Shoe and said, "Let's see what the fourth number is." He unraveled the bill before snapping it flat between his fingers. "The number is five," BB said with a wide smile. He turned over his hand and showed the number he wrote down to Shoe. "Number six is the real deal and will be hard to beat." BB leaned forward and pushed his glasses up along the bridge of his nose while waiting to see Shoe's number."

Shoe grinned as he showed his palm to BB. "'Bakatcha'. My number is

4.68 and that means I win. You better get on your way."

BB's eyes went wide, and his words came in sputters. "That's not right. You can't use 4.68 because that's not a whole number! You cheated!"

Shoe pointed a finger very close to BB's nose. "Take a chill pill. You said pick a number. You never said pick a *whole* number. You made the rules. I followed them and still won. So, stop stalling, and get out of the freaking van before the sun comes up."

BB, exhausted of excuses, finally said, "Okay, I'll go. Pass me the tin in the glove box. I brought it for you, but it looks like I'll need it."

Shoe pulled back some papers and retrieved the tin. As he handed it to BB, he read the label - *J.J. Shoe Polish*. BB opened the tin and pressed his fingers into the black gel. He rubbed it into his face beginning at his forehead, then worked his way down. He saw Shoe's lips turn up into a grin and then open as he was about to speak.

"If I were you, I wouldn't say a freaking word right now," BB grumbled.

Shoe crossed his arms, and he kept his mouth shut, but he maintained the smile while watching BB finish the job.

BB mumbled, "Yes, I'm black, and this shoe polish is even darker black. Hell, even black football players use it on their cheeks, so the sun doesn't reflect into their eyes."

"I didn't say a word," Shoe said.

"You better not—especially to Jack or Mario. You catch my drift?"

"I won't say anything as long as we get going right now!" Shoe urged.

Both BB and Shoe exited the van while being very careful to silently close the doors. They hugged the fence line as they tip-toed up the laneway toward Bart Wilkin's real estate office.

Once there, Shoe peered through the wooden fence slats. He turned back to BB and whispered, "You look good to go. All the lights are out, and it's as quiet as an argument between two mutes." Shoe had been carrying a small, black bag, and now, he unzipped the top. Reaching in, he pulled out a flashlight and a walkie-talkie. "Clip the walkie-talkie on your belt, and every few minutes call to let me know what you're seeing."

BB nodded and his brow furrowed as Shoe retrieved a pair of dark, wrap-around sunglasses and handed them to him. "Ya whanker. What do I need these for?" BB asked.

Shoe felt the need to motivate BB with words that would inspire him.

"Think of your hero Malcolm X. He almost always wore dark glasses. It was his signature thing, and if he was here right now, he would hand you these himself and say, 'Go forth and bust a move, brother.'"

"Ya effin maggot—Malcolm X wore regular glasses, not sunglasses."

Shoe rubbed his chin. "Okay, I'll be honest with you. Your clothes are black, and your skin is black, so, when you open your eyes, it's like being blinded by the high beams of a car coming over a hill. If you don't want to be seen, put these on."

BB's hand snapped out and grasped the glasses. "You're as bad as Mario with your screwed-up words. You say, 'I'll be honest with you,' which really means everything you tell me without the disclaimer is pure *shite*."

Shoe's mouth opened, but he didn't have a good come back.

"This is the time you should just shut your gob, and cut your losses," BB declared.

Shoe intertwined his fingers and held them in front of himself. "Put your foot here, and I'll give you a boost over the fence."

"This will be easier," BB said as he walked to the corner of the fence. There was a one-foot gap between the fence posts of the two properties. He turned sideways and sucked in his gut, as he pushed his body through the narrow opening. He managed to move half his body through when he got stuck. He groaned as he tried unsuccessfully to push further through. He muttered, "Ya gobshite twerp."

BB had the dark glasses on, but Shoe knew BB was looking at him when he uttered the words.

"Get over here and help me. I'm stuck!" BB exclaimed.

Shoe pushed one foot behind him as leverage and pushed with both hands on BB's shoulder.

BB's voice was quivering as he said, "Please—get me out of here. I don't want to be stuck here when the police come. They'll take my picture and post it at the station. They won't even put it under *criminal* mug shots. They'll bin it under *stupid people doing stupid things*."

BB wasn't budging from Shoe's efforts. Shoe retreated to the other side of the laneway. He started to run, and when he was five feet from BB, he launched himself through the air at his friend. They both grunted as Shoe bounced off like a bird smacking into a window.

"Ya eejit. I think you broke my arm!" BB said.

"Keep quiet. You're going to wake someone up," Shoe replied as he rubbed his chin. "Let me think about this."

Shoe pulled at the post and then saw there was a large rock propped up against the bottom of it. He squatted down as the fingers of both hands grasped the raw, far edge. He pulled and pulled, each time rocking his body to gain momentum. The rock rolled half over but then fell back into place. On the next pull, the rock rolled right over as Shoe toppled onto his back.

As a result, the post at BB's chest loosened. It was only half an inch, but it was enough pressure relief for BB to fall over onto his side in the back yard of the real estate office. He got up, dusted off his knees and mumbled, "Freaking gobshite twerp."

Shoe knew the words were for him, but he didn't care. BB was on his way. He whispered to BB, "No pain—no gain, so keep going."

BB could barely see through the dark glasses. He ran across the backyard until he pasted his back against the thick trunk of a maple tree. Peering around it, he saw the coast was clear. He ran across the yard toward the house, but after only two steps, his size 15 shoe caught on an exposed tree root. He went flying forward, resulting in his face dragging along the ground. He spit out bits of grass and soil, rose to his feet and once again dusted off his knees.

Shoe was watching through the wooden fence planks but couldn't focus very well through the darkness. He heard the loud thump and then, once again, the barely audible words, "Freaking gobshite twerp."

BB was more careful now. He crouched low and slowly walked to the basement window at the back of the real estate office. Turning the flashlight on, he placed it on the grass, pointed at the wood covering the broken window. He pushed on it, and, as they anticipated earlier in the day, it was only thin plywood. He pushed on a corner of the wood, and it pushed inwards easily. With his extremely long arm, he was able to twist his hand around the wood and unlatch the window lock.

BB pointed the flashlight into the room and saw it was a storage area with an old desk under the window. He turned his long body around with his feet at the opening and started shimmying backwards. His feet moved backwards and down until they were on the desk. Squatting, he pointed the light around the room, seeing it was filled with nothing but old junk.

BB held the button on the walkie-talkie. "The eagle has landed."

There was a static click and then Shoe's voice in response. "Eagle what?"

"Never mind. I'm in," BB reported.

"Good. There must be a records storage area in the building. Find it, and look for three land purchase deals in Amish country."

"It's a big house. I could be here forever."

"Use your brain! Who does the filing?"

After thinking for a second, BB said, "A secretary."

"Wonderful," Shoe said. "The secretary's desk is probably by the front door, and I bet there are filing cabinets nearby."

BB didn't bother to respond and clipped the walkie-talkie back onto his belt. Being as quiet as possible, he opened the door to the room. Poking his head out, his gaze followed the light to a dead-end at one end of the hallway. Turning to look in the other direction, he saw stairs leading up. He passed two doors having real estate agent name plates affixed to them as he moved toward the stairs. Silently walking upward, he was careful to not shine the flashlight out the front windows. On the main level, he found himself in the main reception area, and by the front door was a desk. *That must be the secretary's desk,* he thought. On the side wall was a row of eight filing cabinets. "Bingo," he whispered.

BB had no idea where to begin, but he saw the labels on the front of the filing cabinets indicating the system was alphabetical. He opened one of the cabinets and inspected several folders. He did the same in two other file cabinets before calling Shoe on the walkie-talkie. "This will be impossible," he told Shoe. "All these papers are filed alphabetically by the owners of the sold properties. Unless we have those names, I won't find what we're looking for."

Shoe, still in the laneway, squatted with his back against the fence post and said, "There must be some type of cross reference, otherwise how would they find anything? Look for a clipboard, a book or a binder."

BB panned the flashlight around the room and across the top of the filing cabinets. Sure enough, there on top was a black binder. "Bingo squared," BB whispered.

Pulling open the binder, he could see sales were documented, but the listings were by date. He started to work backwards through the book, and there on a page, with entries from three weeks ago, he saw three unusual entries. Each entry was labeled with the owner's name, address and the type of sale, whether it was residential, commercial, industrial or agricultural. Here, BB saw there were three farms sold within three days with sizes of 100, 250 and 300 acres. He had performed enough reconnaissance in Amish country to know these farms were all within the heart of it, and he knew these three farms backed onto each other.

When BB initially scanned the office, he saw a cabinet labelled - *Cameras*. He moved toward it and found three polaroid instamatic cameras in the top drawer. In the drawer below, he found film cartridges. *How predictable,* he thought.

Taking one camera, he loaded the film into it as he walked over to the cabinet labelled - *D to F.* Quickly, he found the name of the owner of the first farm and the purchase papers for it. He read through them but was disappointed to find the only identification of the buyer was a numbered business with a Canton address. He took a picture of the form and was surprised by such a bright flash. "Oh shite," he whispered.

He replaced the file folder and found the paperwork for the second farm, then the third. Surprisingly, he saw all three farms were purchased by the same company – Business 324867. BB took the files into a side office and took pictures of these forms before replacing them in the filing cabinets.

"Shoe—are you there?" BB said into the walkie-talkie.

"I'm here."

"I have the files for the three farms, so I'm coming out," BB said.

"You still have time. Check out Wilkin's office, and see if there is anything worthwhile in there," Shoe responded.

"I'm getting nervous," BB said. "It's too dark and quiet in here, and it's creeping me out."

"It might seem like longer, but you've only been in there 20 minutes. Take ten more minutes and check out the boss's office," Shoe encouraged.

BB clipped the walkie-talkie on his belt and walked down the hallway toward the back of the house. There, he saw the nameplate *Wilkins* on a door. The creak of the hinges sounded deafening as BB opened the door and stepped in. It took only four lanky steps for BB to reach the desk and lower himself into the plush chair behind it. Holding the thin flashlight between his teeth, he opened a top drawer, but in it he found only pens, pencils and paper. The next drawer held a pair of shoes and foot powder. *That's gross,* he thought.

The bottom drawer was full of magazines. The top few were *Popular Mechanics* and *Sport Fishing,* but then he found something more interesting. "Hello," he whispered as he pulled out three *Penthouse* magazines. He opened one to the centerfold, quietly whistling before his gaze came back to the drawer. At the bottom was a book.

BB pulled it out and realized it was a notebook, and as he opened it, he recognized it was set up as a ledger. Going back by date, his eyes went wide as he saw there were entries for many land sales. Beside each was a note and a dollar value. Some were smaller, but some were as large as 20 thousand dollars. A few pages into the book, he saw the three land purchases he was interested in. His brow furrowed when he saw the dollar value beside the purchase entries because they were not dollar values at all. Rather, beside each of these entries was the value—*five million yen*. As he read across, his expression went from confusion to eye-popping surprise. Beside each farm sale entry was the note - *As per C.B., payable to the House of Aliens*. BB's surprise instantly changed to shock. With shaking hands, he took a picture of the pertinent entries and placed the books and magazines back into the drawer.

He retraced his steps into the reception area and down the stairs where he froze in horror. At the end of the hallway, the previous darkness was now being intermittently lit by a bright-red, flashing light. *I must have triggered an alarm!* The thought screamed in his mind.

It was at this point he realized he still had the camera strap slung around his neck, and there was no time to return it. He ran down the hallway and into the storage room. He jumped up on the desk and all but flew out the little window. Somehow, the camera strap was still attached to his shoulder when he pulled the walkie-talkie from the belt clip. He pushed the button and yelled, "Head for the van! Head for the van!"

BB ran for the fence, but this time, with the running start, he showed his athleticism. As he jumped, his foot landed on the top of the fence, and he easily slung himself over. As sirens could be heard in the distance, he saw Shoe running for the van ahead of him.

BB arrived at the van only a second after Shoe and flung himself into the driver seat. He started the van and put it into gear. "We're fucked. I set off some kind of alarm!"

"Dude—that's bad, but don't go too fast. We'll look so guilty if you scream out of here," Shoe urged.

At a comfortably legal pace, BB drove the van out of the laneway and down the main road toward the highway. "Look. That's weird. Do you see that guy running down the sidewalk? It looks like Jack's mystery guy with the blue jeans and black hoodie—the same guy Jack has seen a few times in the past few weeks."

"We don't have time for that now," Shoe said. "Just keep going and keep everything copacetic."

Ten minutes later, they were on the highway and headed toward Shoe's pad at Wooster. "Did you get anything worthwhile from Wilkin's office?"

Shoe asked.

The adrenaline was still rushing through BB's body. He was proud of himself. "Oh yeah. I got everything and more. I have the details of the land sales, and there was a key person involved in each."

Shoe shot up straight in the passenger seat. "What do you mean?"

"I found a hidden ledger, and it looked like a very secret ledger. That probably means illegal. I found monetary entries linked to the House of Aliens, and beside each sale date was the initials, C.B." BB gave Shoe a satisfied, determined grin.

Shoe's jaw dropped. "You don't mean…"

"Oh yeah—Governor Carter Breed," BB whispered.

Chapter 8: Chipmunk 12

"Can you see anything?" Shoe asked.

"The rain is coming down so hard it's tough to see any further than the hood of the van." Jack pulled the binoculars from his eyes and handed them to Shoe who was sitting in the passenger seat.

It was 10:00 a.m. Friday, and the four boys were together in BB's van. They decided to check out the numbered company BB came across when he pulled the land purchase files from Bart Wilkin's real estate office. They were parked across the road from the address of Business 324867 in an industrial area of South Canton.

"We don't have to rush," Mario suggested. "Let's wait for the rain to slow down."

Jack glanced at BB in the driver's seat. "How did you manage to get the day off? I thought Fridays were busy at the grocery store—especially in the Butcher Shop."

"I've worked the last three Saturdays, so it wasn't that hard to get a day off. There are two other butchers in the department, and they can cover for me easily enough," BB answered.

Mario turned to Jack. "How about you? Have you found any work yet?"

"I've had two interviews, but they weren't even close to what I'm looking for as an electrical engineer. Besides, I'm not in a rush," Jack responded.

Shoe asked, "It must be nice to have that option. Where are you getting your bread from?"

"Remember, I told you about the patent I have on the variable speed trigger," Jack said.

Shoe nodded as Mario said, "Sure."

"What I didn't tell you is I received an award from the *American Society of Engineers*. It came with a check for 60 thousand dollars," Jack said through a grin.

BB yelled "Dude—wow!"

Mario's mouth gapped open and Shoe whistled.

Jack said, "I've only spent what little I need to keep me going. The rest,

I'm keeping for something big when it comes along. Oh—I did spend a few bucks fixing up my dad's old car."

"You mean the 'X-mobile.' It's still kicking?" Mario said.

"It's in the shop right now getting a tune up, but I'll get it back in about a week," Jack replied.

"Awesome," BB said. "You didn't change the effin color, did you?"

"Chillax guys. It's still mint-green and has the dark-green Matador X stripe matching the vinyl roof. American Motors didn't make many of the X coupe model," Jack explained.

Shoe interrupted. "The rain is dying down." He pulled the binoculars to his eyes and looked across the road at the large two-story office building. "There's a sign out front. It reads - *American Development Consultants.*"

"That doesn't tell us much," Jack said.

"There's something strange," Shoe continued. "They have a large parking lot, but it's empty except for three cars in reserved parking along what looks like executive row."

"It's not a holiday, is it?" Jack queried.

"Negatory. That would be my boss acting quite the maggot if he gave me the day off when it was really a holiday," BB said through a snicker. "Can you read the names on the executive parking spots?"

Shoe refined the focus on the binoculars. "I read a Dennis Green and John Potter." Shoe panned his gaze across the seven signs indicating reserved parking. He pulled the glasses from his eyes and looked at his three fellow passengers. "The other five signs all have Japanese names on them." Returning the binoculars to his eyes, he read off the names. "Soma Kishi, Ryo Ozawa and Ki-ha Park, are the first three names."

Jack interrupted. "Weird—I think Ki-ha Park is Korean, not Japanese."

"It's all the same," Shoe said. "They both lost to us in a war and they eat raw food in both countries. And look at that. The three cars are a Mazda 626, a Datsun 280Z and a Honda Civic."

"Listen to me, guys. This is important." Mario waited for Shoe to remove the binoculars from his eyes, so he had the attention of all three of his friends. There was still a very light rain spattering the roof, but it was quiet enough for Mario to speak in a hushed whisper. "When we went to Commander Peri Winkle's place, we met Red Velvet who told us of a Japanese man who met with Bart Wilkins. Then, BB found what looked like documentation of a payoff in Bart Wilkins secret ledger, but the payoff was in Japanese yen. It was equal to a little over 20 thousand dollars for each of the three farms sold. Now, even though the sign on the building says *American*, the names of the executives are *Japanese*, and the cars are *Japanese*." Mario leaned a little closer to the central point between his friends, and as if they were magnets, each of them was slowly drawn in.

Mario continued. "You know what this means. Japanese—that's the common dominator."

BB slammed his palm into the steering wheel. Shoe threw his head back and laughed uproariously.

Jack grinned and shook his head. "Mario, you spaz! It's common *denominator*, not *dominator*. Do you know what a *dominator* is?"

Mario shrugged. "I thought it was the number on the bottom of a fraction."

"*Dominator* is a sexual term. It refers to a kinky relationship where one sex partner holds control over, or dominates, the other partner." Jack explained.

"A couple of missing letters—so what?" Mario offered.

"From math term to sex freak in one simple lesson—with justification even," Shoe quipped.

"Guys, enough of the word games. We need to get more information from inside the office building," BB determined. "Jack, do you remember when we needed to find a way into Mark Irving's party?"

"For sure," Jack replied as the memory brought a smile to his face.

"Then, time to bust a move. Jack, you're with me. Shoe and Mario, you two wait here, and be ready to bug out," BB directed.

Jack and BB exited the van, ran across the road in the light rain, and they quickly arrived at the impressive, glass double-doors fronting American Development Consultants.

"You ready?" Jack asked.

"BB had an evil smile on his face. "My Irish ass was born ready."

Jack threw open the door and rushed in followed by BB. There was a cute, dark-haired receptionist behind a high counter across the back of the foyer. Jack cried, "We need help!"

Behind Jack, BB was jumping up and down. His knees were held tightly together, but his feet angled up into the air with each jump. "He groaned, "It's 'cominggg.'"

The receptionist jumped up from her stool. "Oh my god. What's the matter?"

Jack rushed to the counter. "Where's your bathroom?"

The receptionist's eyebrows rose with her confusion. "Bathroom..."

"I'm going to shite myself! Hurry!" BB yelled. The jumping stopped, but his hands were clasped over his groin as he paced back and forth around a small table in the foyer. Miniature steps were the best he could do while clenching his sphincter.

"The office area is secure. I can't let you in," the receptionist explained.

BB waddled over to the counter and threw his palm down on the marble surface with a loud *slap*. His eyes were wide as he lifted his other hand, pointing a finger behind the counter. "Give me that freaking garbage can. I'm going to dump a savage shite in it!"

The flustered receptionist jumped back a step as BB's words assaulted her. She reached under the counter, pressed a button, and a glass door to the right of the counter sprung open. "Third door to your right! Oh my god. Hurry!" the receptionist urged.

BB ran for the door and slid six feet on the slippery soles of his shoes just before grasping the handle. He veered up the hallway as the door swung closed behind him.

"That was close. You averted a major catastrophe," Jack said to the receptionist.

"I let your friend in because no one is working today. It is a very rare exception," the receptionist replied.

Jack said, "Miss..."

"My name is Ryo—Ryo Ozawa."

Jack came prepared with his own stage name. "I'm Raul. Why isn't anyone working today?"

Ryo's eyes became moist. "We received terrible news yesterday. Our president, Ki-ha Park, died of a heart attack."

Jack took a moment. "I'm very sorry. It'll be difficult without your president. What does your company do?"

Ryo shook her head as she regained her composure. "We advise on investments. More than that, I am not allowed to say."

"My friend is taking a long time. Can I go and check on him?"

Ryo didn't answer, but she pressed the button under the counter for a second time. Jack passed through the open doorway where he saw there were offices on either side of the hallway. Some had nameplates. He poked his head into a larger common office area where he saw BB rifling through papers on a desk. "We have to boogie in two minutes," Jack said.

Moving back to a door he passed a moment ago, Jack read the name plate for a second time – *Board Room*. He pushed the door open and turned the lights on. Inside was a twenty-foot-long table surrounded by cushioned chairs. On the far wall were six pictures of the Board executives. Four of the men were Japanese although one looked Korean. *I have to hurry*, Jack thought.

Jack walked around the table to a cabinet below the pictures. He opened one drawer after another, finding each empty except for the middle drawer on the left side. He pulled it open, and in it was a thick paper bound book. On its cover it read, *American Development Consultants, 1977 Annual Report*.

BB pushed open the door to the conference room. "We need to book it."

Jack stuffed the book down the belt line at the back of his trousers, then pulled his tee-shirt over it. "Did you find anything?" he asked BB.

"Nothing I can use. A lot of foreign language papers, including loads of what looks like Japanese documents," BB replied.

Jack moved out of the board room and up the hallway followed by BB. Once they were in the foyer, Jack moved to the counter to see a much-relieved Ryo. "We appreciate your help," Jack said.

"It was very stressful, and I am glad it is over," She responded.

"What's this?" The words came from BB who was pointing to a plant under a glass enclosure by the far wall.

Ryo said, "That is a Bonsai tree. It is very old and very valuable."

"What eejit does that? Who puts a tiny, fat tree inside a glass box?" BB questioned.

"Growing and manicuring Bonsai trees is an art form in Japan," she explained.

BB turned toward the counter, and put his hands on his hips. "This isn't Japan. This is America." His voice had an edge to it.

Ryo bowed her head. "Yes, of course..."

"What's going on here?" BB interrupted as he continued the derogatory questions.

Jack rolled his eyes. *Here we go,* he thought.

"BB tapped the top of the glass cabinet. "A Japanese plant, Japanese executives driving Japanese cars and you're Japanese! How can you have *American* in the name of your company? It sounds like a big box of bollocks to me."

Ryo gaze lifted, and there was anger in her eyes. "I was born in California and am more American than you will ever be. Listen to your words. You sound like a lousy 'Mick!'"

"Mick!" BB repeated. "I'll show you who is more American." BB's fingers moved quickly to undo his belt buckle, and before Jack could stop him, BB's pants were around his ankles. BB snapped his hand to his forehead in a smart salute.

"Oh crap," Jack muttered. BB was wearing boxers with red and white horizontal stripes. In the top left corner was a blue square with white stars emblazoned on it.

Jack ran toward BB as BB began to sing at the top of his lungs. "Oh, say can you see…"

Jack grabbed him by his free arm and started to drag him toward the door. This proved difficult as BB could only waddle with his pants tangled around his feet.

However, BB maintained the salute as he turned to look behind him at Ryo. "By the dawn's early light…"

Ryo's hand rose in the air. She lifted her middle finger to BB as she scowled.

Jack kept BB moving toward the door where BB grabbed the handle and poked his head back inside. "What so proudly we hailed…"

Once outside, BB finally pulled up his pants, and they ran across to the van. BB was still singing when he got in the Shaggin-wagon.

"I'm afraid to ask what that was about," Shoe said.

"You really don't want to know," Jack responded. "BB, let's go."

The engine roared to life, and the van sped down the road as Shoe asked, "Did you find anything worthwhile?"

Jack pulled the annual report from under his shirt and passed it to Shoe. "We'll have to go through this in more detail when we have time. But to make a long story short, we didn't see anything alien except a multitude of

Japanese documents."

"God damn Japanese," Shoe complained. "We beat their ass in the war, and we gave them money to rebuild. Now they're kicking our ass. Mark my words, soon they'll be building Japanese cars right here in Ohio!"

"If they were making the cars here, they would be *American* cars," Mario corrected.

"Piece of shit," Shoe muttered.

"Where we going now?" Jack asked.

Mario answered sarcastically. "This piece of shit called the owner of one of the three farms that were sold. I talked to the owner's daughter who said they would be glad to give an interview."

"Why would they talk to us?" Shoe asked.

"I told them we worked for the *Wooster College Times*," Mario replied.

Shoe winked at Mario. "The piece of shit did good."

It took 20 minutes for the boys to arrive at the farm. A red-brick farm house with white shutters was prominent on the property. There was a long drive leading up to the house, and just behind it was a large barn. To the left of the barn was a field of corn as far as the eye could see. On the right side were paddocks of grazing land segmented by brown board fencing. There were cows in the front enclosure while in the back, four horses could be seen grazing.

"The place looks very busy. I wonder why they would sell?" Jack asked.

"That's what we're here to find out," Mario replied.

BB parked the van and the four boys walked up onto the wrap around porch.

A young woman in blue jeans and a plaid shirt answered the door after Mario pushed the doorbell. "Can I help you?" She had a puzzled look on her face.

"Mario smiled. "I'm Mario. We talked on the phone. I'm the reporter from the *Wooster College Times*."

"Oh sure. I remember now. I'm Tracy. Come on in," she said.

Mario introduced his three friends, and after a quick hello to each, she led them to a parlor off the left side of the main hallway. "I have to see my brother in the barn for a few minutes. Peepaw and meemaw will keep you company until I get back." She turned to an older man and woman who were both sitting in lazy boy chairs, and in a loud voice she said, "These boys are going to keep you company for a few minutes until I get back."

The older man dubbed peepaw didn't respond. His legs were covered with a blanket, and he maintained an unbroken gaze out the front picture window. His eyes were glazed over, and both corners of his mouth drooped down with a small drop of drool at one corner.

Meemaw turned her face to her daughter. "The potatoes won't grow in it."

"I'll be back in a minute, boys. Have a seat," Tracy said as she smiled at her mom and then scooted out of the room.

BB, Shoe and Mario sat on a couch in front of the window, facing meemaw and peepaw. Jack lowered down into a side chair beside the couch, facing the large fireplace on the opposite wall.

Since peepaw was still staring blankly out the window, Mario said to meemaw, "The farm looks very busy. We're wondering why you sold your farm?"

Meemaw looked at Mario and said, "The Titanic never hit an iceberg."

The four boys looked from one to the other, baffled.

Mario tried again. "Who came here when you sold your farm?"

"I have white shoes and red shoes, but no black shoes," meemaw offered as she smiled wide at Mario.

"They're whacked," Shoe said. "He's out of it altogether—like living on Neptune. She's out there as well but maybe only as far as Mars. She talks, but she doesn't have a clue."

Using slow words BB asked meemaw, "Do—you—know—where—you—are?"

A brightness came to her eyes as she returned BB's gaze. "Yes," she said.

There just might be hope, Jack thought. *Maybe something useful will come of this.*

BB repeated, "Where—are—you?"

She leaned forward and smiled wide. "I'm in the Hershey Chocolate Factory!"

"Oh shite," BB said.

Mario said, "Maybe their brains got fried by the electromagnetic field of a power tool."

Suddenly, Shoe said, "What's that?"

Mario sniffed. "Holy crap. Did one of you let one go? It's the worst shit smell ever."

"It wasn't me," Jack said.

Shoe pointed at peepaw. "Look at him. The corner of his mouth is lifted. He shot out a silencer, and he's smirking at us."

The other three boys looked at peepaw with his blank stare and then at Shoe like he was the crazy one.

Shoe lifted his finger again and pointed accusingly at peepaw. "He's screwing with us! He just winked at me!"

Tracy came back into the parlor. Right away, she fanned her hand in front of her nose as she chuckled. "Wow! I see peepaw let one go again."

Meemaw turned to her daughter. "A tomato is a fruit, not a vegetable."

Tracy laughed. "So, boys, what can I help you with?"

Mario said, "We're doing a story on farming in Ohio, and we heard you sold your farm as did two of your neighbors. Why did you sell?"

"You've heard of Bart Wilkins?" Tracy asked.

"Of course. He's quite a character," Mario replied.

"Well, he just knocked on our door one day. He threw out a dollar value, and I said no," she explained. "Then, he came back two days later with a higher number. I said no, again. He came back three more times, and each time the number went up. The last time, he came with another gentleman. Bart implored me to accept the offer. I again said no. The fellow with him whispered into Bart's ear, and then Bart gave me a new number. It was almost double what the farm is worth. I would have been crazy to not accept since back in North Carolina, we could buy a farm double the size of this one."

"I guess it makes sense." Mario said.

"Do you use power tools on the farm?" Shoe interrupted.

"What?" Tracy responded.

"Power tools—Electric drills—electric saws." Shoe leaned forward. "Maybe even electric tooth brushes?"

Tracy laughed. "Well, you boys are peculiar. Of course, we use drills and saws and many other tools. Peepaw was the best. He used them for 20 years before his arthritis got the best of him."

"So, power tools are not alien to him?" Shoe probed.

"Not at all," she replied. "We still have a lot to do today, boys. What else do you have?"

Jack leaned forward. "Why do you think they wanted the land so badly?"

Tracy chuckled. "You don't have to be an engineer to figure it out. This farm is one of four in a big square. They bought three of them, and they're trying hard to get the fourth farm. I'm not sure they'll succeed as the other owners are Amish. You might want to visit the Fischer's, but the important point is, just north of our big square, there's a proposed mega industrial park. If there was ever a zoning change here, the land would be worth double what we're being paid for it."

"We might just call on the Fischer's," Jack said as he rose to his feet followed by his three friends. As he walked out of the parlor, he snapped his fingers and stopped. "One other thing, Tracy. Who was the man who whispered in Bart Wilken's ear?"

"He was very aloof and didn't introduce himself. I'm not even sure he spoke English. Then, last week, just by chance, I saw his picture in the newspaper," Tracy explained.

"Do you still have the paper," Mario asked.

Tracy turned and said over her shoulder. "Let me see if I can find it." She came back a minute later with the paper, and she turned to page six where she pointed to the picture. "This is Governor Carter Breed giving a speech at a local Rotary Club meeting. Do you see these people in the background?" She tapped the face of a dark-haired man. "That's him."

Shoe's eyes narrowed as he grumbled, "Freaking Japanese."

Jack ignored Shoe's comment and peered at the picture as Mario said, "Can we keep the paper?"

Jack cut him off. "We don't need the paper. Thanks for everything, Tracy."

They walked out the front door toward the van when Mario said, "We needed the picture!"

"Nope," Jack said. "I know who he is."

Mario grabbed Jack's arm, and the four boys stopped. Mario asked, "Who is he?"

"His picture was on the wall in the boardroom at the American Development Consultants office. His name is Ki-ha Park and he is freaking

Korean, not Japanese." Jack explained.

"Double shite," BB said.

"Unbelievable," Mario said.

BB, Shoe and Mario turned and walked toward the van. Jack, hearing a noise behind them, paused and turned where he saw the most curious sight. From the barn, he saw two large dogs running toward him. He started to walk backwards but knew he didn't have time to make the van. As the dogs came closer, he chuckled when he saw they weren't dogs at all. They were two freakishly small miniature horses, no more than 30 inches tall. Jack held out a hand, thinking, *they look so cute with their short legs and long manes.* One was pure white while the other was white with patches of brown.

Wow, they can run fast, Jack thought as they were now very close. One peeled around behind him while the other ran headlong into Jack's gut with its head. Jack expelled a grunt of air as he fell over backward. He rose to a crouch with one mini horse in front of him and one behind. He turned his head to look at the van. It was rocking with Shoe laughing and slamming his fist into the dashboard. BB was in his own uproar as he slapped the steering wheel, and behind them, he could see Mario howling as well.

"Some freaking friends," Jack muttered.

Jack refocused on the two tiny horses who were both now in front of him. They were neighing while hot breaths snorted out their nostrils. Their pink lips were pulled back in a snarl, and they crouched low on their front legs, ready to spring at him with the slightest provocation.

Jack recalled a lesson from his father, at least as it pertained to dogs, and he remembered his words. "Never show fear. Make sure you let them know you're the alpha male, and they're just submissive followers." With that in mind, Jack rose to his feet, making himself an even larger visage. This caused the one horse to froth at the mouth, but Jack was not deterred. He lifted his finger, pointed at the barn and yelled, "Get the fuck back over there!"

"Ow!" Jack hollered.

"It's all over with," the nurse said. "You won't need another tetanus shot for ten years."

"Thanks," Jack said as he got up to leave the Emergency Ward at the hospital.

"Who would have thought horses bite people like that?" Mario said through his snicker. Two hours had passed since the attack, but he was still having trouble keeping his laughter in.

As they walked out into the corridor, Jack pulled on his leather jacket and inspected the torn sleeve. *It's done for,* he thought.

Mario couldn't let it go. "It was amazing Jack. Those tiny horses were acting like pack animals, circling you until they struck. You were on the ground in a second with one chewing your arm and the other holding onto your pant leg."

"Buzz off. Go find BB and Shoe," Jack said, "Tell them to pick me up at the front entrance. That way, I don't have to listen to any more of your shit."

Mario grinned but complied as he walked off toward the paid parking. Jack headed in the other direction toward the front entrance. Once there, he saw the rain had started once again, and it was just coming to dusk. Both factors made it difficult to see, but the hair on the back of Jack's neck suddenly stood up on end. Out the window, across the wide driveway, he once again saw the mysterious stalker wearing blue jeans and the black hoodie with the hood pulled over his head.

Then, there was a flash of lightning. For an instant Jack saw the face, and his jaw dropped. He rubbed his eyes, not believing what he saw. When he looked again, the dark figure was gone.

Jack was shocked. The man was in fact no man. It was a girl—his girl! It was Carley!

Chapter 9: Hectic Eclectic

Mario heard the knock, walked to the door of his pad and opened it. "Wow. All three of you showed up at the same time. I've never seen that happen before."

"We're clever like that," Shoe said as he brushed by Mario, followed by BB and Jack.

"My Mom was doing some laundry, so I threw your swim shorts in with my stuff. You'll find them clean and on the kitchen table," Mario said.

Walking back into the kitchen after them, Mario opened the fridge door and pulled out four ice-cold cans of beer. He pushed the fridge door closed with his butt and picked up the two large bags of chips on his way past the kitchen table. The cold beers were wedged between his arm and stomach. The hardening of his nipples urged him out the door and toward the hot water in the tub. Mario's quick steps continued directly into the hot tub where he placed the chips and beers on the ledge before taking his customary place at the far end of the bench. Mario's three friends came out of the guest house with their freshly-scented swim shorts on, and each of them picked up a beer as they lowered into the hot water.

"How's Carley?" Mario asked Jack. "Still living the dream?"

Carley was constantly on Jack's mind. They had been going out together for some time now, and when he was with her, Jack felt comfortable. That all changed when he saw her as the hooded person following he and his friends. At first, Jack thought to confront her but quickly had second thoughts. He couldn't help but think she was involved in this less than clear conspiracy, be it involving Japanese, Amish, the governor or even aliens. Jack thought it would be better to very carefully let their relationship play out and see what clues it leads to.

"We're doing great!" Jack replied.

Shoe snickered. "Oh really. Best friends now and always?"

BB interrupted. "Don't get carried away. Jack and his girl can't be best friends and have a boyfriend – girlfriend relationship at the same time."

"Why not?" Jack said.

BB explained. "Look at the four of us. We're best friends. We know because of the way we accept each other, no matter the circumstances."

"You don't think it can be like that for Carley and I?" Jack offered.

"Dude, not only for Carley and you but for any boyfriend and girlfriend, or husband and wife." BB continued.

"I don't follow you," Jack said.

"You're acting the muppet, so I'll explain with an example," BB offered. "Let's say we're all sitting here in the hot tub and Mario says something really effin stupid—I mean pure moronic."

"Hey!" Mario interjected.

"Don't worry, ya eejit. It's purely hypothetical." BB turned his gaze from Mario, winking at Jack. "So, we're sitting here, and let's say Mario says something really asinine—like one of his typical fucked up urban sayings. What would you say to Mario, Jack?" BB asked.

"I would tell him he was a freaking idiot and should check what is causing his brain cells to be killed off at such a young age," Jack replied.

"What would you say Shoe?" BB asked.

Shoe rubbed his chin. "I'd tell him what his problem was."

"And what would that be smartass?" Mario asked.

"I would tell you when you were in line waiting for a *brain*, you thought they said *train*, and off you went for a ride," Shoe said through a grin.

Mario scowled as BB held his hand up. "We say shit like that to each other all the time, yet we remain best friends. There's more to us than just words—even if they're brutally honest."

"You're getting me all weepy," Shoe said in a sarcastic tone.

BB continued. "My point is, and it's a question now, what would happen if Jack told any of those comments to Carley after she said something really effin thick?"

"She would understand if I said something like that. It would be copacetic," Jack responded.

BB chuckled. "Really? What color is the sky in your world?"

Jack thought for a second. "You're right. There's no way I would say anything even close to that to Carley. She would kill me."

"I rest my case," BB said. "Calling each other freaking eejits is reserved for best friends and just doesn't work for boyfriend – girlfriend relationships."

Jack didn't want to think about Carley any longer. He already knew their relationship wasn't what it appeared. "San Francisco and New England are playing tonight," he said before tilting his head back for a first swig of beer.

"It's going to be a boring game with San Francisco walking all over the Patriots," Shoe predicted. "We can catch up with it later since we have more important things to talk about."

"What's on your mind?" BB asked.

"My mind feels like it's going to explode with so much going on. We need to decide where we go from here," Shoe offered.

"Before we do that, we need to take an amounting of what we know so far," Mario interjected.

Jack yelled out a "Ha!" and the beer in his mouth spilled out into the hot tub. As he choked, BB slapped him on the back to help stifle the gurgling sounds coming from his throat. Once his breathing returned to normal, Jack leaned against the back of the bench. "Mario, you're one sorry soul. It's not—*take an amounting*. The saying is to—*take an accounting*."

Mario frowned. "That makes no sense at all. If we're talking about reviewing information, and there appears to be a lot of it, *amount* makes much more sense than *account*."

"You're just making it worse for yourself," Jack replied. "The correct term is *account*. I'm sure the term was originally used for mathematical purposes, and people just expanded the use. But in any case, the correct term is *account*, not *amount*."

Mario crossed his arms. "You're wrong."

Jack rolled his eyes. "Okay. Let's take a vote. All those who think *amount* is the correct term, raise your hand."

Mario quickly pushed one hand up in the air. He waited for someone else to follow, but there was no sign of agreement from the others.

After Mario dropped his hand back in the water, Jack said, "And who thinks the correct word is *account*?"

Jack pushed his hand up in the air followed by BB. Shoe hesitated but finally joined his friends, showing his agreement. Through a smirk while glaring at Mario, Shoe whispered, "Piece of shit."

"Enough bolloxology," BB said. "Let's get back on point." He took a long drink from the can of beer, then pushed his glasses up the bridge of his nose with his finger. "We know Bart Wilkins is in cahoots with the governor on the land sales. It looks like there's some kind of payout or bribe, but it's not clear which direction the money is going."

Jack said, "If the money is going from Bart to the governor, then there must be someone else providing the money. I can't think of a reason why a real estate person would bribe the governor unless he was buying the land himself, and he isn't."

"True enough," Shoe said. "We know the American Development Consultants are buying the land, so it makes sense they're the ones buying off the governor with Wilkins as the middle man."

Shoe offered some added information. "We also know there's a Japanese connection. It looks like the American Development Consultants are more Japanese than American. The question is, why do they need to hide?"

Jack sat up quickly and almost spilled his beer. "Shit! I know why. Mario, do you have a copy of today's newspaper?"

"It's inside," Mario replied. "Let me go in and get it." After a minute, he returned, then handed the paper to Jack on his way back into the bubbling, hot water.

Jack leafed through the pages until he got to the business section. He read the headline aloud,

"Governor Announces Innovation Technology Grant."

Mario shrugged. "I don't catch your drift. How is this related?"

Jack tapped the page several times. "If you read the detail, there's only one grant of 500 thousand dollars along with tax breaks for five years. But here is the kicker. The grant is for companies who will productionize a new technology, and the applications are limited to *American* companies."

Mario scratched his head. "I still don't get it."

"Let's say a foreign company wanted to apply for the grant. They would need an American company to work with," Jack hypothesized.

"Is there anything important in the annual report you snuck out of ADC's offices that might provide more detail?" Shoe asked Jack.

There was a small pile of magazines just off to the side of the hot tub. BB rose to his feet and, with his lanky frame, retrieved the annual report from the top. The effort toppled the pile toward Mario, after which he leaned back, picking up the *National Geographic Magazine* closest to him.

BB opened the annual report and searched the pages as Shoe became more agitated. "This might take a few minutes," BB said.

"The Japanese will be taking over our country soon enough!" Shoe said.

"Japanese cars are on our roads. There are more and more Japanese electronics in the stores sold by Americans who, ironically, hang the American flag outside their stores. That's an oxymoron if I ever saw one."

Mario was reading the *National Geographic Magazine*, only half-listening to Shoe's rant, but his eyes lifted as he heard an unfamiliar term. "What's an oxymoron?" he asked.

Shoe took another swig of beer and wiped his mouth with the back of his hand before continuing. "It's a contradiction in terms. Sometimes people say one thing and mean another."

"So is an oxymoron some kind of super-stunned moron?" Mario asked.

"You could say so," Shoe continued, "but the moron in question has to say something that doesn't make sense to the point where he contradicts himself."

Mario tilted his head to the side indicating his lack of understanding.

Shoe rolled his eyes and said, "There are examples. Think about *jumbo shrimp*. *Shrimp* means small, so how can that be jumbo? Or think about a girl who's almost pregnant. You either are or are not pregnant. You can't be almost pregnant."

"Oh, I get it now!" Mario said. But his eyes averted down to the magazine, and he continued to read.

"So, I say any business man who considers himself a true American, and hangs an American flag outside his store, shouldn't sell Japanese products," Shoe concluded.

"Why are Japanese products the only ones that are a problem?" Jack asked.

"They aren't," Shoe answered, "But they're the growing threat." Shoe pointed to the VHS player behind the TV. "At least Mario has the sense to not buy Japanese electronics. JVC is one of the best players around as would be expected from a good German company. German products are the real deal, and they're known for their meticulous, high-quality."

Jack chuckled. "I hate to burst your bubble Shoe, but JVC is a Japanese company."

"No way!" Shoe yelled. "And how would you know?"

Jack answered after he swallowed another swig of beer. "You forget, I have a degree in electrical engineering, and that's only a stone's throw away from electronics. Trust me—JVC is Japanese."

"I thought JVC was bought by RCA, and they're American!" Shoe expounded.

"JVC *used* to be American owned. There was a company called the Victor Talking Machine Company. They did very well and created JVC as a subsidiary in Japan. JVC stands for Japanese Victor Company. When RCA bought the Victor Talking Machine company, they didn't want the Japanese division," Jack explained.

Shoe scratched his head. "JVC just sounds so German. I should've figured the Japanese and the aliens have their fingers in even more electronics than I thought."

"I have to admit, I haven't seen any solid evidence of aliens associated with what's going on with the Japanese, the governor or the real estate deals," Jack said.

Momentarily, BB raised his gaze above his glasses but then continued to flip pages with his priority returning to the annual report. Mario, having lost focus on the conversation, continued to flip through the *National Geographic Magazine*.

Shoe leaned forward. "We just agreed there's a connection between the Japanese, the land deals and the governor. We also know the Japanese have a longstanding history with aliens."

"Like what?" Jack asked.

Shoe thought for a moment and then pushed his finger into the air. "Here's a good example. Godzilla had a long history with attacks on Japan. There's also Mothra and a whole line of other monsters I can't remember right now."

"Godzilla?" Jack had a puzzling look on his face. "That's just a movie."

"A freaking *Japanese* movie," Shoe corrected.

"Besides, Godzilla wasn't an alien," Jack said. "He came from the depths of the ocean."

"No way!" Mario cried. At the same moment, he jumped up out of the water with his face lowered close to the open magazine, and his eyes were shockingly wide.

"What?" Shoe asked.

Mario pointed at the page in the magazine and looked at his three friends. "You think we have problems. Just be glad you don't live in South America. There are many kinds of evil there such as piranha, jaguars and caiman, but this one explained here is pure evil reincarnate."

Jack considered blasting Mario once again for using *evil reincarnate* when the correct term is *evil incarnate*. But it would just be another few seconds of his life he would never get back. He decided to move on. "What are you talking about?" he asked.

Mario looked down at the waves created by the jets of the hot tub. "Where does our water come from?"

Jack leaned back seeing Mario was off on one of his tangents and would only tell them what was bothering him when he was ready. "Our water comes from Lake Erie."

"What kind of fish are in Lake Erie?" Mario asked.

"Nothing unusual," Jack replied. "Trout, walleye, even some salmon."

"How about candiru?" Mario asked in a shaky voice.

"I've never heard of a candiru. What is it?" Jack asked.

Mario lowered his eyes to the magazine and read. "The candiru comes in many sizes, but there's one version that is very small."

"Are the big ones dangerous?" Jack asked.

"It's not the big ones that are the problem." Mario explained. "It's the small ones. There's a rumor along the Amazon River that these small candiru smell the scent of urine, and they follow it." He took a deep breath. "They follow it until they swim up the guy's penis."

"Ahhh!" Shoe and BB screamed, both simultaneously jumping out of the water, holding their groins."

"It's right here in black and white," Mario said as he tapped the page with his finger. "They have barbs on their body, and once they're in your dick they latch on and won't let go."

Jack laughed as he listened to Mario's words. "So how do they get the fish out of someone's dick?"

"By the sounds of it, they don't. There are two examples explained here where, in each case, the native had his penis cut off."

"Ahhh!" Shoe and BB screamed again and hunched over while they both gripped their groins even tighter.

"You guys have lost your minds!" Jack yelled. "There are no penis eating fish in Lake Erie, and even if there were, we have filtration systems and chemicals that would not allow them in the hot tub. So, get back in and get back on topic." He then glared at Mario. "And best bud, you need to check what's causing your brain cells to die off at such a young age."

Mario, BB and Shoe slid back onto the bench in the hot tub even though the vision in their minds of small fish swimming up their penis gave them less comfort than they had before Mario's Amazon report.

"I still say we don't have a lot of solid evidence on how aliens or wall plugs are connected to any of this," Jack said.

"Peri Winkle and Red Velvet have intel that there's a House of Aliens. Bart Wilkins secret journal also refers to the same House of Aliens," Shoe reminded Jack. "This House of Aliens is the key, and we need to find it."

"We need more information," Jack replied. "Maybe we should visit the fourth farm Bart Wilkins is trying to buy. It's the one Tracy said was owned by an Amish family." He shrugged. "Maybe we'll find our Amish-alien connection there."

"We'll probably find a lifetime supply of wall plugs if we look around," Shoe added.

"I say we need to visit the governor," Mario offered.

"You can't just walk into his office and accuse him," Jack said.

"Maybe we can," Mario said. "A plan is beginning to form in my brainless head. I'll let you know when I purge out the moronic and asinine bits, leaving something that makes sense to you."

BB, who had continued reading the annual report through the banter, now interrupted. "Here's something. It reads here at the very end of the report - *The American Development Consultants is a wholly owned subsidiary of West Coast Express Shipping, out of San Francisco.*"

"How do we find out about the West Coast company?" Mario was perplexed. "I wouldn't know where to start."

"I do," Shoe said.

"How?" Jack said.

"I spent quite a bit of time with Professor Johansen at Wooster College before he died. He was investigating aliens, and I think that's why he was killed," Shoe reminded them. "I never thought much of it until BB just mentioned it, but I recall him talking about the West Coast Express Shipping company. It was one of many leads he was investigating."

"Bummer. That lead has dried up," BB said. "We can't get intel from a dead man."

Shoe said, "Not the professor. We need to see someone else he knew. We need to visit the king."

With an eyebrow raised, Jack asked, "The king?"

"Yes," Shoe whispered. "The King of the Hobos."

Chapter 10: Primal Lust and Angel Dust

Mario and BB were sitting across from each other in the booth at Denny's where they were waiting to meet Jack and Shoe for a late breakfast. The bustle of the busy restaurant was interrupted by a low rumble from the parking lot. Mario and BB peered out the window to see Shoe, on his motorcycle, stop in front of the large window fronting the establishment. He removed the awkward head gear and now appeared somewhat normal in his black attire and today's light-blue Converse running shoes.

The waitress came over to their booth just as Shoe slid onto the long bench seat beside BB. "Can I get you guys a drink?" she asked.

Shoe requested a coffee as did BB. Mario asked for a large chocolate milk.

"What are your Saturday specials?" Shoe asked.

Pointing to the small whiteboard on the easel by the door, she said, "They're listed right there, Honey."

Shoe squinted as he read the sign, then turned his face up toward the waitress. "We're waiting for one more person, so we'll order our food then," he said.

As the young woman walked back toward the kitchen, Mario said, "We're actually waiting for two people. Jack said he was bringing Carley."

"You're effin kidding," BB blurted.

Shoe smirked. "So, we finally get to meet his little princess."

"Why do you have to be like that?" Mario asked. "They've been dating about six weeks, and now he's comfortable enough for her to meet us."

"Speaking of meetings, when are we meeting this so-called King of the Hobos?" Mario asked.

"I checked with my sources, and the king is out of town for two more weeks," Shoe replied.

"Out of town?" BB said. "I didn't think 'manky' hobos went on vacation."

Shoe answered, "Dude, it just adds to the many, many things you don't know. Hobos travel on trains and go from city to city. They're organized, and this time of year, there's a large gathering in Iowa. Like any king, he has responsibilities, and right now, they are there."

There was a flash of green outside the window, as the sun reflected off the Matador X pulling into the parking lot. The three boys had their faces pressed against the glass as they watched Jack get out of the driver's side.

"Holy shit," BB said. "He's actually opening the door for her!"

"Isn't that special." Shoe added in a mocking tone. "They're holding hands. I can already see she has him whipped."

"I don't know about *special* or *whipped,* but she's smokin hot!" Mario added.

As Jack opened Denny's front door for Carley, Mario, BB and Shoe straightened themselves in the booth while still targeting the illusion of casualness.

A smile crossed Jack's face as he saw his three friends. He walked toward them with Carley in tow. "Carley, these are my friends BB, Mario and Shoe."

As she sat down beside Mario, and Jack squeezed in at the end of the bench seat, Carley said, "It's great to finally meet his friends. Jack's told me so much about each of you."

Shoe leaned back against the padded, vinyl backing of the seat with his brow furrowed, creating three creases across his forehead. "Actually, we're his *best* friends."

Carley gave Shoe a cute smile. "Technically, you can't all be his best friend. *Best* implies the singular one who is the best."

Shoe leaned forward as Jack rolled his eyes. "Are you saying you might be his best friend?" Shoe asked.

"By no means would I say that—at least not yet. We've only been dating for two months. I'm just saying for you all to be his best friend is impossible. It's like you asking me, 'Which football team is the best team in the NFL?' If I said the Browns and the Eagles, you would laugh and say only one team can be the best," she answered.

Jack buried his face in the menu but gave Shoe a warning gaze above it.

BB mumbled, "She has a point." He looked at Shoe and Mario in an awkward, new light.

Shoe saw the look of hesitation in BB's face and said to him, "Well if there has to be a *best* it couldn't be a dork like you."

"That's pure bollox. Why the eff not?"

"There are many examples," Shoe replied. "Oh, here's a good one. Remember in grade 12 when you took the vitamin C tablets?"

Mario spurted out a loud, "HA!" as his recollection kicked in.

The waitress interrupted by bringing over the two coffees and the chocolate milk. "What can I get for you two?" she asked Jack and Carley.

They both ordered coffee, and Jack asked the waitress for a few more minutes with the menu.

Carley pulled open the menu and as she peered down the breakfast list, said, "I don't see what's so weird about taking vitamin C tablets."

Shoe grinned as, once again, Jack gave him a look of warning. "If I remember correctly, BB was having difficulty going to the bathroom," Shoe explained.

"Yeah, he was all backed up," Mario added.

BB pushed his glasses up the length of his nose with his finger as the sun's rays coming through the window highlighted the hurricane cowlick in his fro. "That's enough, ya whankers."

"Not quite," Shoe said. "The lady deserves an answer. Jack brought a container of vitamin C tablets to school for BB and told him, if he took them, they would cure his constipation. BB opened the bottle and the tablets were huge! They were so large, he questioned how he would be able to swallow them."

BB leaned back in the seat and just shook his head from side to side as the story unfolded.

Shoe continued. "Jack told him they weren't oral tablets. They were suppositories, and BB had to shove one a day up his ass until he had a poop of monumental proportions."

"You're kidding?" Carley said through a chuckle.

"I couldn't make this up if I tried," Shoe said. "BB almost didn't do it until Jack showed BB the fine print on the back of the bottle. He highlighted the words *slow release* and convinced BB the pills were to cure slow release of shit. He took them for seven days before Jack told him the truth."

"Ya gobshite. It was only five days," BB corrected. "And the fact I'm still here after that, along with years of similar pranks, proves I'm his best friend."

"Listen, we can all be best friends," Jack said as he pressed his elbow lightly into Carley's side. "Even in the *Olympics,* when there's a tie, they give both of them the gold medal. It is possible for the best to be a tie."

"Hey, you're right!" Mario said.

"As right as Orville and Wilbur," Jack stated. "Remember, we're the four musketeers—all for one and one for all."

Shoe rubbed his chin and said, "There was a woman involved with the four musketeers. If I remember correctly, one of the musketeers killed her for her treachery." The words came as his gaze floated from Jack to Carley.

"What can I get you to eat?" Thankfully, the waitress was back just in the nick of time.

Mario, BB and Shoe ordered their regular—the Grand Slam breakfast. Jack ordered the same, but Carley interrupted. "He and I are just going to have toast." The waitress looked at Jack, and Jack, in turn, looked at Carley in confusion.

"I have a surprise for our date today, and you don't want to have a heavy stomach," she said.

Jack closed the menu and handed it to the waitress. "That's cool. Toast it is," he said.

"Where are you guys off to today?" Carley asked.

"Shoe and I are going to Beach City to see a friend of ours. His name is Peri Winkle", BB replied.

"Peri Winkle?" Carley said. "You don't mean old Rip Van Winkle—the crazy guy who lives on the big ranch behind the trees waiting for aliens to come down and abduct him? Not that guy?"

The three boys took a moment to look from one to the other. The looks changed from confusion to embarrassment. Shoe laughed awkwardly, then said. "Certainly not that putz. This is a different Winkle."

Carley's sweet gaze turned to Mario, "How about you?"

Her gaze was hypnotic. Mario felt like his spirit was set free, and he could not lie. He said, "I have a confession."

BB cupped his hands around his mouth, imitating a microphone. "Earth to Mario. Earth to Mario."

Jack leaned forward and peered around Carley at Mario. "What do you mean—a confession?"

Mario unlocked his gaze from Jack's girl. "I had signed up for a ten-week course to study hairstyling. Today will be my third class."

"You mean like a barber," BB surmised.

"Not a barber at all," Mario said. "A barber does pretty basic, short hair cuts. I'm talking about cutting and styling hair which is an up-and-coming form of art. It will let me express myself."

Shoe laughed. "Are you gay or what?"

BB reached up, slapping Shoe in the back of the head. "If anyone's gay, it would be you. Do you remember when you had that earring, and we thought you were quite the homo himbo?"

Leaning forward with her chin on her palm and her elbow on the table, Carley said, "Now that sounds like another story I need to hear."

BB snickered at Shoe and said, "Paybacks are a bitch, aren't they?"

The waitress came back to their table with a helper, and all their food was laid out on their table. Shoe hoped the interruption would stop the earring conversation, but this wasn't meant to be one of those days.

"Why didn't I ever hear about this earring?" Jack asked.

"You were off 'chillaxin' in college when Shoe got the piercing," Mario answered. "He only had it for about six months."

BB, having been embarrassed by Shoe, felt compelled to continue the story. "Shoe just showed up one day with the little jewel of an earring in his left ear, and as we learned, it was significant that it was in his *left* ear."

After swallowing a mouthful of toast, Jack asked, "Why's that important?"

"At the time, we also didn't understand, but Shoe gave us the education as I'm sure he'll tell you now," BB said.

Between bites of a slice of bacon held between his fingertips, Shoe explained. "You see, if you have an earring in your left ear, it means you're straight. If you have one in your right ear, you're gay. I'm not gay, so the earring was pierced in my left ear."

Carley asked, "Why didn't it last for more than six months?"

BB cut in and answered. "Just as Jack doesn't know now, we didn't know, then. Barely anyone knows about this stunned rule regarding the left and right ear. The exception is, if you were gay, you knew Shoe was straight. But all the rest of the people would see the earring and think he was gay. Straight people don't know the rule and don't care if it's the left or right ear."

"Let me make sure I have this right," Carley said. "You got an earring in your left ear to show everyone you were straight, and the only ones who understood it were the gay people. The straight people still thought you were gay."

"Exactly," Shoe said. "It seemed hip at the time, but that's why the earring went away."

The group ate the rest of their breakfast in silence until Carley said, "Jack, we had better get going or we'll be late." She looked at Jack's friends and gave them a wide smile. "It was great and even entertaining getting to know each of you better. I hope to learn even more about Mario the up-and-coming hairstylist, Shoe without the earring and *Vitamin C BB*." She laughed. "That rhymes! How about that."

They all said their goodbyes as Jack laid a 20-dollar bill on the table. "See you guys Monday at hot tub night." That said, he and Carley left the table and headed out toward the X-mobile. Jack helped Carley into the passenger seat and closed his side door after he was seated.

As he drove out of the parking lot, Carley said "Head for the local Canton Airport."

"The small airport out on highway ten? What are we doing there?"

"You've picked all our dates, so it's my turn to surprise you. You'll see when we get there."

Jack directed the car toward highway ten, thinking, *don't eat a big breakfast and an airport. This isn't sounding good at all.*

It didn't take long for the Matador X to turn onto the gravel driveway of the airport. Jack could see there were two manicured grass runways, crossing each other to form an *X*. On this side of the runways were at least 20 small parked planes. On their right, were three larger hangers and a smaller one at the far end of the row.

"Head for the smaller hanger," Carley directed.

Jack saw two cars parked beside the smaller hanger and parked his vehicle beside them. Instantly, Carley opened the door and said "C'mon Jack. We're going to have some fun."

As Jack exited the vehicle, he thought, *this isn't looking good at all*. He followed Carley through the large open hanger doors and past the turboprop plane parked there. They continued toward the back of the hanger where a large man was laid back on an exercise bench, pumping a bar laden with two monstrous weights hanging from the ends. He turned his head sideways, pressed the bar up onto its supports and sat up on the bench. "Carley—baby. How are things?"

Carley smiled and lifted her hand. The large man gave her a high-five. She said, "This is my friend, Jack."

When Jack came up beside her, the man rose to his feet. Jack's gaze kept going up as the man rose to his six-foot-six-inch height. He was wearing a black jump suit rolled down around his waist. His chest was huge, and his abs were ripped above a narrow waist. Above the muscled physique was a square-jawed face highlighted by a thick, handle-bar moustache, the corners of which extended down below his chin. Above his brown eyes, adorned with thick black eyebrows, was like-colored hair cut an inch in length and standing straight up, military style.

"Jack, I am Zoltan," the big man said. "I have heard so much about you from Carley. It is splendid to finally meet." He stuck his monstrous hand out toward Jack.

Jack smiled through his curiosity. The big man had a thick Eastern-European accent. He shook the offered hand and said, "Zoltan, isn't that Romanian?"

After almost crushing Jack's hand, Zoltan let it go, then put both his hands on his hips. "Very clever, Jacko. Carley told me you were a smart one, but you are only a little right." He held up his finger and thumb an inch apart, so Jack could visualize it. "I am from Transylvania which today is technically in Romania. But as everyone in Transylvania knows, Transylvania is Hungarian."

"Hungarian it is then," Jack replied. He turned to Carley. "So, what are we doing?"

Zoltan looked at Carley and asked, "Is it his first time?"

She grinned. "Yes, it is."

Jack frowned. "No, I've flown in a plane several times."

Zoltan's lips closed in a stern, straight line. They barely moved as he said, "Jacko, we are not talking about flying in a plane. We are talking about *jumping out* of a plane." He slapped Jack on the back and threw his head back in laughter."

"Hold on a minute," Jack said as he looked from Carley to Zoltan.

"How do they say it in this country? Take a chill pill!" Zoltan said as his laughter subsided. "Are you afraid of flying?"

"Well, no…"

"Good," Zoltan said. "Because flying is a good thing. It is the falling you should be afraid of—the *splat*." Zoltan dragged his hand sideways, palm down, in front of Jack to emphasize his words.

"How high up do we go to jump?" Jack asked.

"About 12 thousand feet," Zoltan answered. "But again, that is irrelevant. If something goes wrong, it is only the last foot that matters—*splat*." Again, the large man dragged his hand across the front of Jack's chest.

"You're not helping at all!" Carley said as she punched Zoltan in the arm. "Where's Ricky?"

Zoltan chuckled and pointed to a door on his left. Carley walked toward it with Jack by his side. Jack said, "Who's Ricky?"

Carley turned the knob on the door and pushed it open as she said, "He's the pilot."

When the door opened, a gust of fog came out of the office. Through the fog, Jack could see a man sitting on the other side of a desk with his feet propped up on it. He was smoking and blowing even more smoke into the contaminated room.

Jack looked at Carley. "You're kidding? He's the pilot and he's stoned on pot?"

As they entered the office, Carley said, "Don't worry. I've been up with him many times. The pot actually calms his nerves." She turned to Ricky and said, "This is Jack. We're going to get changed. We'll meet you by the plane in 15 minutes."

Carley grabbed Jack's hand, pulling him out of the office toward another door on the same wall. She pulled him through it into a storage room where there were a few lockers on one side and two benches just in front of them. Carley headed to one of the lockers and selected two jump suits. She kept a black one and handed a powder-blue one to Jack. "You can use this locker over here. I'm going to use one over there," she stated.

Jack was very hesitant. Carley wasn't being honest with him, to say the least. She was following he and his friends around. She had some ulterior motive, and now, suddenly, she wants to throw me out of a plane from 12 thousand feet. And if I resist, she has the hulking Hungarian to help her.

"Why am I wearing light-blue, and you get black? This looks gay," Jack said.

"It's not my idea. It's airport rules. Being your first jump, all novices have to wear these light-blue flight suits."

"Why?"

"Many years ago, a rookie went up, and his parachute malfunctioned. It didn't open properly, and he had a black suit on. They couldn't find what was left of him for three days," she explained.

Jack's jaw opened in amazement. "You mean to tell me I have to wear this light-blue suit in case I go *splat*, and it'll be easier to find what's left of me?"

She grinned. "I did tell Zoltan you were the clever one."

Jack continued staring at the locker as he considered the flight suit in his hand. He thought, *what was she really up to?* "Carley, I really don't think I can do this."

From behind him, her voice, a bit deeper than normal, floated toward him. "If you do this for me, perhaps I'll do something for you."

Jack turned and there *she* was. Her clothes were removed except for the skimpy black bra, and there *it* was—the sexy green thong he had been dreaming about since their first date at Kmart. She was smiling, but now it was not so sweet and innocent.

Jack turned back toward the locker, roughly kicked off his shoes. He undid his belt buckle and undressed. The whole time he was cursing under his breath, "God damn women. They shouldn't be allowed to do that."

Once dressed, with helmets in hand, they traversed the hanger to the plane where Zoltan was waiting. He handed Carley a parachute and Jack asked, "Where's mine?"

The big man said, "Jacko, you go up strapped to me in this special buddy harness. You will have your back to me, and I will hold you tight, making sure nothing bad happens."

It was at this time, as Zoltan was putting on his helmet, that Jack noticed the big man had an earring, and it was in his right ear! *Holy fuck!* Jack thought. *The man is gay!* Once again, he almost ran for the change room, but a glance at Carley changed his mind. He saw her in the black jump suit, but in his mind, he saw right through it and visualized only the sexy, green thong.

Ten minutes later, the DE Havilland Otter was speeding down the runway and lifted into the air. They slowly gained altitude, and Zoltan showed Jack the altitude indicator on his wrist. It was difficult to hear with the roar of the engines, so the big man leaned over, yelling in Jack's ear. "We are at eight thousand feet, so it's time to get you buckled up." Zoltan stood up and grabbed Jack by the shoulder. He spun him around and grasped Jack's other shoulder with his free hand. Zoltan pulled back on Jack until Jack felt the contact of the big man behind him. Zoltan threw around harnesses and buckles and finally pulled them tight. Since Zoltan was taller, the tightening action pulled Jack up, leaving his toes dangling several inches off the plane's floor.

It was at that time, Jack felt a lump pressing into his butt. He looked around and down finally discovering the huge size of the big man's feet. His eyes went wide as Zoltan's lips came close to Jack's ear. Zoltan said, "Don't worry. I will take good care of you—buddy."

Jack looked at Carley, expecting some type of help. She just smiled coyly, and Jack's thoughts went back to the green thong. *Freaking women,* he thought.

Zoltan jumped to his feet. He checked his watch, and it showed 12 thousand feet. "It's time to go." He walked over toward the open side door of the plane. Jack instinctively held the sides with a firm grip while the air rushed past just in front of him.

Zoltan showed Jack the altitude gage and said, "To be safe we have to open the parachute by two thousand, five hundred feet." Jack felt the bulge against his ass growing as Zoltan leaned in against his ear. The big man said, "I get so excited when I jump with a virgin."

Jack's eyeballs bulged under the goggles and he yelled, "Nooo!" The words were lost to the wind as the push from Zoltan forced Jack's grip to release. The onslaught of air buffeted them as they spun head over heel. Jack's yell finally subsided once Zoltan gained control of their fall. Jack was now under Zoltan, and the ground was rushing up toward them. Off to his left, Jack could see Carley falling with her hair flowing behind her.

Jack lost all thought of the bulge. He just didn't want to die. His life was passing before his eyes, and he silently vowed he would never mock Mario and his mixed-up words if only he comes through this alive. He saw Carley disappear from view as she rushed upwards after her chute opened. Zoltan moved his arm in front of Jack and showed him the altitude displayed on the watch. The needle was moving quickly as it passed two thousand, five hundred feet. It seemed even quicker as it passed two thousand feet at which point Jack started to flail his arms. Maybe Zoltan was unconscious or maybe he was suicidal. Jack almost puked as either scenario ended with the *splat* Zoltan already mentioned several times.

The ground seemed to rush toward them even faster when the needle hit one thousand, five hundred feet, then one thousand. Finally, he felt the straps pull against him as they were sucked upwards. Jack looked up and could see the parachute fully deployed above them. Zoltan had two handles he was using to manipulate their direction, and he pressed his lips close to Jack's ears. Now, Jack felt the bulge even larger as the big man said, "I failed to mention deployment at two thousand, five hundred feet, is for pussies."

Jack felt like he was going to poop his drawers, but at least the worst part of the ordeal was over. They just had to land on the soft grass of the airfield. However, although their vertical speed had slowed, their horizontal speed was increasing.

Zoltan said in Jack's ear. "This will be fun, Jacko. Keep your feet up and forward so you don't break them."

Jack thought, *whatever.* He had given up on having any control over this. His fate was in the hands of the big, gay man. As they were now close to the ground, Jack raised his feet in front of him as best he could. He felt like he was in a position akin to taking a shit when Zoltan yelled, "Here we go!"

They skimmed the top of the grass until Zoltan's feet hit the ground. They skidded for 30 yards until the pair tumbled forward, rolling twice. They ended up with Jack on his stomach under Zoltan. Jack opened his eyes that had closed during the roll, and he saw Carley land neatly on her feet on the other side of the airfield. He didn't care about their own style. He kissed the ground, and there was only one thought that kept running through his mind. *I am alive! I am alive!*

Chapter 11: Ashtray Heart

Carley's butt hit the door of her apartment as Jack pressed into her body and her warm lips. She fumbled with the lock behind her back while Jack's lips moved down to her neck. Their need for each other began after their skydiving adventure earlier in the day, and now, after speeding to her apartment house, their lust was cresting to a fervent height.

Carley's hands roughly pushed Jack away, ripping his lips from hers, but her fingers curled into his t-shirt and halted his backward plunge. She pulled him back toward her but spun them in a tight circle so that Jack's butt thumped into the door. Now Carley leaned into him with her mouth open and pressed to his in a hard, sensuous kiss. Jack, lost in the kiss, didn't hear Carley slip the key into the lock and turn the door knob.

Intertwined, they both stumbled into the apartment with Carley managing to slam the door closed behind them. They spun and fell into the plush couch as both sets of hands set about the task of removing bits of clothing so the exploration could be more intense. Jack, now minus his shirt, didn't forget about the green thong she was wearing under her jeans, but the thoughts went further in anticipation of what lay under the delicate piece of cloth. The clothing was now nothing but annoying encumbrances and were quickly removed without a second thought. Exploration and deep kissing were escalating when Jack felt a sharp smack on his ass. His eyes opened wide in surprise as she pulled away from him, and he saw the evil grin on her face. He snickered, slapping her ass in return but held on as his fingers tightened into the soft flesh.

"I see you like it a little rough," Jack said between deep breaths.

"Maybe," she whispered in a husky tone.

As their lips came together once again, her fingers raked up his back and tightened in his hair. She pulled down hard, and his lips were ripped from hers once again. Adding to the pain of his hair being pulled, was the sting of her hard slap across his face.

The entire sequence only took a second, but now Carley let go of him. He looked down at her with playful anger and pushed his hands forward to grab her. However, she was too quick, rolling onto the carpeted floor before he could catch her. She was laughing and crawling away quickly when Jack threw himself after her, catching her slender ankle with his fingers. He grinned and said, "You're in so much trouble."

Ninety minutes later, Jack rolled off of her and sat up on the side of the bed. He turned his head around to look at her. She was still splayed out on the bed with each wrist securely tied to a bedpost. Her hair was a wild tangle around her beautiful face highlighted by flushed cheeks. Her eyes were closed, and light purring noises came from her lips.

Jack rose, stepped out of the bedroom and relieved himself in the bathroom. His mind was confused. He had very real feelings for Carley, and what they just shared was absolutely amazing, but she was covertly following he and his friends around. She was definitely hiding something.

When he returned to the bedroom, her eyes were open, and she was squirming her ass from side to side in the bed. "You can untie me now," she purred.

"No."

She laughed and repeated her request.

"Nope. I'm not untying you just yet," Jack stated.

Carley's brows furrowed. "Okay. The fun is over, and it's no longer funny or sexy. Untie me."

Jack sat on the edge of the bed close to her. "I'm not untying you until you tell me what's going on."

She looked at one bed post and then the other as she pulled against the restraints. "Have you lost your marbles? What are you talking about?"

"I know you've been following my friends and I," Jack said.

"You *have* lost your mind!" she screamed. "Un-fucking-tie me!"

"So, do you deny it?"

"Of course, I do," she said through clenched teeth.

Jack rose from the bed, and walked to the dresser. He opened the drawers and searched through the clothes.

"You've no right to go through my things!" she screamed.

When Jack opened the bottom drawer, he was surprised to find it filled with small troll dolls. There had to be at least 30 of them. They all had long, colorful hair, dressed as tiny doctors, firemen, spacemen and many other occupations. Squatting down and resting on his haunches, he turned to her and said, "I don't know if they're cute, or just plain creepy."

She lifted her shoulders off the bed and threw her head back, yelling, "Untie meee!"

Jack pushed down on his thighs and rose to his feet. Walking to the closet, he slid open the bifold door. The closet was crammed with shoe boxes on the floor and clothes on the hangers. He turned his eyes upwards where even more tiny trolls stared down at him. He grimaced as they all carried the same creepy, smiling face. They were lined up like soldiers as if ready to pounce on him. He turned and looked at Carley. "What's with all the troll dolls?"

"Don't you touch them! I like them and collect them. Some of them are worth lots of money."

As Jack listened, he was searching through the hung clothes and there it was. He pulled out the garment and walked back to the bed. "Here's the black hoodie you've been wearing."

"A lot of people have black hoodies," she responded.

Jack's eyes narrowed. "I saw your face in this hoodie at the hospital when I hurt my arm."

Her eyes grew even wider in her anger. "You mean when you went at night during the thunderstorm. You must have really good eyesight to see the details of a face across the parking lot. You're such a putz."

"How did you know it was at the parking lot?" Jack asked.

Caught in her lie, and not knowing how to respond, her lips were pursed tight until they finally burst open. "Untie meee!"

As the scream subsided, there was a loud knock on the door of the apartment. "I'll take care of that," Jack mumbled as he closed the bedroom door behind him. On the way to the front door, he quickly pulled on his jeans and t-shirt.

He opened the front door, and standing there, with wide smiles, was a clean-cut young man and an attractive young woman with a ponytail in her hair. She carried some smaller pamphlets and he carried a bible.

The young man wore a smart pressed, black suit and black shoes shined to a high glossy hue. He looked confidently into Jack's eyes and said, "I know it's close to dinner time, and you must be very busy, but have you thought about how God is helping you today?"

Jack smiled and said, "You're right. I'm busy and my mind was distracted from God this afternoon."

Jack pushed on the door knob to close it, but the man's free hand came up, pressing on the face of the door. The man said, "That's okay since we are here to share a very brief but important message with you." On cue, the young woman snapped one of the small pamphlets toward Jack's hand. Jack read the title - *Watchtower*, across the top of the pamphlet.

"I'll do some reading later," Jack offered as he stepped back and once again attempted to close the door. There was a light *thud* when it hit the man's shoe, with six inches left from the door to the jamb.

Jack thrust open the door and was about to yell at them, but the man was quicker with his words. "Wouldn't you appreciate an absolute assurance of salvation?"

Jack grinned back as he said. "Salvation—why didn't you say so? Who wouldn't want their salvation assured?" He stepped aside as he opened the door wide. His arm opened and coaxed the young couple toward the couch.

The two Jehovah's smiled happily at each other and took seats on the couch. It was just the three of them: the woman, the man and the man's bible. Jack lowered himself into the side chair beside the couch and said, "Tell me about salvation."

The man leaned forward and said, "Well..."

"Untie meee!" Carley's yell came through the thin bedroom door.

The man and woman looked at each other, then the man said to Jack, "Is that your wife? Maybe she should join us."

"That's Carley you hear, and she's not my wife. She's just a friend," Jack said.

"If she could join us, we could invite the two of you to our Hall tomorrow. We would be very happy to welcome you to our community," the woman said in a sweet voice.

There was another yell from the bedroom. "Jack, you get in here right now!"

Jack ignored the yell and said, "Honestly, she really is tied up right now."

"She must be doing her Saturday cleaning," the young man said.

Jack leaned forward in the chair. "You're thinking too hard, my new-found friend. Listen to my words. When I say she's tied up, I mean we just had jungle-monkey sex all afternoon, and I haven't yet untied her from the bed."

The man's jaw dropped as the woman reached down beside the couch and picked up a small piece of cloth from the floor. She held it out and said, "What's this?"

Jack laughed. "That's Carley's underwear. We started out here on the couch and haven't had time to clean up."

The man started to squirm on the couch as the woman turned the thong backwards and forwards. "Where is the rest of it?"

"That's all of it," Jack assured her. He looked at the man whose jaw was still gapped open. "Your wife must have some of these at home hidden away in a drawer—no? If not, well I'm only here on Saturday's, but Carley does have Wednesday nights open to entertain."

"Certainly not," the young woman stated.

"No worries," Jack said. "Carley isn't jealous, and she likes women as well as men. You could come along and participate, or just watch if that's your thing."

"Untie me, Jack!"

The man and woman shot up from the couch. The man said, "We really need to go now."

Jack rose to his feet and blocked their path. "I would be a horrible host if I let you go so soon." He put one hand on each of their shoulders and pushed them back into the couch. Leaning down, he moved his face very close to theirs. "And of course, you can tell I really do need salvation and directions to your Hall, for tomorrow."

The young man began to shake. He looked like he would pee his pants. The woman came to the moral forefront and yelled, "You won't get salvation from us! You will burn in hell! So, let us go right now!"

There was a loud knock on the door. "Canton Police! Open the door!"

Jack slapped his knee and mumbled, "This is too funny." He ran to the bedroom door and peeked his head in. Carley lifted her head, and her smoldering eyes bored into him. Jack said, "The freaking police are here. Be quiet and I'll untie you when they leave." Before she could answer, he closed the bedroom door and ran across to the front door, opening it wide.

A burly, older policeman filled the doorway as his eyes searched out the room behind Jack. "What's with all the yellin?" he asked in a heavy Irish accent. "We have had two calls from your neighbors complaining about the noise."

Jack wiped his brow with his wrist and turned his face into a look of relief. "Thank god you're here. I have two visitors, and they just won't leave.

I told them I didn't have time for them, but they all but forced their way in. They were getting aggressive, and I thought they might actually get violent."

Jack stepped aside and let the policeman in. He tipped his hat back off his forehead, placed his fist on his hips and said, "Are you two causin a commotion?"

The two young people rose to their feet and began talking over each other. The young woman finally placed a strong slap on the young man's hand and yelled, "Shut up!"

Jack leaned over toward the policeman. "See what I mean—very aggressive."

The woman's eyes smoldered as she tried to hold back her anger. "We aren't the aggressive ones. We were kidnapped! He wouldn't let us leave." She snapped her hand out, pointing a finger to the bedroom. "He has someone tied up in there. She's been the one screaming!"

The policeman frowned. "I suggest ya keep your voice down. I don't hear any screaming from the bedroom. What I did hear was someone scream out, 'Ya will burn in hell!' Was that the person in the bedroom?"

"Well, no. That was me," the woman confessed.

"And did you two force your way in here?" the policeman asked.

The two young people both shook their heads from side to side. Jack reached down, picked up the pamphlet and gave it to the policeman. The policeman looked down at it and read the title - *Watchtower*. He rolled his eyes. "Okay, you two—let's go. I want ya out of the apartment right now. If either of ya say a word, I'll arrest the both of ya for disorderly conduct." He walked back to the door leaving it open for the two to follow him through it. Head down, the young man picked up his bible and quickly walked out the door with the woman just behind him.

As the woman walked by Jack, he whispered, "I still need the address for the Hall."
The woman's face flashed the evilest look toward Jack as her lips mouthed the word, *asshole*. It was the same look Carley had on her face when he peeked in the bedroom a few minutes earlier. He remembered, *Oh shit, Carley!*

Jack hurried into the bedroom and sat on the edge of the bed. Carley had calmed down, and her breathing had slowed while she stared at the ceiling. Jack said, "Listen, I like you more than you would know. I love my time with you, and a smile comes to my face every time I think about you. I don't even have to think about the smile. It just happens the way breathing does."

Carley turned her face toward Jack, and a tear was sliding down her cheek. "I work for the *CIA*, Jack."

Now it was Jack's turn for his jaw to drop. "The *CIA*? Isn't that something you should have told me?"

"Working for the *CIA*, I'm not allowed to divulge things about myself or the work I do. We were tracking Professor Johansen from Wooster College, and that led us to Shoe then Mario and finally to you at the airport the day we met."

"You believe the idea of this link between Amish, aliens and wall plugs?" Jack asked.

"There's enough there so that a special task force was set up. We know there's something fishy going on at the governor's mansion, and we're looking for the House of Aliens. Jack, I could get fired if the *CIA* found out I just told you I work for them," she replied.

"Then, why did you tell me?" he asked.

She grinned momentarily. "Well, for one, you have me tied up. Second, you also don't know how strong my feelings are for you. I thought we were the real deal."

Jack averted his gaze and looked down at his feet. He heard the *past tense* reference to their relationship, and it deflated him the same as if he just got kicked in the gut. "I don't know what to think. You haven't been honest with me. You let me have sex with you while you were being dishonest with me. It's really uncool, and I can't wrap my head around that."

Carley's soft voice came to him. "Look at me, Jack."

Her voice was hypnotic, and he couldn't help himself. He turned his gaze back to her.

"This might sound a bit convoluted, but in a way, you were just as uncool with me."

"How so?" Jack asked.

"You just made passionate love with me even though you knew I was following you and not being truthful. That didn't stop you. If you were totally honorable, you would have asked me about the hoodie before you took me."

As much as Jack didn't like having his honor questioned, he knew she was right. He had wanted her and took her even though he knew that, at the end of the day, they might well be done for. "Can we start over now that we have all the cards laid out on the table?"

"I think that would be wonderful," she said.

"Then it's time to untie you," Jack said as he reached for the knot.

"Not yet Jack," she purred. "You can untie me a bit later."

Chapter 12: Marengo to Marado

Jack turned the X-mobile up the driveway at Mario's pad. The large, green vehicle was as sluggish as a fat lady making the turn at a swimming pool, but he liked the big car feel and the power from the large V8 engine.

He received a call from Mario earlier in the morning, telling him he needed to get over to his place right away. "They had a mission," are the words Mario used. The word *mission* along with the sight of a pink Ford Mustang parked in the driveway beside Mario's Vega should have prompted Jack to turn around right then. However, just as the crippled guy in the wheelchair always goes to investigate the scream in the horror movie, curiosity got the best of him, so he continued on.

The main door was open, and Jack could see in through the screen door. Mario heard him and waved for him to enter. Jack walked into the kitchen area where he saw Mario and an attractive, young woman, in a short, green dress and a great pair of yellow high heels.

"Hi Jack," Mario said. "This is Trina."

With her hands behind her, she leaned back against the edge of the counter. Trina said, "Hey Jack. Nice to meet you."

Jack was intrigued, but at the same time, he thought to himself, *I'm in deep shit.* "Nice to meet you too, Trina." He turned to Mario. "So, what's so important this morning?"

The answer was interrupted by the sound of the screen door opening once again. BB walked toward them wearing a tight, black suit over a pressed, white shirt. The shoes, wrap-around sunglasses and thin tie, matched the color of the pressed suit. "I have the same question as Jack, but add, why am I the only eejit wearing the fancy threads?"

When Jack saw BB in the suit, his thought changed to, *I'm in deep fucking shit.*

Mario gave a wide smile, and it was obvious that it was forced. "Let's all sit down, keep cool, and I'll explain. BB, this is Trina." Mario's hand rose and his thumb pointed toward the young woman.

BB tipped his head forward as he surveyed Trina over the sunglasses. He gave her a quick smile as he took a seat at the kitchen table. Trina, Jack and Mario also sat down while Mario rubbed his hands together as if the heat would help fuel his mind.

"We've been given an assignment from Commander Peri Winkle," Mario stated. "We need to go visit the governor."

Jack slapped his thigh and laughed. "What—are we just going to walk in and say, 'stand aside because we're looking for aliens and wall plugs?'"

"Not quite," Mario replied. "I've arranged an invitation."

Jack closed his eyelids to tiny slits. "What have you done, Mario?"

Mario continued. "Okay, everyone take a chill pill, and let me explain. My father is on the council of the *Italian Americans of Ohio*. This is important to the governor because there are over 40 thousand Americans of Italian descent in Ohio, and the group has close to four thousand registered members."

"Get to the point," Jack coaxed.

"I can do a great Italian accent and an even better impression of my father. I used it to call Governor Creed's secretary, and I've arranged for a young man from the Italian American's group and his great uncle from Italy, to pay the governor a visit."

Jack's sphincter began to pucker as he listened to Mario unravel the plot. "Even so, why would the governor see an Italian American kid and an old man from Italy?"

"Mario chuckled nervously. "Dude, because the old man is donating 200 thousand dollars to the *Italian Americans of Ohio*."

Slack on his neck, Jack's head fell forward as he shook it from side to side. When he brought his face back up, Mario was standing with a large silver briefcase held in front of him, the glint from it matching that from his fake smile.

"It looks like there's money in here, and I'm a young Italian American," Mario offered.

Jack turned his gaze from Mario to BB, then to Trina. A sudden realization hit him. "Not a chance! I'm not Italian and I'm not old!"

"That's why Trina's here," Mario said. "I know her from the hair styling shop where I'm an apprentice. She has a sister who does makeup in Hollywood and Trina follows in the same footsteps."

Jack looked at Mario as if he was crazy. "Her sister might do miracles, but it doesn't mean she can."

"C'mon Jack! It's our turn to bust a move. You didn't hear BB complaining when he and Shoe broke into Bart Wilkin's place?" Mario offered.

BB extended his hand high in the air. "Actually, I complained a lot."

Mario rolled his eyes at BB. "Don't make this about your insecurity!" His gaze turned back to Jack. "Don't worry. The plan is set. It'll be a piece of pie."

Jack seemed to be shaking his head nonstop when he was with Mario. "The saying is, *it'll be a piece of cake—a piece of cake*, not *pie!*"

"Well, we're all agreed then. It'll be a piece of cake!" Mario said through his wide smile.

Fifteen minutes later, the kitchen table had been pushed aside, and Jack was sitting in a chair in the middle of the space. A large, thin cape was draped over him, tied neatly at the neck, and Trina was by the counter preparing her materials.

Sitting across from Jack, BB and Mario provided the audience. BB turned to Mario and said, "In this grand *shebang* of yours, Trina is doing the makeup. Jack's the manky, old Italian, and you're the young *wannabe* Italian whanker. What am I doing here?"

"You're the driver," Mario answered.

"The driver?" BB said through clenched teeth. "Am I the driver because I'm the black guy?"

"No, you dork. You're the driver because you can't expect an Italian dignitary to drive himself, especially on an Italian license. Second, since you're so good at snooping during break-ins, while Jack and I are distracting the governor and his staff, you'll sneak into his office," Mario said.

"Nice plan Mario. The black guy has to drive, and the black guy has to be the burglar. You're not only a moron, but a predictable, bigoted moron," BB said.

Mario replied, "It's a doggie-doggie world out there, so we all have to do our bit."

Jack interrupted. "What the hell is 'doggie-doggie?'"

"You don't know that saying?" Mario replied. "I can't believe I got one right, and you don't know it. You say it when you want to indicate there's a very rough world out there."

Jack glared at Mario. "BB is right. You're a predictable moron—a consistently, predictable moron. "The saying is—it's a dog *eat* dog world."

Trina's form blocked Jack's view of Mario as she stepped in front of him.

"First, I need you over by the sink. I'm going to dye your hair white," she said to Jack.

Jack laughed. "Maybe in your dreams."

Trina curled two fingers inside the collar of the cape at his neck, pulling Jack to his feet. "Don't have a cow. The dye washes out easily with hot water." She dragged Jack over to the sink and pulled her hand free to obtain a small plastic bottle. "Head over the sink, please."

Ten minutes later, Jack was back in the chair, but now his hair was a silver-white color. It already added quite a few years to his appearance. Mario and BB snickered from their seats as Trina said, "Now, I'm going to start the real aging process. I'm applying lighter foundation to the inside of your face and a darker foundation to the jawline, chin and cheekbones. The shadowing will represent what you would look like when you're older."

As she applied the makeup, Jack said to Mario, "One problem we have is I can't do a good Italian accent."

Mario said, "I thought of that. You won't speak any English at all. I'll teach you two or three phrases in Italian, and you'll say them every once in a while, so the governor doesn't think you have dementia."

"What if the governor speaks Italian?" Jack asked in an effort to abort their mission.

"I thought about that and did some research," Mario answered. The governor is American, two generations back, and from that point, he's of German descent. He hates Italians and Italian Americans. We know because we tell all the Italian Americans of Ohio not to vote for him. That's why he's seeing us, so he can get more ethnic votes."

"If I remember correctly, you don't speak much Italian at all," Jack recalled. "What are you going to have me say?"

"Every good Italian kid in America, even if they don't know how to speak the language, at least knows how to swear in Italian," Mario said.

Trina mumbled, "Now, I'm going to use some liner to highlight the natural creases in your face."

Jack ignored her and let her work as he said to Mario, "I'm not going to swear at the governor."

"He won't know the difference. It'll sound Italian, and you only have to open your mouth once in a while to make it sound genuine. Other than that, you whisper in my ear, and I'll give the appearance of translating your words to Governor Breed," Mario answered.

Trina picked up a makeup brush and said, "Now just a bit of blending and we'll be done."

Mario began the swearing lesson. "There are some common sayings in Italian. In English, we say shit face or dick face. In Italian face is *faccia*. Dick is *cazo*. Ass is *culo*. Shit is *merda*. Balls are *testicoli* and pussy is *figa*. So, dick face is *faccia di cazo*. Shit face is *faccia di merda* and pussy face is *faccia di figa*."

Jack said, "And it follows ball face is *faccia di testicoli* and ass face is *faccia di culo*."

Mario smiled as Jack picked it up quickly. "You can put a nice twist on it and say, *bacha ma culo*, which means *kiss my ass*."

Trina sighed and rolled her eyes. "If you want me to get this right, stop talking for a bit." Jack complied as Trina put a light-colored lipstick on him. "As people get older, they lose some of the pigment in their lips." She rubbed the lipstick to blend it in, then pressed a small amount of white makeup into his eyebrows, giving them a final appearance of grey.

When she moved behind him, Mario and BB saw Jack's face. Both sets of eyebrows rose in amazement. "Holy shite!" BB said. "You wouldn't believe how old and Italian you look."

Trina applied a liberal amount of gel in Jack's hair, and brushed it straight back. Mario walked over to the counter and picked up a pair of dark wrap-around sunglasses. He handed them to Jack.

Jack put them on and Mario said, "Damn, that's good. You look like you're fresh off the boat, or more correctly, a yacht on the Italian Riviera." Mario snapped his fingers and rushed off to his bedroom. He returned with a dark-green, pin striped, double-breasted suit. "This is my dad's, but it'll fit you nice."

"I can't believe we're doing this," Jack said as he grabbed the suit hanger and headed for the bedroom to change.

Mario yelled after him. "Stop whining! It's our turn to come to the dump!"

Jack, having just entered the bedroom, tilted his head back out. "It's come to the *pump*, you spaz."

A few minutes later, Jack came into the kitchen. Mario pushed up the knot of Jack's white tie and set the matching pocket handkerchief properly. To finish the look, Mario flipped a white, silk scarf over Jack's shoulder, wrapped it once loosely around his neck, and let the remainder fall down his chest. Mario took a step back to stand beside BB. His chin was held in his hand as he said, "What do you think BB?"

BB grinned. "It's brilliant! This just might work."

Mario thanked Trina as she left, and then he went to the bedroom for his own suit. It was dark-blue, and, if you looked closely, you could see the subtle plaid pattern in it. He handed Jack a pair of his fathers' shoes. They were shined to a high gloss, highlighting the brogue pattern.

"We're supposed to meet the governor at his mansion in Columbus. We have a bit of time, but we better boogie in case we hit some traffic." Mario picked up Jack's car keys off the counter and threw them to BB.

"We aren't taking my car," Jack stated.

"You don't expect us to roll up to the governor's mansion in the Shaggin-wagon or my Vega, do you?" Mario responded. He walked toward the front door as he added, "Jack, this is a good time for you to start practicing not speaking English."

Jack picked up the industrial-style, silver briefcase and groaned with the weight. "What did you put in here?"

As they walked to the car, Mario said. "Money weighs a lot. I put six old encyclopedias in it. The large briefcase is heavy on its own, as it's airtight, reinforced and has a dial combination lock on it. My dad used it when he had to deliver payroll money."

Jack and Mario sat in the back seat while BB drove. As they turned onto the highway, BB asked, "So, what are the details of the plan?"

As Mario looked out the window, he explained, "The governor receives his guests in a first-floor parlor on the west side of the building. Sometimes he brings them into a conference room beside the parlor. BB, you'll wait in the front foyer. The governor has a secret service guy, but he'll likely be in with us. Governor Breed's quarters are on the second floor. You shouldn't see anyone else on the first floor as you find a way into the governor's private office in the east wing of the first floor. Other than that, play it by rear."

Jack looked in the rear-view mirror and could see BB's reflection laughing at Mario's misuse of words again. Jack turned to Mario, "What is my name supposed to be?"

"Glad you reminded me," Mario replied. From the car seat beside him, he pulled open a newspaper. "My dad gets these sent from the old country." On the front page, he nonchalantly ran his finger down until it came across a name. "Here you go—Emilio Francesco Martino. It sounds very diplomatic."

It took two hours to drive to the governor's mansion in Bexley, a suburb of Columbus. The trip was quiet other than Mario reinforcing the swear terms to Jack and teaching him a few more. The large, white, stone mansion was set back on the expertly manicured property. The three occupants of the Matador X were stopped at the gatehouse, and after giving Mario's name, they were allowed to continue. Once at the double, oak front doors, a secret service agent opened the door, letting them in. He led Jack and Mario to the parlor where the governor was seated.

Governor Breed rose to his feet and gave the three of them a wide, vote-recruiting smile. Meeting them at the wide opening from the hallway to the parlor, he held his hand out. "Good afternoon gentlemen. I'm Carter Breed. Welcome to Columbus."

Mario grasped the governor's handshake. "It's a pleasure to meet you. My name is Mario Dimeo, from Canton. This is my great uncle from Sicily, Emilio Francesco Martino."

The governor slipped his hand from Mario's and pushed it toward Jack. "That name certainly is a handful."

Jack slid the silver briefcase from his right hand to his left, freeing the right to grasp Breed's sweaty hand as he now fully transformed into his Sicilian persona. As they shook hands, Emilio said, "Faccia di merda, Governatore Breed." *This was the moment of truth,* Emelio thought. *I wonder if the governor will realize I just called him face of shit.*

Mario interrupted the confused look on the governor's face. "My great uncle doesn't speak English. He just told you how happy he is to meet you."

The confused look remained on the governor's face for only a few seconds, but to Emilio and Mario, it seemed painfully longer.

Finally, the governor laughed and put his hand on Emilio's shoulder, coaxing him into the parlor. He looked at Mario. "Tell Emilio I really appreciate him coming all this way to visit our great state of Ohio."

Mario moved to the other side of Emilio and whispered in his ear, "So far, so good."

There were four plush arm-chairs set in the middle of the room around a large, round, oak table. Governor Breed ushered Emilio into one of the chairs, and Mario stood beside Emilio so he could translate while Governor Breed sat across from them.

As Emilio sat, he placed the briefcase down beside him and said, "*Grazie.*" But he was nervous and it didn't sound like enough of a response. "Bacha ma culo," he added.

Mario smiled and held back his laughter, as he just heard Emilio tell the governor to kiss his ass.

The secret service agent moved just inside the parlor wall and faced the governor. Once the agent disappeared from BB's view, BB moved into action and walked briskly down the long hallway into the east wing of the building. After furtively looking from side to side and behind him, he turned a corner, and there, in front of him, was a desk. Sitting behind it was a middle-aged lady.

She was startled by his sudden appearance, but, after composing herself, said, "Are you lost? Can I help you?" As she said this her hand slipped on top of the phone receiver.

BB had to think quickly, and he did. "I'm waiting for the governor's guests. I was looking for the kitchen to get a drink of water."

She paused for a moment before her hand slid off the receiver. "The kitchen is upstairs and off limits, but there is a kitchenette and pantry back the way you came. Down the hallway you will see an open door on your right." She looked down and returned to her paperwork. It was a clear message to BB that he was dismissed.

BB looked over top of the secretary and saw the governor's office door on the opposite side of the room behind her. He gave a deep, frustrating exhale as he turned and headed toward the kitchenette where he did pour himself a glass of water. He contemplated what he could do, but he had no idea.

The governor leaned back in his chair and crossed one knee over the other, tapping the fingertips of one hand against those of the other. "So, what brings you to Ohio, Mr. Martino? My secretary said something about a donation."

Mario leaned down and whispered in Emilio's ear, "Stay cool." He waited there a few seconds before rising up to his full height. "My great uncle recognizes Ohio has a very large Italian population. In fact, it's one of the largest groups of Italians outside of Italy. Every year he visits one of these Italian communities and makes a donation to further Italian culture," Mario explained.

"That's commendable," the governor said. "How much is he donating here in Ohio?"

Mario replied, "200 thousand dollars."

The governor's jaw dropped.

Emilio held his hands, palms up, in front of him and shrugged. "*Cazo si, faccia di figa.*" Emilio thought the governor's look of shock and wanting deserved the words, *fuck you, face of pussy.*

BB heard footsteps heading toward the room he was in. He moved toward the doorway to see the secretary walking down the hallway toward him, carrying a small parcel. BB smiled and said, "Have a good night Ma'am."

The woman heard him, gave a perfunctory smile and then not even a second thought. A dozen steps behind her, BB followed until he was looking into the front foyer. There, a maid dusting the stair railing, said, "Goodnight, Jackie."

The secretary didn't stop, but said on her way by, "Same to you, Mary Ellen. The governor asked me to drop off this package on the way home, so I really need to run."

BB smiled as he backed into the hallway. *Good effin things come to those who wait,* he thought. His steps quickened as he moved down the hallway and right by the secretary's desk. His hand was on the door knob to Carter Breed's office, and he turned it, hopefully. *Thank Christ,* he thought as the knob turned, and the door to the governor's office opened. Once inside, he realized he didn't know what he was looking for. He decided he would start at one end of the office, work his way to the other, and see what he could come up with.

"Will you be leaving a check with me?" the governor asked.

Mario and Emilio looked at each other and chuckled. Mario said, "My great uncle believes in the old ways when you dealt with people face to face. Your handshake was your word and became your bond."

Emilio looked up at Mario and thought, *Mario must have practiced that. It was good, and there were no mixed-up words.*

"And…" the governor said.

"And he only deals in cash." Mario glanced at the silver briefcase. "He'll be giving it directly to the council of the *Italian Americans of Ohio.* We'll tell them how hospitable you have been, and I'm sure they'll welcome your advice on how it should be spent."

BB scrutinized the bookcase and the two filing cabinets against the wall, but he found nothing of importance. He also found a safe behind a painting on the wall, but it was locked. Turning to the desk, he again found nothing relating Governor Breed to the Japanese or the House of Aliens. There was no more time, so he left the office, closed the door, then headed toward the hallway. As he passed the secretary's desk, he skidded to a stop. The desk was a mess, allowing the three colored folders, neatly in the corner, to stick out like a sore thumb. The folders were labelled: *To Do, For my people to do* and *Bullshit file*. BB looked through each and found nothing of importance until he opened the Bullshit file.

There was only one set of stapled papers in it. The title page read,

Funeral Invitation list for Ki-ha Park, President, ADC.

Whamo slamo, BB thought. *I just hit the motherload.*

He turned to the second page where the secretary had written a note to the governor. It read,

Governor,

K. Park, funeral is this weekend. They have asked for recommendations for any invitees they might have missed.

Her name was signed underneath. Below it, were two names in a different writing style. These would have been the governor's additions, he surmised. Opening the middle desk drawer, he retrieved a pen and scribbled on one of the insignificant pieces of paper on the secretary's desk. Once he discovered the pen color matched the governor's, mimicking the governor's style as best he could, he added—*Jack Decker and Shoe Smith*. He wrote their addresses after their names.

The sudden sound of a vacuum being started in the hallway spooked him. He slammed the folder closed before he had the opportunity to add Mario's name, or his own. He placed the folders back in their original position and the pen in the desk. Fortunately, the maid was facing away from him when he walked by her. She had a fright as he said, "Excuse me," from behind her.

"Bless me. I was startled," she said as she held her clenched fist to her heart. Her eyes opened even wider and she turned off the vacuum. "BB? BB O'Neil? Is that you?"

BB stopped and turned his head around to face the maid while pushing his glasses up the bridge of his nose. Then, the connection was made in his mind. The secretary called the maid, Mary Ellen, and as he looked at her, his gaze was drawn to her large bosom. *Holy Shite*, he thought. It's Mary

Ellen Perfect Tits all grown up! In his last year of high school, Mary Ellen developed a crush on him. He could see by the wide smile on her pretty face that the attraction was most likely still there.

"Mary Ellen. Wow! It's been a long time, and you look as smashing as ever," BB said as he walked back to her.

She eyed him up and down. "You also. What are you doing here?"

"I moonlight as a driver, and I'm here with the governor's guests," he replied.

"We really need to get together and catch up," she said.

"That would be great, Mary Ellen," he said as he put his hand on her forearm. "But right now, I need to go. I think the guests are waiting for me."

"Oh, wait just a minute." Mary Ellen pulled a pen from her shirt pocket and a small pad from the pocket in her apron. She scribbled her phone number on the pad, tore off the page and handed it to BB. "Make sure you call me." She looked up at him while giving her best smile.

BB smiled back. He put the paper in his pocket, turned around, then continued toward the foyer. Once there, BB took a couple of delicate steps up the stairs until he caught sight of Emilio and Mario. Mario looked over and saw BB replacing his eyeglasses with his sunglasses. This was the signal BB's search was done.

"We should be going, Governor," Mario said. "Since we're in your State, we just wanted to make sure you knew of our intentions."

The three men rose and followed the secret service agent back toward the front door. Governor Breed shook Mario's hand and then extended it toward Emilio. "Thank you again for coming all this way."

Emilio grasped the offered hand, clenching it. He put his other hand on top. "*Intro culo di mammata.*"

Mario grasped Emilio's arm and pulled him toward the door. As they walked out, Mario whispered, "I never taught you that last saying—*up your mother's ass.*"

Emilio grinned, happy for the ordeal to be over with. "You're not the only one who knows how to swear internationally."

BB followed them out and opened the door allowing Emilio and Mario to enter the rear compartment of the car. The governor didn't wait to watch them leave, as he was already back in the Parlor and dialing a number on the phone there. He waited for an answer, then said, "I have something for you to do for me."

"What now?"

"Two men—Mario Dimeo and his old fart of a great uncle are in town. They have an oversized, silver briefcase with 200 thousand dollars in it," he said.

"A lot of money," was the response.

The governor continued. "I want it, and you're going to get it for me."

"You will owe us a very big favor."

"Don't worry, I'll make it worth your while," the governor replied before he hung up the phone.

The X-mobile passed the guardhouse and turned right, headed toward the highway. They didn't take notice of the white van parked on the side of the road across from the mansion, the small antenna mounted on its roof, or the man holding the camera at the window taking pictures as BB drove by.

Inside the van, the taller man turned back toward the smaller man. "Okay, I got the pictures. What's so important about these guys?"

The smaller man removed the earphones from his head and said to the man with the camera, "There's only one set of earphones, so only I could hear the importance of the visitor. The boss will need to know who's in our town, and he'll want to know right away."

"No one of importance comes to Ohio. Who is he?"

"The audio bugs we have in the governor's mansion finally paid off," the smaller man said. "The old man in the car is Emelio Francesco Martino."

The taller man almost dropped the camera as he stumbled back onto a small stool. Running his fingers back through his hair, he said, "You don't mean *thee* Emelio Francesco Martino?"

The smaller man whispered, "The one and only."

Chapter 13: It's all a Blur

"Jack, you need to get over to my place right now!"

When Jack picked up the phone receiver at his mom's house and said, "hello," those were the first words BB blurted out.

Jack said, "BB, what's going on?"

"I don't have time to explain. I need your help, and I need it right now. Get over here!" BB screamed over the phone line before he hung up.

Pushing down the two little levers in the base of the phone to disconnect the call, Jack waited a few seconds before releasing them and dialing Mario's number. As soon as he heard Mario say, "hello," he blurted out, "Mario, you need to meet me over at BB's place right now!"

Mario said, "What..."

Jack cut him off. "I don't have time to explain. He needs our help, and he needs it right now. Get over there!" He hung up the phone, grinning as he thought, *the mimicking of BB wasn't very creative, but it was effective.*

As Jack headed for the front hallway, he saw his mom in the living room and said, "I have to go. BB has some type of emergency."

She looked up from the newspaper. "Oh no! You were supposed to be seeing Carley this morning."

"Whatever BB's emergency is, I'm not wasting a lot of time on it. He probably just needs someone to hold his hand for a bit."

He pushed open the screen door and was quickly in the X-mobile for the ten-minute drive to BB's apartment. After their adventure at the governor's mansion, Mario had forgotten the large, silver briefcase in his car. Since Mario would most certainly meet them momentarily, he pulled it from the back-seat area, and with it suspended from his hand, he headed for the front entryway of the apartment building. BB lived on the second floor of a triplex, and since there was no elevator, Jack took the stairs two at a time.

He knocked on the door, whereby BB immediately yelled out, "C'mon in—quick!"

Jack pushed open the door and put the briefcase down in the hallway. He rubbed his forearm as the muscles relaxed after carrying the weight of the encyclopedias still within it. Looking into BB's living room, he saw his friend at the far side of his couch, looking down behind it at something on the floor. BB's large afro was vibrating as his body shook. He tilted his face toward Jack. "I don't know what to do."

Jack felt a little queasy in anticipation of what BB was viewing behind the couch. He walked over slowly and peeked his head over the arm. His eyes widened as he said, "Is it dead?"

"Of course it's effin dead, ya maggot!" BB answered. "The dog chewed on the electrical wire while I was in the kitchen. I heard the *zap* and came running in. The dog's teeth were clamped on the cord, and his legs were flailing, at least initially."

Jack leaned over, poking the small Jack Russell Terrier in the side. The open eyes didn't move. "Yup. He's dead."

"'She,'" BB said.

"What?" Jack asked.

"It's an effin 'she,' not a 'he.' You don't see a dick on her, do you?" BB replied.

Jack rose to his full height. "Dogs have an 'innie,' so it's hard to tell, and I assume on a dog that has just been electrocuted, it would be a 'super-innie.'"

"This isn't funny. The dog belongs to my neighbors who live upstairs. I was looking after it while they're on vacation in Florida. What should I do?" Beads of sweat broke out on BB's brow as he continued to shake.

"You need to call them, and see what *they* want to do with their dog. Most owners are close to their pet, so they'll probably fly right home and give the dog a proper burial," Jack offered.

They were interrupted by loud steps coming up the stairs, and shortly thereafter, Mario appeared at the open doorway. He saw his dad's silver briefcase by the door and made a mental note to pick it up on the way out. Seeing BB and Jack by the couch, Mario said, "Where's the fire?"

The words Mario chose to describe the possible emergency were ill advised, and he knew it as soon as he saw the fried dog beside the couch.

BB looked at Jack and said, "Did you call him?"

"I did because I can't stay long. I'm already late going to Carley's house. Once we have a plan, I'm outta here," Jack stated.

"What should I do?" BB asked.

"Call the owner right now. Let them know what happened, and ask them what *they* want to do," Jack replied.

BB walked to the kitchen, followed by Jack and Mario. He picked up the receiver of the phone hanging off the wall, and he read the phone number on the small card jammed behind the edge of the phone's base. His fingers were shaking as he dialed while he was hoping there wouldn't be an answer.

After five rings there was a "hello" from the other end of the line.

"Mr. Robertson, this is BB. How is your trip going?"

"It's good BB," Mr. Robertson replied. There was concern in his voice. "Something must be wrong for you to call Helen and I. Out with it."

There was a pause as BB formulated the words. "It's your dog, Mr. Robertson. I have bad news. Ringo is dead. He chewed on a wire when I wasn't looking. He got himself electrocuted," BB explained.

"Ringo—he's dead," came the whisper over the phone.

"I'm really sorry, Mr. Robertson. It was quick though. He didn't feel a lot of pain," BB whispered back.

Mr. Robertson said, "I don't care if it was quick! Thank god that little piss of a dog is dead!"

"I don't understand," BB stammered.

"Listen BB. You've done me a great service. The dog belonged to Helen, and I hated that vindictive little fur ball. Every time I would sit beside my wife, Ringo would try to bite me. If I would try and get out the door, Ringo would always come running and, half the time, trip me up. I was number two in Helen's life, but number one is now dead!" Mr. Robertson said with glee.

BB words came slowly with his confusion. "You better at least tell Mrs. Robertson."

"Not a chance—at least not yet. It would ruin her vacation as much as you have improved mine. I'll tell her when we get off the plane on the way home."

"What do you want me to do with Ringo?" BB glanced over at the white Terrier. Even though its gums were pulled back showing the teeth still clamped on the wire, it had a cute appearance with the one black spot on its face and a larger brown one on its side.

"I don't really care BB. It's probably best to call a veterinarian and ask them to get rid of Ringo. They can cremate her or bury her—whatever is the least amount of money. I'll reimburse you when we get home."

There was a click on the receiver as Mr. Robertson hung up.

BB turned to Mario and Jack, and said, "He wasn't in love with the dog. He says, 'take it to a vet and get rid of it.'"

"That makes it 'easy-pleasy,'" Jack said. "Find the phone number of the closest veterinarian and find some type of case that seals up tight. Plastic works best. Stuff the dog in it, and take the dog to the vet." With his input complete, Jack clapped his hands together before walking toward the door.

"Where are we going to get a large plastic container, and where are you going, ya whanker?" BB asked.

Jack kept walking. "I'm already late for my date with Carley. You and Mario can figure out the container. Be creative, if need be, but remember to meet up at Denny's at 2:00 p.m. Be there or be square." Before either of the other two young men could answer, Jack turned the corner and walked down the hallway toward the stairs. He made his way to his car and saw Mario's silver Vega parked beside it. He didn't take notice of the two dark-haired men in the blue Honda Civic parked on the road, two buildings down.

Several hours later, Jack pulled his Matador X into the parking lot at Denny's. He turned to Carley and said, "Right on. There's an open spot right by the front door."

Jack and Carley enjoyed each other's company. They had spent the morning hours in a secluded part of a quiet park. Carley had made a picnic breakfast, and since the October weather was getting cooler, they wrapped the large blanket around them and snuggled together. They kissed and touched, but it wasn't so much exploratory any longer, as they had come to enjoy each other many times.

"I can't believe I'm hungry so soon after breakfast," Carley said as she exited the car.

Jack chuckled as he met her in front of the car and wrapped his arm around her waist. "Well, we did burn off some energy and need to refuel."

She slapped his ass and said, "You're so bad!"

They walked in the front door, and Jack instantly caught sight of Shoe sitting in their familiar booth by the front window. As they walked over, Carley reminded Jack, "Don't say anything about me working for the *CIA*. Just say I'm joining the team."

"No problem," Jack replied just as he pushed himself into the bench seat opposite Shoe.

Shoe looked up from his strawberry milkshake and said his hellos. "You guys have bad timing. I was just about to head to the bathroom, so give me a minute." He winked at Carley. "Don't let Jack drink any of my milkshake." Pushing down with his hands several times, he bounced across the red bench seat, then made his way to the bathroom.

Once Shoe was out of earshot, Jack said, "You mentioned *CIA*, and it reminded me. You did call them off?"

She nodded her head up and down. "Yes. I told them I have a lead needing some space, so put any plans on hold."

Jack said, "Plans—what plans did they have?"

Carley chuckled. "They were actually considering picking one of you guys up for interrogation."

Jack's smile faded. "You gotta be kidding me."

Their conversation was interrupted by Shoe's return followed by the waitress. Jack did envy Shoe for his milkshake and ordered one for himself. Carley also ordered one, but it was chocolate flavored. When the waitress brought them back, Jack said, "We're waiting for two more people before we order our food."

The woman, who had pulled out her paper pad, tucked it back away. "'Okie-dokie.'"

Between slurps on his straw, Jack said to Shoe. "You heard what BB found at the governor's mansion?"

Shoe froze for a second, looked at Carley and then at Jack. "We shouldn't be talking about that with Carley here. It'll bore her."

Jack leaned back in the cushioned seat. "It's all copacetic. Carley is a smart girl and could tell we were up to something. She had most of it figured out when I filled in the holes for her. She wants to be part of the team."

Shoe shook his head. "No offense Carley, but you can't just *be part of the team*. To be part of the team, you have to take risks for the team. BB and I broke into a real estate office. Jack impersonated an Italian dignitary, and he, along with Mario, duped the governor on his own turf."

Jack, with some annoyance in his voice, felt he needed to protect Carley. "What do you think she should do?"

Before Shoe could answer, Carley put her hand on Jack's arm. "I'm ready to do my bit, Shoe. When the team feels the time is right, I'll do my fair share."

"What about your part?" Jack asked Shoe. "It's been three weeks since you mentioned we needed to go see the King of the Hobos, yet we're still waiting."

"Guilty as charged," Shoe replied. "My contact tells me the king's delayed, but is expected soon. When he arrives back in Akron, my guy will let me know."

"I know I'm just getting into this," Carly said, "but you need to see a hobo?"

Shoe shook his head. "No, not a hobo. We need to see the *King* of the Hobos."

Carley chuckled. "I would have thought you begin with a duke or a prince of hobos, but you go right to the king. That's impressive."

Shoe ignored Carley and said to Jack, "Are you sure she's going to be of some value, or is she just going to sit around and make sarcastic comments?"

Jack turned to Carley. "I don't know what the hobo connection is all about, but Shoe hasn't steered us wrong, yet. If he says we need to go see the king, I'm compelled to give him the benefit of the doubt." Turning back to Shoe he said, "I'm curious. How the heck do you know hobos?"

"It's better, especially with Carley here, if I only tell you what you need to know. It leaves you with plausible denial in case things go south. Suffice it to say, I know a hobo who knows a hobo, and that hobo knows a hobo."

Carley said, "It sounds like the pony—no—I mean the hobo express in a twisted, demented way."

"Jack, best you tighten the leash on this girl of yours. Although, in a twisted, demented way, I like her spunk, but she's pushing the envelope."

They all laughed as Shoe glanced out the window and saw the Shaggin-wagon pull into the parking lot. Earlier, Jack had been lucky to find a parking spot directly in front of Denny's. The first two rows of parking spots were now full, leaving only the third row at the far end of the lot with available spots. Shoe watched as BB backed the van into the corner spot. He didn't notice the blue Civic pulling into the parking spot at the opposite corner of the same row.

The two men in the Honda Civic were brothers, consequently they looked similar. They both had black hair and dark eyes and were more easily differentiated by the clothes they wore. Although they both wore black pants, the driver wore a red sweater while the passenger wore a similar sweater in dark-green.

The driver said, "Are you sure they're both in the van?"

The passenger in the green sweater said, "Yes. Wait one minute and you will see."

The man in the red sweater said, "Did you see the money briefcase?"

"We were a little too far away for me to confirm it, but I think so," the passenger responded.

A few seconds later, the two men saw BB and Mario exit the van and walk toward the front door of the restaurant.

The man in the green sweater said, "Look there! The Italian guy has the briefcase!"
"It's time for us to make our move," the driver said. He put on a black pair of thin gloves, as did his brother, before they exited the Honda.

Shoe watched BB and Mario walking toward the restaurant, and he now noticed the two Japanese men also walking toward the door from the opposite side of the parking lot. With the team's ongoing investigation, his Japanese phobia had grown. "God damn Japanese," he muttered.

While BB and Mario moved through the second row of cars, there was a squeal as a white van flashed out from the alley beside Denny's. It continued down the first row right into BB and Mario's path. The van's brakes made a second squeal as it careened to a stop. The two rear panel doors were flung open, and four burly men jumped out. Two of them ran toward Mario while the other two attacked BB. Both BB and Mario screamed and tried to run. Mario had the advantage of the heavy, silver briefcase which he threw at the first man facing him. It gave him the two extra seconds he needed to slip free of his attackers. BB wasn't as fortunate. He tried to escape, but the two burly men had BB in their tight grasp.

One of the men holding BB said to the other men, "Don't worry about the Italian guy. Grab the briefcase and let's get out of here!"

By that time, Jack, Shoe and Carley were rushing to the front door just as BB was thrown into the back of the white van. The four attackers followed him in with the last man carrying the briefcase. Jack burst open the front door of Denny's just as the rear tires of the van began spinning. As it lurched forward, Jack read the wording on the side of the van. It read,

Pusiak Fine Polish Pastries.

He watched the van speed out of the parking lot, and with their focus there, he took no notice of the Blue Civic that followed it.

Mario, sweating and disheveled from his narrow escape, ran up to Jack, Carley and Shoe. Jack, seeing Mario was unharmed, turned to Carley and said, "I thought you told me you called off your *CIA* friends."

Before Carley could answer, Shoe said, "Those were *CIA* guys in a Polish pastry van?"

Jack put his hands on his waist and glared at Carley, waiting for an answer.

Carley stamped her foot on the ground and pointed at Jack's face. "They weren't *CIA* agents!"

"How do you know? Maybe these guys were hired by your fellow agents," Jack said in a crisp tone.

Carley spun away from Jack and growled. Then, she turned back with her finger once again in Jack's face. "I know, because I'm not with the *CIA*!"

Jack's eyes opened wide, and he took a step back. "I don't get it. You told me you were with the *CIA*."

Carley rolled her eyes. "What did you expect me to say? We just had sex, and I was tied to the bed. The truth of it is, you never would have believed me or untied me if, under those less than Amish circumstances, I told you I'm Amish!"

Mario and Shoe both grinned while Mario gave Jack a light punch in the shoulder. "Atta boy Jack."

Jack glared at Carley for a few moments before turning his frustration on his two friends. "Get your heads on straight! BB just got kidnapped."

Many of the patrons in the restaurant had come outside in the commotion, and one of them, in a jogging suit, bumped into Mario's shoulder as he walked by him. He slipped a small piece of folded paper into Mario's hand as he whispered into his ear, "Follow the instructions."

Mario spun around with the bump and turned to face Jack. He opened up the paper and said, "That guy just passed me this note."

"What does it say?" Jack asked.

Mario unfolded the paper and read it aloud to his friends.

"To Emelio Francesco Martino:

We do not appreciate the Italian Mafia coming into our area. The Polish Mafia has controlled Northern Ohio from Cleveland to Columbus for many years as agreed to by the New York Italian families. You will meet us at the old tire warehouse on 13th Avenue, in Akron, on Saturday night at midnight. You will bring your agreement to abstain from bringing the Italian Mafia to Ohio. In return, we will return your friend, but your money in the suitcase is forfeit. If you do not come and agree to these terms, your friend's life will also be forfeit.

Peter Pusiak."

Jack, Carley, Shoe and Mario looked from one to the other in bewilderment for some time until Shoe blurted, "What the fuck are they talking about? Italian Mafia and Polish Mafia—are they kidding?"

Jack thought for a moment, and then a curiosity hit him. "Wait a minute," he mumbled. He stepped around Mario and opened the door to his Matador. He pulled out the Italian newspaper Mario left there after their adventure at the governor's mansion. As he walked back toward the group, he ran his finger down the front page. He stopped the motion when he found Martino's name and took the time to review the article.

He took a deep, involuntary inhale and choked on it. His eyes were wide as he lifted his gaze to Mario. "You dork! Didn't you read this before you gave me the name, Emilio Francesco Martino?"

"Jack, you're asking stupid questions. You know I don't speak Italian, so it's obvious I don't *read* Italian. After all, how could a name from five thousand miles away mean anything of importance here?" Mario replied.

Jack turned the newspaper over and pointed into it so hard his finger almost went through it. His teeth were clenched together as he said, "See here where it says *Sicilia*. What does that mean?"
"That's easy Jack. It would be Sicily," Mario replied.

Jack continued. "And here, it says *Mafioso*? What does your pea brain think that would be?"

"That would be Mafia," Mario stated.

"Lastly," Jack said, "I worked a couple of summer jobs with your dad at the construction site. He was the big boss, so what did the guys call him?"

Mario thought back. "They called him, *Capo*."

Jack had a mocking tone. "Oh, look here then. Here are the words *Capo*, *mafioso* and *Sicilia* in the same sentence with the name, Emelio Francesco Martino. Even with your lack of Italian, what do you think that would mean?"

Shoe snickered as Mario thought for a moment, putting his finger to his chin. "It must mean Emilio Francesco Martino is the Boss of the Sicilian Mafia," Mario concluded.

Jack pursed his lips together as he rolled up the newspaper and smacked Mario in the side of the head. "Exactly! They think Martino is in town, and they think I am Martino, the head of the Sicilian Mafia!"

"It could be worse," Mario offered.

Jack rolled his eyes to the sky and said, "How could this possibly be worse?"

Mario said, "It could be raining."

Jack glared at Mario. "BB just got kidnapped by the Polish Mafia because they think he is part of the Italian Mafia, and they think I am the leader of the Italian Mafia. They also think they just stole 200 thousand dollars in the locked briefcase. We have no idea what to do, yet you can make a joke?"

Carley regained her composure and interrupted. "I know what we have to do."

Jack glared at her. "You haven't been part of this, so how could you possibly know what to do?"

She put her hand lightly on Jack's arm. "Hear me out. I'm sorry I lied to you about working for the *CIA*, but I'm from the Amish community. As is Amish custom, at 16 years of age, we go out into the conventional world and taste the evils and sins we've abstained from. We can then make a choice to remain in the world you would know, or return to the Amish lifestyle."

Jack put his hand on hers. "We don't have time for this, Carley."

"Let me finish," she said. "I know you're very curious about the three farms that were sold, brokered by Bart Wilkins. Initially, that's why I got involved in this. He's putting a lot of pressure on the fourth farm owners to sell. There's also some illegal pressure from a fifth farm that also has Amish owners. Specifically, they've cut off the water flow to the fourth farm you know of."

"I still don't understand where this fits in," Jack said.

"Then understand this," she said. "The owners of the fourth farm, now without a water supply, are my parents. I'm telling you this because I recognized one of the kidnappers. He works on the fifth farm that cut off our water. If we find him, we find BB."

Chapter 14: Munchville

Jack pulled the X-mobile off Highway 30 into the parking area of the reststop. He hadn't been to this location since their adventure at Millar's Hardware Store. He parked beside Shoe's motorcycle, then exited his vehicle. Carley exited the passenger side at the same time and pulled the front seat-back forward.

Shoe and Mario, seated at a wooden picnic table, waved when they saw Jack and Carley, but their hands froze in the air when they saw a splash of bright-green in the rear seat—and it was moving. It became larger and larger as the large man exited the car, then straightened to his full height.

Once Jack walked to the picnic table with Carley, he said, "Mario and Shoe, this is Zoltan."

Zoltan pushed one long leg over the bench seat of the picnic table and then the other as he sat down. "My pleasure to meet you both," he said with a thick accent.

Jack and Carley also sat down as Shoe looked suspiciously at the large man in the green Adidas track suit with white striping down the side of the arms and legs. Shoe's gaze turned back to Jack as he asked, "Who's Zoltan, and why's he here?"

"Zoltan's a big man and we might need his muscle if things go bad at the Amish farms," Jack replied. "He's a friend of Carley's."

Shoe's eyelids lowered, narrowing his gaze. "Zoltan—that's not an American name. If I remember correctly, there was a guy named Zoltan on the old Flash Gordon show. Zoltan is an *alien* name."

Jack shook his head from side to side. "Don't be a moron. The guy on the TV show is Doctor Zarkov, not Zoltan, and Doctor Zarkov is from Earth."

"I stand corrected," Shoe said while maintaining the accusing tone. "I remember correctly now. Zarkov was Russian."

Zoltan smiled while slapping his large hand down on the table. "Then, we are all very good because I am Hungarian, not Russian."

"Shouldn't we get back on topic," Carley said. "It's very possible BB is being held at the Yoder's farm."

"I know I can be a bit slow at times," Mario said. "Humor me and tell me why we're here."

Jack gave a long exhale before explaining. "The American Development Consultants have bought up three farms in Amish country. Bart Wilkins is the real estate agent working for them, and Governor Breed is involved. We suspect the American Development Consultants is really a front for a Japanese interest. They want the land and a state grant to develop new technology, then build a manufacturing plant here in Ohio. Governor Breed is being bought off by the Japanese, and the money is being filtered through Bart Wilkins."

Mario scratched his head. "That's confusing."

"Carley's Amish parents own a large farm next to the three farms already purchased. They're getting a lot of pressure to sell, but their farm has been in their family for a long time. They're resisting the pressure to sell," Jack said.

"How are they putting pressure on your parents?" Mario asked Carley.

"My father grows wheat and oats, and we've produced a large portion of our communities grain products for over 100 years. We have a mill on the farm, and it's driven by a large water wheel pushed by the flowing water of the river snaking through our property. A few months ago, the flowing river changed into a small trickle. As a result, the mill's grinding wheel no longer turns," she explained.

"Was there some tact of god that stopped the river?" Mario asked.

Jack was about to respond when Zoltan said, "Don't you mean—*act of god?*"

"Same thing," Mario said.

Zoltan shrugged. "Perhaps the river just stopped. As they sometimes say, 'shit occurs.'"

Mario smirked and took a second to give Shoe and Jack an *I'll take care of this* look. "Zoltan, it's not, *shit occurs*. The saying is, *shit happens*." For a few seconds Mario relished the change from being corrected to corrector.

Mario's gloating was interrupted as Carley finally answered the question of the river's lack of flow. "Just north of our farm is the Yoder's farm. Jon Yoder and his family live there. They've created a dam across the river flowing through the woods at the back of their property. As a result, the area is flooded."

Shoe asked, "Isn't that illegal?"

"You would think so," Carley answered. "If the blockage was man-made and the flow was completely stopped—that is illegal. However, there's a small amount of water flow, and the blockage is not man-made."

Zoltan interrupted. "When Carley and Jack told me we were going to investigate some beaver, I told them I was not interested." The big man winked at Mario. "You see, my preference is not for pussy, and of course when they said beaver, I thought they meant the pussy variety of beaver."

"Of course, you did," Shoe said in a sarcastic tone, now realizing the big Hungarian was a big, gay Hungarian. "I've heard of mixed metaphors, but this is the first time I've heard of mixed animals in such a perverted light."

Zoltan waggled a finger. "They corrected my confusion when they explained they were investigating real beavers with long teeth and big, flat tails."

"Get lost! Beavers built the dam? How is that possible? I haven't seen a beaver in Ohio—ever," Mario stated, his voice agitated.

"I agree, Mario," Carley said. "The Yoder's had help. Two strangers showed up just before the dam was built. We thought they were Amish friends of the Yoder's from Indiana until they imported several huge beavers from Canada."

Mario gasped. "Big, Canadian beavers—here in Ohio!"

"At Denny's, I recognized one of these two strangers we thought were from Indiana as one of the four attackers who kidnapped BB earlier today. From the note Mario was handed, it's clear somehow old man Yoder has hired the Polish Mafia."

Jack said, "It's more likely, Governor Breed has hired the Polish Mafia and placed them on the Yoder's farm, but why would the Yoder's want to harm your family?" Jack asked Carley.

"They never liked our family much because we are a bit different," Carley replied.

Mario was zoned out, shaking his head from side to side and mumbling, "I can't believe there are Canadian beavers here. I've heard they are huge and ferocious, and I once read Canadian beavers, if provoked, will carry away small children."

Jack glared at Mario and yelled, "Dude—don't be stupid! Let Carley finish her story."

Carley continued, "Most of the Amish here in Ohio are Pennsylvania Dutch, but there are a few families of Swiss Amish who've also lived here for over a century. My family descends from Pennsylvania Dutch and the Yoder's are strict Swiss Amish."

"Who cares?" Shoe said. "You can be from Holland or Switzerland and still be Amish."

Carley looked at Shoe. "Actually, Pennsylvania Dutch is German descent. We say Dutch, but it's really *Deutsch*."

"That's stupid," Shoe said. "Why not just say Deutsch then?"

Mario continued his run of cerebral brilliance as he said, "It's not stupid. It's actually smart." He puffed out his chest and looked down on Shoe. "How do you think Americans would have thought of Pennsylvania Deutsch during World War Two? They would have been branded as Nazi's for sure and likely rounded up into American concentration camps!"

Jack waved his hand. "I'm not sure that's altogether the reason, but let's accept that for the sake of moving on."

Carley once again continued after the interruption. "The Swiss Amish are what we refer to as *Old Order Amish,* and they're very strict in their following. More and more of the Pennsylvania Dutch are New Order and take a more liberal view of the Amish culture. For the most part we accept each other, but Mr. Yoder does not."

Mario saw his opportunity and was confident he would continue his streak of astounding wordsmithing. By now the sun had set, and the night was quiet except for the rustle of leaves from the slight wind as Mario said, "Then it seems Mr. Yoder is the deception to the rule."

Carley, recognizing Mario's incorrect use of the word *deception* in place of *exception*, frowned and looked at Zoltan. "If Mario opens his mouth again before I finish, hit him."

"Of course, my dear," Zoltan said just before he pursed his lips. There was a slight popping noise as his lips parted to complete the kiss toward Mario.

Carley said, "A few years ago, there was an incident that caused Yoder's limited tolerance of New Order Amish to turn to all-out hatred. There was a terrible bundling incident."

"What is bundling?" Shoe asked.

"Bundling is a courtship event between a young Amish man and woman. The two are bundled together very tightly, face to face, in a blanket and left overnight to get to know each other better. It's a precursor to marriage, so the bundle is tight, so they cannot do anything inappropriate," Carley explained.

"Bummer. That's no fun at all," Shoe said.

"The bundling incident from a few years ago involved Yoder's daughter and the young man she was engaged to, who was Pennsylvania, New Order Amish. No one knows what really happened or how, but six weeks later it was very clear Yoder's daughter was pregnant," Carley said.

Shoe said, "Well, if you don't know how it happens…" He made an inappropriate gesture with the finger and thumb of one hand forming a ring, and the forefinger of the other hand pushing through it."

Carley once again turned to Zoltan. "Also make sure Shoe doesn't interrupt again." She then continued to address the group. "It wasn't nice at all for Mr. Yoder. He was the laughing stock of the community, and that is the origin of his generalized hatred toward New Order Amish."

"So, it seems Mr. Yoder is in cahoots with the governor, Bart Wilkins and the Polish Mafia in an effort to get Carley's New Order Amish family out of the community," Jack concluded.

Mario said, "What's the plan?" He leaned back a bit as he peered at Zoltan.

Upon hearing Mario's words, the big Hungarian's eyes widened before one closed into a playful wink toward the young Italian American.

Jack answered, "The Polish Mafia set a meeting for Saturday night, but we're going to try and catch them with their pants down."

"Oh, that would be nice," Zoltan said as he clasped his hands together and bit down on his lower lip.

"There's a good chance BB is stashed away in the Yoder's house. Our goal is to find him. The second goal is to see if we can dislodge the dam and free up the river," Jack said.

"I'll look for BB," Mario volunteered as he raised his hand.

"No. You're going to the dam, and the big guy is going with you," Jack decided.

"Awesome!" Zoltan blurted. He reached across, and his fingers dug into Mario's shoulder, giving it a vigorous shake. "We are a team. I will look after you—buddy."

Jack continued, "Carley, Shoe and I are going to the house to find BB."

"You and Carley look for BB. I am going to focus on finding evidence of aliens," Shoe said to Jack. "I expect there's a big wall full of freaking wall plugs in there."

Jack pulled a map from his back pocket and spread it out on the table. Carley, pulled a small flashlight from her pocket and shone it on the map.

"We're here," Jack said. "Carley, Shoe and I will go in the X-mobile and park here, one half mile from the house. Mario, you take Zoltan in the Vega along this road around to the back of the Yoder's farm. Leave the car here." Jack pointed at a spot on the map. "Then, make your way through the woods to the dam."

Zoltan looked at Mario and said, "Just stay behind me. In my green outfit, I will blend into the foliage like a *ninja*—an invisible one." His eyebrows rose as he had an epiphany. "This is good. I will be a *ghost ninja!*"

Jack said to Zoltan, "Just take it slow and subtle. They might have Polish Mafia in the woods."

Mario reached to the center of the table with his fist up. Jack recognized the motion and placed his own fist on top of Mario's followed by Shoe. It took a few seconds for Carley to catch on, but she eventually shrugged and placed her fist on top of Shoe's. Zoltan was smiling wide as he placed his fist, easily double the size of anyone else's, on top of Carley's and said, "This is so much fun!"

Jack said, "Good luck!" and pushed upwards with his hand resulting in the row of fists separating. "The time for talking is over. Be careful."

The group walked to the cars. Zoltan reached into the back of the X-mobile and pulled out a large backpack. He pushed his large arms through the straps and said, "I brought some tools to help dismantle the dam."

Shoe reached into the Vega and pulled out the same two walkie-talkies used in the Bart Wilkins break in. He hooked one on his belt and threw the other to Mario. "Keep the volume on low."

Mario nodded as he clipped on the walkie-talkie before sitting in the driver's seat. Zoltan reached under the front passenger seat and lifted the lever with one hand while pushing the seat to its full rearward position.

The two vehicles exited the parking area of the reststop, and ten minutes later, the X-mobile was parked on the side of the road, south of the Yoder's farm. Shoe, Jack and Carley exited the vehicle, and in a monkey like squat, ran to a berm between the road and the farm. Once there, they threw themselves onto their bellies and crawled to the top of the slight rise. Visibility to the farm, 60 yards away, was low. The night sky was cloud covered, and the Amish discipline of not using electricity made inspection of the Yoder's farmhouse difficult. Jack, predicting this possibility, pulled the binoculars from his back pocket. He raised them to his eyes and panned slowly from side to side across the wood frame building.

"What do you see?" Shoe asked.

Jack took another minute of inspection before answering. "It's difficult to see with the only light coming from the lantern light spilling out from the house windows. However, I can see one man outside. It looks like he's doing rounds."

"That sucks to the max," Shoe mumbled.

"I've been here a few times, watching and trying to discover a solution to the water problem," Carley added. "The rounds they do outside aren't very thorough and only take about five minutes."

They stayed quiet with only the intermittent sound of crickets breaking the pensive silence when Shoe asked an awkward question. "Do you two believe in God or at least some type of higher power?"

"Shoe, it's not usually a stupid question, but since the timing is stupid, right now it makes the question a very stupid one," Jack said as he continued to peer through the binoculars.

Carley, feeling sorry for Shoe, whispered, "I believe in God."

Shoe propped himself up on his elbows and said, "It's a very relevant question, considering what we're about to do."

Jack pulled the binoculars from his eyes and gave Shoe a frustrating look. "How so?"

"I think there's a good chance there are aliens in the house. I'm not sure what I would say to them. I was wondering, if there is a god, did he make English speaking aliens?"

Jack pulled the binoculars back to his eyes and continued to follow the one man doing the rounds. "Why would you think aliens speak English?"

"I'm thinking of *Star Trek*," Shoe explained. "Haven't you noticed, no matter which planet the Enterprise goes to, all the aliens speak English. If people watching the show can go along with Klingons and Romulans speaking English, maybe it's not such a reach to believe all aliens speak English."

Carley said, "Not all the aliens in the show speak English. There are a few episodes where the aliens aren't really humanoid, and they communicate through a universal translator."

Shoe snapped his fingers. "You're right. So, if I'm facing an alien and they look like us, then I should talk normally to it in English. However, if it's some type of blob and not looking like us at all, then I should just bug out."

"Correct, unless the non-humanoid alien looks like it has a communicator that might be a translator," Carley clarified.

"Then again, who knows? Seeing as the Polish Mafia is at the center of this, maybe all the aliens speak Polish!" Shoe offered.

"Unbelievable," Jack muttered just as the front door of the house was thrust open. There was a flood of lantern light along with a loud yell from the man in the doorway.

Carley tried to hold back her laughter. "Did I just hear what I think I heard?"

Inside the house, Mr. Yoder was seated in the kitchen and said to the man at the door, "Janus, you should respect the nephew of your boss."

Janus, turned and scowled at Yoder before turning and cupping his hand to his mouth, yelling out for a second time, "Little Penis!"

Old Man Yoder shook his head and said, "It's behavior like this that forced me to send my family to my brother's house until the land issue next door is resolved."

Janus looked out the door, peering in one direction then the other and mumbled, "Where the hell is he?" In an even louder tone than before, he yelled, "Little Penis!"

Yoder asked again, "Why do you keep calling him that? He's Paul Pusiak, the nephew of Piotr Pusiak, the head of the Polish Mafia."

Janus turned toward Yoder as Paul Pusiak brushed passed him into the kitchen. Janus grinned and said, "There you are, Little Penis." After Paul sat down across from Yoder, Janus put his hand on Paul's shoulder and said to Yoder, "We all call him Little Penis because his uncle is a Big Dick!"

Paul snapped his head around and gazed at Janus. "Too bad you don't have the balls to call me Little Penis, or my uncle a Big Dick, in front of him."

"If I did, that would be very deep trouble for me. It would be the same for you if you told of your nick name. The big prick would think you a rat unable to solve your own problems," Janus explained. "Unfortunately, you will be known as Little Penis until you prove yourself to our Polish brotherhood."

Across the field, once the door was closed, Jack said, "It's time for us to move."

Jack, Carley and Shoe shot up and ran across the field and then the stone driveway until they were flat against the west wall of the house. Jack slid along the wall and turned his face to look in the window. It was the living room, and it was empty.

He looked back and motioned Carley and Shoe to follow him. With soft footsteps, they moved to the back of the house where there were two windows, and between them was a back door. Jack looked in the first window, and as expected it was a second window to the empty living room. They skirted past the door and stopped just before the second window. Jack peered into the kitchen through the half-closed curtains. Inside, Yoder and two men were seated at the large pine table. Jack recognized both men as two of those attacking BB at Denny's. The glass window was cracked open, allowing Jack to hear the conversation.

Yoder said, "Is there anything else we can do to get rid of the Fisher's from the farm next door?"

Janus replied, "It will not take much longer for the blocked river to force them to sell. The governor hired us to do all the dirty work. Your part, and you are well paid for it, is to provide the land for the placement of the dam."

Janus threw his hand to the side in annoyance. "The money isn't so important. I just want the Pennsylvania Dutch family and their blasphemous ways gone. Now, you tell me the Italian Mafia is here, and that could cause even more problems."

"Before our activities this morning, that would be true," Janus confided. "Now, since we kidnapped one of the Italian operatives, the Italian Mafia leader will see he should not challenge the Polish Mafia, especially on our home turf!"

Hearing this, Jack turned and scurried back to Carley and Shoe by the back door. He told them, "It's not clear, but BB might be inside." He ran his fingers back through his hair. "We still need to get into the house. A diversion would be awesome right about now."

There was a light crackle from the walkie-talkie clipped to Shoe's belt. In a faint tone they heard the word, "Duck."

The three of them looked at each other with confusion. Shoe lifted the walkie-talkie to his lips and whispered, "Goose."

As Jack looked curiously at Shoe, Shoe's face was lit up by a bright, reflected light. In fact, as they looked back toward the woods at the back of the farm, a large, orange fireball was lifting 50 feet into the air. A second later, the crashing sound of the explosion reached them, followed by small pieces of wood and beaver fur falling all around them. In the light, through the smoke and flying debris, they saw two figures in the woods running away from the carnage. At this distance, they wouldn't have recognized them except for the white, patent-leather shoes the one man wore and the ghost-ninja-like, bright-green outfit of the bigger man.

"That's gonna leave a mark," Shoe muttered.

"Holy shit," Jack whispered. "What happened to slow and subtle?"

The three of them knew the men in the house would come and investigate, so they flattened themselves against the back wall. A moment later, as expected, old man Yoder, Janus and Paul, crashed through the back door, running as fast as they could toward the fire burning in the woods.

As they disappeared into the foliage, Jack, Carley and Shoe entered the back door. Jack said, "Carley and I will check the first floor. Shoe, you check upstairs."

Shoe reached into his jacket and pulled out the large vibrator. Turning it on, he said, "I'm not taking any chances."

Glancing at the large device, Carley grinned and said, "What—in case you meet aliens or wanton women?"

Shoe couldn't remove the silly grin forming on his face.

"You should be ashamed of yourself for bringing that into Amish country," Carley said.

"Being brought up in an Amish family, you should be ashamed of yourself for knowing what it is," Shoe retorted.

Shoe took the steps upwards, two at a time, while Jack and Carley moved to scour the kitchen for evidence BB might have been there. They came up with nothing and arrived at the same result in the living room, dining room and a first-floor bedroom. A few minutes later, back at the rear door, they met with Shoe as he came down the stairs.

Jack asked, "Find anything?"

Shoe replied, "No BB. No aliens. No wanton women." He turned the vibrator off as he gave his report.

"Let's get back to the car before the Polish guys come back," Jack mumbled in disappointment.

Twenty minutes later, the Matador X was driven back into the parking area of the reststop. Jack, Carley and Shoe walked over to the picnic table where Mario and Zoltan were sitting on the table top, both enjoying a cigar. Both their faces and clothes were spattered with black soot, and the ends of Zoltan's eyebrow hairs were curled from the close presence of extreme heat.

"What happened to slow and subtle?" Jack asked.

Zoltan had a silly grin plastered on his face as Mario answered. "Who would've thought Russians trained Hungarian military personnel in the use of explosives? According to Zoltan, by Russian standards, the explosion caused by the dynamite he carried in his back pack, was subtle."

"At least the water is flowing again," Carley offered.

Mario exhaled a puff of smoke and asked, "Any sign of BB?"

Jack gruffly replied, "Freaking nothing. He wasn't there."

Shoe offered, "We didn't check the barn."

"They would have kept BB close by. There was no reason not to. So, if he was there, he would have been in the house," Jack rationalized.

"What do we do now?" Carley asked.

Jack's eyes were dark with anger. "I'll tell you what we're going to do." He looked at Zoltan. "Do you have a suit—I mean something that's not green, and doesn't say Adidas on it?"

"Of course, Jacko," the big man responded. "I clean up very nice when I have to."

"Good!" He looked to his friends, both the ones from his childhood and the ones recently found. "On Saturday night we're going to meet with the Polish Mafia and get BB back."

"How are you going to do that?" Shoe asked.

"I'm not going to do it," Jack answered. He turned to Mario. "Call Trina and tell her we're going to need her. These Polish bozos will be sorry they decided to screw with Emilio Francesco Martino and the Sicilian Mafia!"

Chapter 15: Salamander Slick

"I don't know how you guys do it." Jack said.

"Do what?" Sitting beside Jack, Mario replied from the back seat of the X-mobile. They were once again dressed in the sharp suits befitting members of the Italian Mafia. Jack was no longer Jack. Rather, an older, very sophisticated gentleman in a pin-striped suit had taken over Jack's persona. For this trip to meet the Polish Mafia, Mario added an extra touch. As he looked at Emilio Francesco Martino sitting beside him, on top of Emilio's head was a dark-green felt hat. On it, just above the brim, was a white ribbon matching the color of the scarf around Emilio's neck.

Jack turned to Mario and said, "I mean, I don't know how you guys get so involved in such a convoluted affair as this alien suspicion has turned into. We still haven't found a lick of solid evidence of aliens, yet somehow, through our fumbling investigations, we've uncovered criminal activities coordinated by no less than the governor of the state."

"Shoe didn't find any evidence of aliens at the Yoder's farm," Carley added.

They had decided before they left Mario's pad that Carley would drive the car to the warehouse, and Zoltan, looking sharp in a black suit, would sit in the passenger seat.

"We better find something soon," Jack stated. "I keep getting told the key is the House of Aliens. We need a clue to its whereabouts, or I'll lose the motivation to continue."

"We should save that discussion for later," Mario said. "Let's focus on what we need to do to get BB back. Jack, I know you have a plan, but I'm freaking out since I need to do all the talking. If you recall, Emilio doesn't speak English."

Jack replied, "Don't worry. I've been working on the Italian accent, so I'll do the speaking in broken English."

"You think your lousy attempt at an Italian accent will fool the Polish dudes?" Carley asked as she turned the car onto the highway toward Akron.

"Remember, my mother is Polish, and I was brought up in a Polish neighborhood. The only thing worse than a Polish American guy trying to fool people with an Italian accent are Polish Americans trying to evaluate an Italian accent," Jack concluded. "They won't have a clue."

Zoltan twisted his head on his neck to look back at Jack. "What do you want me to do? Maybe I should threaten to break someone's balls."

"I think it's better if you don't say anything," Jack said. "If you speak with your Hungarian accent, that is something the Polish guys would recognize. It would screw up their heads and make them suspicious. Just keep behind Mario and I, looking big and mean."

Zoltan thought for a second before replying. "How do I look big and mean?"

Jack grinned as he evaluated Zoltan. The squarely cropped hair on the top of his head almost brushed the headliner of the car. His long moustache was nicely trimmed but there was a day's growth of stubble on the rest of his face and neck. "Just keep doing what you're doing," Jack replied.

Carley looked up in the rearview mirror and saw the motorcycle following them. "What's Shoe going to do?"

"He's going to circle around to the back of the complex. He has a walkie-talkie, and Mario has the other. If things go bad, we can call him, so he can call the police," Jack explained.

Carley slowed the X-mobile as she approached a cross road with an industrial complex on the right side. "Is this the right place?" she asked.

"Yes. Turn right and the warehouse we want is near the end of the road," Jack directed.

There were no street lights, only the lights from the signs on the warehouses. As they approached a large warehouse covered in silver, steel cladding, Jack said, "That's the building we want."

Carley slowly pulled the car into the driveway and stopped, waiting for some sign of the people they were to meet. "Now what?"

There was an overhead flood light at each corner of the building. A figure appeared under the light at the rear corner of the warehouse, waving for them to come forward.

Jack muttered, "Here we go."

Carley drove down the laneway beside the warehouse. Being aware of a possible ambush, her eyes glanced from side to side. As they rounded the corner of the building, Jack said, "Everyone knows what to do, right?"

Zoltan said, "We keep our mouths shut. We look big and mean."

"Exactly, and remember, from this point, Jack is not here, only Emilio

Francesco Martino," he said as the car stopped in front of a door at the top of a flight of five stairs beside a roll-up garage door. Two sinister men, with shaved heads, stood at the bottom of the stairs.

Zoltan exited the passenger door of the Matador X and held it open as Emilio stepped out. Mario slid across the back seat and followed Emilio out of the vehicle. As they walked toward the stairs, one of the Polish henchmen stepped aside while the other went up the stairs and held the steel door open. Emilio was going to lead, but Zoltan put his hand against Emilio's chest. Zoltan went first and poked his head in the door, looking from side to side. After seeing it was safe, he motioned for Emilio and Mario to follow.

Once they were in the building, nearby conversation brought their attention to their left, where 15 men were standing in an aisle between rows of crates. These men noticed the Italians walking toward them, and they moved into the cross aisles between the crates. With the aisle cleared, a lone, tall man with a large beer gut stood at the end of it. He looked 45 years old with blonde, thinning hair. It was long and tied back in a pony tail.

Emilio led them toward the man, then suddenly pushed one arm out to each side, stopping both Mario and Zoltan behind him. He raised his neck slightly as he looked from side to side while the fingers of one hand scratched his neck. He knew this was a critical time to set the tone, so he lowered his stoic face and bored his gaze into the other man's eyes. After a few seconds of stare down, Emilio said, "Who the fuck are you?"

The other man laughed, and as his laughter became louder, he looked from one side of the aisle to the other, at his men. In seconds they were all laughing uproariously.

The man clapped his hands together, and the laughter stopped instantly. "I'm the fucking guy who has your man," he said through a thick Polish accent. It was quite different from the Italian accent Emilio spoke with.

"And does said fucking guy have a name?" Emilio asked.

"You know who I am. I'm Piotr Pusiak, head of the Polish Mafia in this area," the man replied as he lifted his hand and pointed a threatening finger at Emilio. "I'm also the man who is giving you a very good deal today. You tried to infringe on our turf with no warning or introduction. You have insulted us."

Emilio said nothing and shrugged at the man. He pulled the hat from his head and brushed the dust from it before handing it to Zoltan.

Piotr continued. "We took your man and your briefcase of money to show we do not appreciate your insult."

Emilio opened his mouth to respond, but Piotr raised his finger above his head and yelled, "I'm not finished!" Piotr added, "We have a long-standing agreement from the Italian mob in New York that this is our turf. We don't go there, and they don't come here, so everyone is happy. Then you visit the governor with a briefcase of money. Do you want to know what you are going to do?"

Emilio smiled. "Please."

"First, you're going to give us the combination to the briefcase. I have not seen one like it before. It's more like a safe with a handle. We thought of blowing it up, but the money would be damaged."

Emilio said, "Then it was a smart decision not to."

"What is smart is for you to agree to leave our area and never come back," Piotr said. "You get on the next olive oil boat back to Sicily, and never come back. Do you understand?"

Emilio turned and looked at Zoltan and Mario, shrugging at each of them. Each of them shrugged back before Emilio returned his attention to Piotr. The warehouse was deadly quiet, and the tension was thick in the air as Emilio whispered, "I have a stone in my shoe."

Piotr's eyebrows lowered. "What?"

Emilio twisted his lips and bulged his cheeks just before he spat on the ground. He repeated, "I have a stone in my shoe."

Piotr looked past Emilio to Mario and said, "What's he talking about?"

Mario said nothing. Emilio lifted his foot and shook it. Placing it back on the cement floor, he said, in broken English, "I hate that. It's only a small stone—so small it means nothing, yet it irritates me. It can't really hurt me, but it pokes into my foot and gets my attention. Then, I think, is it worth it to even waste the energy to take my shoe off and shake the stone out? Finally, I do and I would look at the pathetic little stone. You would think you could kick it away or just stomp on it and crush it from existence." He smiled at Piotr. "What is the right word in English? Is it *annihilate*, or *exterminate*—maybe *obliterate*? Maybe the right term is—" and Emilio was now yelling "—reign hell's bloody fire on its ass!"

Piotr, 20 feet away, was looking at Emilio in shock with his eyes wide and his mouth gapped open. He realized this was no longer about a little stone, and he was no longer in control.

Emilio waggled a finger at Piotr. "Sometimes you look at the little stone and consider it's really nothing more than a very pathetic little stone. It doesn't know any better, so maybe it's not its fault. As a result, you don't

146

obliterate the stone, but it is important to understand you need to give that stupid, little stone a kick, so it doesn't get in your way ever again."

Emilio had the silent attention of Piotr and his men. Looking at Piotr, he asked, "Do *you* understand?"

The Polish Mafia boss opened his mouth to respond.

Emilio interrupted and said, "Good. We have the beginning of an understanding. Just as I don't want that stone to irritate me again, you don't want to fuck with Emilio Francesco Martino, the head of the Sicilian 'famiglia.'"

Piotr's shoulders sagged. "What do you want from us?"

Emilio knew he'd won. "Bring BB out here."

Piotr nodded to one of his men, but he was frozen in shock. Piotr yelled, repeating the request. "Get BB down here!"

The man looked confused and beads of sweat formed on his brow. "But you are PP."

"You *idiota*! I am PP—Piotr Pusiak. Their man is *BB*, not *PP*. Go get BB!"

The Polish henchman looked like he just shit his pants, but he quickly moved toward a set of stairs leading to an upstairs office.

Emilio continued. "Second, stop speaking with that fake accent. It's terrible. Where were you born?"

Piotr was confused. "I'm from Cleveland."

"Then why are you speaking with that fake Polish accent?" Emilio asked.

"We're proud of being the Polish Mafia as that is our ancestry. It wouldn't be right for the head of the Polish Mafia to not at least have an accent," Piotr explained.

"You're the head of the Polish Mafia, and you don't speak Polish?" Emilio asked.

"Well—no."

Jack raised his hand in the air while pushing his fingertips together. "Faccia da figa!" he yelled. He grinned as he saw Piotr's face turn red. The Polish man knew Emilio just called him a pussy face.

BB came down the stairs followed by the man sent for him. The man had BB's arm in his grip and moved him to a spot beside Piotr.

Emilio smiled at BB and then turned his attention back to Piotr. "Help me with a curiosity. What does *Piotr Pusiak* mean?"

Piotr maintained the thick Polish accent. "It translates to *Peter*."

Jack had a Polish mother and knew the answer to the question he was about to ask. "And the last name?"

Piotr started to shuffle and fidget. "*Pussy*. In English, my name is *Peter Pussy*.

One of Piotr's men had enough of the insults. He blurted out, "Peter da Pussy, boss of the Polish Mafia!"

Emilio turned and said to Zoltan, "If that man tries to speak again, make sure he does not."

Zoltan turned slightly to face the man as he put his hand inside the lapel of his jacket. The boisterous Polish man deflated and shrank back behind two of his colleagues.

Emilio waved to BB to come over to him. Taking small steps, BB walked across and Emilio said to Piotr, "So which one is it? Is it Peter *the* Pussy?" Emilio mimicked the Polish accent. "Or is it Peter *da* Pussy?"

Piotr finally got the message and stopped the accent. "It's Peter the Pussy, or Peter Pussy, or just Peter, if you like."

"That's right," Emilio agreed, switching back to his bad Italian accent. "Whatever I like. We now need to discuss compensation."

Piotr waved his hand in front of himself. "No, we don't. We don't want any trouble. You take your man and we'll call this a misunderstanding."

Emilio began to slowly pace back and forth. "No, *you* have a misunderstanding. I'm now talking about the compensation *you* will give to us."

"Ouch," Piotr muttered as he looked down at his shoes.

As he continued pacing, Emilio pointed at Piotr. "Of course, we want our briefcase back." Inside, Emilio was laughing. Everyone in the room, except he and Mario, thought there was 200 thousand dollars in the briefcase. If only they knew it was filled with old encyclopedias. Then, Emilio stopped and turned to look at the Polish Mafia boss. "I have a second problem I need your help with."

Piotr was defeated and gave Jack the *what now* look.

Emilio looked upwards as he continued. "When we get in these turf wars, it's very stressful. Often, it doesn't end until I've killed every one of the pigs trying to tell me what to do—just as you tried to do."

Now Piotr was the one sweating, and it was profuse with a large wet stain visible under each armpit.

Emilio continued. "But you can't always just obliterate everyone. If you recall, I just told you about the pathetic little stone. But within the merciful decision, there must be compensation."

"How much?" Piotr muttered.

"My man BB was insulted," Emilio said. "That will cost you 50 thousand dollars."

Piotr almost choked on his deep gasp of breath.

"There's more," Emilio added. "You have insulted my Sicilian family, and as the head, I take it personally. When you ask for my forgiveness, it will come with an additional 50 thousand dollars compensation."

The blood drained from Piotr's face, and his lips moved slowly. "Ask for your forgiveness?"

Emilio smiled and said, "Then you are indeed forgiven! There's one last problem, and it is a delicate one. You can help me with a deed of valor and at the same time feel very good about yourself."

Mario was so worried, he felt like he was going to puke. Piotr hadn't yet called Emilio's bluff, but Emilio might be pushing things too far.

Emilio said, "I have a wife back in Sicily. Unfortunately, when I get in a bad mood, my wife gets the brunt of it. I talked to her earlier in the day, and she has already begun to receive the repercussions of my pissed off mood."

Not knowing where this was going, Piotr thought it better to remain silent even though he wanted to scream from his sphincter puckering so tight.

Emilio pressed on. "So, we can solve this last problem with a deed of Polish valor. You'll give me an additional 100 thousand dollars. It's—what is the right word in English?" Emilio turned and looked at Mario.

Mario said, "The word is *deterrent*, Great Uncle."

"Thank you," Emilio replied. He turned his gaze back to Piotr. "Earlier, I called it a kick, but it's a deterrent, and it will pay for the dog I need to buy for my wife."

Piotr's face turned from white to red, and he said through clenched teeth. "A dog for 100 thousand dollars?"

Emilio pushed his finger into his chin as he said, "It might sound excessive, but the average dog lives 14 years. That's 14 years of dog food, vet bills and of course, dog treats. If you consider a cost-of-living increase in pricing of 2.5 percent, annually, over 14 years, I think you'll agree 100 thousand dollars is not excessive at all. In fact, it's a steal if you consider it's the cost of the Sicilian Mafia agreeing to never come into your turf again."

"So, the total amount of money you want in exchange for an agreement to leave our turf is 200 thousand dollars," Piotr summarized.

"That and my briefcase returned intact," Emilio corrected.

Piotr considered this. He could say the 200 thousand dollars was not extorted. Rather, he could spin the story so that the money was seen as a payment to complete a business transaction. He would gain face having dealt with the powerful Sicilian Mafia! Piotr said to his man, "Go upstairs again. Get 200 thousand dollars from the safe and also the silver briefcase."

The man said, "Yes Sir," and headed to the office for a second time.

As they waited, Emilio slapped BB on the shoulder and asked, "Is everything okay? They didn't feed you too many perogies, did they?"

BB snickered. "Nothing that a big plate of spaghetti and meatballs can't fix."

Emilio said to Piotr, "Do you know what the biggest joke in Italy is?"

"What?" Piotr replied.

"You call yourself the Polish Mafia even though you aren't really Polish. This is a common theme around the world. Everyone wants to say they're the Mafia, but Mafia is an Italian term originating in Italy. So, around the world, we see this happen often. You say you're Polish, but you're not. By saying you're Mafia, the implication is you're Italian, but you're not. That's fucked up and terribly funny to real members of the Mafia in Italy."

The discussion was interrupted by a yell from the top of the stairs. "The briefcase is gone!"

Beads of sweat instantly formed On Emilio's brow. This was something unexpected. He needed to roll with it and said to Piotr, "Bring me the 200 thousand dollars."

The man came down the stairs with a brown paper bag and handed it to Piotr. Piotr, in turn, immediately walked across the 20 feet between them and held out the bag to Emilio. Emilio clamped his hand over Piotr's and squeezed tight.

Piotr thought, *Chrystus, the old man has the grip of a 20-year-old!*

Emilio leaned forward and whispered in Piotr's ear. "Don't fuck with me, little stone. You have two days to bring me my briefcase, or a reign of burning Sicilian fire will fall on every Polish person in Ohio."

Emilio pulled the bag from Piotr's hand and turned without waiting for a response. He snapped his fingers in the air as he walked between Mario and Zoltan. "Come along!"

Half way to the exit, Emilio stopped and turned. "I just remembered something, Mr. Pussy. Mario and I went for a drive in the country and went through an Amish area. These people are so quaint with women wearing bonnets and the men in thick beards. I have come to like them very much."

Piotr walked toward Emilio, wondering where this was leading.

"I like them enough so that I don't want any harm to come to them. If I hear of more Polish interference, things could become even more explosive." Emilio had a wry grin on his face, and lifted the fingers of each hand beside his ears. As he thrust them outwards, he said, "Boom!"

Piotr's jaw dropped. "That was you?"

Emilio's only response was a wink to add to his grin before he turned and headed for the exit. One of the Polish men opened the door for Emilio as he and his two friends left the warehouse. Emilio was waiting for the other shoe to drop and thought, *Carley—start the fuckin car! Start the fuckin car!*

As if she heard the telepathic message, the car roared to life and the headlights bathed the laneway in light. Zoltan opened the passenger door. Mario entered, followed by BB and, finally, Emilio. No one tried to stop them. There was silence in the car until they turned out of the Industrial Park, and the single light of a motorcycle was behind them.

Carley asked, "What's in the bag?"

The impersonation was now over. Jack was in a daze and muttered, "Holy shit."

"There's shit in the bag?" Carley asked.

Jack cleared his head. "No, I think I shit my pants. I'm not sure when, but when I sat down it felt like shit was in my underwear."

Mario, sounding like he was in confession, said, "I thought the smell was coming from me. I farted, or at least I thought it was a fart, but I got the same wet feeling when I sat down."

Zoltan said, "You too? That makes three of us."

BB looked from one to the other and said, "Am I the only one who doesn't have shit in his pants?"

There was no response, so BB continued. "Shite! I get kidnapped. I'm tied up, and you're the guys who shit your drawers."

"Did you learn anything?" Jack asked.

"Learn anything? You have to be kidding. I was kidnapped and fearful for my life. You think I had enough focus to catch tips?" BB was dumbfounded.

Mario's face turned red. "You are very freaking welcome for saving your life, you selfish, Black-assed Irishman!"

"Best you shut up," BB warned.

There was silence in the car for a minute, but Mario was such that he had to have the last word and said, "You ride me up a wall."

Carley spit out a laugh she had been holding back. "Mario, the saying isn't, *you ride me up a wall.* It's, *you drive me up a wall.*"

BB gave the lesson some finality when he added, "Ya Whanker!"

Shoe, riding behind the car, thought the occupants of the car had gone crazy. They had just defied the Polish Mafia, yet even though the windows were starting to steam up, he could see his friends were all laughing uproariously.

Chapter 16: Scare de Cat

"Name please," the security guard said.

"Jack Decker and Shoe Smith," Jack answered through the window opening of his mom's Jeep Cherokee Chief.

The security guard, in a black uniform, flipped several pages back and forth on the clipboard. He made one checkmark, then a second. Leaning toward the Jeep, he pointed to the left side of the long, curved driveway disappearing into a line of thick trees. "Follow the driveway, and after the trees you'll see another guard directing drivers to the parking area."

Jack said, "Thanks," and then slowly proceeded down the freshly paved driveway.

Shoe looked ahead through the windshield at the line of cars backed up through the tree line. "I don't understand why I have to come to this Japanese funeral," he said.

Jack, now having reached the last car in the line, was driving even slower. "Unfortunately, BB only had time to jot down your name and my name on the invitation list before he was interrupted. In addition, the governor will be here, and he would recognize Mario and BB from our visit to his mansion. He won't recognize you or I."

"I never wear a sports jacket, so this one I borrowed from Carley feels awkward," Shoe said as he stretched his arms forward to exemplify the tightness.

"Maybe it feels weird because it's a woman's jacket," Jack offered.

Shoe looked at Jack and said, "Both you and Carley told me you couldn't tell it was a woman's jacket!"

"Chillax," Jack said. "It looks fine and it matches your all black, Johnny Cash attire." Jack was also wearing a black sports jacket, a white shirt and black jeans, so he looked similar to Shoe.

As the Jeep finally arrived at the far side of the line of trees, another security guard directed them to their left where already some 100 cars were parked on the expansive lawn. They parked in the spot they were directed to and made their way to the main house. In the midday sun, they saw the house was huge as well as quite unique. As they came closer to the pagoda style, wood-beam house topped with a black roof, Jack estimated the size to be at least seven thousand square feet over three floors. In striking contrast, the large double doors leading into the front foyer were highlighted by a huge, round, orange sun painted on the front of them.

There, once again, a security guard asked their names and gave each of them a name tag. As Jack pinned on the tag, he evaluated the three-story high front foyer. There was a triple-wide staircase leading up to the second floor, and when they entered the building, he saw an indoor stream along the left wall of the entryway. Lazily swimming in the water, were several of the largest and most colorful koi Jack had ever seen.

Jack's amazement was interrupted by Shoe's finger prod. Shoe said, "We're in. What's the plan from here?"

"It looks like all the guests are in the back yard, so let's check it out first," Jack replied.

Jack, but especially Shoe, with his spiked, black hair, received a few unusual stares from the mostly Japanese attendees. As they walked through the double doors on the far side of the staircase, they entered a receiving area where wall to wall windows looked out on the back of the estate. The windows were actually sliding doors that were fully open for the funeral, and it gave the reception room an open-air environment.

Shoe picked up an agenda from a side table and reviewed it with Jack looking over his shoulder. One side was filled with Japanese hieroglyphics, but, thankfully, the reverse side was in English. As they were reading it, Jack felt a tap on his shoulder.

As Jack turned around, the attractive Japanese woman said, "Hello again. I am surprised to see you here."

Jack was stunned for a moment but upon recovery said, "Hello. If I remember correctly, your name is Ryo from the American Development Consultants front desk."

She smiled even though her eyes did not hide her curiosity. "Ryo Ozawa to be accurate," she said. "Why are you here?"

Jack had to think quick. "I'm a member of the *Polish Americans of Ohio*. The society was asked to send a representative to Mr. Park's funeral. I saw the request, and to make up for our poor showing at our last meeting, I volunteered to come."

"We," Shoe said as he poked his head around Jack and smiled at Ryo.

Jack half turned. "I'm sorry. Ryo, this is Shoe—well actually Tommy Smith, but we all call him Shoe."

Shoe smiled and said, "Hello." He held up the agenda and asked, "Could you help us? This is our first Japanese funeral, and we don't want to accidentally insult someone. Could you explain the schedule?"

The worried look left her face as she responded, "Of course." She took the agenda from Shoe's hand and continued. "First, I will tell you Mr. Park was a very traditional Japanese man, so he felt it important to follow our customs. But he did have some unusual quirks. This funeral is one of them."

"How so?" Jack asked.

"It is Japanese custom for a body to be cremated. It is also custom for the major bones to be picked out of the ashes with chop sticks and stored in an urn within the family tomb," she explained.

"Chop sticks like the ones you eat with?" Shoe questioned.

Ryo covered her mouth with her hand to hide her laughter. "They are the same type but not the same ones. You don't eat and then use the same chop sticks for the bones. You also do not pick up the bones and then eat with the same chop sticks."

Shoe's fake laugh joined with hers as he said, "Thanks for the clarification."

Ryo turned to Jack. "You have some weird friends. First, there was the rude negro at our first meeting and now this curious man with spiked hair."

"If you're talking about BB, he is black, not negro," Shoe corrected. "But you're right. He has his rude moments."

Jack thought they were getting way off topic. Pointing to the agenda, he said, "Can you explain this to us?"

"Of course. We are here now," she said, pointing to a spot on the paper. "We have another 45 minutes, then the ceremonial reading from a Buddhist priest lasting another 30 minutes. The last 45 minutes is for the burning of the remains."

Jack waved his hand for Ryo to stop. "I am confused. If he's already cremated, what is there to burn on a pyre?"

"That is one of Mr. Park's quirks I mentioned," she said. "When he died, his body was shipped back to Japan. He was cremated there, and his bones were pulled from the ashes."

"With chop sticks!" Shoe added.

Ryo giggled. "Stop making me laugh at a funeral," she whispered. "Yes, with chop sticks." Turning her gaze to Jack, she commented, "Your friend is very funny."

"Yes. He is very ha-ha," Jack agreed. "Weren't his bones then put in the family tomb?"

"They certainly were, but Mr. Park had a strange request in his will. He wanted to have his remaining ashes, minus the bones, brought back to this country and burned here, ceremonially, for a second time. He wanted to show his appreciation to America by letting his ashes float free on the wind."

"Like the appreciation many Japanese had for America in 1941," Shoe muttered.

"I don't follow you?" Ryo said.

Jack put his hand on Ryo's shoulder, deflecting the question. He recognized Shoe just made a smart-assed comment about the 1941 attack on Pearl Harbor. "We appreciate your help Ryo, but we don't want to keep you away from the ceremony any longer," Jack said.

As she walked away from them, Shoe asked, "What now?"

The pair of men walked over to the opening to the rear garden, and Jack pointed to a Caucasian man speaking with two Japanese men. "That's what's next," Jack advised. His finger was pointing toward Governor Carter Breed.

"You take on the governor," Shoe said. "I'm going to snoop around the house and see what I can find." Shoe's fingers grasped the bottom of his tightly-fitting, woman's jacket, and he pulled down in an *I mean action* movement.

As the jacket was straightened, Jack noticed the area at Shoe's chest bulge outwards. His eyes narrowed. "What do you have in your inside pocket?"

Nothing you need to worry about," Shoe answered.

"Tell me you didn't bring a gun," Jack whispered.

"Don't be silly. I brought, Greta," Shoe replied.

"Tell me Greta isn't a weapon," Jack said.

"Greta isn't a weapon. Greta is a distraction," Shoe said with a wry smile.

Jack shook his head from side to side. "You're stunned. I have no idea what you're talking about, but whatever it is, I have no more time for it." He headed down the wide, stone steps toward the governor.

Shoe moved back through the wide opening and into the reception area. Here, he looked at the hallways leading off the large room. There were two on his left and one on his right. No one took much notice of him as he casually entered the hallway on his right. The chatter from the reception area faded away as he moved down the length of the hallway. He passed several closed doors until another narrower hallway appeared on his left. Deciding to follow it, he saw it was short and ended at another long hallway running parallel to the first one he entered. By now, he was moving in absolute silence as this area was restricted from guests, and all the servants were busy with the reception. He turned right, moving deeper into the house until he came upon another staircase. He looked upwards but didn't hear or see anything unusual. He decided to travel up the stairs, and at the top, as he turned, he saw a security guard halfway down the second-floor hallway.

Shoe thought, *that's odd. The whole house appears empty except for the guard at this one door. It must be important.*

The guard didn't see Shoe, as he was facing away from him, but Shoe decided to confront the man. As he walked toward the guard Shoe said, "Excuse me!"

The guard turned instantly and glared at Shoe. His eyelids narrowed even more than they were naturally. "Guests are not allowed in this area," he said.

"Unfortunately, I'm lost and looking for a bathroom," Shoe explained.

Shoe was now at the door the man was guarding, and he saw the door had a plate on it reading - *Private.* The guard pointed over Shoe's shoulder and said, "You need to follow this hallway all the way to its end. There's a stairway back to the first-floor reception area where you'll see a sign indicating the guest bathrooms are there."

Shoe said, "I saw those ones, but I need to find a different bathroom. There must be many in a house this size."

"I'm sorry, Sir. I must insist you leave this area," the guard reiterated.

Shoe raised both his hands to waist height and shook them slowly up and down. "Relax and listen to me. I need you to understand my situation."

"Situation?" the guard said.

"People have unique natural skills. Some can run very fast. Some can swim like a fish while there are others who are mathematical geniuses. I need you to understand I cannot have a crap in the same toilet others are using," Shoe explained.

The Japanese guard rattled his head. "You aren't making any sense."

Shoe produced a deep, dramatic exhale. "Sometimes these special abilities are really something very different. My unique skill is actually a curse."

"I'm totally confused," the guard stated.

"My shit really stinks," Shoe confessed.

Creases formed on the guard's brow as he said, "Toilets smell like shit. There's no avoiding it."

"No, you don't understand the enormity of what I'm telling you. It really, really stinks. Not only would the bathroom be unusable for at least an hour, but the stink would travel and fill the reception room. Everyone will think someone just died!"

Placing both hands, curled into fists, on his hips, the guard scowled at Shoe.

"Okay—bad choice of words. I know someone did die, but you know what I mean," Shoe implored.

The guard did not relent. "I'm sorry for your condition, Sir, but I must insist you leave this area immediately."

Shoe pointed to the plate on the door. "Is that a private bathroom I could use?"

"No. it was Mr. Park's private office," the guard explained. He put his hand on the radio microphone clipped to a shoulder band on his shirt. "If you don't leave right now, I'll call another guard to escort you back to reception."

Shoe smiled. "Fine, but if anyone complains about the shit stench on the first floor, I'll give them your name."

"My name is Yoshida", the guard said as he pointed down the hallway."

Shoe's smile turned to an even wider grin as he accomplished what he set out to do. As he walked toward the stairs, he now knew the guarded room was Ki-ha Park's office. He just needed to find a way to get the guard away from that door.

Out on the manicured lawn, Jack pulled a glass of ginger ale off a tray carried by a waiter in a white jacket. He sipped it slowly and looked around the large garden while always keeping Governor Breed and the two Japanese men within his peripheral vision. Jack could discern the two Japanese men were brothers. In fact, they looked like twins. At one point, one of the brothers pointed toward the corner of the house. The governor nodded his head and followed the two men down the stone pathway toward it.

Keeping a good distance behind, Jack followed in turn. The three men ahead of him rounded the corner of the house, and when Jack reached the same point, he poked his head through a deep-red bush to see the governor entering a side door to the house. As he heard the door close, Jack ran to it. Luckily, it had a small window in the middle that Jack could peer through. With their backs to Jack, the three men entered a doorway on their right. Jack checked the door knob and found it was unlocked. He entered the hallway and was careful to look into each room before scooting across. The last open door was a closet, and just beyond it was the room the governor and his two associates entered. With his back flat against the wall, Jack shimmied toward the door carelessly left open a crack. Through it, he was able to hear the conversation within. Jack didn't know which brother was speaking, but it wasn't the governor. He remembered the governor's voice from his previous visit to the mansion.

"We've done as you asked," the man said. "Now we need your help."

As most politicians would have, the governor had a loud voice, and it made it easy for Jack to hear what he was saying. "I appreciate that. Whatever I can do to help you, I will. I mean, that's part of our agreement. You scratch my back and I'll scratch yours."

"We need help laundering money so our people here have cash on hand," the man said.

There was a pause for a few seconds before the governor answered. "I'll have to give that some thought, but I'll get back to you."

"We have an idea for you so your thinking is accelerated," the man replied.

"What do you have in mind?" the governor asked.

"We've given you payments in return for the help you're giving us with the land purchases, and, as we previously agreed, you'll give us the technology grant. You have also agreed to help us with zoning changes so we can build our factory, and you have ongoing payments for all of that. Are you still laundering your money through that estate out in the country?" the man asked.

"You mean what we refer to as the House of Aliens?" the governor asked.

Jack, listening outside the door, dug his fingers into his thigh as he thought, *I wish I would've brought a tape recorder.*

The governor continued. "Yes, I push the money through the House of Aliens and get back about 70 cents on the dollar."

The Japanese man said, "That's an acceptable rate for us. We'll give you an additional 20 thousand dollars a month, for five months, and you'll give us back 14 thousand for each of those disbursements."

"Hold on a minute," the governor said. "I can't flow that much money through the estate. Right now, there are ten guests, but we say there are 30 on the books."

"Put 60 guests down in the books," the man recommended.

"That would be too much of a reach. I can't make the expenses add up."

"Then, find ten more residents to make the ratio the same," the man answered.

"Where do I find ten more aliens? They don't grow on trees or just fall from the sky," the governor stated.

"Look, Governor, it might be a challenge, but you have resources. Make it happen and the money will keep flowing to you."

The underlying threat of *less* money was understood by the governor. "Sure. I'll find a way. We just need to keep it quiet, so my wife doesn't find out. She would be pissed if she found out the ownership of the House of Aliens was in her name."

The man said, "What about the fourth Amish farm we're trying to purchase? What's the delay?"

"I have a minor problem. The Polish men I hired to help move that along are in need of a recalibration. I'm meeting them in a few days, and we'll get back on track."

"We are patient, but it's not endless," the man said. "If you don't get this done soon, we'll need to bring in our own men, but that would mean a reduction in your payments."

The governor thought, *I don't need god damn four-fingered Yakuza in my state.* "It's being handled," he said.

"Then we better get back out to the ceremony," the man said.

Jack heard the footsteps coming toward the door, so he slid into the deep hallway closet. Leaving the door open, he hid behind the winter coats stored within. He sat on a blanket-covered box as he peeked through the coats and saw three pairs of feet pass by. Jack waited a minute before getting up. As he did so, he felt a pain in his ass cheek. He rubbed it as he turned and looked accusingly at the blanket. He was curious, so he pulled it aside with one hand while splitting the line of hanging coats with the other. The light from the hallway lit up the silver box. Chuckling, he saw the handle on top of the box having dug into his ass, and he immediately recognized their encyclopedia-filled, silver briefcase!

This is priceless, he thought as he walked back down the hallway to the side door. Outside, as he rounded the corner of the house, he saw the governor heading toward the many rows of seats in front of the pyre. Many people were now filling the seats, and Jack found one, three rows behind Governor Breed.

After leaving the guard, Shoe didn't follow his directions, exactly. He went back down the same set of stairs he previously came up and arrived at the still-empty first floor hallway. He still had time to explore, so he walked down it, opening door after door until he came to a side door exiting the house. It seemed the rooms in this wing were servant's quarters. He saw several bedrooms, a large living room and adjoined to it, a full kitchen.

He was headed back the way he came when he heard voices nearby just outside the side door of the mansion. Shoe ran the few steps to the kitchen and entered. He closed the door over just before he heard the side door open.

He heard a woman with an Asian accent say, "Where should we put Mr. Park's ashes?"

A man's voice answered. "The servant's living room is just ahead. We still have 30 minutes before we need to take his remains out to the pyre."

Shoe pressed his tiny form into the corner behind the kitchen door. He hoped they didn't enter in this direction, and, fortunately, this was the case. Looking through the small crack between the door and jamb, he saw the two attendants walk past, carrying a black box. Shoe heard them enter the living room next to the kitchen through the main door.

"Where should we put him?" the lady asked."

"There on the sofa table," was the reply.

A few seconds later, Shoe heard the living room door close. He almost jumped out of his skin as he saw the door he was hiding behind begin to move. Thankfully, to ensure the security of the urn, the attendants were closing this door as well.

Shoe's curiosity got the better of him, and he went through the adjoining door from the kitchen into what he now saw was a large living area. Behind the sofa was a high table, and on it was the urn. He moved closer and admired the beauty of the black, lacquered box. It was the size of a one-foot cube and had a pagoda shaped lid on it. Covering all sides were cherry blossom flowers painted a bright pink.

It's a shame they're going to burn it, Shoe thought. His curiosity continued as he placed his fingers under the corners of the urn and lifted it off the sofa table. It was lighter than he expected.

He felt the rub against his shin just before he heard the light purr. It startled him, and he jumped backwards. Unfortunately, his hands slipped out from under the urn, and it twisted, slamming into the hardwood floor. The box flipped once before the lid flew off.

When the clatter stopped, Shoe looked down to see a large mound of ashes on the floor and a dusting of gray on his black running shoes. Beside Mr. Park's remains was a blue-eyed Siamese cat, looking innocently up at him.

Shoe's eyes went wide. "Holy shit," he whispered. "What am I going to do?" His fingers curled in his spiked hair, pulling upwards as he continued to talk to himself. "I need to get the ashes back in the box. There must be a broom in the kitchen."

He ran into the adjoining room, randomly opening cupboards and drawers in search of a dustpan and a brush. He didn't have any success until he opened a larger pantry door. Just inside, was a broom, and attached to it was a dustpan.

Fan-fucking-tastic! Shoe thought. Grabbing the broom handle, he ran toward the living room. Grasping the jamb, it helped him make the turn until he abruptly skidded to a stop. In front of him was the light-brown cat, squatting over the pile of ashes. Her stream of pee just finished, and she looked up at Shoe with a satisfied smile.

Shoe's repetition began with a mutter and ended with a yell as he said, "No. No. No!" He ran toward the evil little cat, but a bad situation became even worse. The cat stepped forward, and several kicks with her dark-brown back feet sent up a spray of gray, pee-laden ash into a dust cloud four feet high.

"You satanic bitch!" Shoe yelled at the cat. "What do you want me to do now?"

The cat gave him a loud meow in response.

There wasn't enough ash left on the floor or in the box, so he swept the residual amount under the couch. He ran back into the kitchen. Shoe knew the attendants would recognize the missing weight when they picked up the urn, so he needed to replace it with something. Searching the upper cupboards, he finally found a row of tins and remembered the location of a can opener from his earlier search for the dustpan. He walked back into the living room with two cans, the can opener and a plan forming in his head.

Once it was finalized, he placed the lid back on the urn. Picking up the lacquered box, he evaluated the weight and thought, *that'll work.*

An evil smile crossed his face as he figured he still had 15 minutes before the attendants came back for the urn. There was a patio door on the far wall, and Shoe opened it. He yelled out, "Here kitty-kitty-kitty! Here kitty-kitty!"

The Siamese cat, having heard the door opening and the call, came running from the kitchen. As it was passing by, Shoe reached down and grabbed it by the collar. He kicked the door closed and lifted the cat up, whispering in its ear, "Not yet. I have a plan for you."

Jack had been seated amongst the crowd of at least 200 people for 30 minutes. There were two Buddhist priests on a small stage beside the pyre. They would alternate with one repeating prayers in Japanese while the other would speak in English. Their prayers finished when they saw two attendants carrying the urn from the house. They came around the right side of the gathering and handed the urn to a man who must be the son of Mr. Park, Jack thought. The younger Mr. Park, in turn, placed the urn on top of the wood pyre. There was only a very slight wind, and the intent was for the ashes and smoke to blow toward the lake behind the pyre.

An older woman, who must have been Mr. Park's wife, held a torch into a fire that had been burning throughout the day. She hesitated only for a moment before placing the lit torch into an opening under the pyre. Of course, there was complete silence. The flames burned around the urn until a larger flame erupted as the black, lacquered wood caught. At first, the smoke went toward the lake, as planned, but then it swirled, circled and stretched outward, turning into a slight haze. People in the front few rows began to look from one to the other, and some held their noses in the air.

Jack, in the third row, also lifted his nose in the air and realized it wasn't the smoke itself that caught the people's attention. The Japanese were confused, but Jack had spent four years in residency at college. He ate enough canned food to recognize the scent. His stomach grumbled as he thought, *that smells just like Chef-Boy-Ar-Dee spaghetti!*

After Shoe let the cat out the door, he moved back to the staircase just below the guard at Mr. Kishi's office. There was a darkened corner under the staircase, and Shoe squatted down, hiding there. He was still panting for breath from his activities with the cat, and he hoped his plan would work. He just had to wait.

Back out in the garden, the pyre was now a pile of red-hot embers with only small flames licking upwards. The confusion caused by the unusual scent was over, but the calm was not long-lasting. There was a scream as a Japanese woman, several rows behind Jack, shot up to her feet. When Jack turned around to look, she was shaking and pointing at the end of the row of chairs. There, bobbing up and down in the wind, was a life size blow-up doll. The red lips, creating a hole at the mouth, were only slightly darker than the red hair on its plastic head. She was dressed in a sexy maid outfit complete with high heels, fish-net stocking and crotchless panties. Large plastic breasts adorned the doll, and handwritten across them in black marker, was - *Yoshida sucks.*

There were several more screams, and it only took a few seconds for the young Mr. Park to yell out, "Guards, get that vulgar thing!"

Several guards shot up from chairs while others came from the side garden areas. At least ten men were running toward the blow-up doll that Jack could now see was attached to something on the ground by a thin string. Jack slapped his thigh and thought, *that must be Greta.*

The speediest guard was almost at Greta when she shot down an empty aisle at a very fast pace. People in the row just in front scattered. It was like the sinking of the Titanic with people climbing over others with an, *every man or woman for themselves,* mentality. Greta shot three feet upwards, and the crowd could now see a Siamese cat balancing on a chair-back. They could also see the thin string from Greta's high heel attached to the cat's collar.

As the cat gave a loud *meow,* young Mr. Park yelled, "Get that pussy!"

There was a communal gasp from the crowd.

Mr. Park said, "Not that pussy! I meant get the cat!"

Jack stayed for another five minutes, watching the guards try to catch the agile feline. It reminded him of his boyhood when he watched the *Keystone Cops* on TV. Several times the guards ran into each other, and several times the cat seemed trapped but would slither away at the last second. Jack was laughing so loud his side hurt, but he knew this distraction gave him time. He finally rose up in the ongoing, hysterical confusion and headed toward the mansion.

Shoe didn't have to wait long for the first scream. Within a minute, it sounded like mass pandemonium in the garden. There was an electrical, static sound from Yoshida's radio, just up the stairs, followed by a loud "Yes

Sir!"

Shoe heard the pounding footsteps as Yoshida ran down the hallway toward the main stairs to the reception area. As Shoe hoped, Yoshida was called away for the emergency. Emerging from his concealment, Shoe turned up the stairs, two at a time. He twisted the knob of the private office and finding it unlocked, whispered, "Yes." As he entered and closed the door behind him, Shoe surmised he had no more than 15 minutes before he had to leave.

He searched each desk drawer and each drawer of the three filing cabinets against the far wall. His first pass was quick and superficial, so he began the loop again with a more detailed review. This time, in one of the filing cabinet drawers, he found a file folder, and inside it were three reports. As he read them, his eyes went wider and wider. Knowing his time was up, his hands were shaking as he stuffed the three reports inside his shirt. Shoe had one last look into the office. Satisfied it looked undisturbed, he closed the door and headed for the main stairs to the reception area.

Jack was still laughing as he walked around the side of the house, and reentered. He didn't waste time as he reached into the closet and pulled out the large silver briefcase. *These morons aren't going to keep Mario's encyclopedias,* he thought. He ran down the hallway, but this time, as he exited the side door, he turned right toward the front garden.

Shoe walked casually down the front stairs to the foyer and saw one guard—only one guard to get by and he was home free! The guard looked nervous as loud, frantic orders continued through the speaker of his radio. As Shoe came close, he raised a hand and started chuckling. "Who would've known Yoshida was such a comedian!"

Confusion added to the guard's nervousness, and he didn't know what to do other than let Shoe pass. From under the spikes of black hair, Shoe grinned as he made a clean getaway toward Jack's Jeep. He heard a yell from his left and turned his head to see Jack jogging toward him. Shoe laughed as he pointed to the silver briefcase. As Jack came within earshot, Shoe said, "This is too funny. I guess we can add the Japanese to the list of people who think there's 200 thousand dollars in that stupid briefcase."

Jack also laughed as he said, "I would love to see their faces if they could open it and see only a bunch of old encyclopedias." He poked Shoe's arm and urged him toward the parking area. "We better get out of here."

It was fortunate for them security was set up to keep unwanted guests from attending the event, but they didn't care who left. As such, the gate on the right side of the guardhouse was wide open when Jack drove the Jeep through it.

Once they were on the highway back to Shoe's pad in Wooster, Shoe asked, "Did you get anything other than the briefcase?"

"I sure did," Jack answered. "I overheard a conversation between the governor and two Japanese guys. For five minutes they talked about the House of Aliens. They said 'there are ten occupants there right now.'"

Shoe almost jumped out of the passenger seat as he slapped Jack on the shoulder. "Un-freaking-believable! There are ten live aliens there!"

"I'm having a hard time believing it, but that's what they were talking about," Jack admitted.

"Anything else?"

"Yes, something that might come in handy later. Apparently, the House of Aliens is an estate owned by the governor's wife. The governor is using it to launder his illegal buyoff payments, and he has agreed to launder money for the Japanese," Jack explained.

"What are you going to do with that?"

Jack replied, "Right now, nothing, but leverage is very important in today's world. We'll keep this in our back pocket until the appropriate time arises. What did you find?"

"I almost forgot!" Shoe exclaimed. "I was so excited about your news, I forgot about these." He reached into his shirt and pulled out the three reports.

"What are they?" Jack asked.

"I found these in Park's office. Give me a second to go over them." Shoe took a minute to read the first page and asked, "Have you ever heard of a company named - Obata Manufacturing LLC?"

"Of course. I learned about them when I was in college. They're a huge Japanese conglomerate, and they have many subsidiaries, but their bread and butter are plastic moldings and metal stampings," Jack explained.

Shoe continued reading from the first page. "It says here, in 1977, Obata had 900 million dollars in revenue. There's a pie-chart showing a breakdown by division. The plastics division had the most revenue at 600 million dollars." Shoe turned to the second page and examined it. "There's another pie chart on this page showing the breakdown of the Plastics division. The largest producer in this division is Ridgewell Plastics out of England. Their revenue is 200 million all by themselves."

Jack scratched his head. "I've seen that name Ridgewell somewhere before. I just can't put my finger on it."

Shoe was reading the third page and yelled out, "Shit!" He turned the page to Jack and said, "Look at this! This is a pie chart of Ridgewell's revenue. It's by product, so it shows a section for bottles, automotive trim, aerospace, and look here—the smallest piece of the pie at 15 million dollars is wall plugs!"

Jack bounced in his seat. "That's it! When we went to Miller's Hardware and looked at those boxes of wall plugs, the manufacturer was Ridgewell!"

"Look what it says here. There's a hand written note and a line pointing to a circle around the 15 million number. Shoe read aloud.

"Ki-ha:

This is unacceptable. America is a huge, untapped market. By 1981 this number must be 50 million dollars."

There was an unrecognizable signature at the bottom.

Shoe put the papers in his lap. "You know what this means?"

"It's likely Park was not on track, and he was killed," Jack hypothesized.

"That might very well be, but let's put together all the facts," Shoe said. "A Japanese company is hiding as an American company and buying prime land in Ohio. They have the governor in their back pocket, and there's direction to increase sales of wall plugs. If we put two and two together, it's clear they're planning on making a factory here to manufacture wall plugs!"

Jack replied, "I don't want to believe it, but those are the facts."

"Maybe the most important link is these guys want to build a wall plug factory in the same state as the House of Aliens that we now, indisputably, know exists. That's very convenient," Shoe concluded.

"I can't argue with that either," Jack offered. "But there's something here that doesn't make sense and still bugs me."

Shoe asked, "What's that?"

"This seems to be all about the Japanese. We see a Japanese parent company, and in the last few months I've seen more Japanese people and Japanese cars than I have seen in my lifetime. We just attended a Japanese funeral with a Japanese urn and even Japanese koi in the lobby pond."

It all connects," Shoe replied. "It's all about Japanese, so, what's bothering you?"

Jack scowled. "I still can't figure one thing out. You see, Ki-ha Park is not a Japanese name. It's Korean and he is Korean! I can't wrap my head around that!"

Chapter 17: Cranium Leak

Jack, Mario and Shoe had been waiting on the Canton Train Station platform for 15 minutes. It was dusk, and only three other passengers were sitting on a bench at the little-used train stop.

"Dude, are you sure we're at the right place?" Jack asked Shoe.

"This is the only train station in Canton, so this has to be it," Shoe replied. "My contact told me the King of the Hobos would meet us here."

"I still don't understand what the King of the Hobos could possibly know about the House of Aliens," Jack stated.

Mario put his finger to his lips and said, "Shhh! Be quiet. Someone could be listening."

BB heard Mario as he joined them on the platform. "Don't be such an eejit! The people at the other end of the platform don't look like *KGB* or *CIA*."

Shoe looked up at BB. "Why don't you not be such a piece of shit—you piece of shit? Speaking of shit, what took you so long?"

BB pushed his glasses up his nose as he replied, "I had a ferociously large lunch, and when it's time to go, it's time."

"Are you guys just going to dig into each other's Kool-Aid all night long?" Jack asked. "I said I would come along because Shoe said the King of the Hobos could shed some light on the location of aliens in Ohio even though he won't give us any information as to how he knows this."

Jack's accusation was interrupted by a shrill whistle from the north end of the platform. There, a man in faded blue jeans, black tee shirt and an old, brown, leather jacket was waving his hand.

All four of them turned toward the man when, from behind them, they heard, "What do you want?"

Jack turned to see the older man of the other three passengers, up on his feet, pointing to his chest. The man in the brown jacket shook his head from side to side.

Shoe pointed to his own chest, and the man shook his head up and down.

Again, from behind them they heard, "What is it?"

Jack turned to the older man. "Chillax. He's a friend of ours, and he's looking for *us*."

The old man shrugged and sat down while Jack, BB, Shoe and Mario moved to the other end of the platform to meet the man who they assumed must be the King of the Hobos.

The man in the brown jacket pointed and said, "You must be Shoe?"

"How did you know?" Shoe asked.

"The king told me to look for a guy with spiked hair," the man answered.

Jack interrupted. "You're not the king?"

"They call me Stun-gun Stu."

Shoe jumped off the platform and introduced his friends. "We were expecting to meet the king."

"I know," Stun-gun said. "The king is a very careful man, so we're going to meet him at a different location." Stun-gun turned and started to walk north between the tracks and the thick brush line running parallel to them. "Follow me," he ordered.

The four young men ran a few steps to catch up with Stun-gun. Shoe asked, "Is Stun-gun your real name?"

"Is Shoe your real name?" the man replied and then threw his head back, laughing. "Almost all the hobos have nicknames. It's a way the life we left behind—is left behind. They call me Stun-gun because I really like the old *Flash Gordon* TV shows."

"How far are we going?" BB asked.

"Just around the bend ahead, we'll be catching a ride," Stun-gun stated as a high-pitched whistle in the distance announced an approaching train. After walking for a few more minutes, the hobo said, "This is the spot. Get into the bushes."

The four young men joined Stun-gun Stu in the bushes. Jack asked, "What are we waiting for?"

The hobo pointed to his left, and through the bushes they could see an oncoming light. "That's our ride," he said.

Two locomotives slowly rode the tracks by their hiding spot, followed by a line of freight cars as far as they could see.

"Do you want us to jump on?" Mario asked.

"No need," Stun-gun answered. "It'll stop."

"How do you know it'll stop here?" Jack asked.

Stun-gun's frown showed his irritation with the ongoing questions. "Son, I've been riding the rails for 30 years. I don't need a schedule to know which trains travel the tracks or when they do. That's why I know there's a cross-track half a mile ahead, and flying down that track in five minutes will be the CSX freight headed for Columbus. The train coming to a stop in front of us has to wait."

Stun-gun was true to his words as the freight train came to a full stop. Three cars down from their location the side door of the freight car was pulled open. A large head with unkempt, long hair and an even longer black beard, peered out. He put two fingers to his mouth and whistled. Stun-gun returned the whistle, then stepped out of the bushes followed by the four young men.

Stun-gun looked up at the man and said, "How are you doing ya asshole?"

The black-bearded man replied, "Doing great." He looked at the four men behind Stun-gun and asked, "Are these guys the package?"

"That they are," Stun-gun answered. "Where's that other asshole?" On cue, a second much older, bald man appeared beside the first hobo at the door of the freight car.

Shoe came up beside Stun-gun and whispered, "You must know these guys really well to be calling them assholes."

Stun-gun slapped his thigh and laughed. "I guess I should explain. The guy with the black beard is Whistlin Anus Al, and his friend is Uranus Bill. When they're together, we just call them a couple of assholes because their nicknames literally identify them as—a couple of assholes."

Stun-gun helped each of the young men up the metal ladder leading to the wide freight doorway. There were several wooden crates on the freight car, and they each found one to sit on.

As the train lurched forward, Jack realized he had no idea what the plan was. "Isn't it about time you told us where we're going?"

Stun-gun lit a large flashlight and closed the freight car door. "We're going about one hour up the tracks to the Cleveland yard. That's where the king is."

"How are we supposed to get back?" Jack questioned.

Stun-gun rubbed his chin and said, "I don't really know the answer to that question, seeing as I haven't thought that far ahead."

"Oh great," Jack muttered.

Stun-gun frowned. "I can tell by your bad, smart-assed attitude that you're well educated. I'm sure you have some important college degree."

Jack nodded his head up and down.

Stun-gun grinned and said, "I'm sure a fella with a high-level degree, supported by his friends, surely doesn't need three dumbass hobos to help you get from Cleveland back to Canton after your meeting."

Mario put up his hand. "I'll take the help. I need to be lost in Cleveland like I need a hole in my head."

Jack reached over and clamped on Mario's wrist before pulling it down. "What's all the talk about a hole in the head?" Jack asked. "They're just hobos, not killers—I think."

Jack looked at Stun-gun for some sign of confirmation, but the man's cold gaze, from his stone face, bored into Jack. It lasted long enough for Jack to begin nervously fidgeting until Stun-gun slapped his thigh and threw his head back in laughter once again.

Mimicking Stun-gun, Jack also slapped his thigh and joined the hobo's laughter before sarcastically saying, "Do all you hobos have such a great sense of humor?"

"Smartass Jack," Uranus Bill said.

"Pardon," Jack replied.

Uranus Bill said, "If you're being a hobo, even for an hour, ya need a nickname. Based on what little I've seen so far, Smartass Jack fits."

Jack opened his mouth to disagree, but his words were cut off.

"I agree," Stun-gun said.

"Me too," said Whistlin Anus Al. "What about these other three?"

Stun-gun pointed to Shoe and said, "He already has a nickname."

"If you're going to change it, make it something patriotic. I've had my fill of Japanese, Italian and Polish groups lately," Shoe offered.

"Let me think," Stun-gun mumbled. Then he snapped his fingers. "I have it! Considering your hair, we'll call you Shoes-n-Spikes. It's a play on Stars and Stripes except individualized for you. Yeah, Shoes-n-Spikes it'll be."

Shoe laughed. "Whatever."

Uranus Bill lifted his chin, pointing it toward Mario. "What about him there?"

Mario sat up straight and blurted out, "*Senore* Style! It takes into account my Italian heritage and my desire to be a hair stylist."

"Like a barber?" Whistlin Anus Al questioned while Shoe snickered.

Stun-gun waved his hand. "Nah. That's way too formal. It would be much cooler for you to be known as—the Stylemeister."

Mario clapped his hands together. "That sounds freaking awesome! The Stylemeister!"

"What about me?" BB asked.

Stun-gun pointed to BB's head and said to the two assholes, "Do you see it?"

"Can't miss it," Uranus Bill responded.

Stun-gun turned to Smartass Jack. "I figure you'll tell me the truth. How long has he had that thing on the side of his head?"

Smartass Jack laughed. "You mean the cowlick in his afro? He's had that since he was a kid."

"It's not like he'll go home, wash his hair, and it'll go away?" Stun-gun asked.

"Not in this reality," Jack verified.

Stun-gun turned back to BB. "That makes it simple, then. Long as you're riding the trains, you'll be Whirlwind."

"That's not right," BB said. "These guys all have their real name or trait incorporated into their nickname. Whirlwind has nothing to do with BB."

"You have a point," Stun-gun said. "Let's add the *B's* and call you BhirlBind instead of Whirlwind."

"That doesn't sound right at all," BB said.

Stun-guns eyes lit up. "I know. I know. But say it with a lisp."

"A lisp—I'm totally confused," BB offered.

Leaning forward, Stun-gun said, "Say BhirlBind."

BB repeated the name.

Stun-gun said, "Say it faster!"

BB said, "*It faster!*"

"No—you're stunned. Say the name BhirlBind, faster!"

BB repeated the name again.

"Louder and faster!" Stun-gun implored.

Again, BB yelled out the name.

"Faster!"

BB yelled out BhirlBind, over and over. Between each occurrence, Stun-gun urged him to say it faster and louder. Then it happened. Lost in the repetition, as his lips moved faster than his brain, BB yelled out, "Whirlwind!"

Slapping his hands together and then pointing at BB, Stun-gun yelled, "There it is! Whirlwind! It's just BhirlBind with a lisp!"

BB rolled his eyes. "Okay, I get it. After consideration, Whirlwind will do fine."

The two assholes laughed as the train made a right turn, pushing all the occupants toward the left side of the freight car. BB pushed his glasses up his nose and glared at Stun-gun. For the next 30 minutes the freight car was silent. Stun-gun leaned back against the wall of the freight car and rested his chin on his chest. Within a few seconds, the heavy breaths told the others he was fast asleep. After a time, the train finally reduced its speed, and on cue, Stun-gun awoke. "Get ready."

"Ready for what?" Shoes-n-Spikes asked.

Uranus Bill said, "We have to get off the train before we get into the heart of the Clarke Avenue Rail Yard. The Bulls tolerate us as long as we don't get in the way."

"Bulls?" Smartass Jack asked.

"That's what we call the railway police," Stun-gun explained. The train continued to slow and Stun-gun said to Uranus Bill, "Open the door. It's almost time to jump."

The train slowed even more, but the boys still had some trepidation, as they had never jumped off a moving train before. Stun-gun went first. He moved to the bottom rung of the ladder and expertly leapt to the gravel bed. His feet landed in the running motion required to keep pace with the train. Uranus Bill followed Stun-gun, showing the same level of skill in departing the train.

Whistlin Anus Al grabbed Smartass Jack by the shoulder and said, "Your turn."

Smartass Jack moved down the ladder and hesitated a second before leaping from the train. He tried to mimic the running motion landing, but he only lasted two steps before his forward momentum forced him to duck and roll. To his credit, he lessened the embarrassment, as he finishing the roll by expertly popping up to his feet.

Shoes-n-Spikes did well in his departure. Stun-gun gave him a thumbs up, impressed with how fast he could move his short legs. As Smartass Jack watched, he realized they should have departed in a different order. Now that the train was moving even slower, Whirlwind's long legs made his departure look simple.

The Stylemeister was next. At the bottom rung of the ladder, his knuckles were white as he held onto the metal railing. He was frozen there until Whistlin Anus Al slapped him on the back of the head. His fingers let go, and he stumbled. At first, Smartass Jack thought he would make it until one of the Stylemeister's white, patent-leather shoes hit a rut in the gravel. Consequently, he sprawled face forward into the tall weeds growing alongside the forest's edge.

Whistlin Anus Al jumped off next, after which they all gathered at the Stylemeister. He pulled himself up, spitting dirt out of his mouth and felt embarrassed being the only one to do a face plant.

But then Stun-gun grabbed Mario by the shoulder. "Dude—that was awesome!"

Jack slapped Mario on the back and added, "We wouldn't expect less from the Stylemeister!"

Uranus Bill said, "It's been dark for a while, but we still don't want to be seen out here in the open."

"True enough," Stun-gun said. He walked along the gravel bed for a few yards before seeing a worn path cutting into the woods. The four newly named hobos came after, followed by the two assholes. Stun-gun had traversed this path many times and did not need a light. But after Shoe tripped and fell over a tree root, Stun-gun handed him the flashlight. They walked further into the forest, and shortly thereafter, the darkness ahead of them was broken by small spots of light between the trees. As they drew closer, the spots of lights revealed themselves to be campfires. Moving out of the forest into the clearing, they could see the fires were numerous, and huddled by each were groups of men and even some women. In many places they saw small tents, and in others, tarps were strung between the branches of the few trees dotting the clearing.

On the far side of the camp was an old brick building. As Smartass Jack moved closer to it, he could see it was an abandoned warehouse. They stopped at two double doors where two hobos were standing guard.

Stun-gun smiled at the burlier man. "How are things going, Cheesequake?"

"Things are good," Cheesequake replied. "What can I do for you?"

"These guys are here to see the king. Can you let him know we're here?" Stun-gun said.

"No problem." Cheesequake turned and went through one of the metal double doors.

They had a few minutes, whereby Smartass Jack took the time to examine the hobo camp. Just a few yards away, sitting on a bench beside the wall of the warehouse, was a curiosity. He walked toward the bench and saw a small man in a heavy fur coat with a matching hood. On his feet were what appeared to be seal-skin boots. The man heard Smartass Jack's steps and lifted his face. In the dim light, Smartass Jack saw a wrinkled red face, proof of a long life in bright sunlight. Adorning the chiseled face was a scraggly, gray beard of uneven whiskers.

Smartass Jack couldn't help but ask, "Who are you? You look like an eskimo."

The old man shrugged. "The term eskimo has been considered inappropriate for quite a few years."

Smartass Jack said, "Sorry for that, but why are you here?"

The old man continued in a slow, low voice, "I'm the token indigenous person taking the opportunity to give your story a sense of political correctness."

Smartass Jack blinked several times. The old man looked at Smartass Jack and smiled.

When Smartass Jack returned to the double doors of the warehouse, Stun-gun had returned and was ushering them into the building. Surprisingly, the inside was clean and lit by electricity. They walked by several rooms set up as offices until they came to a large wooden door at the end of the hallway. Stun-gun knocked, and the door was opened by a huge mountain of a hobo. Though most surprising was the fact this hobo was a woman.

As they walked through, Stun-gun said, "Thanks Winnie."

The newcomers saw they were in a large room with three couches on their left. There were several wooden chairs against the wall, and facing the three couches was a weathered, blue lazy-boy recliner. Just behind it, through a wide doorway, a short, thin man wearing a brown duckbill cap, entered.

The man, although small in stature, had a larger man's voice as he clapped his hands together and bellowed, "Welcome!"

Stun-gun Stu stepped forward. "Guys, this is King Ludvig Skywise, the King of the Hobos." Then he turned to the king and introduced the four newly anointed hobos. He pointed to each in turn. "This is Shoes-n-Spikes, Smartass Jack, Whirlwind and the Stylemeister."

The King smiled through a mouth and lips seeming too large for his face. He spread his arm open toward the couches. "Please sit."

The boys did as requested, and the king paced back and forth in front of them. He stopped in front of Shoes-n-Spikes and said, "Your description precedes you. I was told you worked with Professor Sebastian Johansen at Wooster College."

"Yes," Shoes-n-Spikes replied. "He told me if I ever needed to find out information about unwanted visitors in Ohio, I should see you." Shoes-n-Spikes, lowered his voice to a whisper as he finished the words while looking suspiciously at the other hobos in the room.

King Skywise grinned, then settled himself down into the lazy-boy recliner the boys now realized was an aberrant hobo throne. "You don't have to worry about them. They have my absolute confidence," the king stated. "Both Stun-gun and Winnipeg Winnie have been with me for over 20 years."

Smartass Jack interrupted and said, "I'm not really even sure why we're here or who you really are."

King Skywise looked at Stun-gun and gave him a thumbs up. "Awesome name that is—Smartass Jack." Turning his gaze back to Smartass Jack, he said, "However, Shoes-n-Spikes I know of, but the three of you I know nothing about, so I have no trust at all."

"How do we fix that?" the Stylemeister asked.

"Cheesequake!" the king bellowed. "Time for the test."

Cheesequake chuckled as he walked to an old, broken-down dresser against the far wall. From it, he pulled out an electric drill. Next, he retrieved a long extension cord and connected it between the drill and the electrical outlet. The large man walked over to a spot in front of the couch the four boys sat in, and said, "Who's first?"

The king nonchalantly waved his hand. "Let's go left to right."

Cheesequake nodded his agreement and moved to a spot in front of the Stylemeister. He pulled the trigger several times to test the speed of the power tool.

Realizing he was to be first, the Stylemeister's eyes went wide in horror, seeing the quarter-inch drill bit spinning in the chuck. He jumped to his feet as he said, "Stun-gun said they wouldn't put holes in our heads! He promised!"

Winnipeg Winnie was behind the couch, and her massive hands caught on the Stylemeister's shoulders as he shot up, only to thrust him back firmly into the cushion. The Stylemeister tried to squirm free, but the woman was unusually strong, and as a result, he was held firmly in place. Pressing the trigger of the drill, Cheesequake brought the spinning drill bit closer and closer until it was half an inch from the tip of the Stylemeister's nose.

The Stylemeister tried to retract his head deeper into the back cushion as the king asked, "Well, how are his eyes?"

Cheesequake released the trigger. "Normal—no quivering."

The same process was performed on Smartass Jack and Whirlwind with the same conclusion from Cheesequake.

King Skywise clapped his hands together. "Good. Now that you've passed the power tool test, we can talk safely."

By now, Smartass Jack might have been better named *Pissed Off Jack* as he said to the king, "This is stunned. Talk about what? We still don't know who you are or why you would know anything."

Looking at Shoes-n-Spikes while pointing at Smartass Jack, the king said, "You really didn't tell these guys anything?"

"Without your permission, I didn't want to," Shoes-n-Spikes replied.

King Skywise leaned forward in the lazy-boy as he addressed the four boys. "Shoes-n-Spikes has told you about Professor Sebastian Johansen who worked at Wooster College, but you're probably wondering why would a reputable college professor be bothering to investigate aliens."

"Good point," Whirlwind said.

"The story really begins a little over 20 years ago. You see, Professor Johansen had a brother who worked for a top-secret space agency at an even more secret location," the king explained.

"You mean Area 51 in Nevada?" the Stylemeister asked.

The king laughed. "Not at all. Area 51 was a *red herring* the Air Force put out there to keep all the conspiracy theorists distracted. The real work with aliens and spacecraft was done at Area 43 in Colorado."

The Stylemeister scratched his head. "I never heard of Area 43."

"Don't be so thick," the king said as he shook his head in dismay. "You never hearing of Area 43, is what we call—the plan working!"

The Stylemeister slunk back down into the couch, promising himself to keep his mouth shut.

The king continued. "Johansen's brother worked at the facility where he saw aliens and even a couple of alien spaceships. There were more aliens there than you would think. They were poked and prodded, and a couple of them died. That gave the scientists the opportunity to dissect them."

"That's effin disgusting," Whirlwind said.

"Yes, it was," the king agreed. "Johansen's brother was an up-and-coming physicist, but he was young and had to work his way up. At the time of the disgusting work, he was an assistant janitor at the secret facility, and as the assistant janitor, he was the one who discovered a breakthrough in alien behavior."

Smartass Jack sarcastically quipped, "He must have been promoted from assistant janitor to full-fledged janitor for that."

The king turned to Stun-gun, and this time gave him two thumbs up. "Awesome name that—Smartass Jack!"

By now, Whirlwind was sitting on the edge of the cushion, engrossed in the story. "Don't mind the gobshite. What was the breakthrough?"

"One day, young Johansen was asked to put up a cork board in a conference room in the facility. The wall he was working on backed onto a complex of holding pens where aliens were held. He needed to put holes in the wall, then wall plugs and finally screws. When he began drilling, there were horrific screams from the other side of the wall. Several military guards and a doctor rushed by the door to investigate, but the screams stopped when he stopped drilling.

The doctor returned past the conference room door scratching her head. Young Johansen shrugged and once again started to drill. As sure as flies attract to shit, the screaming began once again. Johansen laughed and turned the drill on and off several times. He realized *he* controlled the screams."

"Awesome! What happened next?" Whirlwind asked.

"Johansen was promoted to a full-fledged janitor, but the new knowledge he accidentally came across was used to torture the aliens. His ambitions were downtrodden, and he just wanted out. A month later, he broke into the doctor's office and packed as many documents and files into his duffle bag as he could. He escaped and no one in any government agency has heard from him since."

"How do you know all this?" Smartass Jack questioned.

"The king pushed his cap back on his head and replied, "I know because my real name is Ludvig Johansen, and I'm the brother of Professor Sebastien Johansen."

"Holy freaking shite!" Whirlwind cried as a chill went up his spine.

Smartass Jack was not as easily impressed. "How does a prominent physicist turn into a hobo?"

"What better place to hide?" King Skywise responded. "I needed to stay way under the radar, and this is about as far under as it gets." He clapped his hands together, once again. "But right now, it's nothing more than a tall tale. You want some proof, do you not?"

Before Smartass Jack could answer, the king was on his feet, walking toward the back doorway. "Come along," he said.

They went into the back room, then through another door into a smaller room. When the king flicked the light switch on, they could see a small desk and an old, narrow bed. King Skywise reached under the bed and pulled out a trunk. His old fingers deftly dialed the combination lock, and he threw open the curved lid. "Go ahead and have a look. There's your evidence."

Shoes-n-Spikes and the Stylemeister dropped to their knees while Smartass Jack and Whirlwind looked over them as file after file was retrieved and opened. It was past midnight when they looked at each other in amazement and shock. There were documents showing the results of various tests on aliens. They also learned there were various types of aliens. There were the *Grays*, who were smaller, skinny aliens. There were the aliens known as the *Giants*, who averaged nine feet tall. They even found a file on a *Reptilian* who looked exactly as the name described them. However, they were shapeshifters and could take human form.

But the ones who were the biggest concern was the fourth group of aliens who looked just like humans. At one point, Shoes-n-Spikes asked, "Did they look Japanese?"

He was disappointed when the king replied, "All the aliens in this group looked Caucasian."

After putting all the documents back into the trunk, the king pushed it back under his bed. He said, "I know it's a lot all at once. Do you have any other questions?"

"I only have one," Smartass Jack said. "How the hell are we going to get home?"

The king chuckled and slapped Smartass Jack on the shoulder. "You're starting to grow on me. You don't think a king wouldn't have a car, do ya?"

"I have another question," Shoes-n-Spikes said. "Have you ever heard of the House of Aliens?"

The king's eyebrows relaxed with relief. He moved to the wooden desk and from the bottom drawer pulled out an envelope, yellowed with age. He handed it to Shoes-n-Spikes. "My brother told me, 'If a weird looking guy named Shoe came calling and asked about the House of Aliens, give him this.'"

As Shoes-n-Spikes opened the seal on the envelope and pulled out the paper within, the three friends and the king looked over his shoulder. On the piece of paper was a name. it read - *Leo Denebola.*

Whirlwind asked, "Who the shite is Leo Denebola?"

The king grinned and said to Shoes-n-Spikes, "Are you going to tell them, or am I?"

Smartass Jack quipped, "I don't care who tells us, just someone tell us!"

When Shoes-n-Spikes lifted his face, there was a life in his eyes his friends had never seen before. "We have to go back to the planetarium at Wooster College."

"Why?" the Stylemeister asked.

Grabbing the Stylemeister by his shirt collar, Shoes-n-Spikes explained. "Because it's not who. Leo Denebola isn't a who. It's a what!"

Chapter 18: The One After the Last Thing

Stun-gun drove the four boys back to the Canton Rail Station where they all piled into BB's van. Jack and Mario were dozing off, and even BB, who was doing his best to keep the van from going off the road, was having difficulty keeping his eyes open. Fortunately, Shoe, who was energized with his proprietary knowledge of Leo Denebola, was wide awake. Every time BB's chin would drop to his chest, Shoe would slap him in the shoulder, returning BB's focus to his driving—at least until the next doze and slap cycle.

By the time they arrived at Shoe's basement apartment in Wooster, the darkness of the night was just being broken by the oncoming sunrise. As much as they wanted to rush over to the college planetarium so Shoe would explain the mystery, when they entered the apartment, they all found a soft spot on a bed or couch, or in Mario's case, on the shag carpet in Shoe's trophy room. Soon they were all asleep.

Jack's sleep was restless. Of the four friends, he was the one who had doubted the theory of aliens in Ohio, but the hobo king provided evidence that was hard to refute. Consequently, at noon, he was the first to wake and, in turn, awaken each of his friends. Shoe made a large pot of coffee, and each of them held a mug of the hot brew as they sat in the living room, contemplating their next move.

"Are you now going to give us the skinny about what Leo Denebola is?" Jack asked Shoe.

"You won't understand," Shoe answered. "We have to go to the Planetarium, and once there, I'll show you, so hang loose just a bit longer."

"We're not effin retards," BB said. "Just tell us."

"As soon as we finish our coffee, we'll go there. It's Sunday, so there won't be anyone around, but I can use my service key to get us in."

Mario sat forward on the couch and blurted out, "Spill the peas already!"

Jack slapped his forehead and shook his head from side to side. "You want to be a hairstylist, and I've never been to one, but I do go to a barber. It seems chit-chat is a requirement. I sure hope it's not the same for hair stylists."

"What did I do? Of course, hairstylists chit-chat," Mario replied.

Jack said, "You know, you have this weird condition where you fart out of both ends of your body. Just as we all do, you have shitty farts coming out of your ass. However, your nuance is that you also have brain farts coming out of your mouth with regularity."

"I've no idea what you're talking about," Mario replied with a perplexed look on his face.

"You're right. You have no idea what you're talking about," Jack agreed. "You said, 'spill the peas.' That's incorrect. The correct saying is, *spill the beans.*"

"You guys take this way too serious," Mario concluded. "Beans and peas—they're both green, and both are about the same size. Can you dig that?"

"You're assuming the saying is about *green* beans," BB interjected. "They could be talking about *brown* beans. Also, green beans only look like snap peas, but if they're peas out of the pod, or if they're talking about split peas, the similarities aren't there."

"I say we do two things," Mario offered. "First, all three of you fuck right off. Second, let's leg it to the planetarium."

BB rose to his feet. "I agree. Let's go, but before we do, everyone give me five dollars."

Shoe choked as a spray of coffee left his mouth. "Are you stunned? Why would we give you money?"

BB pushed his glasses up along his nose. "We just came out of a gas crisis, and everyone thinks it's only a matter of time before the next one arrives. I'm always the one driving, so you all need to give me some bread for gas."

Shoe muttered, "Piece of shit," while he reached into his pocket for the five-dollar bill. Mario and Jack did the same.

They headed for the door to the apartment where Shoe held it open. Jack and Mario passed by, but Shoe put his palm on BB's chest and brought him to a stop. "I should let you know there's a Sunday admission fee to the planetarium."

"How much?" BB asked.

Shoe grinned as he turned over his hand with his palm up. "Five dollars."

"Ya effin maggot!" BB yelled as he slapped away Shoe's hand while walking past him.

Ten minutes later, BB was parking the Shaggin-wagon in front of the planetarium. For early November, it was a relatively warm day, and there wasn't a cloud in the sky. Shoe led them down several hallways to a locked metal door. After unlocking it, they entered as Shoe turned on the banks of lights, illuminating the large, spherical room.

"Okay—we're here," Jack said. "Spill the peas." He laughed at his joke and was joined by Shoe and BB. Mario glared at Jack, clearly with a lack of the same amusement.

Shoe walked to the curved, side wall where a ramp led him to a three-foot-high, elevated walkway. He turned to BB, Jack and Mario. "Behind me is a mural showing the constellations, and each constellation is a configuration of stars." He turned to face the large, round map and pointed to his left. "Over there is the constellation, Leo. It's the constellation of the lion, so now you know what Leo is."

"And Denebola?" Jack asked.

Shoe walked to his left until he stood right in front of the constellation, Leo. "Each star in the constellation has a name. With his finger he lightly traced out the lion from the head to the star at the tip of its tail. "This star here—the one in the middle of the tail, is called Denebola." As the explanation emitted from his lips, he lifted his hand and pressed the finger into the star on the mural. "Hey!" he exclaimed, as his finger didn't stop at the paper; rather, it buried into the wall.

"What's that?" BB asked.

Shoe pushed his finger in a second time, then a third. "There's a hole behind the mural." He bent over and ripped the mural to create a larger opening, revealing a fist-sized hole in the concrete block. Reaching his hand further in, he searched around and pulled out a key. Moving to the railing along the edge of the elevated walkway, he leaned down and showed his friends the key. It was gold with a bright red handle. On it, also in gold, was the number – 38."

"What are we supposed to do with that?" Jack said.

"Dude, the key could be used anywhere," Mario added. "It's like searching for a needle in a haystack."

BB had a huge smile on his face.

"What?" Jack said.

BB grabbed Mario's hand and shook it violently. "First of all—congratulations for using an urban saying and not fucking it up. Second, I know where the key goes."

"Dream on! That's impossible," Shoe retorted.

BB waggled his finger. "'Nay-nay.' You remember yesterday when we were waiting at the Canton Railway Station."

"Sure," Jack said in an impatient tone.

"Well, you'll also remember I went to the bathroom to leave a monumental deposit. Along the south wall of the building, the wall is blue, and that is the women's bathroom area."

"Get to it!" Jack yelled. "You're like my freaking mother telling a story. It's painful!"

"Wait for it," BB replied. "The north wall is red, and this is where the men's bathroom is, but the important point is that along each wall, beside the doors, are lockers. Again, blue ones at the women's end, and red ones at the men's end." He looked at Shoe. "That key you're holding is identical to the ones used in the red lockers."

"Are you sure?" Jack asked.

"Gold key with a red, square handle and gold numbers—yup, this key belongs to one of those lockers," BB verified.

"What are we waiting for?" Shoe said as he pounced for the exit.

The three friends followed and quickly made their way back to BB's van where they all piled in. Within moments, they were on the highway back to Canton.

"I don't think I'm that thick, but I don't get it," BB said. "Why is the professor making it so hard for us to find the House of Aliens? Why didn't he just tell you before he died?"

"I'm not really sure," Shoe replied. "I can only assume he wasn't sure how serious I was about the danger of aliens in Ohio. Maybe by making us work for it, he was making sure we really were as interested as he was."

"This path is certainly creative," BB added. "What do you think will be in the locker?"

"Even more important, what if we can't figure out the next clue?" Jack said.

Mario interjected, "We'll be at the train station in 30 minutes, so let's cross that ledge when we get to it."

"Piece of shit," Shoe muttered.

Mario crossed his arms. "What now?"

Jack was lying on the bed across the back of the van looking up at the ceiling. "You just farted out of your mouth again. You said, 'let's cross that *ledge* when we get to it.' The correct saying is, *let's cross that bridge when we get to it.*"

Mario brought his finger up to his chin. "There are nine words in the saying, and I got eight of them right. That would be 90 percent correct. When was the last time you got anything 90 percent right?" Mario asked as he glared at Jack.

Jack replied, "Remember, I took engineering in school, and it's more exact in application. When you're speaking English, it's either right or wrong, and eight words right out of nine is 89 per cent, not 90."

Mario smirked. "Well, 'la-de-da,' Mr. High and Mighty Engineer."

Shoe turned around from the front seat, ignored Mario, and said to Jack, "Maybe Mario thinks speaking English is like throwing a hand grenade or dropping an atomic bomb where usually close is good enough."

The fact Shoe was talking about him like he wasn't even in the van was not lost on Mario. "Hey, I'm in the fucking van!" he yelled as he waved his hand in front of Shoe's face.

There was a sudden screech as BB slammed on the brakes. Shoe's eyes went wide as his body was lifted off the front seat and pressed against the seat belt being stretched to the limit. The side of Mario's face slapped against the back of the front seat, flattening it like a pancake while Jack, thrown off the bed, rolled several times until he came to a stop against Shoe's sneakers.

The braking action was only momentary, and then BB pressed the gas pedal to bring them back up to speed. BB said, "I couldn't take your bollocks anymore—whining like little, old ladies."

Jack lifted his head and said, "So you tried to kill us, you black, Irish moron!"

BB laughed. "It served its purpose." He leaned forward, turning the volume knob of the radio to a high enough setting so that Jack's response was totally drowned out.

There were no trains scheduled for Sunday, so the parking lot at Canton Station was empty, except for one car. When they entered the small terminal building, it was also empty except for the face that poked through the ticket window on the far wall. "You want to buy tickets for later in the week?" the man asked.

"No thanks," Shoe replied.

"Well, there are no trains today."

"We'll only be a few minutes," Shoe replied. "We need to get something out of a locker." He held up the red and gold key as they walked toward the red row of lockers by the men's washroom.

Almost every locker had a key in it, but sure enough, locker number 38 didn't. As they grouped around it, Shoe engaged the key, turned it and subsequently pulled the locker door open. They all paused a moment as they peered inside. It was empty except for a red can. BB reached in and pulled it out where, in the increased level of light, they saw it was, in fact, a red coffee tin. BB's large fingers turned the lid, removing it, before he peered inside.

"BB said, "What the effin hell," as he pulled out a red viewmaster.

Jack took the viewmaster from BB. "Wow! I haven't seen one of these in a while. Is there a set of pictures to view? I'm not sure what they call the round disc with the pictures on it."

BB peered into the tin. "Nope. It's empty."

"I have one of these at home," Mario added. "The disc is called a reel and there are 14 pictures on it. But the 14 pictures are actually doubles, so when you look with both eyes, the double picture produces a 3D effect."

"If I'm understanding you correctly, the 14 pictures let you see seven images in 3D," Shoe said.

"Yes, except we don't have a reel," Mario replied.

There was a loud clang as BB, in his frustration, threw the red tin on the floor. It clanged twice more as it bounced off a locker, then the corner of a bench in front of the line of lockers. "I can't believe I wasted the gas in my van for this!"

With the racket, the man's face appeared once again at the ticket window. "You guys need any help?"

Shoe waved his hand. "No. We're just leaving!"

Jack picked up the tin as they walked toward the door to the terminal. Jack spun it in his hand several times. He felt a dent in the bottom where it had hit the corner of the bench. He tossed it to BB. "You dented the bottom when you threw it."

BB looked inside the tin and then at Jack. "Ya whanker. There's no dent."

Jack's brows furrowed as he took the tin can back from BB. He looked inside at the bottom of the can, and, sure enough, there was no dent.

However, turning it over, he saw there was a dent on the bottom surface. His brows lowered even more as he held out his free hand and said to BB, "Give me your pocket knife."

BB replied, "How do you know I have a knife?"

"You're black and you're Irish. Why wouldn't you have a knife?" Jack responded with a snicker.

"Aren't ya brilliant, ya eejit," BB said as he reached into his pocket and pulled out his pocket knife. The knife was red with a white cross on it. "I know. It's shocking, but the knife is small enough to be legal."

Jack had already zoned out BB as he took the knife and pulled the blade clear of the handle. He worked at the short circular hem running around the bottom of the tin. After opening the hem around half of the circumference, he was able to pull back the bottom. As the four of them looked into the gap created, they could now see the false bottom, and on it was a white viewmaster reel.

Shoe grinned. "Excellent work, Jack. Let's go outside in the better light and see what's on the reel."

Once outside, Shoe pressed the reel into the viewmaster and held it up to the sun's rays. As he brought down the side lever, the picture changed, and each time he saw a picture of a different old house. He went through it several times before handing it to Jack, who did the same. BB was next and then Mario.

Finally, Mario lowered the viewmaster and said, "I don't get it."

"It must be another clue," Shoe added.

Jack took the viewmaster from Mario and pulled out the reel. In the middle of the reel, it read - *Historical Houses of Ohio*. He pulled it back up to his eyes as he said, "The envelope was given to Shoe by the hobo king because he asked about the House of Aliens. Now, here we are looking at pictures of seven houses. We have to think the professor is telling us the House of Aliens is one of these houses."

"But which one?" BB asked.

Jack reinserted the reel and pulled the lever numerous times, trying to find something in the pictures when Mario yelled, "I have it!"

Shoe slapped Mario on the shoulder and said, "It's about time. You haven't farted out of your mouth in a while."

"You're just jealous because I know what's going on, and you don't," Mario replied with a grin.

Jack continued to pull the lever, cycling the pictures as he said, "What do you have Mario?"

In his excitement, as many Italians do, he talked quickly, and his hands moved with each word. "There's a theme. The theme is a color, and the color is red. The locker is red. The tin can is red and the viewmaster is red."

"That's your idea of knowing what's going on." Shoe quipped.

Jack continued to pull the lever, mumbling, "Hold on. He's right."

Shoe threw up his arms. "About what?"

Mario grinned. "Jack see's it now."

Jack pulled the viewmaster down from his eyes and handed it to Shoe. "There are seven pictures of houses on the disc. Only one has red brick. That house must be the House of Aliens."

Shoe flipped the viewmaster up to his eyes and verified Jack's conclusion. He examined the red-brick house which, in fact, was really a very large mansion surrounded by a high, red-brick, segmented, wall broken by sections of wrought-iron fencing. He adjusted the viewmaster's angle to get a brighter view. "In the background, behind the brick wall, there's a green sign, but it's too blurry to read what's on it."

"Then it won't help us," BB said.

"Maybe it can," Shoe replied. "There's a photography club at the college. "We might be able to read it if the image is enlarged."

The four young men walked back to the Shaggin-wagon in a very good mood with the possibility of a solution to the House of Aliens within sight. In fact, they were all very jovial.

Jack said to Mario, "So, what did we do?"

"We just might have found the needle in the haystack."

"How did we do that?" Jack asked.

Mario was getting pumped. "By crossing the bridge when we got to it!"

"And, what did you do?" Jack continued the encouragement.

Mario's pulse was rising in his fervor, and his voice was loud. "Red! Red! I came up with the common denominator!"

"Jack raised his hand, and Mario gave him a hard high-five. "You're on a roll my friend. How did we get here?"

Mario's eyes were wide, and the words blurted out. "We persevered and let no one get in our way. We didn't waste a lot of time, and we didn't beat the bush around!"

Mario was on such a roll until the last brain fart was expelled. Jack could do nothing but admire his friend. Through his laughter, the only words Jack could think of were, *Mario, you're awesome!*

Chapter 19: Unconcho

"Ever since Jack met Carley, he's always late," Mario said.

"He's known Carley since he got back from Philadelphia, so your comparison must go back several years—to before he went to college," BB clarified as he looked out the large picture window from their regular booth at Denny's.

Mario looked at his watch. "Jack did say to meet here at 1 p.m. for lunch, did he not?"

"Chillax. He'll be here soon enough," BB said before he took a drink from the straw hanging out of his glass of Dr. Pepper.

"We haven't talked about the money for a while now. Have you thought about what you'll use it for?" Mario asked.

"You mean our share of the 200 thousand dollars we coerced from the Polish mafia?" BB replied.

"Yup."

BB pushed the glasses up the edge of his nose and leaned in, whispering, "Keep your voice down. We don't want anyone to know we have that amount of money, or how we got it."

"I was doing the math, and with 50 thousand dollars I could open my own hair styling shop," Mario whispered.

"Your numbers are a bit off," BB corrected. "We agreed that Jack, Shoe, you and I would each get an even split, but only after Carley and Zoltan got a small cut. They got five thousand dollars each. The remainder was divided four ways, so we each got 49 thousand dollars."

"To be exact, that would be 49 thousand and five hundred dollars each," Mario said with a smile.

"Your father has the money stored away for us?" BB asked.

"Of course," Mario responded. "He has four safety deposit boxes around town, but two of them are never used. I put the money in a duffle bag but told my father it was your stamp collection needing to be stored for a while. The duffle bag is in one of the safety deposit boxes he never uses."

"You should have used the silver briefcase of yours instead of the duffle bag. It has a combination lock, so no one could inadvertently come across the money in case they access the safety deposit box," BB offered.

Mario leaned in and looked across the restaurant before responding. "You're stunned BB. The only other person who might go into the safety deposit box is my father, and it's his briefcase, so he knows the combination."

BB smirked. "That's effin brilliant—you telling me off for saying something stupid."

Still whispering through clenched teeth, Mario said, "No more talk of the silver briefcase. You know very well why I couldn't use it."

BB nodded and leaned back as he looked out the window where he saw Jack's green X-mobile drive into the parking lot. Almost before the car came to a stop, the passenger side door was flung open. Carley deftly exited and was clear before the large door rebounded off the hinges and slammed shut. The pavement was still wet from an early morning rain, but Carley paid no attention to the small puddles as she stomped through them, sending up a spray of water droplets with each step.

BB laughed and said, "Looks like there's trouble in paradise."

With Mario's attention brought to the parking lot, his gaze moved to the Matador X where Jack was now exiting. "I think maybe they have crossed the hump now."

"What hump?" BB asked.

Mario pointed at Jack. "He has that same look on his face that many married people have. He looks satisfied but confused and, honestly—a bit defeated."

"That's daft," BB replied. "How can he be satisfied and defeated at the same time?"

Mario winked at BB. "Remember, it's Saturday, and this is their *sex in the morning*—morning."

BB's eyes widened. "You don't mean…"

There was a loud clang from the metal-framed, glass door of the restaurant slamming into the jamb as it shut behind Carley. As she walked toward the booth occupied by BB and Mario, Mario rose to move to the other side. It was a small courtesy allowing Jack to sit beside his girl. However, Mario was only halfway off the bench when Carley placed her hand on Mario's shoulder and forcibly pushed him against the outside wall of the booth. She said, "Move the hell over," as she dropped onto the cushion beside him.

BB shrank back into the opposite corner of the booth and said to Mario, "I think you're right."

"Right about what?" Jack asked as he slid into the booth beside BB.

Mario explained, "Well, it's a sensitive topic and one you might not want to discuss."

Jack ran his fingers back through his black hair. "We've been through a lot together. We're all buds and we can talk about anything."

Carley looked up and glared at Jack. Her face was flushed, and her blue eyes seemed a shade darker than normal. She contorted her face into one resembling a five-year-old, and in a mocking voice, she repeated, "That's right. We're all best buds!"

BB leaned forward. "Okay, I'll cut through the tension here. It's Saturday, and on Saturday morning's you guys have sex, so how can you be mad at each other?"

Carley's hand flashed forward as she pointed at Jack. "Correction—he had sex!"

Men have a strange bond at times. Upon Carley's accusation, Jack, BB and Mario felt like they just got simultaneously kicked in their groins. There was the pain and the feeling like their nuts shrunk up inside themselves while in unison they whispered, "Ouch."

"That's not fair," Jack said.

Carley's finger was still pointed at Jack but it was now shaking. "I'll tell you what's not fair. You finishing and leaving me hanging."

BB said, "Hanging?"

Mario Interjected, "BB, you moron. She didn't orgasm, so she wasn't satisfied, and Jack obviously was."

Carley grasped Mario's shoulder, and her fingers dug into the muscles there as she said, "Well, at least you understand the problem here."

Mario gave a wide smile. "I'm Italian and Italy is a nation of lovers. We understand the art of intimacy."

"Awesome," Carley said. "Maybe you should give your *bud* some lessons."

"Chill out Carley!" Jack implored. "We've had a lot of sex, and this is the first time I did my thing a bit early. It's never happened that way before."

"Why do you think this time was different?" Mario asked.

Jack laughed. "What—are you my sex therapist now?"

Carley's eyes narrowed. "Jack, you answer his question, or I'm going to slap you and not in a kinky way."

BB pushed Jack out of the booth and he got up. "This is gross and I've heard enough. I need to go to the can so I can puke."

Jack returned to the bench and thought for a second. "I don't think anything was any different."

Mario rested his chin on his hand. "Maybe that's the problem. Perhaps you're getting into a routine and becoming too predictable."

Carley raised an eyebrow and looked curiously at Mario. "What would you recommend?"

"Good sex comes from observing and adjusting," Mario explained.

"I'm not sure I understand." Carley replied.

Mario was feeling good about himself now that he had a captive audience. "A good partner watches and listens to what works and what doesn't work. Adjust to what works, and lose what doesn't," Mario clarified.

Jack rolled his eyes. "What would you know? You think you're some kind of Italian Dr. Freud?"

Carley slammed her hand down on the table as her growing frustration with Jack added to her tension. "Where's Shoe?"

"He said he would be late, but why do you need Shoe?" Mario asked.

"Shoe carries around that monster vibrator with him and right now, I could use it more than him!" Her finger was once again pointed at Jack.

"That doesn't sound very sanitary," Mario said just before he dry-heaved.

BB, just returning from the bathroom, smiled sarcastically and said, "I see you two have made up."

Her eyes flashed at BB. "Dream on. Give me the keys to your van."

"Why?" BB replied.

The three young men looked from one to the other as a noise came from Carley's throat. It was not a word. It was some type of guttural sound from deep within the pit of Carley's stomach. She just held her hand out, and BB thought better than to disobey the demand. He put the van keys in her hand, then she rose from the bench seat. As she walked by Jack, she grabbed the lapel of his leather jacket, wrenching him out of the booth.

"This morning's error in judgement was your 'mulligan.' It's now time for redemption." Carley's words faded as she walked toward the front door while pulling Jack behind her.

"Don't make a mess!" BB said, but Carley set a fast pace that already had the young couple out the door and beyond earshot.

BB sat down and scratched his head. "That's 15 minutes of my life I'll never get back."

Thinking they might be waiting for a while, BB and Mario ordered burgers and fries for their lunch. As they ate, they watched the Shaggin-wagon now living up to its nickname. The van was rocking back and forth from front to back in a steady rhythm. Then, suddenly, the rhythm stopped for a few seconds. Following this, there was a *thump,* and the van was jarred down on the back shocks. The rhythmic cycle repeated several times, testing the van's suspension.

After 30 minutes, the double back doors of the van were slung open. There, kneeling on the bed, was Carley, but she looked completely different. Her hair was tangled and twice as high as when she entered the Shaggin-wagon. She raised her face to the sky and inhaled deeply followed by her tongue running across her upper lip. BB and Mario saw all of this through the picture window. Mario was frozen with a french-fry half way to his gapped mouth.

BB said, "Do you see that? She looks like a lion who just finished feeding on a carcass."

Carley pounced out from the back of the van and waited for Jack who jumped down after her. He closed the back doors and leaned over, rubbing a knee. He then stretched backwards while holding his sides, and finally, he limped along behind Carley toward Denny's.

"And there is the carcass," BB mumbled.

"Dude—I think I need to get me an Amish girlfriend," Mario added.

As Jack and Carley walked back toward the booth, Carley waved the waitress over to them. Carley lowered an eyebrow and said to Mario, "What are you doing—move already."

"Looks like everything is back to normal," Mario said as he slid out and moved to the opposite bench beside BB.

Carley slid into the bench seat first, followed by Jack just as the waitress arrived.

Even before the waitress could ask, Carley said, "I'll have a cheeseburger combo with fries and also a hotdog on the side."

"You sure?" the waitress asked. "That's a lot of food for a small thing like you."

Carley winked at the woman. "I'm still saving room for pie."

Jack added, "I'll just have the cheeseburger and fries."

As the waitress headed for the kitchen, Carley leaned her cheek against Jack's shoulder and closed her eyes. Jack tossed the van keys back to BB who trapped them against the table. Taking the napkin, he wiped off every face of each key before placing them back in his pocket.

BB's face contorted as if he just smelled a really bad fart. "What's that noise she's making?"

Mario answered, "I think she's purring."

With her eyes still closed, Carley smiled and then a, "meow," escaped her lips.

"Shite—I think I'm going to puke again," BB said.

"Relax," Jack said. "We need to talk business and maybe clear up a few loose ends."

"Like what?" Mario asked.

"One thing I keep forgetting to ask you, in all the hectic travels, did you give the silver briefcase back to your father?" Jack asked.

"Mario paused for a second before answering. "No. It's at BB's supermarket. We thought it might come in handy again, so we hid it in one of the meat coolers there."

Jack lowered an eyebrow, but then as he thought about it, he smiled. "That's actually a good idea. There are quite a few people after the money they think is in the briefcase, and you never know when that leverage might come in handy again."

"What do you mean?" BB asked.

"Think about it," Jack explained. "The Japanese are still out there working with the governor. The Polish are also working for the governor and satisfied for the time being, but who knows when they will turn on us?"

"What's the update on the House of Aliens?" Mario asked.

"That's why Shoe is late. The photography club at Wooster College was just finishing doing their magic on the viewmaster reel and the picture of the red-brick building," Jack explained. "There are two open issues, then. We have to find the House of Aliens and we need to stop the governor."

"How are we going to stop the governor?" Mario blurted. "Why don't we just give all the info we have to the FBI?"

"We could," Jack replied. "But I'm not sure how far the corruption goes or whom we can trust. Even though the governor would be removed, the Japanese might still get the grant."

"What do we do?" Mario asked.

Jack grinned. "I can only come up with one way to stop the Japanese from getting the grant, and that's for the governor to give *me* the grant."

BB almost choked as he lost his breath. "Why the effin hell would the governor give you the grant?"

"Mario just indicated we have a lot of incriminating information that would take the governor down. We need the opportunity to meet the governor and trade our silence for the 500-thousand-dollar technology grant. And remember, I have the patent for the variable speed trigger which is very new technology. If the grant money was used to support production of it, then it's all actually quite legit," Jack replied.

The waitress brought the plates of food for Jack and Carley as Mario and BB considered Jack's plan of action.

"How do you expect to get up close and personal with the governor?" BB asked.

Jack finished chewing a handful of french-fries. "It looks like you're going to be the key to our access to the governor."

"Why do I feel like something bad is going to happen to me," BB said as he pushed his glasses higher up on his nose.

"You recall Mary Ellen Wright works at the governor's mansion," Jack said.

BB's eyes narrowed as he muttered, "Something really, really bad."

"There's a reception and cocktail party at the governor's mansion where he'll announce the winner of the technology grant. We need you to convince Mary Ellen to sneak us in," Jack added.

"I haven't seen Mary Ellen for years, other than saying a quick hello at the mansion during our recent visit," BB replied. "She probably wouldn't even give me the time of day."

"Ohhh, I think she would," Jack said with a wry grin."

BB was stone faced. "What the eff did you do?"

"It wasn't me," Jack answered. "She knew you and Shoe were tight and she called him to find out your status. She was hot for your black ass in high school, and it seems that hasn't changed."

"Status—black ass?"

"Yeah. She wanted to know if you're straight, gay, married or single. In other words, she's very interested to know if your black ass is still available," Mario added.

BB turned his gaze to Mario. "What—does everyone know about this except me?"

Mario grinned. "Pretty much—but listen. It's really simple. She's involved in the Thanksgivings Day Parade, and she said if you dropped by and gave her a hello, it would mean a lot to her."

Jack added, "Make sure you understand, you need to do whatever it takes to get us into the governor's reception." He waggled his eyebrows to highlight the inference.

"Or it could take a very special helllooo," Mario interjected.

BB rolled his eyes as the sound of a motorcycle from outside the window signaled Shoe's arrival. They watched as Shoe removed the boxing headgear and tried to fix the flattened spikes of black hair as best he could. Once he entered Denny's and sat down at the booth, the others saw he carried a large, manila envelope.

Jack pointed at the envelope and said, "I hope you have something good in there."

Shoe replied, "That's why I'm late. The guy I know, who's a member of the photography club, is very good, but he's freaking tame. He blew up the photo from the viewmaster ten times magnification and then 20 times. He cropped it each time, sharpened it, but still the green sign on the far side of the house was not clear enough to read."

Shoe pulled two page-size photographs from the envelope and laid them on the table. Everyone sitting at the table each took a turn, pulling the photographs in front of themselves, trying to decipher the wording on the green sign.

"You're right Shoe, there's no way to read the wording on the sign," Jack said.

"My friend was ready to give up, but I told him he could do better. 'Do one more magnification,' I said." As he explained, Shoe pulled a last picture out of the envelope. "This picture shows the sign magnified 70 times." Putting a finger in the middle of the picture, he slid it along the table in front of Jack.

Jack tilted his face down, and the green sign filled the photo. The image was still rough, but clearly, in white letters, he could read -

Burton City

10 miles

"Burton City—that rings a bell," Jack said.

"It should," Shoe said as he pulled a roadmap from the envelope. He unfolded it before laying it down on the table in front of the team. He tapped his finger down and said, "This is Burton City. It's about halfway between Canton and Wooster and just about ten miles north of the main highway."

With his elbows on the table, BB leaned over. "So, the sign beside the House of Aliens is ten miles from Burton City."

"That's still a large area to search," Mario offered.

"Don't be such a putz," Shoe blurted as his finger danced across the map. "There are only two main roads going through Burton City. In the east-west direction, Burton City Road cuts through the town. In the north-south direction, the main thoroughfare is named, Mt. Eaton Road."

"That means the House of Aliens is ten miles down one of these roads in one of four directions from Burton City," BB added.

"Outa sight! What are we waiting for?" Mario said as he shot to his feet.

"Take a chill pill there, Mario," Jack urged. "It's 4:30 p.m. and the sun will still be bright in the sky for two more hours."

"Then, are we going tonight?" Shoe asked.

Jack nodded his chin up and down. "Damn straight we are. Our favorite highway reststop isn't far from Burton City." He pointed to a spot on the map. "We'll go home, get some sleep, and then meet at the reststop at midnight."

Mario clapped his hands together. "Right on! I love it when a plan comes together!"

Minutes later, the group members were all on the road going in different directions away from Denny's. Jack pulled up in front of Carley's apartment where she reminded him, she had to go to her father's farm the next day. She couldn't go to Burton City with him. Jack smiled, gave her a kiss, then assured her that wouldn't be a problem. Actually, he felt relieved. He wasn't sure exactly what they would do at the House of Aliens, but it was likely some illegal activities would be involved.

After Carley left the X-mobile, Jack pulled out of the parking lot and headed for his mother's house. Once inside, his mother, who heard the front door open, yelled out, "Hello, Jack!"

Jack turned right and entered the living room where his mom was sitting on the couch, watching TV. "Hi, Mom. What are you up to?"

Jack's mother pushed herself to her feet and began walking to the kitchen. She said, "There's some dinner in the oven. Let me get it out for you."

"No, that's okay. We just ate at Denny's," Jack replied.

Grabbing the door jamb, Jack's mother spun around. She folded her free hand into a fist and pressed it against her side. "You eat way too much food at Denny's."

"I'm sorry, Mom, but I really am full."

Jack's mom smiled. "Did you save room for a piece of pie?"

Jack's eyebrows rose. "Banana cream?"

"Coconut cream," she replied.

Jack grinned as he followed his mother into the kitchen. She cut a piece of pie for him and sat down across the kitchen table as he pressed the fork into the homemade pie.

"How's Carley?" she asked.

"She's doing fine. Tomorrow she's spending the day at the family farm. Now that the river water is flowing again, there's a lot of wheat to be milled," Jack answered.

"Aren't you going to help?" she asked.

Jack didn't want to tell her he had pressing plans with his friends later tonight that would leave farm work impossible for tomorrow. Rather, he changed the subject with something that had been on his mind for some time.

"Mom, you're still very active in the Polish community, are you not?"

"Yes," she replied. "I volunteer and lead a seniors yoga class at the Polish Center, and I help organize the July 4th fair every year. Why do you ask?"

Her son finished the pie and placed the fork on the plate. "Have you ever heard of Piotr Pusiak?" Jack asked.

For a moment she froze, and her face went pale. She cleared her throat. "The only Pusiak I have heard of is the one who owns the Pusiak Pastries bakery chain."

Jack nodded. "It's the same guy. I met him a few weeks ago, and he seemed an odd fellow."

Jack's mom rose to her feet, picked up the pie plate and then moved to the sink. While rinsing the plate, she said, "When you brought up Peter Pusiak, out of the blue, I wondered how you came about that. I figured it was more than the taste of coconut cream pie that brought you to think of his bakeries. I've heard he is a dangerous man, so you keep away from him."

"How do you know he goes by Peter?" Jack asked.

His mother turned and leaned back while placing both hands on the counter behind her. She took a deep breath. "I know Peter very well, or I should say your father and I knew Peter very well a lifetime ago."

"It sounds to me like there's a story there," Jack said as he looked curiously at his mother.

"Yes. It's a story I probably should have told you a long time ago." She shrugged. "But Peter was out of our lives, and it seemed better to leave it that way."

Jack rubbed his chin. "That means, at some time, Peter Pusiak was *in* our lives."

Mrs. Decker walked over to a kitchen chair and sat down. "As you know, your father served in the Korean war. Of course, he met many other soldiers, but your father didn't make friends easily in that environment. With all the deaths, his thought was it was better to lose a fellow soldier instead of a friend."

Jack leaned forward with interest and set his chin on his hand with his elbow on the table.

"Peter Pusiak was in your father's army regiment. Your father knew little of him other than his name. That changed, one day, when your father was on an unfortunate patrol. The patrol defeated the Chinese attackers, but your father got lost in the jungle. He was half-starved and his water can was empty, when after five days, Peter Pusiak found him."

"Small world," Jack said.

"Peter was the only one willing to go out and look for your father while the rest of the company just assumed your father was dead. Since Peter undertook the mission without authorization, he was put in the brig for a week."

"You're kidding? They court marshalled him?"

"They would have except the media got a hold of the story, and they proclaimed Peter a war hero. He was released, and it was then that Peter and your father became the best of friends."

"So far this is a good story," Jack concluded.

"Up until that point, yes," she agreed. "Peter and your father came back from the war and remained the best of friends. We would have dinner with Peter every Sunday, and he was very good to us, always bringing expensive gifts."

"Something must have happened," Jack surmised.

"When Peter was in Korea, he made some unscrupulous acquaintances, and through them, learned about gambling, prostitution and drugs. Your father wasn't aware of this, nor was he aware that Peter brought these skills back to America with him. These activities brought Peter the money he needed to start the bakery chain, but the chain was also a front for his illegal activities," she explained.

"And that led him to be the head of the Polish Mafia," Jack offered.

"You know this?" his mother asked as her eyes lit up. "And you still associate with him?"

"Relax, Mom. I never said I associate with him. I said I met him."

Jack's mother's face was flushed as she leaned closer to her son. "Does he know who you are? Does he know your last name?"

Jack shook his head from side to side. "No, but you look panicked. Why?"

Her face softened and her eyes were moist. For a moment she looked much older than her years. "This is a bit embarrassing. You see, your father and Peter had been back in Ohio for about five years before your father found out about Peter's illegal activities. Jack, I'm so sorry. By then it was too late!"

"Too late for what?" he asked.

"Peter Pusiak is your godfather!"

Chapter 20: Music for the Mildly Disturbed

Mario's silver Vega shot down Highway 30 toward Dalton. Just prior to it, they would reach the reststop where the four friends would meet up. Jack's jaw vibrated with a yawn while he stretched his arms outwards.

"Didn't you get enough sleep?" Mario asked as he drove the car down the dark road.

"I slept but not really well," Jack answered from the passenger seat. "I'm hopeful we'll find the House of Aliens tonight."

Mario turned his face to Jack for a moment. "I like that you're so positive. This investigation we're doing is the only excitement I get. Other than it, I'm a couch tomato."

Jack chuckled. "That would be a couch *potato*."

Mario joined Jack with his own laughter. "Hey, I'm Italian and a pasta lover, so I'll stick with couch tomato!"

Jack slapped Mario on the shoulder. "Dude, keep right. We're almost at the reststop."

Mario pressed the brake pedal, and the Vega slowed before turning into the gravel driveway of the reststop. He parked beside the Shaggin-wagon, then Jack and Mario left the Vega to join Shoe and BB under the small flood light hanging off the small brick building.

"We're going in the van, aren't we?" Shoe asked.

"That's what I thought," Jack responded.

"Where's your stuff?" Shoe said.

"What stuff?" Jack asked, his eyebrows lowered in confusion.

"What's wrong with you two whankers?" BB interjected. "We're going to the House of Aliens, and if we see an alien, we're going to freaking nab it."

"Don't have a cow. I didn't really think that far ahead," Jack admitted.

Shoe threw up his arms. "For an engineer, that's disappointing."

"What did you bring?" Mario asked.

BB slapped Mario on the back. "Follow me."

The four young men walked to the back of the Shaggin-wagon where BB pulled open the double doors. There, leaning forward, was an aluminum ladder, and beside it was a long coil of rope. BB leaned into the van and pulled out a small, black toolbox. After opening it, he pulled out several items. First there was a six-pack of black, plastic gloves and then two black balaclavas. Finally, he pulled out Shoe's magic wand vibrator and an electric toothbrush.

BB waved the electric toothbrush at Mario and Jack. "I'm bringing this for my own personal defense. Shoe has the vibrator. What are you two going to defend yourself with?"

"So, you two plan on going in looking like burglars?" Jack questioned.

BB pointed the electric toothbrush at Jack. "You aren't allowed to answer my question with a question, ya eejit."

"Think about it," Jack explained. "If you two go into the House of Aliens looking like burglars and we get caught, we'll surely get charged with break and enter or at least trespass."

BB's afro shook as he laughed. "You think somehow we can just say we got lost, if we get caught?"

"If we get caught, that's the card I will be playing," Jack continued. "I mean, look at Mario. He's wearing his white leather shoes. They're almost glow in the dark, so who in their right mind would think he was doing a break and enter? He would get a good laugh and a ride home, but you two, in your balaclavas and black gloves, would get a ride directly to jail."

BB slammed the back doors of the van closed. "Always the know-it-all engineer," he mumbled. "Let's get going as we're putting the cart before the horse. First we have to *find* the House of Aliens."

A few minutes later, they were in the Shaggin-wagon heading north to Burton City. "We are close to ten miles out, so keep an eye out for a red-brick building or the green sign," Shoe directed.

The van slowed slightly, and all four of them kept a keen eye out with two of them looking out each side window. They were disappointed to reach the outskirts of the town and not find their target.

"No worries," BB said. "We'll keep going north."

As they searched, Jack said, "Guys, there's something I said this afternoon that's bothering me."

"Like what?" Shoe asked as his gaze stayed on the passing buildings.

"I talked about the grant and said I should get it, so the Japanese don't get it. Considering we've been in this together from the start and we've all taken risks, that's not fair," Jack confessed.

"You're the one with the technical patent, so you're the only one who would qualify for the grant," BB reminded Jack.

"True enough, but I've thought of a way around that. I think if we're successful, and I get the grant, I'll give each of you a share of the company as investors. What do you think?" Jack asked.

"That's cool with me," Mario concluded.

Jack continued. "I also think, if the company does well and the funds are available, I'll buy out your shares, so you can use the funds for your own endeavors, if that's what you choose."

"That sounds like a good way to share what we've all been working on," Shoe said.

BB interrupted. "We've gone about 12 miles north of the city and there's no red building resembling what we're looking for."

"Let's turn around, and when we hit Burton City Road West, turn right," Shoe directed.

BB nodded as he pulled a U turn and headed south. When they were almost at the center of the sleepy town, the van turned west onto a pot-hole-covered road. Once out of the city limit, the road was repaved, allowing for a smoother ride. On this side of the city, the roadway curved one way, then the other, as it snaked through low hills. At the same time, oncoming night-clouds obscured the moonlight that had been helping their search.

BB, who was watching the odometer, said, "We're 15 miles from town. I'm turning around."

BB made a sharp turn, and they were on their way back to Burton City. No one spoke of it, but they were all thinking, *perhaps this wasn't their night to find the House of Aliens. Perhaps the information they collected was wrong.*

Their thoughts were broken by a yell from Mario. "Stop! I think I saw something."

BB pressed the brake pedal bringing the van to a screeching halt. "What the *eff?*" he said.

Waving his hand toward the rear of the van, Mario said, "Go back about 50 yards. There's something on the side of the road."

As the Shaggin-wagon was guided slowly backwards, Shoe watched their progress through the side-view mirror. After a minute of rearward movement, Shoe said, "I don't see anything."

Mario hit BB on the shoulder. "Stop right here and let me out."

Once the van pulled well onto the shoulder and stopped, Shoe exited the van out the passenger door followed by Mario.

As Jack and BB also exited the van, Mario walked into the thigh-high grass alongside the roadway, first peering to his right, then his left. There, once again, he caught the glint of steel he saw a few moments ago from the van. "There! There's something in the grass!" he yelled.

Led by Mario, the four young men walked west through the long grass and rocks. Once at his destination, Mario squatted down and pulled long grass and weeds from the metal object almost perfectly hidden from view. Sure enough, it was an old road sign consisting of a metal post and a square metal plate on the top. It must have been toppled quite some time ago, considering both the post and the sign were covered in orange rust.

Mario heaved on the post where it met the sign. It didn't budge. Shoe quickly joined him, and as the two of them heaved a second time, the top of the sign bent upwards until it was standing vertically, once again. As they moved to the other now visible side of the sign, they saw it was covered in mud. Mario pulled off the caked-on mud, and they could see this side of the sign was also very rusty. However, there were sections of green and white, and as BB shone a flashlight toward it, they could see letters. It was difficult to read but not impossible. As such, they all read,

Burton City

10 miles

Jack scratched his head. "I'm stumped. That looks like the right sign, but the red house isn't here."

The three others understood what Jack meant. In the picture from the viewmaster reel, the sign was beside a red-brick and wrought iron fence. As their gaze moved outwards from the road, there was a fence, and it was red, but there was no sign of brick or wrought iron. The fence they were seeing was made of six-foot planks of cedar.

They walked toward the fence where Jack, Mario and Shoe tried to peek through the gaps in the fence. Once BB was at the fence, his longer frame easily allowed him to peer over the top of it. After a few seconds he gave a loud whoop. "This is the place! The house in the middle of the estate matches the picture from the viewmaster."

"Are you sure?" Shoe asked.

BB turned and squatted down with his back leaning against the fence. "As sure as there's hair on my arse. The fences on the other three sides of the property are made of red-brick and wrought iron sections. It looks like something traumatic happened on this side, and based on the condition of the damaged sign, I suspect a truck must have crashed through here."

"The fence on this side was replaced!" Jack added in his excitement.

"Guys, we're finally here. Are we doing this?" Mario asked.

"Grab the ladder and the rope," Jack directed. "Leave the burglar stuff."

BB and Shoe went back to the van, and when they returned with the ladder and rope, but not the burglar gear, Jack exhaled with relief. The fact BB had his electric toothbrush hanging out of his front pocket and Shoe carried the mother of all vibrators, would only add to their story of four lost, crazy guys, in the event they were caught.

BB leaned the ladder against the fence, allowing Jack, Mario and Shoe to scamper up and then jump down into the property. BB followed and after he was on the estate side, pulled the ladder over, hiding it behind some overgrown bushes. As they squatted down, they looked at the house and saw very few lights. There was one light under the center of the roof covering the long front porch. There were three windows on this side of the large house lit by interior lights, and the rest of the house was dark.

"What do you think?" BB whispered.

"Let's head for the back of the house," Jack suggested.

Slumped over, they shuffled across the recently cut grass toward the rear corner of the large building. If anyone would have been watching, "chimpanzees" would have been the first word coming to mind. As they made their way across the property, Jack saw there were three stories, and on this shorter side there were four windows on each level. It might have surprised his friends to see so few lights lit, but it was 1:30 a.m. and Jack remembered overhearing the governor. He said there were only ten residents of the House of Aliens even though, for money laundering purposes, they had 30 residents on the books.

Once they arrived at the house, they pasted their backs to the brick wall, breathing heavily with their exertions. Jack didn't have to say any words as he ran around the back of the building, staying close to the wall. He knew his three friends would follow, and they did. They ducked under each dark window they passed until they reached the middle of the structure where they found a back door.

"Try it," Jack whispered.

BB wrapped his fingers around the long, silver handle and pulled. He pulled a second time with more force, but the door didn't budge. His head nodding from side to side told Jack the door was locked.

Jack, followed by his friends, slid along the back wall. At each dark window, he pulled upwards on the lower frame. The first two were locked, but the third window creaked open. Quietly, Jack pulled the lower frame up until it was six inches open. He turned, holding his hand out and was about to ask, but BB knew what Jack wanted. BB laid the flashlight in Jack's palm before the words came out.

Raising the lower frame to its fully open position, Jack pulled aside the sheer curtain within and poked his head into the room. His hand with the flash light followed, and as he pressed the switch, the far wall was lit by a large circle of yellow light. He moved the projected light around the room and saw it was a small, unoccupied bedroom. *Awesome*, he thought as he put his free hand on the window frame and pushed his body through. As his hips passed the window, he rolled to a one-legged, kneeling position just before BB's face appeared through the window. Jack held up his hand, and for a second time, he inspected the drab room. Once he was satisfied, he motioned for BB to come through followed by Shoe and Mario.

"No turning back now," Jack offered.

"Actually, that isn't correct," Mario said. "We could go back out the window and climb back over the wall. It's about 20 minutes back to the reststop, and we could all be back in our beds an hour after that."

"That's not what I meant," Jack whispered through clenched teeth. "I meant, we've so much invested, and we've come so far. We can't turn back now," Jack explained.

Mario had a confused look on his face. "I'm not saying I want to go back. I'm just saying we could if we wanted to."

"You're thick as a brick," BB said as Jack moved to the door. There was a small squeak, as Jack turned the door handle. He opened it a crack and peered down the hallway. It was dark except for a red and silver emergency light at the end of it.

BB pressed his hand onto Jack's shoulder, coaxing his attention back into the abandoned bedroom. "You better let me go first."

"Why?" Jack asked.

"You three have glow in the dark faces and I'm black, so I have a lot more stealth capability," BB said.

Shoe snickered, but Jack knew it was a good idea. "Okay, you go first.

We'll be right behind you."

After opening the door, BB was out in the dark hallway. He didn't waste time in shuffling down it's relatively short length. Four faces peered around the corner, one on top of the other, as they looked toward what they knew was the front of the house. This hallway leading toward it was also dark with only the light at the end to guide them. Once again, BB pasted himself against the wall as he moved down the hallway. At the end of it, he stopped abruptly and squatted down. Behind him, the other three musketeers did the same. BB raised his fist, and with his other hand, he pointed toward the front of the house. He then pulled this hand back and raised two fingers before finally pointing toward the front of the house for a second time.

What the fuck, Shoe thought. BB's acting like we're Navy Seals.

No matter the theatrics, they understood BB's message. As they peered into the front entryway, they saw a large cubicle. The lower half was covered with paneling, and the top half was constructed of glass. It was wide enough to cover the entire front entryway except for a small passageway allowing for the movement of patients or visitors moving in and out of the building. Inside the large cubicle there were two women in white uniforms. One was slim while the other was easily six feet tall and heavy set. It was easy to see who handled security, should the need arise.

BB poked his head out, peering around the corner. The long hallway to their left was as dark as the one they were in. On their right was the only other hallway ending at the front entryway, and it was the only one that was lit.

BB turned toward Jack and whispered, "We need to get down the hallway to our right."

"Understood," Jack replied.

The four of them slunk back into the darkness of the hallway and huddled together. Jack said, "I'll give the signal when the women aren't looking. Then we'll silently shoot across to the cubicle, keeping very low. Once there, we'll mold ourselves against the floor while keeping us out of sight of the women."

Before waiting for any feedback, Jack headed back to the front hallway with his three friends crowded behind him. One woman was sitting facing the front door of the house, but the larger one was talking and pacing back and forth from one side of the cubicle to the other. *C'mon—c'mon* Jack thought. *Stop moving your fat ass around.*

Jack's wish was granted as the chime of a bell was heard. The heavy-set woman moved to the far corner of the large cubicle and pulled two pieces of toast from the top of the toaster. She opened the cupboard door and searched for something to spread on them. Seeing her distracted, Jack took the opportunity. His body shot forward while bent over 90 degrees, and slid across the hallway until he was against the paneled half-wall. BB, Shoe and Mario followed as they spread out across the wall, hidden from view. They inched forward, crawling like soldiers, propelled by the motion of their knees and elbows. They did this until all four of them were in the lit-up hallway. Once they were out of view of the two women, they saw their path was blocked by a heavy metal door, and set within it was a large wire-mesh window.

BB led the way once again as he pulled on the silver handle. He cringed, suspecting an alarm might sound, but there was only silence as it opened, and they passed through. Looking further down the long hallway, they saw the walls were painted light-green, and there were six doors on either side.

Jack held his finger up to his lips and whispered, "shhhh," as he saw three of the doors were propped open.

As they walked by the first two closed doors, opposite to each other, they saw red lights pulsing above each door. At each of these doors, hanging on the wall, was a clipboard and a key.

BB pulled on the door as he inspected the key. Turning, he said, "The doors are locked from the outside."

They passed two more doors, one having the red light pulsing, and the other didn't have the light illuminated. This door didn't have a clipboard.

Jack whispered, "The red light above the doors means there's someone in the room."

Shoe's hand tightened on the coil of rope slung over his shoulder. "Fucking aliens," he said. "We're finally going to catch one."

Once again, Jack lifted his finger to his pursed lips. "The next door is open, and the red light is on. Everyone be on high alert."

As they moved into the doorway, then through it, they saw before them a very bland room. The walls were covered with the same green paint, and there was a narrow bed tucked into the far corner. The sparse room had a chair in the middle of it, and sitting on it was a man who was in front of an easel, painting. He was so engrossed in his work, he didn't hear the four men walk in until Jack lightly knocked on the wall.

The man turned his head and smiled through a thick beard. He rose to his feet. "Ah visitors."

Jack smiled back and said, "Hello."

The bearded man was casually dressed in light-brown slacks and a polo sweater. His brown loafers finished the less than interesting look. "It's a bit late for visitors. Are you new arrivals?"

Shoe leaned toward Jack's ear and whispered, "What's he hiding under that beard?"

Jack noticed the accent the man spoke with and replied, "My apologies, but we are indeed new arrivals. Where are you from?"

Again, Shoe whispered to Jack, "See that painting. No one paints that badly. In fact, it looks like an alien landscape. We should take him."

The man's eyes glazed over as he said, "I'm from far away." He remained frozen for a few seconds before he continued. "But soon I will leave here."

Jack nodded and said, "That's awesome. We'll let you get back to your painting." Jack turned and pushed his three friends out of the room.

Once they were back in the hallway, Shoe said, "What are you doing? He's small enough that we can easily take him."

"True enough, but he's not going anywhere," Jack said. "We have two more rooms to check."

Jack led them to the next room on their right. As they came closer, they could hear the sound of music, and once in the doorway, Jack saw it originated from the room in question. This room looked similar to the last one except there was no easel, and on a chair sat an attractive woman. She wore a beautiful dress, although it had a style that belonged in the 1930's. Held to her chin was a violin which she was playing with her eyes closed. Again, Jack knocked on the wall to catch her attention, which it did. Her eyes opened, and she shot to her feet.

"I didn't mean to startle you, especially with the beautiful music you were playing," Jack offered.

The woman tilted her head shyly as her hands slid down the sides of her dress. Her face was flushed as she blushed. "I always like visitors. I just wish they could give me a little more notice."

Jack said, "We won't be any trouble. We just wanted to say hello."

Her face thrust up and her eyes went bright. "Will you stay for some tea?"

"Tea?" Jack asked.

"Of course. We must have tea." She lifted her hand and pressed together the tip of one finger and her thumb. She shook it as if an invisible bell was there. "They will bring tea in a moment. Would you like to sit down?" She opened her arm, offering the side of the empty room.

One side of Jack's lips turned up in a grin. "We have one more visitor to see, and then we'll be back."

She raised up on her tip toes. "Make sure you come back soon. I'll be leaving here very shortly."

Jack funneled his friends out of the room until they were back out in the hallway.

"Holy shite," BB said. "She's having an effin hard time assimilating."

Jack headed for the last open door and entered under the flashing red light. Once he was there with his friends, their jaws dropped. In this room the bed and a small table were the only two pieces of furniture within. In front of the table was an older man who was bald yet had a long, white beard hanging down to his navel. More surprising than this was the fact he was butt naked with his clothes pooled at his feet.

The man was motionless, his eyes fixed on the large, black dot painted on the green wall. He didn't notice the entry of the four men until Jack issued a, "Hello."

The old man's body didn't move, but his face turned toward the visitors. "Before you ask dumb questions, I'll tell you right now, I'm fucking nuts and I'll never get out of here!"

On the last word, the frail man lifted his arm. A wrinkled finger curled out and pointed at Jack as his head leaned back. At the same time, his crazy, black eyes bored into the group of four men.

"What the fuck?" Shoe whispered. "He's scaring the shit out of me!"

As the naked man's free arm tilted down to the small table in front of him, the strange, old man picked up a small white and red box. At first, Jack thought they were Marlboro cigarettes, but he could read the wording and realized they were actually *Marboro* candy cigarettes. The man's finger began vibrating toward the group, while in his other hand, the Marboro box was turned upside down. Four candy cigarettes dropped to the floor, and as they bounced, the man raised the open end of the box to his mouth. His cheeks blew up, filling with air, then, as he expelled the air, a high-pitched screech came from the box.

"Faccia de figa!" Mario said.

They fell over each other and spilled back into the hallway. The old man followed as he continued to blow into the box. Jack jumped out of his path, not wanting to catch whatever affliction the man had, whether it be of this world or some other. The old man moved quickly, reaching the red, metal box on the far wall of the hallway. He pulled the lever of the fire alarm, and the sound of a whooping, loud alarm filled the building. The old man pulled the candy box from his lips but maintained his finger pointed at Shoe.

Shoe's entire body was vibrating. "Go back to where you came from you—you Spawn of Satan!"

Initially, Jack thought Shoe was shaking with fear until he saw the giant enabled vibrator held tightly in his white-knuckled fist. Jack's focus returned to the problem at hand. He saw, with the alarm set off, all the locked doors were automatically opened. There was a loud yell, and a painting came flying out from one of the doorways, crashing against the far wall. The bearded man rushed out of the room and yelled at the boys. "How am I supposed to paint with all this noise?" He strode toward the four young men with angry, determined strides.

As he walked past the next door, a blur appeared behind him as a violin crashed into the back of his head. It shattered into a thousand pieces as he fell to the floor. The girl in the pretty dress held her quivering hand to her chin as she yelled, "Run for your lives!"

"This is like a horror movie!" BB screamed.

"It can't be!" Mario yelled back. "None of us are in a wheelchair!"

Jack was still on the saner side of panic as he looked down the hallway, trying to find a point of exit. Coming out of another doorway was a small man in a robe and slippers. He was pacing from one side of the hallway to the other. Each time he hit the wall, he would turn like some type of psycho wind-up toy and say, "This is not a drill. This is not a drill."

Just beyond him was a mountain of a man. He looked like a long-haired biker, covered in tattoos. Leaning back against the wall with his eyes closed, his face was set in a grimace. His hand was in the shape of an odd fist with his fingers straight except for the last set of knuckles that were curled in. He was repeatedly hitting the strange fist into his forehead, and each time he said, "The fucking bells! The fucking bells!"

BB, wide-eyed, stared at the scene and hollered, "They're as mad as an army of blind frogs in a box of fat crickets!"

Jack saw enough. He yelled, "Make a run for it!"

Led by Jack, they sped for the door at the end of the hallway. Jack jumped over the bearded man and spun out of the reach of the girl. He timed his run to pass the robed man, and finally, he steered well clear of the biker dude. As Jack pressed the handle bar on the door, it flung open, and he heard two thumps. The first was the door hitting the heavy-set woman, and the second was the heavy-set woman getting pasted against the wall. Just behind this carnage, the thinner woman was thrown back off her feet, allowing the four men to fly by her.

Jack made a right turn at the front cubicle and sped down the passageway toward the front door. In full flight, he lifted his foot and kicked the silver handle bar of the front door. It flung open, and all four of them were in the safety of the night air. Jack slid to a stop, waiting for his three friends to pass by. As he did this, he looked up at the stonework above the doorway. There, chiseled into the stone was a phrase. It read,

> *Maison D'aliénés.*

As they continued their run down the driveway to the main gate, Jack thought about the etched words. They were somewhat familiar. Turning the corner, the group ran to the main road, then to the van. BB jumped in and brought the engine to life with a roar.

Mario said, "What about the ladder?"

Shoe, through panting breaths, said, "Don't worry about the god damn ladder. We have to get out of here before the police arrive."

With everyone in the van, BB floored the gas pedal. The rear wheels spun until the Shaggin-wagon shot forward like a bullet.

Jack was sitting in the passenger seat still trying to catch his breath. He thought on the phrase in the stone, and then he hit his forehead with his hand. "You fucking idiots!" he yelled.

"Dude—chillax! We got away," Shoe said.

Jack said, "Not that. Not that at all. We're all freaking morons!"

"I'm not following you," BB replied.

"Above the door, it read - Maison D'aliénés. Do you know what that means?" Jack asked.

Mario answered. "I remember Maison means *house* in French. So, Maison D'aliénés means House of Aliens, but we know that."

Jack shook his head from side to side. "There are no freaking aliens," he mumbled.

"You're still not making sense," BB said as he drove the van through Burton City.

Jack looked from one to the other of his three friends. "I said I would follow the alien trail as long as things made sense. Now, it finally *does* make sense. In college, I took French as an elective, and Mario is correct in that the first word means house."

"And?" Mario said.

"The second word doesn't mean *aliens*," Jack explained. "*Aliénés* doesn't translate to *alien*. The actual English translation of the French word *aliénés* is—*Lunatics*."

"What!" BB yelled.

"Yes," Jack replied. "We finally found the House of Aliens, but there are no aliens. It's a House of Lunatics—an insane asylum!"

There was silence until they returned to the reststop. Before they got out, Shoe said, "What about the professor, the King of the Hobos and all the evidence he has?"

"The universe is huge," Jack answered. "There are a billion solar systems and even more planets. I would say, in all of that, thinking we're the only living beings, is naïve. I'm sure there are aliens out there. There's a very good possibility they've been here, but not now, and not here in Ohio."

Shoe was still having difficulty accepting the reality they discovered. He grabbed Jack's collar and said, "The governor called it the House of Aliens. Even the Japanese called it the House of Aliens."

Jack put his hand on Shoe's shoulder. "We're Americans. For many years we've been spoiled, and we tend to be a bit arrogant and lazy. It sounds like there are people who just find it easier to call it a bastardized name like, House of Aliens."

Shoe's eyes were moist as he whispered. "What are we going to do?"

"We need to save the aliens, power tools and wall plugs for another day," Jack said. "Now, we can be much more focused on the one task we have left."

"The governor?" Mario said.

"Oh yeah." Jack spoke with a renewed resolve in his voice. "We're going to make sure the Japanese don't get the technology grant. We're the only arrogant, lazy, American bastards who are getting that freaking money!"

Chapter 21: Oink da Boink

Jim Huber took his family to the Canton Thanksgiving Day Parade every year. It was always on the third Thursday of November, and this was his family's favorite holiday. This year, Jim was fortunate enough to have a prime spot right on the curb. They were situated just after the main intersection where the head of the parade had made a right turn and was now flowing by them. Two bands walked past with their instruments swaying back and forth to the beat of the music. Between them was a group of trick riders, and a farmer walking with the biggest cow he'd ever seen.

His wife stood beside him, clapping her hands each time a new float turned the corner and passed by them. His ten-year-old son stood on his other side and wasn't as excited as he was in years past. On the other hand, his four-year-old daughter Margie, was sitting on his shoulders, and this year, she was old enough to really appreciate the music but especially the clowns that intermittently danced by. They had watched for half an hour, and Margie had a perpetual smile on her face only broken by her laughter as she clapped her hands nonstop.

They heard cheers from around the corner where the remaining floats had not yet reached the main intersection. First, there was one roar, then another. Each was louder as the parade's signature float came closer. Governor Breed used some of the tax dollars to sponsor a large float celebrating the first meeting of the pilgrims with the native Americans. On the float, the execution of pilgrim John Smith was being played out. As the story goes, when Pocahontas's father was going to kill John Smith with his war club, his daughter placed her head on top of John's, forcing her father to cancel the execution.

Margie made her father read the story of Pocahontas every night for the last week in preparation for the parade, so she squealed with delight when they finally saw the large, green tractor turn the corner. The even larger three-level float made a wide arc behind it and came toward their location. Each level of the float was four feet high with the lower one shrouded in fake, green shrubs. The middle level had a ledge, and on it was a multitude of sculptures of forest animals. There were deer, turkeys, rabbits, bull frogs and even a black bear. The top level was surrounded by a waist-high fence made of old timbers, and on it stood a pilgrim representing John Smith, but Pocahontas was nowhere to be seen.

Margie's constant, irritating clapping stopped and she said, "Where is

Pocahontas?"

Her father said, "I'm sure she'll come out in a minute."

But still, only the pilgrim waved from the top platform of the float.

"Where is Pocahontas!" Margie yelled in a high-pitched voice so much louder than expected from such a small, sweet girl.

Jim Huber hoped Pocahontas would appear soon and salvage the parade for his daughter.

"I want Pocahontas! I want Pocahontas!" Margie yelled, beginning a cadence where, on each repetition, she slapped her father on one ear, then the other.

As Margie continued to scream, the float was now passing right in front of them. His son tugged on his father's coat sleeve. "What's going on, Dad? There are two huge clown feet hanging out of the shrubs at the back of the float."

Jim Huber now saw it as well. The two huge, red feet were upside down and pressed out through the curtain surrounding the lower level.

Through his daughter's constant pummeling on his ears and her crying screams, he heard his wife's voice. "That doesn't look very safe. Do you see how the whole float is rocking back and forth? The suspension must be shot!"

Jim didn't answer because he had no answers. This day with his family was ruined. His eyes narrowed as he looked up at the figure of John Smith with a wide smile on his face, waving from the top platform of the float. Jim mumbled, "Fucking pilgrims."

One day earlier:

The doorbell rang and Mary Decker rose from her seat in the dining room. "I'll be right back."

Carley, BB and Shoe had all arrived at the Decker household within the last 15 minutes. As Mrs. Decker pulled open the front door, it was to see Mario's wide smile.

"Hello Mrs. D," Mario said as he walked into the front hallway.

"Hey Mario," Jack's mother replied before she poked her head out the doorway. First, she looked down the road in one direction, then the other.

She followed Mario into the dining room and said, "I don't see how Jack can be late for a lunch with his friends that he organized."

As Mario sat down, he said, "I'm sure he'll be here in a moment."

"It's just so embarrassing," Mrs. Decker replied.

The flushness of her cheeks instantly left when she heard the front door being opened. Jack dropped off some small boxes on the kitchen counter before coming into the dining room. He kissed his mom on the forehead. "Hello and sorry I'm late."

She rose from her seat and said, "The sandwiches are made and in the fridge. I'll get them."

As Jack sat down, Shoe said, "You're lucky Jack; your mom is the best. Did your meeting run late?"

Jack brought his finger up to his lips while shaking his head from side to side. "There was no meeting. I just wanted to pick up some dessert for us to have after the sandwiches."

Mrs. Decker came back into the dining room with a frown. "Jack, are those three boxes of sweets from Pusiak's Pastries?"

"You know they are, Mom," Jack replied. "The label on each box says so."

Mrs. Decker put her fists on her hips. "I thought you were going to keep clear of Peter Pusiak?"

Jack tilted his head toward his mom. "I am. It's just three boxes of pastries. It doesn't mean I'm going to join the Mafia!"

Jack's mom went back into the kitchen and promptly returned with two trays of sandwiches. On her second trip, she brought a party pack of soda pop and placed it in the center of the table.

She gave her son an embarrassing kiss on the cheek, then waved to the group. "Have fun. I have my own lunch with a girlfriend, but I hope to see you all again very soon." She gave a special wink to Carley and then scooted out of the room.

They all picked up a sandwich. Jack took a large bite and after he swallowed, said, "I'm going to warn everyone right now. I don't want to hear one word about aliens, power tools or wall plugs."

Shoe, with a disappointing look on his face, was the last to nod his agreement.

"Are we all set for tomorrow?" Jack asked.

"I don't think I'll ever be ready for this," BB responded. "You guys want me to flirt and chat up Mary Ellen Perfect Tits."

"Mario swallowed his mouthful of sandwich and said, "Flirt or do whatever else you have to as long as the result is us getting snuck into the governor's reception."

"She might just smack me in my effin face," BB said. "After all, she liked me in high school, and she let everyone know. When I refused her advances, she was totally pissed."

"I talked to her," Shoe said. "She's still crazy about you. She made it very clear she was very interested in meeting you at the parade."

"I still don't understand, why the parade?" BB added.

Shoe just finished a mouthful of sandwich. "I love these tuna sandwiches!" He took a moment to savor the after taste before turning his face to BB. "She insisted you wear a clown suit, which she has arranged for you with the company of clowns who are hired to perform at the parade. She didn't say it directly, but I got the sense, even though she is hot for you, she wants you to feel some pain."

"Pain?" BB said.

"Yes—payback for your embarrassing high school rejection of her," Shoe clarified.

BB shook his head from side to side. "Freaking shite. Why do women have such a long memory?" he mumbled.

Carley snickered just before Jack said to Shoe, "What are you going to do at the parade?"

"I'm going to mingle in the crowd and be ready to jump in, if need be," Shoe said.

BB lifted his head. "Jump into what?"

Shoe smiled wide. "I'm going to be your spotter!"

BB raised his face, glaring at Shoe. "If you're so sure about how she will feel, why would I need an eejit spotter?"

Shoe said, "Well, we all know it's extremely rare that I'm wrong, but if I see you in a crash and burn scenario, I'll pull you to safety."

Mario turned his sandwich and held it like a model plane. He rolled it toward the plate as he made a sound similar to a sputtering engine. "Ya, crash and burn!" The final word was emphasized by the sandwich squashing into the plate.

BB propped his forehead against his two palms. "Unbelievable. This is such bull-freaking-shite."

Jack rose and walked into the kitchen. On his return, his arms were full with the three boxes of pastries which he set on the table. "Dig in," he said.

Shoe asked Jack, "Are you and Mario all set for the parade?"

"Absolutely," Jack replied. "A group of men from the *Polish American Society* are right behind the float Mary Ellen will be on. I've made arrangements for Mario and I to be part of that group."

"Hold on a minute," Mario said. "I'm not going with the Polish group. My father is on the council of the *Italian Americans of Ohio*, and, with a lot of effort, I've arranged for Jack and I to ride with them."

"Dream on," Jack said through a chuckle. "Why would I ride a minibike when the Polish group ride in very cool go-karts."

Mario glared at Jack. "Why would I wear the stupid red pants and white shirt of the Polish? And I wouldn't be caught dead in those Fez hats with the withered feathers coming out of the top!"

Jack aggressively pointed at Mario. "The Italians wear the same red and white clothes, but they also have a green vest that doesn't match at all. Their headgear is even more asinine. I'm not sure what it's called, but it's just like the hat Napoleon wore except it has a large feather hanging off the front. What's with the feather, and why are they wearing a French hat?"

Mario slammed his fist on the table. "The hat is called a *bicorne* hat, and it's Italian!"

"Why would Napoleon wear an Italian hat?" Jack questioned.

"You know, you ride me up a wall!" Mario exclaimed.

A loud guffaw escaped from Jack's lips. "Oh, really—because you actually *drive* me up a wall!"

"Hold on guys!" Shoe exclaimed as he stretched his arms out between the two verbal combatants. "Italy and Poland both have a very proud heritage. Both countries have a lot of similarities and are good at similar old-world skills."

"What the hell are you talking about?" Jack asked. "What similar skills do the two countries have?"

Shoe's lips began to quiver and then the corners curled up slightly. They continued upwards as his entire face smiled. "Well, you're both good at surrendering!" Shoe blurted out just before the full-on laugh exploded from between his teeth.

Jack slapped his forehead. "What a moron."

Carley placed her hand on Jack's. "Guys, it's a special holiday weekend. We should all be thankful for what we have."

Jack slouched back in the chair and motioned toward Mario. "What could you possibly be thankful for?"

Quick as a whip, Mario responded, "For not being Polish."

"Jack wrinkled his face and said, "Oh, isn't everyone a Comedian today."

Carley squeezed Jack's hand as she snickered. "That was actually pretty good, Mario."

Jack pulled his hand out from under hers. "Maybe you should date your sex therapist," he retorted as he nodded his chin toward Mario.

Carley kissed Jack on the cheek. "No way. Italians are too emotional, and you're so cute when you're sensitive."

As the banter intensified, BB sat back in his chair and watched his friends. They were crazy and fun to be around, but there was very serious business to be taken care of tomorrow. He had to convince Mary Ellen to sneak them into the governor's reception. What if he didn't succeed, and her real goal was to make a fool of him while using the opportunity to slap him in the face? He started to lose his confidence, and the beads of sweat began to form on his forehead.

That night, Carley and Shoe slept over at Jack's house. BB and Mario made the short drive home but returned early the next morning. BB used his van to go to the clown company's tent, accompanied by Shoe—his effin spotter. Jack and Carley left in the X-mobile, and Mario, who was still sore about the conversation the night before, drove his Vega to the staging area for the *Italian Americans of Ohio*.

By 10:00 a.m. they were all ready as a bugle blared, indicating the beginning of the parade. BB rose from his seated position on the curb and heard music start to play from well ahead of the clown contingent's position. It was jumbled, as several bands at different locations in the parade played at the same time. It took several moments for movement from the front of the parade to cascade to them, but finally it did.

BB was wearing large, red clown shoes, and above them, were white and red striped pants. He also wore a pink shirt covered by a yellow vest and black suspenders. The other clowns thought his hair was fine other than it needed, and was given, a dusting of white powder. His face was painted white in contrast to the red lips and oversized rubber nose.

After walking with the parade for five minutes, he mumbled, "I look like a freaking clown."

"That's because you're dressed like a freaking clown!" was replied back to him.

BB looked down to see four adolescent boys standing on the curb. He estimated they were each about 14 years old. The blonde kid said, "You were using your *out loud* voice, ya idiot clown!"

BB just shook his head and ignored the sarcastic kid, but the four youngsters skipped along, keeping pace with BB.

The blonde kid asked, "Why are you so tall?"

BB replied, "Why are you so effin ugly?"

The kid put his hand atop his eyes, blocking out the sun. He looked at BB's hair which was a mix of brown and white, but was highlighted by the massive cowlick. "Is that your real hair?" the kid asked.

"Is that your real face, or did your neck throw up?" BB quipped.

The blonde kid spat on the ground and waved at BB. "See ya! Wouldn't wanna be ya!" he yelled.

Without looking at the punk, BB snapped back, "Smell ya! Shouldn't have to tell ya!" He kept walking while raising his right hand, giving the kid the finger. BB lifted the frilly cuff of his shirt and checked his watch. *Well, I better get going*, he thought. Seeing the Pocahontas float 50 yards ahead, he increased the pace of his long strides toward it.

Jack and nine other members of the *Polish American Society* were seated in their slick, white go-karts. They had wide, black wheels and resembled open-wheeled racers. They made small circles around each other, and the bystanders cheered whenever they came close to the crowd on the curb. The blood-thirsty cheers were even louder when two riders would almost collide. Jack pushed the fez backwards on his head, so the feather did not obstruct his view. The other drivers, although much older, were well versed in the choreographed, *almost-collisions*. On the other hand, he was told to just keep going straight and don't hit anything.

He saw clowns walking back and forth along the sidelines, but they were short in stature. Then, he saw the longer legs, covered in red and white stripes, pass by him. He looked up and laughed at how ridiculous BB looked. BB peeked down, saw his friend laughing and lifted his middle finger into the air for a second time.

Jack watched as BB made his way to the Pocahontas float. Mary Ellen, dressed as the native American, put her hand to her mouth and laughed when she saw BB. He made the best of it, giving a formal bow. When he rose up, she leaned down, allowing for a brief conversation. At one point, BB pointed to his chest as Pocahontas giggled, then nodded her head up and down. Even from this distance, Jack could see the look of surprise on BB's face as he pointed to the lower tier of the float.

That's when Jack heard a higher-pitched motor rev just before he felt a foot hit him in the side. His go-kart slid sideways as he saw Mario glide past on the minibike. When Mario reached the front of the Polish riders, he hit the brake and the minibike skidded around to a stop facing the go-karts.

Jack wondered, *what the fuck* as he saw Mario, in the stupid Napoleon hat, put his hand sideways into the vest. There was no voice, but he mouthed the words, "Game on."

A few moments earlier, from his initial position behind the Polish contingent, Mario also saw BB the clown. He noticed BB struggling with the encounter, and, in that moment, he made a critical decision. BB needed a distraction!

Now, Mario was driving back toward one of the other go-karts as three other minibikes drove through the Polish contingent, from their rear. The minibikes side bumped the go karts, and several of the forward go-karts started to circle back.

An older Polish rider saw Mario coming toward him, whereby he accelerated to meet him in a demented game of chicken. In the end, Mario swerved, and as he passed the side of the Polish rider, the old man snickered and yelled, "Fucking coward!"

It was now complete chaos with go-karts and minibikes circling each other. Arms and legs would thrust out in an attempt to dislodge the enemy. The crowd thought it was all part of the act, and they would gasp each time there was an *almost-collision*. They would also cheer when a minibike wobbled, or when two go-karts would bounce off each other.

To make matters worse, they were in the heart of the parade route where an announcer was describing the parade as it went by. The announcer only moonlighted at the parade. His real job was as the announcer at the local college football games, and, when he saw the action, he went into full play-by-play mode. He called the action by the numbers on the go-karts and minibikes, and somehow the people viewing the parade from the east side of the street would roar every time the Polish riders won a challenge. Those on the west side would yell and throw their fists into the air every time the Italians got the better of the Polish.

It was complete bedlam. The action was at a frenzy when the announcer yelled over the PA system, "Oh, the humanity!"

Jack was giving as good as he got. His pant leg was ripped at the knee, and he had a bruise on his arm. He saw the Pocahontas float ahead of them was making a right turn, and they would be next to go around the bend. It forced them to get in formation and end the battle. Once they were around the corner, they left the roar of the battle behind them. He saw two older Polish riders beside him grin from under their fighter pilot, mirrored sunglasses and give each other a high-five.

Beyond them, Jack scrutinized, first the float, then the crowd. BB was nowhere to be seen! However, he did see Shoe in the crowd beside the float. Jack raised his arms in the air and shrugged. Shoe grinned as he looked at the Pocahontas float with the big, red clown feet hanging out the back. He pointed at it and then at Jack, finally giving Jack a return thumb's up.

Jack was relieved. He didn't understand what was going on, but the thumbs up from Shoe told him things were okay. As he continued to drive forward, he thought, *there was only one thing that wasn't okay*. He didn't understand why the young girl, sitting on her father's shoulders, was screaming and battering her father's ears. After all, it was Thanksgiving!

Chapter 22: Herbally Enhanced

"This is far out," Mario said. "We've never used the hot tub this late in the year."

"I think you just cursed us," Shoe said, looking out from the warmth of the hot tub, protected by the overhanging roof, from which he now noticed the light snowfall.

BB lowered himself down in the hot water until only his head was exposed. "It's a surprisingly early snow for November, and here comes another surprise that'll make the night a whole lot crazier."

Shoe and Mario turned their heads to look in the same direction as BB, to see Jack and Carley approaching, hand in hand.

"Hey guys," Jack said. "I hope you don't mind, but I brought Carley along."

Carley took a step forward and beamed a smile. "Hi. Where can I get changed?"

Jack pointed to Mario's front door and said, "You can change in there. I'll be along in a minute."

As soon as the door closed behind her, Mario slapped the water and said to Jack, "What are you doing?"

"Don't have a cow. What's up?" Jack replied.

Mario explained, "We used this hot tub when we were teenagers, and now, after your return to Ohio, we come here almost every Monday night during football season. Although we've never spelled out rules, it was and is quite obvious this event is for *men* only."

Jack rolled his eyes. "Are you kidding me? Carley has been part of our adventures almost right from the start. She deserves to be let in the hot tub."

"I'm not going to waste my breath," Mario stated. "We'll take a vote, and my vote is no women in the hot tub." He looked to BB to vote next.

"I believe in traditions," BB said almost apologetically. "My vote is no women."

Jack's eyes bored into BB. "Really? You know slavery used to be a tradition!" He turned his gaze to Shoe. "It looks like you have the deciding vote."

Shoe fidgeted and looked up at Jack. "Sorry, but I don't have much choice. I forgot my swim shorts, so I'm sitting here dressed commando. You really think you want her in the tub with me?"

Jack looked confused.

"Exactly," Shoe said. "My vote is no women in the hot tub—at least for tonight."

Their discussion was interrupted by the creak of the front door opening. They all looked over to see Carley standing just outside the doorway in the skimpiest string bikini. It was bright-red and barely covered areas only Jack knew intimately. BB, Mario and Shoe all stared with their jaws slack and with a new found envy for Jack.

Mario was the first to react. "You must be freezing out there. Come sit beside me on my bench."

BB added, "Over here beside me is better. You get a better view of the snowfall."

As the two men made their bids, Carley slowly shuffled over to Jack, curious about his friend's creepy invitations.

Jack firmly grasped her arm and pointed to the empty bench at the far side of the hot tub. "That's where I sit, so wait for me there while I get changed. Make sure you don't go near Mario or BB, otherwise you might catch their 'moronitis,' and make absolutely sure you don't go near Shoe otherwise you might catch—well—who knows what you might catch…"

Carley still looked confused as she lowered down into the tub and took her place on Jack's bench. At the same time, Jack went into the house and changed into his own swim suit. With worries about Carley left alone, he was beside her in record time.

Mario said to Carley, "It's lucky for you this is a Saturday night. We normally meet here on Monday nights while watching the football game. If it was Monday, we would have turned you away."

Carley smiled sarcastically. "Wow! I'm surely blessed. Maybe Saturday night can be Amish Lady's Night!"

Mario laughed. "That's ridiculous. What would we do?"

She splashed water playfully at Mario. "You men could be our bitches. You could wear thongs or speedos and serve us drinks and snacks. Doesn't that sound like fun!"

Now, it was Jack's turn to laugh as Mario, with a frown on his face, reached over and turned on the TV. He hopped through a few channels until a hockey game appeared.

Mario leaned back, and they watched for a few minutes until he said, "Do you guys understand the rules?"

"Sure, that and the Theory of Effin Relativity," BB replied sarcastically.

"I can't see the puck. It's too small," Shoe complained as he began to scoot over to a better vantage point closer to Carley.

Jack snapped his fingers and glared at Shoe. "Get back to your spot!"

Shoe snickered, then slid back to his original location under the warm bubbles of the jet that, thankfully, hid his junk from the others.

"This game is nothing like football," Mario observed. "Some of the fast skaters have Swedish names on their backs. You wouldn't catch Swedish pussies playing American football."

"I'm not sure I would call them pussies," Jack countered. "That puck is flying around really fast, and they're battering the hell out of each other, yet none of them are wearing helmets."

"Just goes to show you there's a fine line between being very brave and very stupid," Shoe added.

"What do you mean?" Mario asked.

"Well, take that guy who just flattened the other player into the boards. It looks like it was well done and took loads of bravery to do it at the speed he was going. If he was off, even by an inch, he splatters his head into the glass. Everyone watching would just say, 'What a freaking moron.'"

BB laughed. "Hero to zero—just like that."

"You guys are missing the most important point," Carley interjected.

"What would that be?" Jack asked.

Carley pointed at the TV screen as she explained. "It's obvious none of them are wearing helmets, yet I bet every one of them is wearing a jock."

"If it was me, I would wear a jock before I would wear a helmet," Mario offered.

"Me too," BB added. "Have to protect the bobbles."

"Typical men," Carley admonished. "You guys would protect your junk before you would protect your brain."

All four men nodded their heads up and down as Mario said, "If I had to choose—yes."

Carley mumbled, "Unbelievable."

BB had been watching the game intently, finally discovering what was bothering him. "Why are there no black players?"

Mario leaned toward the screen. "Even in the stands, there are very few black people. Where's the game coming from?"

Jack replied, "It's from Philadelphia. The Flyers are playing the New York Rangers."

"I don't get it?" BB repeated. "There's lots of black people living in those two cities."

"Yeah, but hockey is a Canadian game," Jack said.

"You're not catching my drift, ya gobshite!" BB exclaimed. "Ya just said it was Philadelphia and New York!"

"Maybe it's because black people don't have mullets," Mario added.

"What the eff are you talking about?" BB replied.

Mario placed his finger on the screen while trying his best to follow the head of one of the skaters. "Look close and you'll see almost every single player has a mullet. Even the coach's hair is a bad-ass mullet!"

"Turn off the TV, ya whanker," BB yelled.

Mario turned and looked at BB. "Hey, it's a close game."

"Turn the effin thing off before I batter ya with it!" BB shouted again.

The TV was turned off, and Mario glanced at Carley. "My apologies. So much for Amish Lady's Night."

Carley laughed. "No worries. Quiet might be better."

Mario returned the smile. "I agree. I had a dream like this once. Sitting in my hot tub on a quiet night—a light snow falling and a beautiful woman to keep me company."

Carley tilted her head, and an evil smile formed on her lips. "My dream was a little different. I was in a hot tub wearing next to nothing with four very sexy men in the tub with me."

BB's one eyebrow shot up, "Oh, really."

"Relax BB. I said four *sexy* men."

"Enough already!" Jack yelled. "In case anyone didn't notice, I'm still sitting here. It's not like I turned invisible."

"So sorry, Darling," Carley said as she winked at her boyfriend.

Jack ignored the silly wink and continued. "BB—you and Mario put it back in your shorts. Shoe, well you just keep it squeezed between your thighs. We need to talk about the governor's reception tomorrow."

"I think we're all set," BB replied.

"Tell us again, so there's no confusion," Jack requested.

"We need to be at Columbus Catering at 2 p.m. tomorrow. Mary Ellen has made arrangements with the caterer to transport us to the governor's mansion, hidden in the back of the freezer truck."

"That'll be cold," Shoe admitted.

"It's only a ten-minute ride, so everyone will be fine," Mario replied.

"What happens once we're inside?" BB asked.

"To a point, we have to play it by ear," Jack explained. "We'll mingle and act like unemployed, spoiled offspring of the elite."

Mario laughed, "Say what?"

"Act like you're a member of a political party and consider that as your sole purpose in life," Jack clarified.

BB added, "I can do that."

"Not you, or Mario," Jack said.

BB pushed the metal-rimmed glasses up the bridge of his nose. "What do you mean?"

"I thought you would have thought about the fact the governor has seen both you and Mario," Jack said to his two friends. "If he recognizes either of you, the whole plan will fall apart."

Both BB and Mario looked defeated. "I really wish you were wrong, but you're right. There's no way around it," BB acquiesced.

Jack smiled and said, "You two still have an important part to play. If things at the reception go south, we need a quick escape route. You two need to wait in the van just outside the mansion's guardhouse."

Both BB and Mario thought about responding, but every time they opened their mouth to begin, they realized they had nothing to say that would refute the facts Jack just stated. That put a damper on the jovial banter that filled the hot tub only a few minutes before, and the rest of the evening was spent in a quieter, relaxing atmosphere.

They all should have known Mario better. He opened the small, plastic box beside the hot tub. He removed two joints and handed one to Shoe. He lifted the lighter and lit the joint now hanging from his lips. As he handed the lighter to Shoe, he took a deep drag of good old "Acapulco Gold."

In contrast to what appeared to be his quiet reflection of the day to come, Mario's mind was actually churning with the creation of his own plan regarding his part to play in Columbus. The plan was halfway complete, but he wasn't sure the joint was helping or holding back his thoughts. He ran his fingers back through his hair and when he felt his own curly mullet, he grinned. Then he smiled even wider. *I have it now,* he thought. *I know exactly what to do.*

Chapter 23: Gatordile

The next morning, Jack was up early and drove to Mario's pad to pick him up. He honked the horn several times, and only after there was no response did he realize Mario's Vega wasn't parked in the driveway. Jack went to the front door of the main house and rang the doorbell.

Mario's father answered the door and gave Jack a wide smile from under his thick moustache. "Jack, nice to see you again."

Jack smiled back. "Nice to see you, too. I was supposed to pick up Mario, but it looks like he's not here."

Mario's father put his hand on Jack's shoulder. "My son told me you would be coming around. He wanted me to tell you he got an early start, and he was picking up BB on the way to Columbus. He will meet you there."

After saying his "thank you" to Mario's father, Jack got back in the X-mobile and headed toward Carley's apartment. After picking her up, they went to Wooster to pick up Shoe before starting the 90-minute drive from there to Columbus.

Arriving in Columbus early, they went to a small family restaurant, ate lunch, then headed toward the catering company. It was situated in a row of shops within a strip mall. After going in the front door, Jack was told to park out back and come in the rear service entrance. As they entered the rear door into a small office area, the same man Jack talked to at the front desk, met them once again.

"We really appreciate you helping us attend the governor's reception," Jack said. "We're avid supporters but missed the cutoff on the invitee list."

The older man closed his eyes and shook his head. "I don't care, and I don't want to hear it. That gives me plausible denial about what you're really up to."

"Well, I still wanted to say, thank you," Jack added.

The older man said, "I'll tell you three the same thing I told your two friends. Mary Ellen told me the only way I would get the catering contract was if I snuck you in."

Jack's brows furrowed. "What two friends?"

The man turned sideways and pointed down the hallway. "The last room on the left—they're in there."

Jack, followed by Carley and then Shoe, walked toward the room in question. Over their shoulders, each of them carried a hanger holding their formal attire for the evening to come. The room they entered was long, and at the far end they saw only one man. He was in a black tuxedo and was looking at himself in a mirror hanging from the wall. There was another door in the far wall that was closed, and light came from under it. Jack assumed it was a bathroom and the second man must be within it. Jack cleared his throat to gain the first man's attention, but it didn't work. He was fixated with his appearance in the mirror, continually running his palm over his bald head.

Jack, trying again in a loud voice, said, "Excuse me."

The man turned and said, "Oh, you guys are here."

Jack, Carley and Shoe walked toward the stranger, and Jack, through his confused look, said, "Do we know you?"

The man in the tuxedo walked toward the three of them, and as he came closer, Jack's brow furrowed even more. The man was familiar as if it was someone he should know. It wasn't until the baffling man was right in front of Jack that the mystery was solved. Jack's eyebrows shot up. "Mario! What the hell! Your hair!"

Behind Jack, Carley smiled and Shoe snickered as Mario ran his palm across his clean-shaven head. "Hair? There is no hair!"

Their shock was interrupted by a *click* as the door of the bathroom was opened. As they looked toward it, they saw a second surreal vision. There, with the light surrounding his profile, was the second, tall man also in a black tuxedo. This man was skinny, and his bald head just fit under the door jamb. It wasn't until the man raised a finger to his face and pushed his metal-rimmed glasses up the edge of his nose that Carley drew in a deep gasp of breath.

"Oh my god! Is that you BB?" she said.

As he stepped further into the room and then walked toward them, they could see it was indeed BB with a similarly shaved head. Shoe slumped over, slapping his thigh. He started to laugh while Carley and Jack were still frozen in shock. Every time Shoe's laughter was about to subside, he would glance up at either of the bald heads, and the uproar would begin once again.

Finally, Jack said, "Guys, what the hell is going on with the shaved heads?"

Mario replied, "You said the governor would recognize us, so we changed our appearance."

"Don't get me wrong. You both get 10 out of 10 for effort, but your faces are still the same," Jack explained.

Mario put both fists on his waist. "Jack, you didn't recognize me until I was right in front of your face, and you've known me for 15 years."

Carley put her hand on Jack's arm. "He's right. The governor won't recognize either one of them."

Shoe, finally finished with his fits of laughter, said, "I agree."

"But we need you in the van parked by the governor's mansion," Jack reminded them.

BB replied, "It's all looked after. Mario followed me to the governor's mansion, and we left the van across the road before continuing here in the Vega."

"I think it's settled then," Carley said. She was already on her way to the bathroom to get changed, not bothering to wait for any further input from Jack. The decision was made.

After 15 minutes, she came back out, and for the second consecutive day, the jaws of the men in the room dropped. The subject of their awe was the way the black evening dress, covered in shiny sequins, hugged her figure. The dress was ankle-length with a long slit up one leg revealing a shapely thigh. She spun on the ball of one foot as she said, "What do you think?"

The men were speechless for a few moments as the spin revealed the low-cut back. Jack came out of the spell first and saw the slack-jawed faces of his three friends. They were staring like parched French Legionnaires at a pool of cool water after marching 30 miles through a scorching desert. Jack wondered if, with a single slap, he could snap all three of them out of the spell.

Instead, Jack yelled, "Earth to the morons! Earth to the morons! Snap out of it!"

As Jack walked by Carley toward the bathroom, he whispered to her, "You're so bad, teasing them like that."

She giggled and whispered back, "Yup."

Shoe changed into his black suit after Jack and just before the catering agent poked his head into the room. "Good. You're ready. It's time to go."

The five of them were an odd sight as they walked through the kitchen area, then onto the loading dock while trying not to brush their formal attire against any loose bits of food. The large panel truck was already loaded with metal carts, each piled with plates of hors d'œuvres. The catering agent hustled the five of them in behind the carts, and then he pulled down the large door, leaving them in darkness.

It didn't take long before the truck lurched forward. Carley said, "Jack, it's freezing in here, and your hands are so cold."

Jack growled, "Those aren't my hands."

There was a sound of a flesh on flesh *slap* as Carley said, "Keep the hands off the merchandise."

Not long after, when the door opened, and their eyes adjusted to the onslaught of light, it was to see Mary Ellen waving frantically. "Hurry!" she said. "None of the guests are here yet, so we need to get you out of sight."

As they stepped out of the truck, employees from the catering company began pulling the metal food racks out from behind them, steering them toward the kitchen. Mary Ellen grasped BB's hand and smiled at him, but she froze when she saw his bald head. Her heartbeat spiked, but after a moment she smiled. "I like it, but I'm sure you'll let me play with it a bit later before I make a final decision. Too bad there's no time for that now." She pulled on his hand and led the group to a set of stairs along the back wall that led to the basement.

After she directed them to a dusty storeroom, she said, "People will be here in about 30 minutes, so come up then, and hopefully no one of importance will notice you." She rose up on the tip toes of her high heels and gave BB a quick kiss before he realized what her intent was. He did not have time to kiss her back or to pull away, if that was his inclination, since she was too quick and scurried out of the room.

They waited quietly until Shoe said, "I'm starving. Is there any food in here?"

"If there was, I certainly wouldn't eat it," Carley answered. "You should have grabbed a couple of hors d oeuvres from the carts in the truck when you had a chance."

"It was dark, and I don't eat anything blind even though I did feel around a bit," Shoe informed them while winking at Carley."

"We should go upstairs in a few minutes," BB said. "What do we do then?"

Jack replied, "It's almost 3:00 p.m. and the announcement informing the guests whom the recipient of the grant will be, is at 5:00 p.m. so we have a bit of time. But within that interval, we need to get the governor alone, so he can be informed of our plan to steal the grant out from under the feet of the American Development Consultants."

"You mean from under the feet of the Japanese," Shoe clarified.

Jack nodded. "Yes, and there'll likely be some unhappy Japanese fellows around, so keep clear of them."

"It's also very likely, since the Polish mafia is paid by the governor, they'll also have a presence upstairs," Mario said. "We need to keep clear of them as well."

Jack waved his hand in front of himself. "Don't worry about the Polish guys. After what we put them through, I don't think they'll bother us."

A confused look came across Mario's face. "Are you not understanding what I'm saying? The Polish guys work for the governor, and we're going to try and strong arm the governor. Yet you're saying, 'Don't worry about the Polish guys.'"

Jack pushed himself up off the box he was sitting on. "You worry too much. Time to go."

Jack led them out of the small room and peered up the staircase, seeing it empty. Slowly moving up it, he was followed by the rest of the group until they were all on the small receiving dock beside the kitchen. From there, they saw a small hallway and followed it past the kitchen entryway until it ended in the main atrium of the mansion.

The group went unnoticed as they sauntered into the atrium and quickly became lost in the multitude of black suits and tuxedos complemented by the women in colorful evening gowns. As they walked toward the governor's parlor, with the double doors thrown open, they could see most of the guests had already arrived.

Jack clasped Carley's hand and pulled her close. BB, Mario and Shoe also leaned in as Jack said, "We should separate and see who's here. There might be someone who might be helpful to our cause. You guys cover the floor while Carley and I shadow the governor's movements."

"When do we meet back up?" BB asked.

"See the bar behind me?" Jack replied. "We'll meet there in 30 minutes."

BB, Shoe and Mario nodded as Jack and Carley turned and headed out into the parlor. As they strolled further into the throng of politicians, lobbyists and their wives or husbands, Jack saw the crowd spilling through another set of double doors at the north end of the large room. After taking glasses of champagne from a server's tray, they headed for the room on the other side of what was now a human spillway. As they moved through it, they came into a huge reception room. Here, they saw the podium at the far end that would be used for the announcement, and just in front of it, the governor and his wife were socializing. There were quite a few political groupie's surrounding the pair, seeking favor, but ultimately, chattering nonsense.

An older woman with a long face pushed her way into the group and grasped the governor's wife's arm. Pulling, she urged Mrs. Breed from the spot beside her husband toward another group of three women. The women greeted each other with fake hugs and kisses before strolling together toward the central atrium of the large house.

Mario and BB saw the group of women enter the atrium and recognized the governor's wife at its center. The boys figured they should stay close and overhear what they were talking about. As they moved closer, they saw Mrs. Breed and one other woman carried small dogs. One was a small, white dog while Mrs. Breed carried an even smaller black poodle.

BB, from the edge of the group, said, "Aren't they cute?"

The women saw the tall, black man and the stylish Italian, eagerly letting them join their circle. The bald heads on top of the black suits gave BB and Mario the appearance of sinister agents filled with intrigue.

"Whom would you two be?" Mrs. Breed said through an alluring smile as her free hand flattened down the side of her dress.

Mario returned a wide smile and put on a thick Italian accent. "My name is Mario, visiting from Sicily, and this is my associate, BB, from Morocco."

The women's eyes lit up as Mrs. Breed exclaimed, "How exotic and mysterious! What brings you two to Ohio?"

Mario stepped up the accent. "We have been sent here by our governments to observe your culture, and as you call it— 'the American dream.'"

As Mrs. Breed smiled her approval, the little, black poodle lifted her snout, placing several licks across Mrs. Breed's chin and lips. She chuckled and leaned into the little doggie kisses.

BB pointed at Mrs. Breed, and in his own completely self-made and inaccurate accent said, "You see, that's something we do not understand in my country."

"You do have dogs in Morocco, don't you?" one of the other ladies asked.

BB brought the fingers of one hand up to his chin, giving the illusion of deeper contemplation of what he just saw. "Of course, we do have dogs. In fact, probably too many, but we do not usually let them lick our faces."

"But they're cute, so why ever not?" Mrs. Breed wondered as the little poodle lifted her nose and gave her chin an added loving lick.

BB's other hand lifted, and he pointed at the black poodle. "Your dog is very cute, but in our country even the cutest of dog's eat their—what is the correct English word? Help me, Mario."

Mario added, "The correct word is *puke*. They eat their own *puke*."

It was very sudden, but the smiles on each of the women dropped.

BB snapped his fingers above his head. "Yes, that is true, but the word I was thinking of was *shit,* not puke. Dogs eat their own *shit,* at times. So, in our country we tend to not let them lick us, especially on our faces." BB opened his mouth and poked his finger in while his face feigned what it would look like if he was about to hurl chunks.

Mrs. Breed twisted her face with her nose slightly raised. "My dog doesn't eat her puke or her shit."

BB clapped his hands together. "That is a miracle! You must tell us the secret allowing for this level of training. I see already the wonder of the American dream!"

Mario smiled apologetically at the ladies. "My friend is just not very good with dogs."

"That would be an understatement," BB corrected. "Once, I was dog-sitting for my neighbor, and the dog was accidentally electrocuted."

Mario poked BB in the side. "You know we are not supposed to talk about Ringo."

"I only bring it up because Ringo used to eat his own shit," BB added.

Mrs. Breed said, "If you want any more information on dog training, you'll need to see my husband under the umbrella of international matters," she said before striding away with her nose still high in the air, followed by her friends.

Shoe was still in the parlor mingling, but his stomach was growling. His hunger hadn't left him, so he checked serving trays as they went by. There were tiny quiche squares and caviar on crackers along with other items that didn't pass his visual test of recognition. He wandered in search of his favorite—shrimp. On more than one table he saw small plates and napkins with tiny shrimp tails on them, so he knew they were in the vicinity—just not his.

He saw another server and checked his tray, but there were no shrimps. "Can you tell me where I could find some shrimp?" he asked.

"I'm sorry," the server replied. "The kitchen has run out of shrimp."

Shoe turned around and mumbled, "This is an important reception. How can there be no shrimp?" As he lifted his eyes, he saw it. On a small table, no more than 15 feet away, was a small plate, and on it were six jumbo shrimp. They were right beside four other tail sections from shrimp already having met their fate. Mesmerized, Shoe walked toward the plate and was about to reach for it when four fat fingers and a thumb picked up one of the enticing shrimps. His eyes followed the path of the fingers as they brought the morsel up to a pair of thick, red lips. They parted and shrimp juice squirted outwards as another shrimp was sacrificed.

Shoe's heart beat faster, as he now saw the ratio of shrimp to discarded tails at five to five. He needed to act quickly. There were three women and one man surrounding the heavy-set woman sitting in the chair beside the shrimps. They were listening to a story from the seated women, and that gave Shoe's heart and stomach, respectively, a reprieve and an opportunity. *As long as she's talking, she can't be eating,* he thought.

The heavy-set woman said, "I'm trying another diet I read about in a magazine. Two of my friends began it, and in the first two weeks they lost ten pounds."

"That's very promising," Shoe said to her.

The heavy woman lifted her eyes. "Why thank you, young man. How nice!"

Shoe saw her glance at the shrimp plate beside her, and he began to panic. *Just keep her talking,* he thought. *She can't eat if she's talking!*

As she started to move her hand toward the shrimp, Shoe asked, "Are you getting enough exercise?"

Her hand paused. "I try, but my doctor says my issue is glandular. Do you know of any diets that work successfully?" she asked Shoe.

Shoe brought his finger up to support his chin as he considered the question. Finally, he replied, "I heard of one from my friend who was in the military."

The heavy-set woman scooted forward onto the edge of her chair. "What was it called?"

Shoe leaned forward, closer to the woman. "If I remember correctly, it's called – 'The Don't Eat So Much Freaking Food Diet!'"

The woman gasped and drew her face back.

Shoe continued. "And as for your gland, whichever one it is, it's a god damn greedy bitch, so stop feeding it so much!"

The woman's eyes became moist as she considered Shoe's words.

Shoe took a deep breath and, in a calmer voice, said, "I know tough love can be difficult, but it begins right here." He put his hand on her shoulder and gave it a reassuring shake as his other hand lifted the plate of five shrimps. As he walked away from the dumbfounded woman toward the bar, he popped one of the shrimps into his mouth. He made sure he ate the remaining shrimps before he reached his friends, and placed the empty plate on the bar top next to his fellow conspirators.

"What now?" BB asked.

"There's too many people here. I'm not sure," Jack said.

Carley rolled her eyes. "Men! I can't believe how thick you guys are."

"Hey, why do you have to be like that?" Mario said.

"Well, really. I've no idea how you got this far. You were after aliens, and you connected power tools and even wall plugs to the search. It must have been pure happenstance that got you on the governor's trail. I think you guys are about as smart as a box of wall plugs. In fact, I think that's a good name for you. I christen thee—The Wall Plug Boys."

"That's awfully derogatory," Jack said.

"I'm not sure what derogatory means, but 'Wall Plug Boys' has a nice ring to it," Mario offered.

Carley turned to BB. "You said you were in the governor's office the last time you were here."

"That's a fact," BB responded.

"Then you guys get to his office and wait there. I'll have Mr. Breed there in ten minutes."

"How the eff are you going to do that?" BB asked.

She did a spin on the ball of one foot, then said, "I didn't wear this sexy dress only for the amusement of the Wall Plug Boys." She winked at them as she set off in search of the governor.

They watched her leave as BB said, "I don't care what she says. There's no way I will ever believe she is or was Amish."

Jack muttered, "You have no idea."

They stared at her figure until she disappeared from view in the crowd. It took Mario's urging to bring them back to reality. "BB, let's go. Lead us to the governor's office."

Ten minutes later, Governor Breed was being pulled down the empty hallway. Carley held his hand as she said, "You said your office is down here?"

"It sure is, Honey," he replied. "But we can't be gone for too long. I have an announcement to make, soon."

Carley pressed up against the governor and whispered in his ear. "Just for a few minutes. You're such an important man, and I love important, powerful men. I would really owe you if you show me where you make all the important, manly decisions."

The governor took a deep breath and moved his hand to grab her ass, but she was quick with her hand pulling him further down the hallway. When they reached the end, the governor flicked on the switch, bathing the outer office with light. Governor Breed headed straight to the door of his private office, but before he could open it, Carley went ahead. She opened the door and disappeared into the darkness.

The governor laughed at her playfulness as he turned on the light to his private office. He closed the door behind him, and when he turned, he saw they were not alone. He tried to put his hand on the door knob, but BB's hand was there first.

"We just need a few minutes of your time, Governor," BB said.

"Hey—what's this?" Governor Breed exclaimed.

Carley walked over to the governor and took his hand, once again. She tugged and said, "I would like you to meet my friends."

The governor resisted, but Carley gave him a mighty tug that almost pulled him off his feet. Once in the center of the room, Carley pointed at her boyfriend and said, "This is Jack Decker." Then she introduced, Shoe, Mario and BB.

Lowering his voice, the governor asked, "What do you guys want?"

Jack said, "It's simple. When you make the announcement at 5:00 p.m. you'll tell everyone in attendance that the grant will be given to me."

A loud guffaw came from Governor Breed's lips. No one else joined his laughter. "You guys can't be serious."

"We absolutely are," Jack clarified.

The governor was quick for a big man and was at his desk in a flash. As he picked up the phone and began dialing, BB moved to intercept him. Jack lifted his hand and shook his head to stop BB's proposed intervention.

A few seconds later, the governor yelled into the phone. "Get to my office right now! I'm in trouble!"

After slamming the phone receiver down, it only took a few seconds for running footsteps to be heard in the outer office. The door was thrust open, and four large men in black suits entered the room. At their lead was Peter Pusiak, the Pastry King of Ohio and Polish Mafia leader.

Pusiak's face was red from his exertion, and through deep breaths, he said, "What the fuck is going on here?"

The governor yelled, "These guys are trying to extort me! Throw them out, and make sure it's a painful departure!"

Pusiak snapped his fingers, and one of his henchmen closed the office door. He slowly walked over to a position in front of Jack. He glanced at Mario and Shoe before returning his attention back to Jack. "You guys messed up. Do you have any idea who you are dealing with?"

Jack didn't flinch as he stood toe to toe with the leader of the Polish Mafia. He raised a hand and poked his finger into Pusiak's lapel. "I know exactly who you are. You're my godfather!"

There was an uncomfortable silence until Pusiak's knees bent and he threw his head back in laughter. When his face came back down, he gave Jack a huge hug. "Of course, I'm your godfather!"

There wasn't a single person in the room who didn't have a *what the fuck look* on their faces.

Pusiak released Jack and said, "How did you like the pastries the other day? After Jack told me he was my godson, of course I provided nothing but the best, no?"

Jack's friend's faces all appeared long due to their mouths gapped open, and it looked even more comical as they nodded their heads up and down in unison.

"Any time you want something sweet, come to one of my shops, and you'll get pastries for almost free," Pusiak continued.

"Pusiak! What the hell are you doing? I gave you an order," the governor said.

Peter Pusiak walked over, curling his fist into the governor's lapel. "I don't work for you anymore. You're bringing the Japanese into Ohio—into my turf? Not a chance, so they aren't getting the grant. Jack is."

The governor was frozen, and his face was white as Jack walked over to join the pair of men. Jack handed a folder to the governor.

"What—what is this?" the governor stuttered.

Jack reached forward with his finger, pulling open the cover. "The first two pages are a copy of the patent I own for a variable speed trigger. This is the new technology that makes me eligible for the grant. The next page is a prepared statement you will read announcing me as the recipient of the grant."

"The Japanese won't accept this," the governor said.

Pusiak's grip on Carter Breed's lapel tightened as Jack continued. "The last page in the folder is another letter. It describes your illegal activities including money laundering of skimmed money through the House of Aliens, tax fraud, and from that, attempting to give the American grant to a foreign company. Of course, using your wife's name without permission as the owner of the House of Aliens, is also included in the long list of infractions."

If it was possible, even more blood drained from the governor's face, and his hand holding the folder began to shake.

"That last letter will be mailed out to the five major newspapers in Ohio if anything happens to us, or if I don't get the grant," Jack added.

Pusiak released the governor and said, "Don't worry. We'll take care of any Japanese problems."

The jostle as Pusiak released the governor brought him out of his stupor. He turned to Jack. "If I do this, what's in it for me?"

"You get to stay on as the governor of this fine state of Ohio," Jack said. "This will be the case as long as you keep things straight for the rest of your term."

The governor swallowed hard, and he pointed accusingly at Jack. "If you send the letter and I go down—you go down. I will tell everyone about this bit of extortion allowing you to get the technology grant."

Jack held his hand out. "Then we have an understanding and a deal?"

The governor pushed his hand forward, but at the last second, stopped. "There's one other thing I want."

"What?" Jack asked.

"Your two friends can't fool me. They shaved their heads, but I recognize them as being friends of the Sicilian Mafia," Governor Breed revealed.

"And?"

"I think they got their silver briefcase back," the governor added. "I want the briefcase of money as part of the deal. I get the 200 thousand dollars in the briefcase, and you get the technology grant for 500 thousand dollars. That's a steal for you!"

Jack sighed impatiently. "We do have the briefcase, but there's no time to get it here before the announcement."

"The governor's face went stone cold. "Then, no deal."

"Actually, there's time to get the briefcase," BB interjected.

"What do you mean?" Jack asked.

"Mario and I thought it might be handy, so we brought it, and it's in the van," BB said.

Jack turned to Peter Pusiak and asked, "Can one of your men go with BB down to the main road to retrieve the briefcase?"

Peter turned and snapped his finger. "Aleksey, go with BB and bring the van up to the VIP parking area."

Ten minutes later, the two men returned, and BB handed Jack the familiar silver briefcase owned by Mario. Jack was relieved to feel the weight of the encyclopedias still within. Walking to the governor's desk, he placed the briefcase down on it and said, "Now do we have a deal?"

The governor turned the briefcase toward him. "Why is it so cold?"

"It was hidden in a freezer," Jack replied.

"No wonder my guys couldn't find it," the governor mumbled. He fumbled with the latch, then said, "Hey—what's the combination?"

Jack snickered. "You think we're stupid? You get the money, and your Japanese friends get us before we leave. Not a chance."

Governor Breed crossed his arms. "What do you propose?"

Jack explained, "You make the announcement. We get in the van and we leave. I call you from a pay phone ten minutes later with the combination. You open the case and you smile. We drive home and we smile."

The governor thought for a minute before pressing his hand out toward

Jack. "Deal."

Jack shook the governor's hand and then looked at his watch. "We're just going to make it if we hurry."

The entire group walked down the hallway, reversing their earlier path until they found themselves at the back of the very crowded reception room. Pusiak and his henchmen jostled a pathway through the throng until they were all by the three stairs leading to the podium. Jack saw several employees of the American Development Consultants also by the stage. Included in the group was Ryo Ozawa whom he felt sorry for. *Boy, they're going to be disappointed*, Jack thought.

Jack and his friends looked to the podium as a government official spoke into the microphone. "Better late than never. Here he is—Governor Carter Breed!"

A wide, bright smile came across the governor's face as he went into full politician mode. He bounced up the steps, shaking several hands along the way. The crowd clapped thunderously, joined by a few yells and cat-calls. Bathing in it, the governor waited a minute before raising his hand to bring the room to silence. In his other hand, the governor held the announcement Jack prepared the day before. He cleared his throat and read it aloud. Governor Breed was a professional and polished speaker, glancing nonchalantly at the paper occasionally while maintaining his focus on the audience of potential voters.

He said, "There were many fine applicants for the technology grant. A team of experts considered their proposals and evaluated their merit. We investigated the technology behind the application and the ability of the applicant to bring the new technology to market. Of course, the grant was only available to native-born Americans, as we are promoting the best country in the world!"

The crowd brought their hands together again as the governor whipped them into a frenzy.

Governor Breed continued. "With that in mind, it's with my great pleasure that I announce the winner of the technology grant. The selection may surprise you as you hear the name of a native-born Ohioan who has a wonderful new patent. We have the confidence he, with our support, will bring the variable speed trigger from paper to the tools you use in your home every day. Ladies and gentleman, I present to you—Jack Decker!"

Jack smiled as he walked up the stairs toward the podium. He looked at the delegation from the American Development Consultants and saw the shock evident on each and every one of their faces. By the time Jack was in front of the microphone, those same faces had turned red with seething anger. The people in the crowd were confused by the unfamiliar name announced. First, there were only a few claps, but, led by the governor, it spread until the entire room was endorsing Jack.

Jack leaned in to the microphone and said, "Thank you." It was drowned out by the crowd cheering for the newest, up and coming businessman of Ohio. Jack saw five dangerous looking Japanese men making their way toward the podium through the crowd. Peter Pusiak raised a finger and ten of his men intercepted them. The disappointed Japanese men were redirected toward the atrium, then out the main exit.

Jack raised his hand and the crowd noise subsided. "I want everyone here to know how thankful I am for this opportunity. Not only am I thrilled with the opportunity to pursue my dream of putting my invention into production, but I'm just as thrilled to bring it to this, my home state. Let's make Ohio great again!" Jack waved and smiled while the crowd burst into boisterous approval of him, and as he walked off the podium, he shook the governor's hand.

The governor still had the fake smile pasted on his face as he whispered in Jack's ear. "Remember—the freaking combination. I'll be waiting in my office for your call."

Jack pulled back and smiled. Hand after hand came in to shake his, and the pulling and jostling led him toward the door to the parlor. The crowd thinned as he, followed by his friends, made their way to the front atrium of the mansion. There were fewer hands to shake and women to hug as he was getting closer and closer to the front door. Finally, with a last wave, he walked out into the late afternoon air.

BB led and said, "This way to the van."

They bustled into the Shaggin-wagon and BB fired up the engine. As BB pushed the gas pedal, Mario said, "I can't believe we just did that!"

Shoe whooped as he fired a fist into the air, and Carley gave Jack a big kiss. She said, "You're the best, Lover Boy."

They whooped and cheered as the van passed the guardhouse, then turned onto the main road.

Interrupting their celebration, Jack said, "Find a payphone, BB."

"You're really going to give him the combination?" Mario asked.

"Oh yeah," Jack explained. "When he sees those encyclopedias, he will know we won this—not him."

As the van slowed to a stop beside a glass booth housing a payphone, Mario said, "The combination is 3811, but remember not to let me ever work for you. You're spiteful."

Jack opened the side door and hopped out of the van. He dialed the governor's private line from the payphone, and it began to ring.

Shoe was rifling through one of the small cupboards in BB's van and said, "I'm really thirsty. Is there anything to drink in here?"

The governor answered the phone and said, "What's the combination?"

In the van, finding one cupboard empty, Shoe moved to the next one. Both Mario and BB simultaneously yelled, "Not there!"

Jack told the governor, "3811," and hung up the phone.

The warning was too late, and the cupboard door in the van was opened. As Jack looked back in the side door of the van, several encyclopedias spilled out onto the floor.

Jack said, "What the hell?"

The governor fell back into his chair in front of the briefcase he just opened. He had mixed feelings of anger and shock but mainly disappointment as he looked into the contents of the plastic bag within the silver briefcase. All he could think, over and over in his mind, was, *Who the fuck puts a dead dog in a briefcase?*

Chapter 24: The Epilogue

Even though Jack told Governor Carter Breed he wouldn't release any incriminating information during the remainder of his tenure, a full term was not in the cards. There were other rivals who suspected the governor had some illegal dealings, including taking bribes and money laundering, but this didn't bother people all that much. After all, he was a politician, and this type of activity was expected.

What was and is not condoned at all, is cruelty to animals, even if it's a small furball of a dog named Ringo. It was purely coincidence, from the day Ringo chewed on the electrical wire in BB's apartment, for his body to travel from the purported Italian Mafia, to the Polish Mafia, to the Japanese contingent and, finally, onto Governor Breed's desk. The governor had very few options, and he selected a poor one.

The day after the reception, a garbageman found Ringo's carcass in the dumpster outside the governor's mansion with his teeth still clamped onto a short length of electrical wire. As any unionized worker worth his weight in salt would do, he took the opportunity to get back at the establishment, and that meant Governor Breed. A quick call to the newspapers, and the headline the next day was – *Governor Breed, Dog Killer.* Underneath it was a picture of poor Ringo.

A representative picture of Ringo appeared on news reports across the country as the story went viral, and sales of Jack Russell terrier puppies took a sharp spike upwards. Protests against cruelty to animals popped up in front of many government buildings with the largest held in front of the Ohio governor's mansion. Over one thousand people stood vigil outside the gates with chants of, "Ringo—Ringo—Ringo!" Placards and banners, held by protesters, were emblazoned with the face of Ringo who was now the *Rock Star* of the dog world.

The story of Ringo had set off every newspaper person in the state, and they turned their bloodhound noses toward Carter Breed's expanded portfolio. Their thought was, *where there's smoke, there's fire.* Ringo was the smoke and the House of Aliens, now revealed, was the fire. As a result of the scrutiny, the insane asylum was confiscated by the state and upgraded to an efficient top-notch facility. Mrs. Breed, now disclosed as the unknowing owner of the facility, was vilified. However, she was given some latitude once she filed for a divorce which was quickly granted.

As for Carter Breed, ironically, it was not corruption that took him down. Rather, cruelty to animals hit a much more sensitive nerve with the American people. Two options came from the state prosecutor. Carter Breed could resign or face criminal charges and jail time. Taking the first option, he disappeared from public view, and his name was stricken from any and all state records. It really was somewhat surreal, but a small Jack Russell terrier named Ringo had taken down the most powerful man in Ohio.

Commander Peri Winkle was despondent when he learned the House of Aliens didn't actually house aliens. In fact, he had a nervous breakdown. When they found him naked in the middle of Beach City, yelling to the skies with a tin foil hat protecting his head, he was incarcerated. Ironically, he was the first guest of the new and improved state insane asylum called the House of Aliens.

Mario Dimeo followed his dream. With his portion of the funds the boys had obtained, and with help from his father, he opened a hair styling studio that would appeal to men. America was being thrust into the 80's, and it was the *Big Hair* era. This was the case for women, but even more so for men. For Mario, *Big Hair* and his salon was a marriage made in heaven. It was not long before he opened a second salon—then a third—and by 1985, Mario owned 18 salons across seven states.

In 1982, Honda built the first Japanese auto plant located in America, in Ohio. Shoe never lost his suspicious nature about Japanese investments, so it wasn't a surprise for that event to be his last straw. He took his share of the funds the boys accumulated and moved to India. First in a tiny hut, then in a small abandoned warehouse, and finally in a large factory, Shoe hired people to make sneakers of his own design. As his business grew, so too did his market share. Rivals tried to buy him out, but he refused to sell. By 1987, when his company went public on the New York Stock Exchange, he was a very wealthy man. He did struggle with one regret. Even though he left America because of foreign investment, while in India, he *was* the foreign investment. That was always difficult for him.

Carley stayed with Jack for the rest of her years. She continued to help the Amish community remain autonomous, and she dabbled in a few business ventures herself. One of those had her create and manufacture her own line of troll dolls. It was a business where it was hard to be original as almost every version of troll doll had already saturated the market. However, one winter, she created her Amish troll doll. Just as Amish culture does not appreciate vanity, these dolls had plain blonde or brown hair, and there were no faces. There were brown and white dolls to cover the ethnic diversity, and she would have created an Asian doll, but with no faces, what was the point? There were female dolls with simple dresses and bonnets. The male dolls were even simpler with white shirts and drab trousers. Their uniqueness came from a selection of three styles of beards. The Amish troll dolls took the market by storm that Christmas, and Carley became financially independent.

Peter Pusiak, having never had any kids of his own, treated Jack as his own son. It changed him, and he left the Polish Mafia behind and even sold all his pastry shops. This left him quite wealthy and with time on his hands. He spent more and more of his time with Jack, and even the weekly Sunday dinners at Jack's mom's place began, once again. At first, Mary Decker was resistant, but over time, she saw how Peter had changed. She was so impressed and later smitten, so that in 1985, when Peter asked for her hand in marriage, she said yes. Jack was both the new son in law and best man at their wedding.

BB stayed with Jack in the building and operation of the power tool factory. They were extremely successful, and within five years, they were able to pay out Mario and Shoe's share of the company. Jack often recollected his fondest memory with the company. They had purchased a plot of land in the new Industrial Complex near the Amish community. It didn't look like much then, as it was covered with tall grass and weeds.

It was the day for the ground breaking ceremony. A tiny swatch of grass had been cleared, and a small bench bleacher was set in place. Several dignitaries from Canton city council were there along with a few news cameras. Just after the first scoopful of dirt was lifted, a TV news reporter interviewed Jack and BB.

The news reporter first turned to Jack and said, "This must be very exciting. Have you thought about a name for the company?"

Jack scratched his chin. "We haven't come up with a final answer yet, but since family is so important to me, it would be good if the company name represented that."

The reporter pushed the microphone under BB's chin and asked, "How about you? What name do you think works?"

BB said, "Family is also important to me, but in this age of oppression, I think we should make a statement for equality whenever we can."

"I'm not sure I understand," the reporter replied.

BB grabbed the microphone from her and raised his other fist into the air. He said, "I mean, I need to do what's right for my people, and I'm Black!"

The reporter took the microphone back and asked Jack, "Any final words Mr. Decker?"

Jack and BB froze as they looked at each other. They had been together for so long, they were connected, and right now, the exact same message flashed in their brains.

BB said, "You think that name works?"

The reporter moved between them and said, "What name?"

Jack said to BB, "I think it's a great name. In fact, it's awesome possum!" He lifted his hand in the air, and BB gave him a high-five. It was a good start for a company that would, years later, be considered part of American culture.

It was an American culture that Jack hoped to change. He would build the company with BB in an atmosphere free of stereotypes and racism. He realized, and it was highlighted by their search for the House of Aliens, that they had all lost sight of the fact their differences actually gave them strength. They had mistakenly separated Italian Americans, Polish Americans, the Amish, Japanese and even the black population. He knew there was a point to BB's priority of promoting black culture, but he also knew there would come a day when it would hurt the cause more than help it. Jack knew that, one day, the country would be better seeing everyone simply as Americans—and even more simply as people where they were all seen as equal and the same.

It was a noble thought, and Jack knew it began now with their failed search for aliens in Ohio that was the spark forever changing them. Never again were they the four musketeers and a vixen. Instead, they had changed into fine adults. However, even though they matured, some things didn't change. BB still called everyone an eejit or a whanker. Mario still fucked up his urban sayings, and Shoe called everyone a piece of shit. Jack continued to be the glue holding them together, and Carley was the drug that kept Jack sane.

As the years went by, they all had kids and then grandkids, leading to huge annual picnics consisting of all four families. All five of them didn't always make it, but their bond remained strong, and they saw each other two or three times a year. Even in their later years, if you visited Canton and drove by Mario's father's house on the night of the first Monday Night Football game of the season, you would see a beat up, rusty, brown van parked in the driveway. Just beyond it, in the hot tub, amongst the cheers and jeers, you would hear the boisterous laughter of four fine men and an even finer, albeit sassy, woman.

Dear Reader:

Reviews are important to every author. We are thankful that many readers take a few moments to return to the purchasing website, in this case, Amazon, and leave a rating and a review.

If you could do so for this story, it would be much appreciated. Keep in mind, a Hollywood style review is not needed. Even a few simple words would be great.

Thanks again, and I hope you enjoyed the story.

Peter Sandor

www.ingramcontent.com/pod-product-compliance
Lightning Source LLC
Chambersburg PA
CBHW021235250626
47155CB00008B/3017